Its power is legendary. It can fulfill every impossible magical desire. But for one young witch seeking redemption, the Northern Circle coven will challenge her skills—and her heart—beyond measure.

One tragic impulsive mistake made Chloe Winslow an outcast to her influential magic family. As a medical student, she wants to combine science with sorcery to heal those she hurt and right her wrongs. But brilliant, charismatic Devlin Marsh re-routes her plans with a once-in-eternity offer: membership in the exclusive Northern Circle, a mysterious Vermont coven known for pushing the limits.

Enthralled by Devlin and their mesmerizing mutual attraction, Chloe makes a dangerous sacrifice to help the Circle's high priestess awaken Merlin himself—and learn his timeless cures. But a foreshadowing soon causes Chloe to doubt the Circle's real motives, as well as Devlin's...

Now Merlin's demonic shade is loose in the human world, while Chloe and Devlin's uneasy alliance will pit them against ancient enemies, malevolent illusions, and shattering betrayal. And with the fate of two realms in the balance, Chloe must risk her untried power against a force she can't defeat—and a passion that could destroy her.

Also by Pat Esden

The Dark Heart series
A Hold on Me
Beyond Your Touch
Reach for You

Published by Kensington Publishing Corp.

HIS DARK MAGIC

A Northern Circle Coven Novel

Pat Esden

LYRICAL PRESS
Kensington Publishing Corp.
www.kensingtonbooks.com

LYRICAL PRESS BOOKS are published by

Kensington Publishing Corp.
119 West 40th Street
New York, NY 10018

All Kensington titles, imprints, and distributed lines are available at special quantity discounts for bulk purchases for sales promotion, premiums, fundraising, educational, or institutional use.

Special book excerpts or customized printings can also be created to fit specific needs. For details, write or phone the office of the Kensington Sales Manager: Kensington Publishing Corp., 119 West 40th Street, New York, NY 10018. Attn. Sales Department. Phone: 1-800-221-2647.

Lyrical Underground and Lyrical Underground logo Reg. US Pat. & TM Off.

First Electronic Edition: December 2018
eISBN-13: 978-1-5161-0630-1
eISBN-10: 1-5161-0630-X

First Print Edition: December 2018
ISBN-13: 978-1-5161-0631-8
ISBN-10: 1-5161-0631-8

Printed in the United States of America

For Russell:

who gave this woman a reason to not return to her hometown.

Acknowledgments

I'd like to thank everyone from the Swinger of Birches writers' retreat. HIS DARK MAGIC went from seed to synopsis there. In so many ways every person there inspired me. To Laura Anderson for that August afternoon when we went down to Lake Champlain and talked. That was when the Northern Circle Coven series truly came to life. I'd be remiss if I didn't give a special nod to Lake Champlain herself. She plays an important role in this novel. Plus, she once again pointed me in the direction of three magical stones that led to the sale of this series. I'm not kidding. Lake Champlain has stones that make wishes come true. It's happened to me twice.

As always, undying gratitude to Jaye Robin Brown, Ginger Churchill, and Jessica Gunn. Enough said, you're the best.

Special thanks to my agent Pooja Menon and my editor Selena James. You'll never know how much your faith, wisdom, and guidance mean to me. Thank you as well to everyone else at Kensington Publishing for your support and help in bringing this new series to life. I truly appreciate each and every one of you.

Finally a huge thank you to readers, booksellers, librarians, reviewers, and bloggers everywhere for supporting books, so authors like me can continue to write and share our stories.

Chapter 1

Earth. Air. Fire. Water.
—Inscribed into a white candle

Chloe padded barefoot across her apartment to the altar on her windowsill. She struck a match and lit a candle. Its light shimmered over a row of crystals and washed into the darkness beyond the open window.

"Spirits of air," she intoned, holding out her hands. "Guardians of thought and intent, grant me your presence today. Spirits of fire, guardians of will and passion…"

A gust of wind sent autumn leaves whirling through the darkness and rustling against the window's screen. She stopped chanting and cupped her hands around the candle, shielding it from the breeze. She shivered. There was a sense of foreboding in the air, a whisper and a chill that a witch like her could not ignore. Someone else with powers was close by. And they were thinking about her—at least that's what her intuition murmured.

She glanced out the window. There was no one in the tiny parking lot, one story below. The windows in the house next door stood dark and silent. She caught a whiff of bacon and hash browns, but the smell was faint and not unexpected. It was almost five-thirty, breakfast time for the couple upstairs.

Quiet as could be, she tiptoed past her bed and a stack of textbooks to the studio apartment's front door. She opened it a crack and glanced out. The hall light was on, its brightness fanning across the hallway between her and the main staircase. But the doors to the other two apartments on her floor were shut, everything dead silent.

Remembering her candle, Chloe swiveled back. "Out," she whispered, flicking her fingers to send a burst of energy at its flame.

The flame obeyed, only a thread of its rosemary-scented smoke trailing behind her as she opened the door all the way and crept down the hallway, the hairs on the back of her neck prickling.

When she reached the top of the staircase, everything was still quiet. But after a moment, a faint *thump-thump* echoed up from the foyer below.

Thump-bang. Bang. Chloe froze, her breath knotting in the back of her throat. It was as if someone had leaned into the front door, hard shouldering it to see if it would give way.

She waited, listening for the noise to happen again. One long second passed, then another. She gritted her teeth and took a cautious step downward.

Her ear caught the swish and clink of something being slid through the mail slot, followed by a hum of magic.

Not daring to breathe, Chloe snuck down the stairs far enough that she could see the foyer and the front entrance. A narrow envelope lay just inside the door, as white as moonlight against the worn floorboards.

She glanced at the window set into the front door. No one was looking in or lurking in the shadows on the porch, so she sprinted down the rest of the stairs and snatched the envelope. Even before she read who it was for, her intuition screamed that it was addressed to her:

Chloe Winslow

The ink was black. The handwriting neat and controlled. Perfectly centered. But it wasn't an envelope. It was handmade, paper folded and held shut by a disk of gold sealing wax stamped with an *N* surrounded by a circle.

She nudged the seal with her index finger. Energy crackled off of it, snaking up her arm. She gasped. Powerful magic. She was certain of it, though if any of the other tenants had found the letter and touched the seal, they wouldn't have felt a thing.

Adrenaline pumped into her veins. A month ago, she'd moved out of her parents' house in Connecticut to take prerequisite courses at the University of Vermont before applying for medical school. In all those weeks, she hadn't encountered any other true witches or magic. No way in hell was she going to let someone drop off a thing like this and then escape before she could meet them.

She shoved the letter into the waistband of her yoga pants, unlocked the front door, and charged out onto the porch. Her gaze flashed to the left. Parked cars lined the dark street. But no one was getting into or out of any of them.

The swish of someone striding through fallen leaves came from the opposite direction. She wheeled and caught a glimpse of him. Definitely a guy, striding down the sidewalk through a glimmer of streetlight. Broad shoulders filled out his dark quilted jacket. Khaki chinos. Lean. Athletic. Confident.

Chloe's long legs took the porch stairs in a single leap. She sprinted down the sidewalk after him, leaves scattering beneath her bare feet.

The guy jogged between two parked cars and crossed the street.

"Wait!" she shouted.

He slowed and glanced back. That was all the time Chloe needed. She willed her legs to go faster and in a dozen strides caught up to him and snagged his sleeve.

His eyes met hers. He looked to be maybe twenty-four or -five. His dark-brown hair curled at the nape of his neck. Deep, brown eyes. Muscular. Classy. Gorgeous. His magic purred in the air around him.

She gulped a breath and toughened her voice. "You owe me an explanation."

His gaze traveled over her slowly, from her bobbed honey-blond hair, past her makeup-free face and stretched out T-shirt, down to her stormy-blue painted toenails, then back up to her eyes. Dimples formed as his lips twitched into a roguish smirk.

"Not afraid of confrontation, are you?" he said.

His voice was warm and deep, liquid danger spiked with an undercurrent of confident innuendo. It sent an excited shiver up her arms. Still she glared at him. "First of all, I suspect you dropped off that letter at this time of morning because you knew I'd be awake and sense you. That means you've been spying on me."

"Is that so?" He shifted closer, his magic sweeping her skin.

Her legs weakened. Desire thrummed low in her belly. Dear Goddess, this hadn't been one of her brighter moves. Maybe she could snuff out a candle with a flick of her fingers, but with seemingly no effort his magic had aroused every inch of her. Clearly, he was extraordinarily gifted—and not just with working spells.

She let go of his sleeve, retreated a step, and found herself trapped against a cedar hedge.

He cocked his head. "Why don't you open the letter if you're so curious?"

Her fingers obeyed, sliding it from her waistband—

She stopped. What the heck was she doing? She'd felt the magic crackle off the seal. If she broke it, there was no telling what kind of spell might be activated.

Chloe pulled herself up to her full height and looked him square in the eyes, which wasn't that hard to do. He was probably five-foot-ten, but she was only a couple of inches shorter even in bare feet. "I've got a better idea. How about if you tell me what it says?"

He frowned as if the idea didn't appeal to him, then surprisingly he stepped back and shrugged. "All right, if you insist. It's an invitation from the Northern Circle coven. Have you heard of us?"

"Umm—no." Her pulse quickened, renewed wariness pumping into her blood. Her parents had mentioned a few older hereditary witches who lived in this area, but never this group.

"It's to a party. A meet and greet. A chance to see if you might be interested in joining us and if we think you're a good fit." He rubbed a hand down the sleeve of his jacket as if deciding whether he should say more. Finally, he went on, "We're dedicated to finding ways to access ancient knowledge. Through out-of-body travel, retrocognition…" He studied her face carefully, as if watching for her reaction.

She pressed her lips together, refusing to give him one—though what he'd said totally enticed her.

Amusement twinkled in his eyes for a second, then he continued. "We believe there are cures to modern diseases and conditions that have been lost to time. The wisdom and magic of Imhotep, Hippocrates, even Merlin." He smiled, slyly. "You are interested in medicine, right?"

Her wariness evaporated and that thrum jumped to life again deep inside her. But this time it had nothing to do with sex. *Magic. Medicine. Secrets lost to time.* None of the classes she was taking or anything she'd come across at the university were even remotely as exciting as this.

She folded her arms across her chest. "Of course you'd know I'm interested in that. You've been keeping tabs on me."

"I—we haven't been spying on you. You don't always use protection spells. We picked up on your energy. That's one of the ways we find new potential members." He stopped, his jaw tensing as if he were holding something back.

She pinned him with a steady look. "And?"

He grimaced. "All right, we have contacts in administration. We may have checked your college records as well: graduated from a community college, taking additional prerequisites before applying for medical school.

Top-ten test scores. Not a great apartment. But somehow you scored it last minute."

Now he sounded like her father, using his connections to screen potential employees. She thrust the letter out. "If this is all so innocent, then why don't you open it? Or does the seal bother you?"

He laughed, tugged the letter from her fingers, and broke the sealing wax. The welcoming scent of sage and lavender perfumed the air, and a trail of green firefly-like sparks twinkled upward, swirling around before vanishing off toward the brightening eastern horizon.

"Better now?" he said, handing the open letter back to her.

She skimmed it, nibbling her bottom lip. Even in the dim street-light, she could see he'd told the truth. It was an engraved invitation signed: *Athena Marsh, high priestess, Northern Circle.*

"You can take a city bus—or text Athena if you want a ride. She'll probably ask me to pick you up, but she's the one doing the organizing. This is her pet project," he continued. "You won't be the only newbie. No one will force you into anything."

His voice settled sugar-sweet in her ear. *Medicine. Magic.* A chance to gain the knowledge from ancient physicians, scholars, and sorcerers. Perhaps even pick the wizard Merlin's brain. How could she say *no*?

Chapter 2

The clouds I saw that morning were shaped like a fool and a red dragon.
I meditated on them, but their meaning remained hidden.
"In time," my mother said. "In time, you will understand."
—Kashari

Magic. Medicine. As Chloe walked back to the apartment house, the words set off a wildfire of possibilities in her mind. But another thought whispered as well. *Protection.*

She sighed and scuffed into her apartment. The guy was right. She hadn't been as careful about protecting herself as she should have been. Sure, she had hung charms and talismans to ward off bad spirits and attract good energy. She had the crystals on her windowsills and a bowl of them on the tiny kitchen bar that doubled as her desk. Her apartment overflowed with candles, herbs, incenses...all the essential tools of the Craft. However, when she'd done her rituals, she cast only the most basic of magic circles to do them in, to save both money and supplies. That negligence could have allowed a coven working in unison to spy on her—or even a single witch with the right skills and interest. She needed to up her protection in that area immediately.

Her chest tightened as she switched on her reading light and settled down on the edge of the couch with the invitation in her lap. She unfolded it, staring at the words but not seeing them. The life changing possibilities they offered were immense. She'd always be a part of her family's coven. But joining the Northern Circle would provide the new beginning she'd longed for, a second coven made up of witches who wouldn't judge her by her past mistakes. And maybe, just maybe, the chance to discover a potion or spell that could reverse the harm she'd caused five years ago and lift the shame she'd brought down on her family.

Chloe folded her arms across her chest and rocked forward, hugging herself as her mind flashed back to that horrible night. Tuesday, June 15th, two days before her seventeenth birthday.

She was babysitting for the Vice-Chancellor of the High Council of Witches and his wife. She'd put their kids to bed and stretched out in a poolside lounge chair with her e-reader. Lights brightened the pool's smooth blue water and illuminated the terrace around her. Soft music played in the background. She sipped an iced tea and swiped her finger across the reader's screen, devouring page after page of the latest issue of *Glamour Magazine*. When she got to page 44, she stopped, mesmerized by the photo of a long-legged model in a red sequined dress: the Vice-Chancellor's wife, his trophy bride. She always looked gorgeous. Spiked heels. Amazing dresses.

Before Chloe knew what she was doing, she'd left her lounge chair and was upstairs in the Vice-Chancellor's bedroom, going through his wife's walk-in closet. The two of them wouldn't be home for hours, and the kids were in bed. There was no way could she could get caught. She flicked through the designer dresses, imagining what it would be like to wear such clothes. Then, there it was, right in front of her, the red sequined dress from page 44. Chloe wriggled out of her T-shirt and shorts, and into the dress. She turned to admire herself in a mirror—

The crash of breaking glass reverberated up from downstairs. She swung away from the mirror, dread squeezing the air from her lungs. A burglar. The kids. The sound had come from somewhere near the pool.

As if trapped in a slow-motion horror movie, Chloe would forever remember the tight silk lining of the red dress cinching her thighs as she flew to the top of the stairs to see what had happened. She'd never forget looking down to where her iced tea glass now lay broken at the edge of the pool. But most of all, she'd never forget the ripples in the blue water...

Nausea surged up Chloe's throat. She swallowed back the bitter taste, jumped up from her couch, and paced to the window. She looked out toward where the guy from the Northern Circle had walked through the glimmer of streetlight only minutes earlier, the wind swirling around him. She'd known in that instant that she was going to catch him, that she had to. Like she'd known that night, all those years ago at the Vice-Chancellor's house, that someday, someway, she had to right the tragedy that she'd caused.

Chloe took a deep breath, easing herself past the memory. Her tension subsided. But it picked up again as her thoughts shifted back to the guy and the heart-pounding sensation of being trapped against the cedar hedge, with nowhere to escape as he stepped closer. Now that she thought about it, Chloe could remember how he smelled too: like bacon and coffee, and cinnamon. Magic. Power. Confidence. His dimples and smirk.

Her stomach tensed and a wave of tingles surged low in her body. She brushed her fingers across her lips, imagining his lips against hers. Spicy and sweet. The kiss deepening. His fingers trailing magic down her arms, caressing the sides of her breasts.

Heat flushed her cheeks. She wheeled from the window. What he smelled like or might taste like or how titillating his witch-touch might feel weren't important. What was vital was the Northern Circle and that they were interested in her.

She retrieved the invitation from her bed. Thanks to the guy breaking the seal, she could read it again without fear.

A thought darted into Chloe's head, wicked and enticing. The last thing she wanted to do was drive the coven off. But that didn't mean she couldn't have a little fun and at the same time show this Athena Marsh and her coven that they weren't the only ones who could play the spy game.

She dropped into her desk chair, closed her eyes, and drew in a long breath through her nose. Then she focused all her energy on the invitation and let the breath out slowly, allowing her magic to flow from her fingertips into the paper's fibers.

"Reveal to me," she murmured.

A tight sensation spread upward from her throat to her ears. Her heartbeat slowed and images rippled into her head, the recent history of the paper:

Feminine fingers, long nails, pale skin scented with lavender oil, holding a stick of gold sealing wax. Her pinky is weighed down by a ring, amber set into gold. Another ring is on her middle finger. An amethyst crystal carved with an N surrounded by an etched circle, its power flowing along with magic into the hot wax. The woman sets down the stick and intones a spell. Her voice reverberates. The scent of burning sage smokes the air.

Chloe focused harder, straining to see the rest of the room, using more power than perhaps she should.

Darkness surrounds the woman, shielding what lies beyond from her view. Just her: Late twenties. Long mink-brown hair tucked behind her ears, shoulders veiled in a red and gold shawl. Hereditary magic, passed down through endless generations. Gifted. Experienced. A black beaded choker encircles her tense neck—

As if she'd been snapped back by the crack of a whip, the connection broke. Maybe Chloe had been negligent about protection, but Athena

Marsh hadn't. And she'd felt the intrusion into her past, like Chloe had hoped. She was equally certain Athena hadn't sensed the full extent of her abilities, despite her turning up the volume a bit.

Satisfied and feeling a bit smug, Chloe smoothed her hand across the invitation and gave it a tap. "Now, my pretty, let's take another look at you."

As Chloe had thought, the information was basic. A meet and greet including dinner at the Northern Circle's complex. RSVP. The address. A number to text for a ride if desired. *Probably a ride with the dangerously handsome guy*, she reminded herself. The get-together was Friday. Two days from now at 7 p.m.

She opened her laptop. Her first class was at eight o'clock. Organic Chemistry. That didn't leave her with a lot of time, but enough to Google the complex's address and have a quick look-see. Maybe she could even find something online about Athena or the other members of the Northern Circle—even the guy. She licked her lips, the fantasy about kissing him flickering back into her mind. Not a good idea, more than likely he already had a girlfriend or two.

A soft knock came at her door and her neighbor Juliet's voice whispered, "Chloe, are you awake?"

"Just a minute." She shoved the invitation under the laptop, then opened the door. What the heck could Juliet want this early?

Juliet streaked past her and into the apartment, the belt on her bathrobe trailing out behind her like a cat's tail. Actually, even without the tail, Juliet looked a lot like a cat—a Persian cat with big, blue eyes and flat face. Chloe didn't know if anyone ever mentioned this similarity to her, but she doubted Juliet would take it as an insult. She was a full-fledged cat lady. In fact, lately she'd been talking about dropping out of college to start a homemade cat toy business instead of sticking with her dream of becoming a vet. Chloe hoped Juliet's Wiccan friends would talk her out of the idea.

Juliet flopped down on the couch, her hands twisting into the fabric of her bathrobe.

"What's wrong?" Chloe asked, shutting the door.

"It's Greta. I needed to tell you something before she corners you."

Greta was the other tenant on their floor, a large woman with graying hair, enormous feet, and permanent PMS. She worked down the street at the Red Cross blood bank.

"You guys had another run in?" Chloe asked. It seemed a little early for that. Like 6 a.m. early.

Juliet's head bobbed. "The kitties and I were looking out the window. I was having tea and they were having some catnip crumbles. First, I saw the guy walk up onto our porch and heard you go downstairs, then Greta started pounding on my door. She was all worked up about smelling smoke. *'I thought the house was on fire, candles should be illegal...'* blah, blah, blah." She skillfully imitated Greta's piercing voice.

"You told Greta it was me not you, right?"

"Of course not. I just didn't want you to contradict what I said." Juliet looked down at her bejeweled kitty slippers, then she glanced up. Her big eyes widened. "So who's the guy?"

"Um—I don't really know him." She was about to change the subject when she realized this was the perfect opportunity to do some digging. Juliet may not be a hereditary witch like she was and probably didn't even realize people with inborn abilities like hers truly existed. But Juliet was a practicing Wiccan, and an active member of the local Wiccan community. She might know something. "He was dropping off an invitation. Have you ever heard of the Northern Circle coven?"

"No. Are they local?"

Chloe got out the invitation and handed it to her. "It's to a party."

"Cool." Juliet beamed. She turned the envelope around and studied the broken seal with excitement. "There probably will be a ton of people there."

Chloe's stomach dropped. *Shit.* Juliet thought it was a general invitation for anyone who wanted to come, like to a music recital or real estate open house. She swallowed hard as Juliet unfolded the paper and read who it was addressed to.

Juliet thrust the invitation back. "Oh. For a minute I thought...I mean, you'll have fun."

"Don't apologize. I'm sorry if I gave you the wrong impression." Chloe tossed the invitation onto the laptop as if she didn't care. Juliet was always doing nice things for her. She shouldn't have shown it to her. She should have said the guy was someone she'd met in class or through some dating app. "I probably won't go anyway. There are a lot of creeps out there. They probably didn't invite you because you already belong to a coven."

Juliet shrugged. "I suppose you're right. There's another possibility too. That guy was cute from what I saw. Maybe he's interested in you—like personally. Anyway, I'll ask around and see if anyone's heard of them." Her sad-kitty mouth turned up. "Or you could forget about that party and come to our Friday night Wicca study group. Seriously, Chloe, we have a great time. Everyone's really supportive. I've learned so much. You would too." She stopped chattering and gave Chloe an eager look.

"I'm not sure about the party or this Friday, yet. Not that I don't want to go with you. Sometime, maybe."

Before she could finish backpedaling her way out, Juliet bounced up from the couch. "Next week, then. We're getting together Wednesday night. I'll tell everyone that you're coming. You're going to love it. It's going to be the best."

Juliet flung her arms around Chloe, hugging her super hard while Chloe stood there like a wilted stalk of celery. For the love of Hecate, how was she going to get out of this without hurting Juliet's feelings? Most likely she'd have to suck it up and put in an appearance. Worst of all, she'd have to pretend to be a newbie witch.

Her lips twitched into a smile. Or she could give up the pretense of being new to the Craft. It would surprise Juliet, but she could teach and share basic rituals instead of hiding. That would be cool, though she'd have to be careful not to overstep. Keeping the world at large unaware of the existence of true magic was the first law every hereditary witch swore to, long before they were even old enough to cast a spell.

The eager thrum that Chloe had felt when she talked to the guy from the Circle once again buzzed inside her. No matter which path she chose, exciting possibilities waited.

* * * *

An hour later, Chloe slipped into a seat at the front of the lecture hall. She got out her phone and scrunched down, hoping she could avoid talking to anyone and do some research before the professor arrived.

It turned out the Northern Circle's complex was located in a revitalized industrial area near the city of Burlington's waterfront. It was really close to Oakledge Park and a bike path, and on a bus route. It was a long walk from her apartment, but not impossible by any stretch of the imagination. According to the aerial map and limited street views, the complex was composed of an old factory and several garages, perhaps surrounded by gardens and a chain-link fence. Artsy looking, it supposedly housed several businesses and living quarters. It was hard to tell exactly what was going on because of the way the addresses and buildings melded together.

She sat back up as the professor entered. No matter how intrigued she was by the coven, she needed to pay attention in Organic Chem if she wanted her med school application to be top-notch. Still, when class finally ended, she didn't waste time hanging around. She just escaped and dashed outdoors.

The sun was warm and the smell of newly mowed lawn and dried leaves hung in the air. On all sides of her, students rushed by. She followed the eddy for a minute, then ducked out of the flow and hoisted herself up on a concrete wall to sit. She'd reached the end of what she could find out about the coven online. There was, however, one other way to potentially learn more, and quickly.

Before she could talk herself out of it, Chloe took out her phone and called her mom.

Her mom answered instantly. "Chloe, sweetheart. What a nice surprise." Her voice faltered. "Is something wrong? Shouldn't you be in class?"

"Nothing's wrong, Mom. I just had a question." She slipped back onto her feet and turned around, facing a display of mum plants instead of the sidewalk. Her mom was a homebody; for years her life had centered on homeschooling Chloe and her older brothers and sisters. Now it revolved around her grandbabies. Mom was less likely to know about the coven than her dad, but she was far less judgmental. Chloe scrunched her toes for luck and took a deep breath. "Have you ever heard of the Northern Circle?"

Silence. A long silence that seemed to stretch on forever. "I think so," her mom said at last. "Here. Let me give the phone to your dad."

Tension pinched behind Chloe's eyes as her mom clamped her hand over the phone and whispered to someone, undoubtedly Dad. She'd never stopped to consider he might be working from home today. But in truth it didn't matter, Mom would have told him about the call eventually.

"Chloe, nice to hear from you." Dad's voice sounded stiffer than usual. "You don't want to get involved with that Northern Circle crew. They've got a bad reputation."

"I was just curious," Chloe said, sounding more defensive than she'd have preferred. Why did talking to her parents always make her feel like a twelve year old? "The Wiccan woman in my building mentioned them, that's all."

"They're a seedy group. Heritage witches, definitely not Wiccan. A young priestess heads it up now. A Marsh girl. Her father's one slippery fellow."

By "slippery" her dad usually meant they used magic to take in gullible people. "You're not talking dangerous, then."

"He was studying at Yale at the same time as me. He's skilled enough, I suppose. But he spent more time partying than honing his craft. Bickering. Hanky-panky. His ex-wife oversaw the coven for a while. They've had a bad reputation since I was a teenager. Even back then, their high priestess died under questionable circumstances."

"Oh?" Wariness fluttered in her belly. That was something to be concerned about, though it was a long time ago.

"Stay as far away as possible from that family and coven."

"Don't worry about that. But I'm glad I asked." She took a fortifying breath and hastily switched the topic, so he'd think she didn't care that much. "I also called to tell Mom about a woman I met downtown at the farmers' market. She makes really pretty glass straws. A while ago, Mom mentioned she wanted some."

"Let me give the phone back to her," he said, then added, "We miss you, Chloe. Let me know if you hear that coven's up to anything questionable. The High Council will want to know."

"Will do," she said. Disreputable. Partying. Hanky-panky. Ex-wife. If she were reading between the lines right, Athena Marsh's father was a womanizer and that was the main reason for the coven's reputation and her father not liking them. That also answered her bigger question. No mentions of dark magic or dubious practices. Nothing wrong with Athena herself. In other words, there was no reason for her not to check them out and see what her generation of Northern Circle witches were up to. She just needed to stay clear of daddy dearest.

Chapter 3

Lead me to the sweet garden of discovery, to joy and truth, and wisdom.
—Chloe Winslow, entreaty to Hecate

"You look amazing. But yellow?" Juliet wrinkled her nose at Chloe's outfit: skinny black jeans, a tight raspberry top, and the offending canary-bright gilet. The gilet was Chloe's absolute favorite new find, totally fun and stylish with a single button at the throat that allowed the vest-like top to flutter open and show a flash of raspberry and skin when she moved. It was the sort of thing she'd always longed to wear, but back home looking chic and sunny had never felt right. Even when she'd pulled the gilet from the rack at the store, her mind had gone back to *Glamour Magazine*, page 44, and the red sequin dress. It had taken all she had to get past the quiver of unworthiness in her stomach and buy it. But she was on the path to right her wrongs. She deserved it and it made her feel powerful.

"If there are other newbies there," Chloe said, "they'll be wearing dark colors—traditional stuff. I'd rather look like me." She held her arm out so Juliet could fasten the clasp on her charm bracelet, its tiny pentacle jingling against the miniature athame and crystal pendulum.

"You mean you'd rather have that guy notice you."

"Well, yeah, partly that," she said, as Juliet finished with the clasp. "Mostly I've been thinking about the way he was dressed the other night. The invitation sounded casual, but I think they're the kind of crowd that calls for stylish and classy."

Juliet hissed, like a tomcat defending its territory. "The Craft isn't about clothes or money. Seriously, if they're like that you should forget them and come to my study group. That is, if you're sincere about learning witchcraft and not just looking for a party."

Her throat clenched. A retort prickled the tip of her tongue, but she took a deep breath and forced herself to sound vaguely unbothered. "You're probably right. But if I don't go, I'll always wonder what I missed."

"I'm sorry. I didn't mean to sound so bitchy. I know you're sincere. It's just, people using the Craft as an excuse to party or pretend to be cool is my hot button."

"Don't worry about it. You were just trying to help. And, for what it's worth, I didn't get a snobby vibe off him." Chloe glanced at her phone, checking the time. "I've got to go. I'm supposed to meet him in the parking lot at six-thirty."

With her suede jacket over her arm and the heels of her ankle boots clicking a sharp cadence, Chloe took off. It wasn't dark yet, but a chill had settled in the air. It stole the heat from her anger and replaced it with a shiver of excitement. To an extent, Juliet was right. Tonight was about partying, not learning. But so what? She deserved some fun. Besides, she totally intended on finding out more about the Circle's plans to access ancient medical knowledge at the same time, so it wouldn't be all fun and games.

Plus, since her phone conversation with her father, meeting the Northern Circle had taken on another significance. The last thing in the world she wanted to do was shame her family further by becoming involved with disreputable witches. But a part of her also wanted to prove her father and his generation of magic practitioners wrong about the Northern Circle. Younger witches were as capable of managing a coven and doing great things as him and his cronies. Chloe didn't know Athena, but she felt sorry for her, pre-judged because her father was a womanizer and the coven had gone to seed under her mother's care, issues that had nothing to do with her. How could her generation become anyone or discover anything new if older witches didn't give them a chance? Or a second chance, if need be.

Chloe hugged her jacket against her chest and scanned the street. Every parking space was taken. A woman with two young kids piled into an SUV. A truck loaded with hay bales and pumpkins rumbled past. She'd swapped a couple of texts with Athena about where and when she'd be picked up. She was right on time. Unfortunately, she'd failed to ask what kind of car she should be on the lookout for.

The sexy coven guy's car. Her lips pressed into a smile. *Devlin*, she reminded herself of his name, saying it slowly, getting used to the feel of it on her tongue. Athena had told Chloe his name a little over an hour ago in a text. She'd been getting out of the shower when her phone chirped.

Standing there naked and wet while she read his name for the first time had felt oddly intimate, ridiculously so.

A car horn blared, bringing Chloe out of her thoughts. An orange BMW coupe with several people inside had double-parked a few yards away. The driver's door opened. Devlin emerged, then bent back into the car and pulled his seat forward as if readying for her to climb into the back.

When she reached him, he greeted her with a smile and a teasing sparkle in his eyes. "I wasn't sure if we'd have to wait for you."

She laughed. "It doesn't take me that long to get ready."

His smile widened. "Either way, you look really nice."

Heat flushed through her, a delicious tension tugging just below her belly. "Thanks, so do you."

She started to get into the back, but discovered only a narrow section of her seat still available. A burly African American guy in a yellow button-down shirt was manspreading across his seat as well as some of hers. Glossy dreadlocks studded with gold beads hung over his shoulders. A carefully trimmed beard outlined his chin. Gold-rimmed glasses. Classy aftershave, bergamot and lavender, if she wasn't mistaken. Anyway, she was grateful he smelled nice, given how much room he took up.

"Hey," she said, greeting him and a woman who sat slouched in the shotgun seat. Actually, the woman was skinny and looked more like a girl, though she probably was in her early to mid-twenties.

The guy eyed Chloe. "I've seen you around campus. You go to UVM, right?"

"Yeah. I'm hoping to get into the med school next year. Right now. I'm just taking a few last prerequisites." She held out her hand. "My name's Chloe. And you're—?"

"Midas." As Devlin put the BMW in gear and headed into the flow of traffic, Midas divulged that he was already in graduate school: geology with a focus on geophysics. He was all excited about his thesis, working on it and as a teaching assistant…

He yammered on as they drove along the University Green, and turned down the steep hill toward Burlington's shopping district. Cars and buses rushed past. In the distance, Lake Champlain stretched across the horizon, stripes of darkness overtaking a fading sunset. Just when Chloe feared no one else would ever be able to get a word in edgewise, the girl in the shotgun seat swiveled around and interrupted him.

"I'm not going to school," she said, softly.

The girl might have been pretty in a delicate china doll sort of way, but even makeup couldn't hide her blotchy skin and the hollows under her eyes. *Drugs*, was the first thought that popped into Chloe's mind, though overuse of magic left the same markers. Whether it was meth or magic or a combination of the two, the girl had done too much of something at some point in the past.

Devlin cleared his throat. "Sorry. I didn't mean to be a bad host." He glanced in the rearview mirror at Chloe, then tilted his head in the girl's direction. "This is Emily."

"Em for short," the girl added. Her haunted eyes met Chloe's. "School's not really my thing. I was staying at a halfway place in Albany, when I learned about the coven." She bowed her head. "I—I mostly just talk to the dead."

"Oh—" That's nice? Awful? Chloe wasn't sure how to respond to that.

Devlin came to her rescue, expanding on what Em had said. "When I was a kid, Northern Circle's home base was in Saratoga Springs, New York—near Albany. The coven's home base has been in various parts of Vermont for almost twenty years, but we still have connections in Upstate New York."

The traffic intensified, and Devlin stopped talking. They passed Church Street with all its shops, and City Hall Park where the farmers' market was held on Saturdays. They headed into blocks of older homes that Chloe was unfamiliar with. Warehouse buildings. Breweries. Art Galleries.

Chloe folded her arms across her chest. It was taking longer to reach the coven than she'd expected, and it was getting darker sooner than she'd counted on. It seemed impossible, but she must have miscalculated the coven's location, somehow.

"Are there going to be any other potential initiates?" Em asked.

Devlin nodded. "One more. He's already at the complex."

Midas leaned forward. "I have another question too. I'm not clear on exactly what the Circle has to offer us—above the normal Sabbats and gatherings. What about mentoring? I heard Athena's not much older than us. Are there elder members? Experienced witches?"

Devlin's energy crackled in the air. He gunned the car, bumping over a set of railroad tracks. His voice toughened. "Don't ever underestimate Athena. By the time she was eighteen she was more skilled than most middle-aged witches. The Circle takes learning and traditions seriously. But mostly we're looking for witches who are innovative—and fearless."

Innovative. Fearless. Her generation. Chloe bit down on a smile. That was exactly what she wanted. New things. Groundbreaking discoveries, like the cures and medicines he'd mentioned the other night. Second chances.

Devlin turned into a driveway with wasteland skirting both sides. "What you want to remember," he corrected himself, "what you *all* need to remember is that tonight is a two-way street. This gathering is as much about us wanting you as your interest in us."

Chloe swallowed hard. When Devlin had mentioned this before, she'd taken it as regular coven spiel meant to suck in new members. But he sounded dead serious now.

She sat up straighter and mentally switched from party mood to full-on competitive mode. If the Circle was looking for impressive and confident, that's what she'd give them. An unwieldy thought slipped in to her mind and she pressed her lips together in a momentary frown. This also meant she needed to forget about flirting with Devlin, at least for tonight. She smiled—though finding out if he was available could still remain a priority.

Ahead, an abandoned three-story brick factory surrounded by a chain-link fence loomed out from the twilight. Its arched windows gaped darkly as if the rooms beyond them were vacant. But as they drove nearer, hints of what truly lay in store for her appeared on either side of the driveway.

Strange glass spheres and pyramids glowed in the weeds and hung from trees. There were junk cars painted with wild colors. Blossoming plants sprouted out of them, vines trailed over them. A concrete angel knelt under a cloak of ivy. Weird, artsy things, strewn everywhere.

They rounded a thicket and came to a place where it looked like the chain-link fence had been ripped open—just wide enough for cars to pass through.

"We're not in Kansas anymore," Em said, craning forward.

Chloe leaned over the front seat to see what Em was looking at. Arching over the hole in the fence was a gateway made out of twisted iron. At the very peak of the gateway were at least a dozen life-size flying monkeys created from car parts and other scrap metal. Some leered down, their fangs bared. Others spread their sheet metal wings, as if readying to take flight.

She swiveled around to catch another glimpse as the car cruised under the gateway. "Those are creepy—and amazing."

"Fucking amazing," Midas said. "Who made them?"

Devlin tapped on the brakes, slowing the car. "Chandler Parrish. She's one of the coven members who lives on the grounds." He nodded towards a cinderblock building off to their left where an old Jeep Cherokee and a kid's bike were parked out front. "That's her apartment and workshop. She'll probably give you a tour if you ask."

He pulled up and parked by the factory's front door, a nondescript entryway that Chloe suspected was purposely plain to contrast with whatever mind-blowing things decorated the inside. She could barely wait for Devlin to get out and pull the front seat forward so she could escape. Well, that was until she brushed against his arm and their eyes met.

Then, for a heartbeat, she forgot all about the flying monkeys and the cool architecture, and what waited inside. She even forgot about the party, and Athena. And even her plan to put medicine and magic first. For a moment, her body hummed and all she wanted was to be alone with him.

Then life snapped back into motion as he herded them toward the front door.

Chapter 4

A girl with death on her hands shall free a demon from darkness,
and he shall scorch the world of man.
—First Prophesies of Merlin

Devlin opened the front door and Chloe strutted into the foyer—
projecting confidence while butterflies tangoed in her stomach. Midas and
Em following right behind her. The foyer was small, nothing more than a
brick-walled box. Straight ahead was an industrial-style sliding door made
out of steel and opaque glass. On the other side of it, a shadowy figure of a
person wavered into view. Chloe couldn't tell if it was a man or a woman,
but when the door slid open, she recognized the figure immediately, from
when she'd used the invitation to look into the past. Athena: long mink-
brown hair and cropped bangs, strong cheekbones, elegant nose and chin, a
taut neck encircled by a black beaded choker. The only difference was that
now her red and gold silk shawl was wrapped around her hips, accenting
the eggplant color of her dress instead of covering her shoulders like before.

"Come in, come in." Athena waved them forward. "Everyone's waiting
downstairs to meet you." All around her the air shimmered and rippled
in an impressive halo, an apt illusion Chloe decided was caused by the
contrast between the darkness they stood in and the vibrant brightness of
the hallway behind Athena.

They all followed Athena out of the foyer into the wide hallway. Even
though Chloe had visited amazing places like the historic Eastern Coast High
Council of Witches headquarters in Connecticut, she found it impossible
to not gawk at everything they passed. To say the building was a factory-
turned-home was an understatement. From the graffiti-splattered brick

wall that ran along one side of the hallway, to the steel beams that stretched across the towering ceiling above, down to the dents and gouges in the wooden floorboards beneath her feet, this wasn't just a restored building. It was an ultra-modern work of industrial art.

Athena turned right, toward where the graffiti-splattered wall gave way to an iron railing and to what looked at a distance to be the top of a wide staircase. As they got closer, Chloe realized they hadn't entered on the first floor like she'd assumed. They were in fact on the second floor, headed for a balcony that overlooked the first story. A heartbeat of music and the hum of voices pulsed up from somewhere below.

Chloe stopped walking. She closed her eyes and took a deep breath, listening to the drone of the sounds and absorbing the earthy-natural scent of the place: sage smoke, burning candles, houseplants, lots of plants. Energy caressed her skin, the touch of air enlivened by the closeness of so many witches. And, for that moment, it was like she was home again on the Summer Solstice with her family's coven. It felt almost too good to be true.

"You did an amazing job with this place," Midas said to Athena. "I assume it's self-sufficient, energy-wise?"

"Yes, for the most part." Athena stroked her throat, drawing a black-polished fingernail along her choker for a second, as though thinking back. "My mother deserves the credit for creating it. Devlin, too. Most of the stonework, water features, and a lot of the gardens are his work."

"Devlin?" Chloe's eyes flashed open. She hadn't expected that. She glanced around looking for him in the hope that he'd explain further. But he wasn't there. What the heck?

"I think he went to park the car," Em said softly.

Athena flagged her hand. "We're lucky he's here tonight at all. He's been hiding away, working on a project for a client who's building an elaborate log home in the Adirondacks."

"What exactly does he do?" Chloe asked. It sounded nosy and she should have been focused on questions about the coven, but she couldn't help being curious. So much of Devlin was a mystery, one she badly wanted to unearth—or better yet, undress.

"He's a landscape architect," Athena said crisply, studying Chloe with shrewd blue eyes as if she'd read her thoughts.

Heat rushed up Chloe's neck. "I guess—I assumed he was still in graduate school." She bit her lip as a sickening fear unfolded inside her. What if Devlin played messenger for the coven and gave people rides not because he was nice or even because he was a coven member or worked for the coven part-time? What if he did things because he had a relationship with Athena, a very personal one? It wouldn't be surprising, but it would really suck.

Athena's dress shushed around her legs as she headed down the open-sided staircase. "Enough about Devlin. There are lots of other members for you to all meet."

For a second, Chloe thought about taking one last run at trying to solve the mystery of Devlin's relationship status, but the stylish grandeur of what lay below stole her attention.

The floor plan was open. On one side of the staircase, an ultra-modern pool table with electric blue felt took up most of the space. A guy and woman circled the table, involved in a furious game of eight ball. Across the room, a fully-stocked bar sat against the wall, glasses and bottles sparkling under blue lights. On the other side of the staircase, a half-dozen people—mostly women—chatted and lounged on chic furniture, amid potted palms and stands covered with flickering candles. Watercolor paintings of oak forests and moonlit skies dotted the brick walls. The furthest walls in that room—as well as in the lounge area—were tall sliding glass doors crosshatched by industrial steel. Beyond them, Chloe could see hints of light weaving through shadowed gardens, and perhaps the outline of a stone monolith.

As they reached the bottom of the staircase, Athena paused and turned to address them. "Feel free to look around and introduce yourselves. I need to finish up in the dining room. I'll join you in a few."

"Do you need help?" Chloe asked. Not offering would have felt wrong, rude in fact.

"Certainly." Athena gave an approving nod. "Come along." She took off at a fast pace, her footsteps clicking smartly on the polished tiles.

"Will your father be here?" Chloe asked, as they strode past the bar and into a lofty, narrow dining room. This was something she really did need to know.

Athena laughed. "Definitely not. He's less than unwelcome here. But it would be amusing."

"Sorry. I didn't realize—"

Athena's expression tightened. "I suspect you told your parents about the invitation and they filled you with stories about the coven and my family's past?"

Chloe lowered her eyes, shame blistering inside her. A small part of her brain argued that she had no reason to be ashamed. After all, Athena had investigated her as well—and she hadn't told her parents anything.

She raised her chin and met Athena's eyes. "But we aren't our parents or our pasts, are we?"

A smile softened Athena's lips. "No we aren't—and I thank you for realizing that. I like you, Chloe, and I truly hope the rest of the coven feels the same way."

Warmth washed over Chloe. She liked her too. Athena was genuinely open minded and self-governed. Not at all what Chloe had expected, after talking to her father. At the heart of things, they had a lot in common. "It's hard enough growing up as a witch without being surrounded by rumors and negativity."

Athena stepped closer to Chloe, resting her hand on her shoulder. Her eyes studied Chloe's, intent and unwavering, her hand moving up onto her cheek. Chloe stiffened, uncomfortable with the sudden intimacy of being close enough to feel the warmth of Athena's breath. But she held still. Covens were like family, right?

The forceful *clank* of a door swinging shut nearby interrupted the stillness, making her jump back.

Athena's hand dropped to her side and her gaze went to someone behind Chloe. "Fantastic. Thank you, Jessica. I was about to do that myself."

Chloe swiveled. Standing in front of a still swinging door that opened into a kitchen was a buxom brunette in a moss-green shirtdress. She'd seen the dress in the Anthropologie catalog. In fact, she might have bought it if she hadn't already blown her budget on the gilet, not to mention a looming phone bill.

The brunette's eyes slanted in her direction, her lips curling up in distaste. "I see the special guests are here."

Athena hurried to the brunette and wiggled a pitcher of ice water from her grip. "Chloe"—she said, glancing back— "this is Jessica. She's the rock of this coven, a generous witch and my assistant. If you have any questions, she's the one to ask."

It didn't take a genius to see that she and Jessica weren't going to be buddies. Not when Jessica was making it very obvious that she found the newbies distasteful. Or, more likely, she didn't like them getting too close to her Athena.

Chloe forced a smile. "I'll remember that."

Athena set the pitcher on the table. "Why don't you two finish in here while I check on the oven to see how everything's coming along?" Without giving them a chance to respond, she swept off and vanished into the kitchen.

Jessica huffed out a loud breath, then fetched a stack of linen napkins from the sideboard.

Chloe kept her smile tacked on. Maybe she didn't have to worry about daddy dearest, but being around this sweetheart wasn't going to be a picnic. They went to work setting the table. The main courses were going to go on a buffet interspersed with clusters of votive candles and bittersweet vine. The salads and trimmings were to be served family style on the table.

For the most part, Jessica glared and Chloe did the talking. Then Chloe figured out that Jessica didn't mind talking about the coven, as long as she didn't ask personal questions about her or Athena. Apparently, not only did Devlin, Athena, and Chandler Parrish—the metal sculptor—live here, but so did a woman named Brooklyn. She was Haitian and twenty-three, and—at least according to Jessica—the most skilled cream and salve maker to ever grace the face of the Earth, which was bullshit. One of Chloe's aunts deserved that title.

Athena reappeared carrying a bowl of iced shrimp. Perhaps it was Jessica rattling on about Brooklyn's mind-blowing skills that filled Chloe with the need to prove herself, but when she was certain Athena and Jessica were watching, Chloe flicked her fingers at the nine-branched candelabra that sat in the center of the table.

"Fire," she said, commanding all the candles to light at the same time.

They flared to life instantly. Chloe turned her attention to an off- kilter napkin, straightening it out while trying to look nonchalant as though she lit that many candles every day and then some.

Jessica sniffed indignantly. "That tells us all we need to know about her."

Athena's eyes went icy. She pushed the bowl of shrimp into Jessica's hands. "Do you mind taking this out to the bar and making sure everyone has drinks? We'll be out in a second."

Chloe swallowed hard, unsure if Athena was angry with Jessica or her. It had to be Jessica. She was the bitch. Chloe had just done something that needed doing; though with a teeny bit more flare than necessary.

Totally silent, Athena waited until Jessica's footsteps faded. Then she glanced over her shoulder at the buffet, pursed her lips, and blew out a single puff of air.

Every votive candle on the buffet lit up at once—two or maybe three dozen of them.

She looked at Chloe and winked.

"How did you do—?" Chloe replayed what Athena had done in her mind. No hand motions. No verbal commands. She had to be a firestarter or in league with a fire spirit, that had to be the answer.

Athena moistened her lips with the tip of her tongue. "I don't have any special talents in this area if that's what you're thinking. Push your words and intention into your breath, focus and gather your magic there instead of in your fingertips. You can use this method for psychometry as well—like when you felt the history of a certain invitation?" She raised a perfectly arched eyebrow.

Chloe grimaced. *Damn.* She *was* good.

"I'm sorry about that." Chloe shrugged. "It wasn't personal. I wanted to know about the coven. You have to admit—the early morning delivery, the spell on the sealing wax—that's not exactly the normal way invitations get delivered."

Athena folded her arms across her chest. "I hope you're past that now because we're looking for witches who aren't just powerful. We want members who can be single-mindedly devoted to the coven and our purpose. Medicine and magic. Coven power, not personal glory. Unquestioning trust." She moved closer and leaned forward, pushing back Chloe's hair. "We aren't looking for showoffs."

Before Chloe could say anything, Athena turned and strode off toward the living room. A chill settled inside Chloe and for the first time it fully sunk in how serious this was. *Magic and Medicine.* This wasn't just a new path for her to explore. This Circle was potentially her new beginning.

But was she ready for it? Was this what she really wanted?

Yes. With all her heart.

Chapter 5

There is something about the heat and sparks,
metal welding to metal, finding form and beauty in what was cast aside.
—WPZI interview with artist Chandler Parrish

Chloe caught up with Athena at the bar where she was opening a bottle of white wine.

"Would you like a glass? This is one of our finest. Of course, if you prefer something else…"

"Wine would be great." Chloe took the glass Athena held out, her mouth watering as the scent of spices and sweet woodruff reached her nose. She took another sniff. "May wine, right?"

"It's our top seller. Personally, I don't care if it's an autumn or spring, it's my go-to favorite."

Chloe set her glass on the bar. "I didn't realize you were in the wine business."

"It's one of our more lucrative ventures," Athena said.

Casual as anything, Chloe rested her wrist on the top of her wine glass and let the tip of the miniature athame on her charm bracelet touch the wine. It didn't change color, indicating the absence of drugs or spells in the wine. Not that she suspected Athena, testing was simply a habit her mom and sisters had drilled into her. A smart habit.

Athena came around the bar, glass in hand. "Enough about business, let me introduce you." She raised her voice, addressing the couple at the pool table. "This is Brooklyn and Matt."

The guy turned toward them. He was a cute, baby-faced blond, an outdoor-redneck kind of guy, his scuffed jeans and flannel shirt tamed down for the occasion by the addition of a gray pullover sweater. "Nice to meet you," he said.

Brooklyn put her pool stick down and favored Chloe with a smile. At least *favored* was how her rich, stormy energy felt as it reached out and welcomed Chloe, deep-rooted magic that smelled dusky and earthy, and spoke of a long lineage of practitioners. Given her Haitian heritage, she might be a servant of the spirits, a follower of some form of Vodou. Perhaps Jessica hadn't exaggerated that much about her salve-making skills.

Brooklyn gestured toward the other half of the room, screened from sight by a short wall and the staircase. "Chandler asked where the two of you were. She's setting up the maze."

Chloe smiled and nodded, but the fact the maze was being *set up* by Chandler the metal sculptor both confused and interested her. "I'm guessing this isn't a standard garden style maze with plants and walking paths?"

"You'll see." Athena draped her arm over Chloe's shoulder and walked her around the stairs. "It's a test, actually. Nothing difficult. However, we did have a man arrive last night who wanted to join us and thanks to the maze he's gone."

"He failed?" Chloe said. Her mouth went dry. How hard was this test?

"You might say that, though he wasn't totally without his uses." Athena pressed her lips together, but not before Chloe caught a glimpse of a smirk.

Chloe took a couple sips of her wine. She didn't want to drink too much before this test, but half a glass might help her relax and keep her head where it belonged.

Everyone—including Em and Midas—were gathered on chairs and floor cushions that had been pulled up close around a glass-topped coffee table. Athena tossed out introductions to the people Chloe hadn't met. There were the two elderly women in black and a man from somewhere near the Canadian border. One of them smelled like pee, and Chloe reminded herself to avoid sitting near them at dinner. There was a couple who lived off the grid and ran the coven's small vineyard. None of them gave off anything more than a slight hum of energy; no doubt their skill level was equally basic.

Chandler Parrish turned out to be in her late twenties or maybe early thirties. She was broad-shouldered with shaved-short hair, large hands, and sleeves of monkey and dragon tattoos. Even with a caftan covering eighty percent of her body, her effortless movement as she hoisted the thick glass top off from the coffee table and rested it against a wall revealed how agile and powerful she was.

"That would be the maze," Athena said, nodding at the coffee table. With the top removed, Chloe could see that the glass had laid overtop a table-size labyrinth created out of rusted gears, nuts and bolts, part of a car radiator, gauges...It was like a giant cross-section of a brain gone steampunk and set on top of four chunky legs.

Midas knelt down on one side of the table and peered over his glasses for a moment. "This is totally awesome. How does it work?"

Chandler settled cross-legged on the floor across from him. "I'll demonstrate how I choose to do it. Then it'll be your turn."

She placed a gray marble in one corner of the maze. With a flick of her fingers, an athame appeared in her grip. Chandler rested the athame's tip at the base of the marble and murmured an incantation. As the tremor of her magic filled the air, the dragon and monkey tattoos on her arms vibrated as if about to come to life. Exhaling, she drew the athame forward. The marble followed, creeping along one of the maze's alleyways as if something of great force fought to hold it back. She drew the marble around a gear and into a straighter alleyway. Suddenly the marble swung away from the athame's tip, veered down a dead-end alley and stopped. Chandler mumbled her incantation again and placed her athame tip against the marble. Energy crackled in the air around her, sparks and tiny blue flames licked up from under the marble. But it didn't move.

Settling back, Chandler withdrew her athame. "Not a recorder breaker for me, but you get the idea."

Chloe studied the maze. This was a test, clearly. But when Chandler had said, *"How I choose to do it,"* Chloe had taken it to mean the test wasn't just about moving a marble from one point to another. It involved using personal magical strengths to succeed, about resourcefulness. Most likely there was magic melded into the maze, but something else was going on as well. She just couldn't quite put her finger on it.

Athena tilted her head at Midas. "You ready?"

"Anytime." He grinned, a shit-eating grin that told Chloe he'd figured out the trick. She also suspected the no showing-off bit was about to go out the window.

"Would you like anything?" Athena asked. "You can request and use any tool of the Craft you desire."

Midas flicked a dreadlock back from his face. "Nope, I got this."

He scooched around the table until he was as close to the marble as possible. Then he placed one hand over the marble and his other hand under the maze, directly beneath the marble.

Chandler smiled approvingly. "I don't believe we've seen it done this way before. Smart move."

Athena leaned closer, eyes wide and glinting with eagerness as he moved his hand over the marble, leading it down an alleyway and deeper into the maze. The marble didn't cling to the metal or resist as it had with Chandler. In fact, it moved almost too freely to the point that Midas had to withdraw his hand for a second and let the marble go still, while he caught his breath and refocused.

Chloe took a sip of wine to hide a grin. Okay. She was starting to get this. The marble resisting and clinging to the metal maze could be caused by magnetism, if the marble was a loadstone or contained magnets. Midas's hand that was beneath the table might be blocking the earth's natural magnetism, somehow magnified by magic. It was pure speculation, but Midas was into geophysics, so it made sense for him to catch on quickly. Chandler could have used the incantation to magnetize her athame. The question was, what could she do without copying either of them? What would play to her strengths instead of feebly imitating theirs?

Her fingers went to her charm bracelet and the tiny crystal pendulum dangling from it. Divining. She was fairly good at that. It seemed like she could figure out something, especially if Em went next and she got a few more minutes to think.

Chloe scanned the group. Where was Em? For that matter, Devlin still wasn't around either.

She widened her search and spotted Em sitting partway up the staircase with her knees pulled up to her chest. Her hands were clamped over her ears and she was rocking rhythmically, as if listening to music.

A heavy feeling gathered in Chloe's chest. She understood that withdrawing was one way to deal with stress. But Em had accepted the invitation. She'd somehow gotten here from New York State and connected with Devlin. It would be a shame if Em blew her chance of joining now by not even trying. The Circle might be her salvation from whatever past she was escaping.

Chloe set her glass on a stand and wound her way through the crowd to the staircase. As she started up, Em raised her head and took her earbuds out.

"Hey," Chloe said, sitting down beside her. "You're going to try the maze, aren't you?"

Em clutched her knees closer. "I'm not sure that's a good idea. I feel like I'm going to puke."

"It's just nerves." Chloe put her arm around Em's shoulder, leaned closer, and whispered. "You're a medium, right?"

She nodded. "But I don't see how that's going to help."

"It's not a normal maze. I think the marble's a magnet." Chloe picked at her bracelet, thinking. "Maybe a spirit could tell you what to do?"

"Maybe, if they wanted to." As Em lapsed into silence, an uneasy feeling prickled Chloe's intuition. Someone was watching her.

She held still for a second, trying to pinpoint the person. Athena might be wondering what she was talking to Em about and why, assessing her actions as part of the maze test. Jessica could be keeping an eye on her.

Tilting her head, Chloe let her intuition guide her gaze over the staircase railing toward the lounge.

Devlin. He was leaning against the bar, looking up at her with bold dark eyes.

Heat flared through her cheeks, and a rush of tingles invaded her belly.

He raised the beer he was holding in a toast and smiled.

Her breath caught in her throat and a chill swept her arms. She smiled back and nodded, but deep inside fear uncoiled. She was too far away to understand the meaning of his toast, to see it reflected in his eyes or in any other subtleties of his body language. She wanted to believe it was purely friendly—or even a hint that he'd been watching her out of a more personal interest. But there was also the possibility that he was saluting her because he thought she was cozying up to Em in hopes of finding a way to succeed at the maze. If that was the case, then he really didn't get her.

"I know." Em's fingers clenched Chloe's arm, bringing her up as she got to her feet. "Electromagnetism and ghosts are like kissing cousins. I can do this."

Em's burst of confidence buoyed Chloe, making her grin like crazy. They hurried down the stairs and rejoined the crowd. Midas still had the marble moving through the maze. But the marble was now on the farthest side of its labyrinth of alleyways and dead-ends. Even his long arms weren't long enough to reach over and beneath the table at the same time. He twisted and stretched like a contortionist. Finally, only one fingertip could reach the marble, then not even that.

Midas threw his hands up in surrender. "Damn. I was so close."

"That was amazing." Chandler applauded and everyone else joined in.

"Good job," Matt added.

Em drifted over to Midas. Hooking her lank hair behind her ears, she gazed down at him. "Done yet?"

"Yeah, I guess." He huffed out a frustrated breath and relinquished his spot.

Em sunk down cross-legged with her hands resting on her knees. Her eyelids fluttered closed. Her breathing slowed. She raised her arms, outstretched, with her palms up. "I beseech you, souls that wander this place." Her voice murmured, like the rustle of a graveyard willow. "Give me aid. Show yourselves. Move the marble that we may see your power. Show us that you're greater than the strength of the maze."

The room hushed. Chloe didn't even dare breathe. Em's voice faded, replaced by the croon of her energy, a sorrowful ballad sweeping the room, calling out to departed souls.

A chill skated up Chloe's spine and her intuition screamed that something powerful was coming.

As if she sensed it too, Athena wheeled and stared at the wall of sliding glass doors. Lips narrowing, she folded her arms across her chest. "I don't like this."

Flash. A blaze of light illuminated the garden, followed by a series of white strobes. Then everything went dark, including the houselights. Only the flicker of candlelight remained.

Chloe's mouth dried. Her pulse hammered in her veins. Whoever the spirit was, they wanted badly to get in. She could feel its insistence building the air, a powerful storm waiting to be unleashed.

The houselights flickered back on. The tension evaporated from the air.

Chloe blew out a relieved breath. Apparently, her intuition had been wrong.

Crackle. Boom. A blindingly bright baseball-size orb streaked from the garden and flew straight at one of the doors, throwing itself against the glass. *Bang. Bang!*

Em leapt to her feet and flung the doors open. "Welcome," she cried, twirling in the circle.

The orb whizzed past her, trailing sparks as it zinged off one wall and then another, like a trapped bird on fire.

Brooklyn and Matt ducked to get out of its way. Jessica froze as the orb flew at her, hovering inches in front of her face before frantically darting off.

"Give me your athame," Athena snapped at Chandler. In a heartbeat, Athena had it in her hand, pointing the tip of its blade at the orb. "Be gone, spirit. You're not welcome—"

Devlin caught Athena's arm, yanking it down. "Let Em finish."

Athena's face went red, her teeth clenched. "If something happens, it's on your head."

"Fine. But let the girl try." Devlin scowled.

Em sailed to the maze. Her voice quivered, bordering on panic. "Please. I beseech you. Move the marble."

Her anguish went right to Chloe's heart. *Please. Help her. Please.* Chloe sent her thoughts out to the orb. *Help Em and we'll help you find peace.*

The orb hesitated, wavering in place. It might have appeared to be nothing more than a mindless glowing ball, shimmering and sparking from gold to bright red. But it was someone's spirit and Chloe sensed that it had turned to look at her. A desperate voice entered her mind. *"Yin. Yang. Betrayal."*

Chloe's mouth fell open, her pulse hammering. She glanced around, searching everyone's faces for signs that they'd heard the voice too. But no else seemed to be reacting beyond their immediate fear and awe at seeing a spirit flinging around the room like a panicked ping-pong ball.

The spirit was talking to her, *her alone.*

Goose bumps rippled up her arms and she trembled. She wasn't the psychic medium in this room, not even close. So why was it talking to her?

The orb flickered. *"Tell Devlin."*

Why me? she asked.

"Tell him," the spirit pleaded.

The orb swung away, then shot down into the maze, white-hot light flashing up from between the metal alleyways as it shrieked and skittered, pushing the marble forward, around gears, and gauges, faster and faster—

"Enough of this!" Athena pointed the athame at the orb. Chloe waved her hands, but before she could tell Athena to stop, she shouted, "Be gone, spirit. I banish thee from this house!"

The orb exploded, a shower of sparks flying outward, then vanishing into thin air.

For a long second uncanny silence filled the room. No one whispered. No one moved. Even the candlelight didn't flicker. Finally, a whimper escaped from Em's mouth. Her gaze lifted to Athena's and she wailed, "You banished it."

Athena stalked toward Em, her voice strained. "Was it a spirit you normally call?"

Em shrank. "No. It just came. It wasn't demonic." She paled. "It wasn't, was it?"

"I didn't like the feel of it," Jessica grumbled.

Everyone started talking at once, about the orb and Em. Chloe fingered the edge of her gilet, an uncomfortable heaviness gathering inside her. She wanted to tell them what the orb had said to her. But it had been explicit about her telling Devlin. And, as much as she respected Athena, she felt more responsible to the spirit and Devlin. Once she told him, he could tell Athena if he wanted to.

Chandler popped open a bottle of champagne. "How about a toast for outsmarting the maze. Well done to Em and Midas!"

As she filled people's glasses, the conversation turned from Em and the orb to Midas and his cleverness. Everyone began dispersing off toward the other side of the room, like the maze tests were done. Athena rested her hand on Em's back, steering her in the same direction.

Chloe glanced at them, then at the maze. She cleared her throat. "I think it's my turn, right?"

Athena gave a throaty laugh. "So it is." She clapped her hands to get everyone's attention. "One last round and then we'll have dinner— vegetarian lasagna and wild turkey that Matt was kind enough to donate to our feast."

Everyone came back over, but they continued to chatter amongst themselves as Chloe sat down at the maze. Anger bristled inside her, making her body tremble. She clenched her hands, forcing herself to still. She got how everyone wanted to start partying in earnest, truly. But couldn't they at least wait a little longer for her to finish?

She took off her bracelet and held it so that the tiny crystal pendulum dangled freely above the marble. She drew in a deep breath, then channeled her energy toward her fingertips, and down into the chain, and into the crystal, as if she were divining. Simultaneously, she withheld some energy, letting its magic mingle with her breath. It was hard to focus on two different intentions at once. *Relax*, she told herself. *Focus. Breathe deep.*

The sounds in the room around her faded into the distance, and the crowd vanished from her field of vision and thoughts. All she saw was the marble. All she felt with her mind's eye was its smoothness and heavy weight, and the labyrinth of alleyways it had to travel for her to succeed. All she heard was the rhythm of her breath and heartbeat.

She exhaled, directing her magic-infused breath at the marble, commanding it to encapsulate the marble in an invisible bubble, to shield it from both the earth's magnetism and the iron maze. Then she asked her pendulum to guide the marble to the other end of the maze.

With the pendulum drawing it along, the encapsulated marble eked forward, up an alleyway, around a turn…A dull headache began to pulse behind Chloe's eyes. Her concentration fumbled and the marble snapped out from under her pendulum. It was game over only minutes after it had begun. Still, she'd succeeded in using her skills to find a solution, even if she hadn't gotten as far as Midas or Em.

She let out her breath, enjoying a mild round of applause as her stress drained away.

"That was really creative," Chandler said.

Athena slipped Chloe a knowing nod and that pleased her more than anything. It was weird. Despite the orb's ominous warning and her need to talk to Devlin in private, she felt overwhelmingly contented. More precisely, it felt like she was taking control of her life and future for a change, in exactly the way she wanted.

* * * *

Dinner was rowdier than Chloe was used to. She ate more than she should have and drank more wine than she'd planned to or needed, not with the buzz she was already getting off the coven's high-octane energy.

She was actually grateful when the older witches and the ones who lived off the grid headed home after dessert.

"I better get going too," Matt said. "I have to be at the park early tomorrow. My boss has been up all our asses about being on time."

Brooklyn smiled. "I better go with you, then—to make sure you don't oversleep."

As they headed up the stairs, Chloe smiled to herself. It was surreal and wonderful to be hanging out with people who had jobs and were working on degrees while still actively being part of a coven. Sure, she'd grown up in exactly this kind of atmosphere. But this felt different, like she was truly an active part of something, not an offshoot of her parents.

With them gone, the mood quieted, especially after Athena invited everyone who was left to join her for an informative meeting in what she called the *teahouse*.

Chloe padded through the sliding glass doors along with the remaining stragglers and into the brisk night air. Scattered spotlights up-lit the garden, outlines of shrubbery and plants blending in with sculptures and stone archways. They passed an obelisk carved with arcane symbols, and monkeys and dragons that resembled Chandler's tattoos. A fountain murmured in the distance and the path under their feet shimmered blue. The whole effect was otherworldly, as if they couldn't possibly be in a city let alone in the remains of an industrial district.

While Athena led the way, Devlin hung back a few yards, bringing up the rear of the group. Chloe slowed her steps, letting everyone else move on.

"Beautiful night," he said to her, smiling skyward.

Chloe hushed her voice. "I need to talk to you about something, privately."

He glanced at her, his brow furrowing with concern. "What is it?"

"When Em was doing the maze, the orb—" She stopped talking. A few yards ahead of them, Midas had swiveled around and was now waiting for them.

"Hey, Devlin." Midas scuffed his foot against the glowing path. "I'm guessing this is solar?"

Devlin slid his hand across the small of Chloe's back. His fingers hesitated for a second as if apologizing for the interruption. "Later, okay?"

"Sure, I guess." Chloe's stomach sank, not just from having to keep such an enormous secret to herself for longer than she'd have preferred, but also from suddenly feeling the cool rush of air on her back where the warmth of his hand had been. The concern on his face a second ago, his lingering touch, everything about him made her breath catch and her hands long to explore his body. What would it be like to kiss him, to feel his touch for much longer than a passing moment—and better yet against her naked skin?

Devlin hurried ahead to catch up with Midas. "It's a commercial product. But I've got an idea about creating a natural solar pavement out of hybrid mushrooms."

"Cool. If you ever need brainstorming partner, let me know."

Chloe joined them. "My aunt raises mushrooms," she said distractedly, still thinking about him touching her, and not realizing that she'd just barged in on their conversation. "Ah—that is, if you need some extra input," she added, a little embarrassed.

"That would be great." Devlin smiled at her, his eyes bright with sincerity.

Chloe returned his smile. "Athena said you designed most of this. Did you two work on it together?"

"To a degree. The gardens are my portfolio—or at least the water features are," he said, once more walking forward. "They're a work in progress."

Glancing down at the luminous path, Chloe searched for a question that would reveal more about his and Athena's relationship. But they'd reached an arched footbridge where Athena and everyone else waited, so she decided to hold off questioning him for another time.

A short ways ahead of them, the teahouse came into view. It was a simple structure, its translucent sliding doors glowing red from the coals of a fire that no doubt smoldered within. They climbed the stairs leading inside, and Chloe discovered she'd indeed been right. At the center of the sparsely decorated room, glowing coals rested in a shallow fire pit, giving just enough warmth for comfort and to keep a kettle of water singing.

She settled down on the mat-covered floor between Em and Chandler. It seemed wiser since Devlin had taken a spot beside Athena. Athena offered them the choice of sake or ginger tea. Chloe chose tea, touching the athame to the steaming liquid to make sure it was safe to drink. But after only a couple of sips her pulse began to race and she felt oddly giddy, though most likely that was a result of the coven's surging energy and the joy in her heart, rather than tampered tea.

She relaxed with her hands braced on the floor behind her, listening while Athena gave an overview of the coven's recent history: her grandfather, Zeus, had apparently bought the complex property about twelve years ago for the coven. Her mother had started the renovations, and Athena had taken over the project a few years ago when she became high priestess.

Her voice shifted, filling with excitement and she got to her feet. "There is something I'd like to show you all."

"What is it?" Midas asked.

She swung around to face them, worry reflected in her eyes. Her gaze moved from Midas, to Em, and finally to Chloe. "I'm not convinced it's wise to show any of you this. Normally, it's something a coven would be shouting off the mountaintops, but because our reputation isn't exactly..." Her voice trailed off and her gaze shifted to Devlin.

He cleared his throat. "Last winter, the High Council confiscated several objects from us, after receiving complaints that we might not be able to safeguard them. As a group, we decided to keep the existence of this recent acquisition to ourselves for the time being. We expect none of you will breathe a word about it."

Chloe's pulse quickened. Acquiring and harboring sacred objects, magical tools, and significant natural items was something covens strived for and prided themselves on, though they kept such things secret from the outside world. Her family's coven had a priceless illuminated manuscript from the fourteenth century and a spectacular meteorite. What had the Circle gotten their hands on?

Midas looked squarely at Devlin. "My lips are sealed."

"Yes, me too," Em murmured.

Chloe nodded, not trusting herself to speak.

Athena's voice hardened. "That's good, because if word of this travels beyond these walls, we will know who was responsible, and we will take action." She looked pointedly at the three of them and then strode to a nearby cabinet, opened a door and took out a cloth-wrapped object the size and shape of a large toaster. "As you are all aware"—she said, returning to her spot on the mat—"the Circle's goal is to communicate with ancient physicians, alchemists, and witches in order to rediscover secrets that could benefit modern medicine." Her eyes glittered as she unwrapped the bundle, revealing a tarnished brass chest. "However, until now you were unaware that we were already in possession of an artifact which will allow us to do this in the very near future."

Chloe scooted closer. "You're kidding."

"Not in the least." Athena patted the brass chest. "Though Merlin's reputation in the field of medicine is less celebrated than others', we have chosen to start our journey with him because of this."

Em gasped. "You have something that belonged to Merlin?"

Athena nodded, the corners of her mouth turning up in a proud smile. Sweat trickled down Chloe's spine. Merlin. She couldn't believe it.

She eyed the box, wondering what would fit in something that size. A scroll, perhaps. Maybe a ritual skullcap. A few weeks ago, she and Keshari—a student she'd first met last spring when she'd come up to tour the university's campus—and some other students had gotten into a debate in Folklore class about the original use of ritual caps and the so-called Golden Hats from the Bronze Age. Unfortunately, it hadn't been like she could announce to the class that she personally knew of a coven in Nuremburg who still used the ancient caps and hats, and what they used them for. Could the Circle have gotten their hands on something like that? She clamped her bottom lip between her teeth, struggling to contain her eagerness.

"This is not a fly by night idea," Athena reassured them. "We believe, with this item, guidance, and the right coven members, the collective energy of the Northern Circle can be used to accomplish the unheard of. Together, our minds and spirits will be able to move out of our bodies and explore places like Ancient China and the Library of Alexandria. We're convinced it's possible."

Jessica sniffed smugly. "You can say that again."

Devlin smiled, his dimples deepening. His voice grew husky as his gaze touched Chloe's. "The possibilities are endless."

For a second, Chloe was certain she caught a hint of innuendo in his tone and she flushed. Then she rolled her eyes at herself. This was far too serious of conversation for him to be implying anything like that. *Get your head out of the gutter, girl*, she chastised herself, turning her attention back to the Athena.

Athena raised a hand, quieting everyone. A coal in the fire pit snapped, sending a flash of light across the room. With a flick of her fingers, she used a burst of magic to open the chest. She picked the chest up and tilted it so everyone could see the contents. In the center of a large nest of dried grass sat an oval cluster of dark purple crystals about the size and shape of a peach.

Midas leaned closer. "An amethyst?"

Athena closed the chest and sat back. "It's much more than that. Few are even aware of its current existence."

"More like, you're lucky you didn't get caught digging it up," Devlin grumbled.

Ignoring him, Athena steepled her fingers on top of the chest and continued. "Jessica, Chandler, and I retrieved it in Wales, on the Isle of Anglesey. It was buried at the base of an oak tree near Aberlleiniog Castle." Her voice deepened with reverence. "It's the crystal from Merlin's staff, his first staff, the one he used long before Arthur, before Nimue deceived and entombed him alive."

Chloe gawked at her, dumbfounded. "You're certain of that?"

Athena dipped her head. "Very much so."

Goose bumps peppered Chloe's skin and she trembled. She wasn't sure if it was from excitement or the fear of being in the presence of such a powerful artifact—most likely both. But even if she had wanted to decipher which one was the stronger emotion, she couldn't have. A sudden surreal, drifting sensation came over her. Fog blanketed her mind and her thoughts became as deadened as they'd been in the months following that night at the Vice-Chancellor's house.

As Athena and Chandler continued on about how they'd acquired the crystal, Chloe closed her eyes, lost in the heavy stupor. Everything felt languid and dreamlike. Merlin's staff crystal. Unbelievable...

"We waited until after midnight, then parked the car alongside the road near the castle ruins," Athena said. "Jessica stayed behind to keep a lookout while Chandler and I hiked in through the woods."

Chandler blew out a noisy breath. "Devlin's right, we were lucky no one caught us."

Athena chuckled. "I was more concerned about one of us breaking a leg. You see, we knew where we had to go. We'd scouted out the spot during the day. But everything looks different at night—and those ruins are overrun by bats."

"The bats didn't bother me," Chandler's deeper tone said. "I was worried that we'd never get the box out from under the oak's roots."

"How did you even know where to look?" Midas asked.

"Runes," Athena said. "But we'll save that story for another time. I believe Jessica has a treat for us. In our travels, we also discovered a technique

Merlin used to divine the future. It involves owl bones and ash berries. Jessica's been practicing, if anyone would like to have their fortunes told."

Athena's voice faded into the background as Chloe let her mind drift, digesting all the bits and pieces of the story. She imagined creeping through the dark woods, uncovering the box, then opening it and seeing the amethyst stone twinkling in the moonlight.... *"With this item, guidance, and the right coven members...our minds and spirits will be able to move out of our bodies and explore places like Ancient China and the Library of Alexandria,"* Athena had said. Incorporeal time travel, even the thought of it was amazing.

The fog in Chloe's head subsided. She blinked. Though it felt like she'd only been daydreaming for a moment, she'd clearly spaced out longer than she'd thought. Devlin and Midas were gone. Jessica and Em sat close together with a handful of small bones and red berries sprawled out between them. Drizzles of condensation now hazed the teahouse's sheer walls.

Em tilted her head to one side and laughed softly. "I think the bones are wrong. Falling in love with a tall, dark-haired, country boy is the last thing I see happening to me anytime soon."

Chloe scooted over to them. "Em?" she said. "Are you ready to go home?" Jessica shot her an irritated look, which she pretended not to see. While she felt badly about interrupting them, Chloe was exhausted and ready to call it a night. Like it or not, she had stuff she needed to do in the morning, like laundry for one thing—and the ever present Organic Chemistry memorization. Where was Devlin anyway?

"You go ahead." Em waved her off. "I'm spending the night here."

Athena smiled. "You're welcome to stay as well."

Jessica snapped a sideways look at Athena, her jaw working like she wanted to say something about the growing guest list.

Chloe saved her the trouble. "Thanks, but I need to get home. Do you know where Devlin and Midas went?"

"They said they were going back to Devlin's apartment." Athena smiled.

Chandler got up from the mat. "I'll show you the way. I've got to get back to the main house anyway. The sitter will be dropping off my son soon."

"I didn't realize you had a son," Chloe said, as she followed Chandler outside. It surprised her, but in retrospect the kid's bike outside Chandler's workshop should have been a big clue.

"His name's Peregrine. He's eight years old. The light of my life." She laughed. "He is a handful, though. All boy, like his father was."

"Was?" Chloe's stomach tensed. She shouldn't have said anything. It sounded like he'd died and the last thing she wanted to do was bring up bad memories for Chandler.

Chandler rested her hand on Chloe's shoulder, guiding her down the path to the footbridge. "I didn't mean it like that. We separated before Peregrine was even born."

"Oh." Chloe fell into silence, unsure what to say next. There was a wistfulness in Chandler's voice that said not all her memories of Peregrine's father were bad, but clearly something had gone wrong.

As they reached the other side of the footbridge, Chandler pointed to the left. "Follow that path. Devlin's apartment is attached to the garage. His BMW will be parked out front."

Despite the lingering thoughts about Chandler and her son, and the general fogginess of her brain, a tingle of excitement danced just below Chloe's stomach. Chandler had just said, *Devlin's apartment*. Athena had said it too. *Devlin's apartment*, as in *his* apartment, not *his and Athena's*.

She had no trouble finding Devlin's place. But his BMW wasn't out front. The garage's overhead door was open and it wasn't in there either. *Damn it*, Chloe thought. He must have left to take Midas home. Who knew how long she'd have to wait for her ride.

A thought crossed her mind and a smile lifted Chloe's lips. Was she crazy? She might not have planned on waiting, but this was perfect. Without Midas around, she could talk to Devlin about the orb uninterrupted. Plus, it would be the perfect time to get the whole scoop on Devlin and Athena, not to mention a read on how he really felt about her.

Next to the open garage door, vines arched over what most likely was the front door to Devlin's apartment. Chloe considered trying the door to see if it was unlocked. She suspected he wouldn't care if she waited inside. But it felt wrong, so she pulled her jacket tight around her and made herself at home on a marble bench in a nearby garden.

Above her, the stars sparkled in the darkness as bright as flecks of crystal. Chloe stretched out on the bench and gazed up. The night was so clear it was perfect. She'd remember this moment forever; even if the coven decided to not let her join and she never had a reason to return to the complex. This was one of those seconds in time where everything felt right and beautiful, so far from her home and family, from her apartment, even away from the high-powered energy of Athena and the rest of the coven. This moment was a different kind of power: still and natural. It fed her soul.

"Which is your favorite?" Devlin's voice eased into the stillness.

Chloe bolted upright, swinging her legs off the edge of the bench. "I didn't hear you drive in."

He sat down next to her. "I left my car in front of the main house. But I ran into Chandler and she told me you were here." He glanced skyward. "So which is your favorite?"

"My favorite? You mean, star?"

"Yeah, which one?"

"Ah—probably the North Star. Though it is a little boring. Too dependable."

He laughed. "Nothing wrong with dependable." He got up. "Why don't we go inside? I'll fix us some coffees. I believe there's something you wanted to tell me?"

"It feels like it almost didn't happen now, but yeah. It's important."

His apartment was a single room like hers, but that's where the similarity ended. His was an ultra-large, L-shaped space with a high ceiling and exposed barn-like beams. First came his kitchen, then a large office and living room area. Off to one side in an alcove was a king-size bed created out of logs, and the door to a bathroom. Everything was neat and classy, a page out of an L.L. Bean catalog. The only thing missing was a golden retriever.

"Make yourself at home," he said, directing her to a jumbo-size couch.

As she sunk down into its cushiony depths, the warmth of the air and the tinkle of a desktop fountain lulled what remained of her senses. She put her feet up on the coffee table. It felt like the kind of place where that was okay.

On the other end of the coffee table, a brass tray filled with pebbles held three beeswax pillar candles with symbols of the Craft etched into them. Geodes glistened on the windowsills. She nestled her head back on a pillow, closed her eyes and breathed in the faint aroma of coffee and cinnamon. The pillow was soft, her eyelids heavy…She had to tell Devlin about the orb. Why had it asked for him? She really didn't know much about Devlin. Where did his greatest magical strength lie?

A hand took her by the arm. Firmly leading her somewhere.

Soft pillow. Smooth sheets. She was laying on a bed.

Her feet were cold. And naked.

And she couldn't move her legs.

Chapter 6

I walked in the mist between worlds,
A ghost among the dead.
A child more lost than those I freed.
—Journal of Emily Adams. New Dawn House. Albany, New York

Chloe jerked awake. She wriggled her toes. Her feet were naked. But now that the heavy fog was lifting from her brain, she could tell her legs were immobilized by tangled blankets and not by something more sinister like duct tape or rope.

Something warm snuggled against her back. *Oh, shit.* Last night came rushing back to her in one quick jolt. Devlin. His apartment.

She swallowed hard and froze, worried that any movement might wake him up. What had she—or more precisely—they done? Anything? Everything? Not that the thought of having sex with him was horrible. She just…She'd have preferred to remember it.

A huge wet nose jabbed her in the ear.

What the hell?

She rolled onto her back. Instantly, the golden retriever—who last night had seemed missing from Devlin's perfect L.L. Bean apartment—was on top of her, rolling and licking.

"Off, off!" she shouted. She pulled the blankets up to her neck and scooched upright until she sat against the pillows. The room swayed, a nauseous feeling swelling upward from her stomach. Oh boy, she didn't just have a hangover. She had the Queen Mother of hangovers.

The dog bounded down from the bed and began sniffing her jeans and yellow gilet that were both meticulously draped over a nearby chair. That explained where some of her clothes were, but what about the rest?

Chloe eased the blankets a few inches away from her body and took a quick inventory. Her top, bra, and panties were all where they belonged. That was a good sign.

"Come on, boy." Devlin's voice whispered from the direction of the kitchen, followed by a soft whistle. "Come on, Henry. You want to go out?"

The dog took off. She heard a door open and close, probably the beast being put outside. A moment later, Devlin walked into view wearing nothing but a pair of worn jeans. His hair was damp and rumpled, every delicious inch of him flushed from a recent shower. Perfect abs. Perfect chest. A tree of life tattoo spanned his muscular upper arm.

He gave Chloe a dimpled smile and her thoughts stuttered to a halt. Last night she'd wondered where his greatest magical strength lay. Right now, she was pretty sure it had to do with electrifying every synapse in her body. Holy Goddess of Lust that boy had it all going on.

As he walked over to the bed, she swallowed about a million times. His bed. The bed she'd spent the night in.

"Sorry about Henry. He snuck inside before I could stop him." He held out a shot glass of what looked like thick, dark beer. "A little something for your hangover."

She grimaced and her voice stammered a little. "I—I don't think it would be smart for me to drink anything right now."

"Trust me. You won't regret it."

Chloe wasn't so sure about the *trust me* part, though she wasn't entirely sure why she shouldn't. Her head was too screwed up to figure out what had happened. Especially with him standing there half-naked and her sitting in his bed. But she suspected he'd been a gentleman.

"Go on," he said. "Raw honey, tomato juice, and a few secret ingredients."

"It looks gross." Her fingers trembled as she took it. At this point, what could it hurt? She lifted it up and chugged it in one sickly-sweet and chunky liverwurst flavored gulp.

"Oh my God. That was disgusting," she said, wrinkling her nose as a bout of shivers gripped her body.

He chuckled. "There's extra toothbrushes in the medicine cabinet. Take a shower if you want. I'll make us breakfast." He took the empty glass from her and smiled. "Most of what you're feeling isn't from the alcohol. You overexposed yourself to the coven's magic. You must have sensed it."

"Yeah, but I didn't realize it was that strong."

"Athena was turning it up pretty high last night. Well, everyone was. Don't worry. But next time, you might want to close yourself off a little more."

He turned to head for the kitchen and she slipped out of bed. She didn't bother to wrap in a blanket. It wasn't like he hadn't gotten an eyeful already. Besides, after swallowing his putrid goop, it seemed wiser to get closer to a toilet as fast as she could. Still, before Chloe shut the bathroom door, she swiveled back. "Hey, Devlin?"

He glanced over his shoulder, the muscles in his back flexing.

"Thanks, for letting me have the bed and being considerate."

He waved off the compliment. "At least I made one person happy. I suspect Athena feels quite differently this morning."

Chloe felt herself pale as she waited for him to expand on that. But he returned to the kitchen and the clatter of utensils being moved filled the air. *Damn, Athena being unhappy didn't sound good*, she thought, closing the bathroom door.

In the bathroom, she didn't just find extra toothbrushes. There was a stack of towels, a washcloth, and a folded *Middlebury College* T-shirt waiting on the vanity. The shower helped. The T-shirt was large—obviously his—but soft and worn to cozy perfection. Once she was done, she wriggled into her jeans.

She found Devlin in the kitchen, standing over a sizzling frying pan. He'd put on a white button-down shirt. Its tails hung out, but that only added to his air of laid-back sophistication.

"Feeling better?" he asked.

"Very much." Chloe smiled. "That disgusting cure of yours is pretty amazing."

"I hope you like frittata." He slid a cast iron frying pan filled with a cheesy mix of bubbling egg and vegetables into the oven. "I'm a one-trick pony when it comes to breakfast."

She wandered over to the coffeemaker and helped herself. "I don't think anyone in their right mind would call you a one-trick pony—chauffeur, landscape architect extraordinaire, maker of the world's best hangover cure, not to mention witch." She took a sip of coffee, pressing her lips against the cup for an extra second while she worked up her nerve. "So I kind of don't remember much after I sat down on your couch."

A wicked twinkle brightened his eyes. "Well, after I put away the trapezes and sent the contortionists home, we stole a car and broke into a liquor store."

Chloe laughed and cuffed his shoulder. "I'm serious."

The humor faded from his voice. "I'm not sure what you're getting at."
"Is there a specific reason Athena isn't happy with you—like because I stayed here?" She edged toward her real question. "Are you two friends? Business partners?"

"Athena's my sister. You didn't know that?"

She clamped her teeth down on her bottom lip to keep from grinning. "Ah—no. Why would I?"

"Technically this place—the complex and everything—is as much mine as hers. Our mother signed it over to both of us when she resigned as high priestess." He scratched at his cheek as if deciding where to go from there. "I was away at college when it happened. Athena devoted herself to rebuilding the coven."

"So the idea of searching for cures was hers?"

"Yes, and one I'm proud to be involved with. That's why I don't mind giving her absolute authority, loyalty, and my respect. I want to see her succeed. I owe it to her."

Chloe glanced into her coffee cup, her reflection staring back. *Medicine and magic.* Chloe didn't know if something had happened in Athena's past to motivate her into pushing the coven in that direction any more than she knew the root of why Devlin *owed* Athena, but Chloe understood being driven by the past.

That night at the Vice-Chancellor's house, she'd learned that there were nightmares as horrible if not worse than drowning. Like being responsible for destroying a young child's life—and all because of her impulsiveness. In four days, it would be five years and four months since the Vice-Chancellor's son went into a coma; lack of oxygen had destroyed his brain beyond repair, even experimental therapies that had created tissue regrowth in some children had failed on him. Five years and four months with no change to his condition, except for his family becoming more and more despondent—all because of her. With all the magic witches had, there had to be some way to repair or reverse the damage she'd caused. But there wasn't one. Not now. Not yet. But maybe, just maybe, there was a plant or potion or spell that could make things right. Something that could heal that little boy's brain.

Chloe lifted her gaze to Devlin's. "I'd be proud to be a part of her plans, too."

He rested his hand on the small of her back, guiding her to the kitchen island to sit. "It is a major obligation. You have to be willing to do as asked without question. Trust and unswerving commitment to the Circle. It will take away from your study time."

She nodded. His tone made it sound ominous, but it was far from that. Being a part of a serious-minded coven with goals that paralleled hers was what she longed for. *Magic and medicine.* Her parents wouldn't be happy, but this was what she needed. "You're forgetting. My family is devoted to the Craft. I know what kind of discipline and commitment is required. As for college, I do better under pressure."

"Why doesn't that surprise me?"

"Ah—maybe because you've been spying on me?" Chloe teased.

He took a seat on the opposite side of the island. "You know I'm sorry about that. I feel bad about the way the invitation was delivered too. That wasn't my idea. My father started that tradition decades ago."

"Don't worry about it. I'm fine with that now. Truthfully, I'm glad I'm here." She raised her coffee cup in a toast, the way he'd done with his beer at the party last night.

His dimples flashed, along with a roguish glint in his eyes. "In truth, Chloe, when I heard who your parents were and read your college records, I never expected you to be such a wildcard." He cleared his throat. "Before I start saying stupid things like how good you look in my T-shirt, I believe there was something you wanted to tell me last night?"

Chloe smacked herself on the forehead. "Oh my Goddess, how could I forget!"

While the aroma of cooking frittata slowly filled the kitchen, she told him what the orb had said. *Yin and yang. Betrayal.* He listened to her closely. When she was done, he reached across the island and squeezed her hand. "I'm glad you told me first, like the orb asked. But I have no idea what it means."

The idea of him not knowing made her uneasy. The orb had been so insistent that she specifically tell him. She was sure the message was vital. But as he rested a reassuring hand on hers, the worry melted away, replaced by a ripple of desire.

She uncrossed her legs and shifted closer, her fingers aching for the touch to lead to more. She studied his lips. Firm and full. Made for kissing—

The connection broke as he took his hand away and sat back. "We need to tell Athena. She was pissed last night because Midas confided some concerns to me that he should have gone straight to her with. I don't want to delay with this."

Chloe took a sip of coffee, buying herself a second to regroup, before she nodded. He certainly knew how to deal with this better than she did.

Devlin called Athena and relayed everything she'd told him about the orb. Chloe was grateful he didn't turn it into a video conference, given her wet hair and wrinkled clothes. But she was thankful he'd used speakerphone.

Athena suspected the spirit was a deceased coven member, someone attracted to the magic they were once a part of. She didn't think there was anything to be concerned about. When she banished the orb from the house, she'd only sensed kinship radiating from it, not fear or anger. She was going to talk to their mother. Perhaps the spirit asked for Devlin because it was reliving a past event, something connected to his teenage years? At the mention of his past, Devlin's lips pressed tight together. He ran his hand over his throat as if contemplating saying something, but then he glanced at the floor instead.

Chloe's stomach sank. Was he not speaking his mind because she was there? For a second, she felt like an intruder into a conversation she had no business being a part of. But then she remembered that the orb had spoken to her. Not Devlin. Not even Athena. She had a right to be here, at least for this.

The timer on the stove buzzed.

"Got to go." Devlin abruptly ended the conversation with Athena, then he rushed over and took the frittata out of the oven. As he served it onto plates, he started to go on at length about how he'd never eaten frittata until a few years ago. The almost too enthusiastic way he'd shifted from talking about the orb's message to discussing cooking convinced Chloe that he was still withholding something, most likely related to Athena's sniping comment about his teenage years.

"I meant to tell you," he said, walking over with the steaming plates. "Last night, Em and Midas used techniques they were familiar with to tackle the maze. But you were impressive. You used your bracelet and a skill that was called for but not easy for you. Resourceful and gutsy."

Chloe blushed. She decided to let her curiosity drop; after all, everyone was entitled to their secrets, herself included. "Honestly, I didn't think anyone was watching me, except Athena."

"Chloe." His voice became husky. "I didn't want to look at anything but you."

She glanced away from him, toward the frying pan and what remained of the frittata. Heat rushed through her body, settling in her stomach and spreading lower. Every inch of her buzzed. Her lips parted as a longing to feel his lips against hers overwhelmed her. She wanted to taste him, touch him, to rip that damn shirt off his body and drag him to that king-size bed. Oh Goddess, she was in trouble.

Chapter 7

Fourteen stones. The one at the east wears the shadow of a demon.
The one at the west whispers a warning: sunset is coming and the moon
will not rise.
—Predictions of Athena Marsh

It was about eleven a.m. when Devlin drove Chloe back to her apartment. If she'd had a choice, she'd have joined the Northern Circle before she left. A coven of friends with goals that matched hers was exactly what she wanted and needed. But according to Devlin, her next step was to officially proclaim her interest to Athena, since she was the one organizing and keeping records of everything. Unfortunately, Athena had gone back to bed, so Chloe surrendered to the fact that she'd have to call her later.

Devlin dropped her off in front of the apartment house. She said a quick thank you, then shoved her hands deep into her jacket pockets, joyously lost in daydreams of him and the coven as she scuffed her way through the fallen leaves and climbed the porch steps.

The couple from the third floor came hurrying out the front door. One of them acknowledged her with a greeting, holding the door open for her to enter. Without meeting their eyes, Chloe smiled and flipped them a wave. She let out a grateful breath when they kept on going without stopping to chat. But it was too late to dive back into her daydreams. The cracks had already formed, the light of reality seeping in as she began to second-guess her decisions that had felt wise a moment earlier.

It didn't seem right to risk disappointing her parents again by joining the Circle without even mentioning it to them. Not when they'd explicitly warned her against fraternizing with them. It also wasn't fair that her parents would end up being blamed for her mistake if something bad happened, like they had with the Vice-Chancellor's son. She needed to weigh that risk against the chance that she might find a cure that could right the past, not to mention that the coven could become a shining example of what her generation of witches were capable of.

Chloe plodded across the foyer and started up the stairs. The whole thing was complicated by the issue of Devlin. He was smart, had ambition and a great profession, he was a witch, everything that would have normally thrilled her parents—and impressed the High Council of Witches. Except, he was Devlin Marsh. Athena Marsh's brother. The son of a man her father had warned her about. Not that she was convinced anything long-term was going to happen between her and Devlin. After all, they'd just met. But...

She reached the top of the stairs and let out a long sigh. Like it or not, she needed to talk this through with someone. *Juliet,* she decided. She'd ask her opinion—without telling her too much about the coven.

Quiet as she could, Chloe crept past Greta's door and knocked on Juliet's. A clunk sounded from inside, followed by several meows. But no one answered, of course. She sighed again. This was a large part of the problem with living in an apartment house populated with grad students and working people. Most of the time everyone was gone. If they weren't, then they were either sleeping in or had people over.

Her thoughts weighed on her as she went into her apartment and flopped down on the couch. She had two choices. Follow her heart and simply join the coven. Or get up her nerve and talk to her mom about it. She laughed at herself. Calling her mother was beyond ridiculous. Mom would have a heart attack, and despite Chloe being an adult, her father would fly to Burlington and physically drag her home by the hair if he had to.

Mom. Chloe's pulse picked up. When she'd talked to her father on the phone the other day, she'd mentioned buying some glass straws for her mom at the farmers' market. Instead of sitting here driving herself nuts or wasting the rest of a gorgeous day studying and doing laundry like she'd planned, she could walk downtown and get them. By the time she got back, Juliet would probably have returned. Plus, as an added bonus, Keshari might working at the market.

Chloe didn't know Keshari that well. Last spring, when she'd come up to get a closer look at the university, Keshari had been her walking-tour guide. They'd hit it off right away and Chloe had been pleasantly surprised when they'd ended up in the same Folklore class. But they'd never managed to get together liked they'd planned, mostly because Keshari was not only working on her bachelor's degree; she also lived at home and helped her parents with their Tibetan import business—including sometimes manning their farmers' market booth. Keshari seemed sweet and open, into meditation and philosophy. A talk with Keshari would be the perfect way to get her head on straight, assuming Keshari was at the market today.

Chloe changed into fresh jeans and a lightweight sweater, tugged on her sneakers, and started for downtown. The warmth of the sunshine on her face and the smell of the leaves crunching beneath her feet energized her. A city bus whooshed to a stop nearby, but she didn't try to catch it. The more she walked and thought, the more it felt like she was right where she was supposed to be.

Fifteen minutes later, she reached City Hall Park where the farmers' market was held. The sidewalks and vendor tents teemed with shoppers, buying pumpkins and pottery, batik scarves and handmade soaps. Chloe's mouth watered from the smells of fresh baked pretzels, breads, and cookies. Working here probably didn't pay much, but next spring she should talk to Keshari and see if any of them needed help. It wasn't like she was going to be able to live on her savings forever.

She picked up a dozen straws from Double Infinity Glassworks, then continued down the line of vendors, sipping a sample of freshly pressed cider. It was delicious, but not as incredible as the bright patchwork jackets under the next canopy. They were orange, spring-green, bright pink, boxy, and embroidered. They had a distinctly Himalayan vibe, and she absolutely adored them. She also suspected she'd found where Keshari worked. Keshari had told her that her grandparents and parents had come to Burlington in the 1990s as refugees from Tibet. They still had family back there, and most of what they imported and sold was handcrafted by them.

Over the rack of jackets, wind chimes and brass bells swung lightly in the breeze. Her charm bracelet clanked against the side of a brass singing bowl and it let out a *gong* that reverberated through her body, right into her bones. Chloe didn't know much about singing bowls, but sound healing was on her list of areas to explore in the future. Maybe they were something the Northern Circle should investigate as well. She'd read somewhere that sound could be used to inspire out of body experiences as well as for healing.

A display of glass gallon jars filled with layered stripes of vivid colored sand caught her eye. Smaller jars sat next to them, their granular contents equally as eye-catching, in various shades of white, pink, and peach. It looked like Himalayan salt, which was way better for protection than the generic table salt she had resorted to using after running out of the purified salt she'd brought from home.

A woman swished out from behind a drape that formed the back wall of the tent. Chloe couldn't see her face well as she stood within the shadows of the tent, but the woman wore black leggings and one of the orange and pink jackets that were hanging on the racks. Her dark hair was bound into sleek pigtails and strings of jade and honey-colored beads hung around her neck. She was pretty sure it was Keshari, but the woman could have been a sister or cousin.

The woman stepped closer and Chloe's doubt fell away. "Hey, Keshari. I was hoping you were working today."

A wide smile crossed Keshari's lips. "Chloe, wonderful to see you. Welcome and blessings." Her voice was as resonate as a singing bowl.

"I've been meaning to call or catch up with you after Folklore, but that class is such a zoo."

Keshari waved a hand at Chloe. "No worries. It is not your fault. I always seem to be rushing." She smiled again, the corners of her eyes crinkling. "I would sit in the front of class with you, if it were not so claustrophobic."

Chloe laughed. "If I don't sit up front, I get distracted."

As Keshari moved into brighter light, a pendant on one of her necklaces sparkled. Chloe leaned forward, squinting at it in the low light. "Wow. That's gorgeous. Is it salt?"

"Yes. Himalayan. My uncle makes them. We have more in the jewelry showcase if you are interested."

Chloe was fascinated by the idea of Keshari's family creating such gorgeous things on one side of the world, then cooperatively selling them on the other. She thought she was from an interesting family. But she was beginning to realize that there were so many others who were equally if not more fascinating. *Like Devlin*, the thought crossed her mind so fast she blinked in surprise. She shook her head and glanced at Keshari's pendant again.

"I love your pendant. But I was hoping you had loose Himalayan salt. Is that what's in those?" She motioned at the jars filled with rainbow colors.

"The smaller ones, yes." Keshari went over and picked up a jar containing pink salt. "The others are sand. Kits for creating basic mandalas. They come with booklets about meditation and the various philosophies."

"What a great idea. I've read about mandalas, but I don't know much."

Keshari's gaze went to Chloe's charm bracelet. "Are you Wiccan?"

"Ah—" Chloe's pulse picked up and she swallowed hard, a lie already forming in her mind. But, of all the students she'd met at the university, Keshari was the one she'd most wanted to get to know better. In class, they always seemed to be on the same side of discussions and debates, like the one the other day about if Bronze Age caps and Golden Hats were crowns for kings or used by ancient wizards. What was the harm in a little bit of honesty? "I practice the Craft. Just not as a Wiccan. Actually, that's why I asked about the salt. I want to use it for protection."

Keshari nodded thoughtfully. "Have you heard of the Tears of Tara, then?"

Chloe frowned. "Tara—like the Goddess?"

"The Tears are a special salt. Gathered from sacred lakes in the mountains in Tibet. The purest in the world. We use it to preserve food and for bartering. Our shamans also use it."

"You sell it here?"

She nodded. "Wait a second, please."

She disappeared into the shadows and behind the drape. While she waited, Chloe pretended to check out the jewelry showcase. In truth, all she could think about were Keshari's words. '*Our* shamans also use it.' That made it sound like Keshari and her family weren't purely Hindu or Buddhist as she'd assumed from their heritage.

Keshari returned a minute later, holding a fist-size satin bag, tied shut with a red ribbon. She undid the ribbon, pinched out a few gray granules and placed them on Chloe's palm. "Taste. They will surprise you."

Chloe licked the grains from her hand. They tasted strong and earthy. But that wasn't what left her stunned. As the salt crystals melted in her mouth, a surge of magic energy tingled across her tongue and gums. The inside of her lips trembled from it. The magic flooded her sinuses, like the heady sensation of peppermint or a shot of whiskey, or what she imagined it would feel like to kiss Devlin. Her scalp prickled and she was certain that if she cast any spell right then it would have come out potent and quick.

"Holy cow," she said. "That's amazing."

Keshari laughed. "I'm not sure about holy cows. But it tells me you are blessed."

Chloe stiffened.

A test.

She glanced toward the tent's exit, wondering if she'd made a big mistake by even looking for Keshari.

"I am sorry," Keshari said, holding out her palms in a placating gesture. "I should not have said anything."

Chloe rubbed a hand across her charm bracelet. Normally, she'd have panicked if someone discovered her abilities. But—if she was totally honest with herself—on several occasions she'd thought she sensed a flicker of magic shimmer off Keshari. She'd decided her own preconceived ideas about Tibetan people being mystical had clouded her judgement and made her imagine the sensation. Witches weren't immune to making blind assumptions and being prejudiced about other cultures. However, Keshari clearly knew true magic existed. "You startled me, that's all."

"I still feel bad. I know better. But it makes me happy to meet someone like myself."

"Yeah. I guess I can understand that." A knot of hesitation lingered in her chest. Her father would have told her to walk away, to look into Keshari thoroughly before opening up. But she totally got how Keshari felt. Meeting fellow practitioners her age was one of the reasons she was considering joining the Northern Circle. This wasn't a reason to panic and back away, but an opportunity to know someone she already liked at a deeper level.

Her fear dissipated and she stepped closer, focusing on the air around Keshari. She had to pay close attention, but she could detect a subtle thrum of magic there. She wet her lips with her still tingling tongue, working up her nerve. "I thought I picked up on your energy before, but I wasn't sure."

"The campus is not exactly a favorable place for noticing such things. Too many emotions and competing energies." Her eyes shone with mirth. "The only thing I ever sense in class is that the professor gets nervous when the two of us gang up to debate his theories, yes?"

Chloe laughed. "That's true." She glanced past Keshari at a woman who'd stopped to look at the price tag on a set of wind chimes. The woman moved on, rejoining the flow of shoppers. The market was one of the city's hubs. It was busy, but it had a more laidback vibe than the university. Over the years, it seemed like Keshari must have picked up on other gifted people, not to mention her family discussing such things. Maybe, just maybe…"You don't happen to be familiar with the Northern Circle?"

Keshari's eyes widened. "I—" This time she was the one who appeared taken aback. "Are you a member?"

"No. But they asked me to join."

She lowered her voice to a whisper. "Me too. Last winter. But my parents said *no*."

An unexpected twinge of guilt uncoiled in Chloe's stomach. If she'd asked her parents like she was supposed to, that's what they would have said for sure, as well. "So you didn't even consider it? I mean, isn't that kind of up to you, not your parents?"

"I know people who belong to the coven. They—" Keshari stopped talking as a slim woman in a red tunic and full-length skirt—most likely in her early fifties judging by the streaks of white in her jet-black hair and the wrinkles at the corners of her eyes—swished into the tent carrying a jug of cider.

The woman's gaze went from Keshari, to the satin bag in her hand, then to Chloe, and back.

"Mama," Keshari greeted her. "I'm glad you're back. I'd like you to meet Chloe, from my Folklore class."

She dipped her head. "Blessings to you, Chloe."

"To you as well," Chloe said.

Keshari held out the bag of salt to Chloe. "For you. A gift," she said, then to her mother, "May I go have coffee with Chloe? We have been wanting to get together."

Her mother eyed the bag again. She frowned and said something to Keshari in what Chloe assumed was their native language. Keshari's voice hardened then lifted, like it did when she was debating in Folklore class. She glanced at Chloe.

Chloe pasted on a polite smile, despite the anxiety flip-flopping inside her. She had the feeling her magic was now general family knowledge.

Keshari's mother grinned and flagged both hands. "Go. Enjoy the sunshine."

"Thank you, Mama." Keshari took Chloe by the hand, towing her out of the tent. Once they were out of earshot, she let go. "Sorry." She cringed. "I told her the truth."

For a moment Chloe's jaw clenched, but a refreshing sense of relief almost instantly replaced her tension. "I'm glad you did. I get so tired of lying."

"It made my mother happy. She believes good fortune brought you to our tent." She stopped beside a coffee stand. "You want to get something to drink?"

Chloe smiled. "Only if I'm paying."

Keshari's voice once again took on the resonance of a singing bowl. "My grandfather has a saying: 'Share a coffee with a man and he shall be remembered for forty years.' I hope the memories of this afternoon and our friendship last even longer."

"Me too," Chloe said, and for the first time in a long time, she felt like it might really come true.

Chapter 8

Lift up your wand and chalice.
Step bravely, hound at your side. The great adventure awaits.
—The Fool Card

Chloe and Keshari wandered away from the farmers' market, sipping coffees and heading toward an equally busy Waterfront Park. As a rule, Chloe usually avoided talking about her family and personal life. But with Keshari, she found herself opening up and whispering one detail after another. Keshari spilled about her life as well.

When they stopped talking to watch a team of runners stream past—all lean and glistening with sweat, their footfalls thudding in unison—Chloe understood why talking to Keshari felt so comfortable. It was more than that they both had abilities. It was that they'd both faced similar challenges because of it. Keshari knew the fear and loneliness of keeping secrets from the outside world, of having only superficial friendships beyond the small circle of her family and fellow practitioners. She understood the devotion, practice, and sacrifices mastering a powerful craft entailed. As Chloe suspected, Keshari's family wasn't Hindu like many of the local Nepalese. They followed an ancient form of Tengrism mixed with some Buddhist traditions. In a lot of ways, their beliefs and craft were in step with the witchcraft Chloe's family practiced.

Despite all that, or perhaps because of it, as they walked along the shoreline, Chloe couldn't help but worry a little. Everything about Keshari and her background indicated she would have fit in with the Northern Circle. Yet she'd turned them down, submitting to her parents' wishes without question. Meanwhile even if Chloe's parents and all her brothers and sisters insisted she shouldn't join, she still planned on doing it. Was there a special reason Keshari's parents had been dead set against her joining? From the little she'd heard and seen, Keshari's mother seemed like a reasonable person. Chloe wasn't sure she was ready to hear the answer, but she respected Keshari's opinions, especially about magical paths.

They threw their empty coffee cups in a recycle bin and sat down on a swinging bench that overlooked the lake. The low sunshine reflected off the tossing waves and the windshields of the boats making their way out beyond the breakwater. Lake Champlain was breathtaking. Stretching all the way north to Canada and west to New York State, it was way larger than Chloe had thought before she came here. But she couldn't just sit and stare at the water in silence forever.

She enjoyed one last swing, then scuffed her feet against the ground, bringing the bench to a halt. She shifted toward Keshari, gave in and asked, "Why didn't you join the coven?"

Keshari met her gaze, her eyes offering nothing except honesty. "My parents thought it was a bad idea."

"Was that the only reason? What did *you* want?"

Keshari's shoulder raised in a half-shrug. "I have a lot to learn about my own beliefs. College. Work. I never seriously considered it. It does not fit with my dreams." She glanced down, her voice hushed. "I want to go to Tibet and study under a shaman—and collect obscure folklore while I'm there."

"That would be amazing."

"But you are considering joining the Circle, yes?"

Chloe nodded. Her gaze returned to the lake. She closed her eyes for a moment, letting her mind reach out to the air and water. Everything felt peaceful, perfect, and right. Everything said she could trust Keshari to keep secrets. So she took a deep breath and then told Keshari about the coven's plans for discovering new cures. Keshari gasped in amazement when Chloe revealed that the coven possessed the crystal from Merlin's staff.

"I didn't even know that existed," Keshari said.

"Neither did I." Chloe swallowed hard. She probably shouldn't have said anything about that, but it felt so wonderful to talk freely for a change. "Please don't say a word to anyone. The coven would kill me."

"Do not worry," Keshari assured her. "The secret is safe with me."

Chloe's instincts told her Keshari was speaking the truth. She breathed a sigh of relief. *Kill* wasn't exactly the right word for what the Circle—or the High Council of Witches for that matter— might do. Wiping her mind clean of memories was a more traditional punishment for revealing secrets.

She shuddered as her thoughts—despite herself and how much she tried to avoid it—went to that boy lying in his hospital bed. Maybe she deserved to have her mind screwed with. Still, in this case, it wasn't like the Circle wouldn't proudly announce the existence of Merlin's crystal to the witching community at some point. This wasn't a forever secret.

"So what was the meet and greet like?" Keshari asked.

Chloe described the maze and told her about the other potential new members—Em and Midas, plus another mystery person that the coven had turned away. She didn't talk about what made joining so vitally important to her. That wasn't something she shared with anyone. "Everything they're doing fits into my dreams. It feels like it was meant to be. I think our parents are wrong."

"Then what holds you back?" Keshari rested her hand on Chloe's arm. "Why didn't you leave the high priestess a note or text her to say you wished to join?"

As the question sank in, fear settled in the pit of Chloe's stomach. Until that moment, she hadn't realized she was delaying, but she knew the answer instantly. "There's this guy, Devlin."

Keshari nodded. "I know him."

"You do?" Chloe's eyes widened. But she shouldn't have been surprised. They were both local. They might have even gone to the same schools.

"He has bought things from us now and then. He also gave me the invitation."

Her excitement shriveled. Okay, so Keshari didn't really know him *that* well.

The corners of Keshari's eyes crinkled as she grinned. "You like him, yes?"

"Yeah, probably too much." With a sigh, Chloe sat back and pushed her feet off the ground, letting the bench swing once more.

Keshari giggled. "I don't blame you. He's gorgeous, and smart."

"I just don't want to mess up my chance of being a part of the coven by getting involved with him. What if we get together, then things fall apart—like next month? And I suspect there's zero chance I'd turn him down if he made a move." Chloe glanced toward the shoreline and to where a guy was hurling sticks into the water for his golden retriever, so much like Devlin's dog. "I wish I knew if this was just a bad case of lust or something deeper."

"You're the only one who can judge that."

Chloe raked her fingers down her pants legs. "I'm also worried about Devlin."

"You are?"

"Kind of." Chloe hesitated, but this wasn't a coven secret. This was hers to share or not as she saw fit, and she really wanted answers. "When Em did the maze, she used her ability as a psychic medium to call up a spirit to help her. It came in the form of an orb. No one else heard it speak, but the spirit gave me a message, a warning for Devlin. '*Yin. Yang. Betrayal*'."

Keshari rubbed one of her necklaces, fingering one bead at a time as if asking her gods or goddesses for their input. She stopped and licked her lips. "I've talked to spirits before. All the women in my family do. I can see why the message worries you. But communicating with spirits can be misleading."

"What do you mean?" She intellectually knew what Keshari meant, but not how it applied in this case.

"How did you feel about the message? Are you certain it was for Devlin?"

"Are you suggesting that it might not have been?"

"Yin and yang. The balance of light and dark. The warning could indicate that the harmonic balance between you and Devlin is off and could lead to betrayal. It could have been one of Devlin's ancestors revealing that its death was the result of a betrayal by someone unbalanced. It could be a message for you."

"Me?" Chloe's breath knotted in her chest. She shook her head. "It couldn't have been. I'm sure it was for him."

"Why do you think it spoke to you and not to anyone else in the room? There were lots of witches there, including the medium. Why you?"

"I assumed it was because it knew I'd keep the warning a secret from everyone except Devlin."

"You're worried that your compassionate motives for joining the coven might be waylaid by your physical desires. Yin and yang. But are you sure of the coven's motives? Are they following an altruistic path? Is this a warning to you from your ancestor?"

"Wow," Chloe said. "You sure got a lot out of a tiny message."

"I'm not an expert in interpreting messages from the spirits, just ask my grandmother. But I know one thing. Spirits can be godsends or tricksters. You need to trust your intuition."

"Honestly?" Chloe shook her head. "It never occurred to me that the coven might want to find out about cures for anything other than helping people. But they aren't living a low-key lifestyle and that takes money. There's this girl, Jessica, for instance, she doesn't exactly wave the I-love-humanity flag."

Keshari folded her hands on her lap. "How you interpret the spirit's message and what path you decide to take belongs to you, not me or your parents." She smiled. "No matter what you decide, I'll be here for you."

Tears welled in Chloe's eyes. Normally she was good at keeping her emotions to herself, but this time they overwhelmed her. She threw her arms around Keshari, hugging her tight. "Thank you. That means the world to me."

Keshari squeezed her back. "So—what does your heart say now?"

"My heart..." Chloe released Keshari and sat back. She closed her eyes, listening to her heart, a steady fast thumping that matched the excitement coursing in her veins, the same thrum she'd felt when Devlin first mentioned the coven's goal. All traces of anxiety and fear had disappeared from her mind. She was going to do this. She'd known that when she'd received the invitation. She opened her eyes, feeling calm and ready. "I'm going to say yes."

Chloe took out her phone and punched in Athena's number. It rang once, twice...Her voicemail picked up. "Bright blessings. You have reached Athena Marsh, I'm currently out of my office. Please leave a message. Joy be with you."

Chloe wet her lips, then spoke into the phone. "I've thought about it and I'd love to join the Northern Circle if you'll have me. Blessing to all of you, Chloe." She put the phone away, turned to Keshari and sighed. "So it went to voicemail. I guess all I can do now is wait and see what happens."

Keshari grimaced. "I don't mean to put a damper on things, but you are going to have to tell your parents eventually."

Chloe nodded. She would worry about that later. "I'm going home for Thanksgiving. I'll tell them then—" Her phone chirped and she stopped talking to glance at it. Her breath stalled. "It's a text from Athena."

"That was quick." Excitement glistened in Keshari's eyes. "What does it say?"

Chloe drew a deep breath, a chill of both excitement and fear spiking through her as she read the message:

That's wonderful news. We will make plans for your initiation. Be prepared. It will happen without warning.

Chapter 9

Happy 10th birthday to my special little witch.
Love, Dad
—Tag on box containing a 14k gold pentagram charm

It was after six by the time Chloe got back to her apartment house carrying the Tears of Tara salt and the straws she'd bought for her mother. What she needed to do was spend the rest of the weekend getting ahead on her household chores and studies, which would give her free time to spend with the coven later, especially with the upcoming initiation.

Lost in thoughts of what the initiation might entail, she climbed the porch steps and went inside. She hoped it wasn't going to be too grueling. But whatever it involved, it would be mentally tough and involve further testing of her magic abilities. Keshari had suggested that Chloe not let them see the full extent of her skills. "Just in case," she had said. Chloe knew what she meant—*in case things went bad*. In her heart Chloe agreed, but she couldn't make herself believe anything bad was going to happen. At the same time, she was sure she'd need everything she had to get through the initiation.

She was halfway up the stairs to her apartment when Juliet came streaking out from a first floor apartment. The apartment's tenants, the Rescue Twins, were on her heels. The Twins were two beanpole-thin guys who always had on their UVM Rescue Squad uniforms, hence Juliet had given them the Twin moniker.

"Perfect timing!" Juliet squealed. "We're going to my place for pizza and beers."

"It's the good stuff." One of the Twins raised a six-pack of Switchback Ale to prove the point. The other hoisted a four-pack of squatty bottles.

"Sounds great. I'm starving." Chloe smiled and started up the stairs again. "I'll just drop off my stuff in my apartment and be right there."

"Don't disappoint us," Juliet called after her.

"Promise. I'll be right there." She wasn't lying either. She was famished, so much so she could probably devour an entire pizza by herself. But as she neared the door to her apartment all thoughts of eating vanished. Something the size and shape of a greeting card was stuck on her apartment door.

Adrenaline surged into her veins. *The initiation.*

She dashed down the hall and was in front of her door in a second. A tarot card. From a Rider-Waite deck. A guy with a rod and bundle over his shoulder and a dog at his side, about to step off a cliff. The Fool card, indicating a journey of self-discovery. She just needed to make the leap. The go-for-it card.

Chloe pulled the card loose from the tape that secured it to the door. She flipped it over, expecting to see directions telling her when and where the initiation would take place. There was nothing. No writing. No map. Only the normal back of a Rider-Waite card.

Her lips twitched into a sly smile. Athena knew she could use psychometry to uncover information. She probably wanted her to dive deeper to get the details.

Unlocking her apartment door, Chloe went inside. The last traces of evening light brightened her windows, but the rest of her room was dark and shadowy. She set the card and things she'd bought on the coffee table and took off her charm bracelet. She reached to turn on the desk lamp—

Her instincts jumped to high alert. She wasn't alone.

Someone grabbed Chloe by the arms, pinning them hard behind her back. She twisted against the grip, struggling to get free.

But then she stopped. *The initiation.* That's what this was.

Her breath seized in her lungs. But what if she was wrong? What if this was something else?

A musty smell flew up her nose as a second person blew a cloud of fine dust into her face. Her head whirled. Her eyes burned. She clamped them shut, tears seeping out the sides. Mushroom spores, *Calvatia caeus.* She'd gotten them in her eyes once when she first started working at her father's botanical supply business. Temporary blindness. It would go away. But there was more to this dust, the dizzying sting of magic.

"Are you ready?" A voice snarled close to her ear.

Shit. It was Jessica.

Chapter 10

With your eyes closed, dreams become more real,
so do nightmares.
—Athena Marsh, high priestess of the Northern Circle

I won't be blind for long, Chloe reminded herself as Jessica shoved her into the back of a car. Not Devlin's car. This one was higher off the ground like an SUV. The back seat wasn't built for comfort. A Jeep Cherokee, maybe, like the one she'd seen at the complex parked in front of Chandler's workshop.

"Hands behind your back," Jessica snapped. She wrapped duct tape around Chloe's wrists, yanking it tight. "Now sit up. No talking. If you refuse to do anything we say or resist in any way, we'll throw you out of the car—and the coven. Understand?"

Sweat stuck Chloe's shirt to her back. She nodded sharply, but kept her face expressionless and her thoughts to herself. No way was she going to give Jessica the pleasure of knowing how angry—and afraid—she was. Initiations weren't supposed to be easy. Still, drugging her and being so rough was taking it to a whole different level.

Jessica slammed the door shut and a minute later they drove off, speeding down the street.

She was certain there were only two people up front. Jessica was on the left, in the driver seat. The other person was riding shotgun.

"We should make her take off her clothes," the second person said. Her voice was unmistakable: Brooklyn. At the party she'd come across as nice. Now she sounded sarcastic as she went on about forcing Chloe to go skyclad—witch's slang for naked—and snakes, bugs, and how it's too bad it wasn't colder.

Chloe ground her teeth. Her hands clenched into fists. She'd misjudged Brooklyn for sure. Once this was over, she would watch her back around the two of them.

The car filled with the smell of a lit joint—weed and a sharper scent Chloe didn't recognize. Whatever it was they were smoking, it wasn't making them mellower. But it was making it harder for her to fight off the dizziness.

"Remember when you shaved that bitch?" Brooklyn said.

Jessica chuckled. "That was nothing compared to the look on the doctor's face when we dropped her off at the emergency room. It wasn't even her blood."

Chloe lifted her chin and shifted more upright. No way was she going to let them think their bullshit was getting to her. And that's what this was, complete bullshit.

Her head whirred and she slouched back down, nausea as well as another huge round of dizziness surging inside her.

Minutes ticked by. More time passed. Chloe swallowed hard, struggling to not throw up. She couldn't help but wonder why they hadn't picked up Midas or Em. Plus, the car was moving faster now, like they were on the interstate heading out of town.

The *fitz* of bottles opening and the smelled of beer filled the car. "To loyalty, and power," Jessica said.

"And stupid bitches." Brooklyn laughed.

As their voices lowered and they switched to talking about banal stuff going on at the coven's winery and Matt's job with Burlington's Recreation Department, Chloe tuned them out. She needed to think. She'd assumed they were driving to where the initiation would take place. But what if the drugging and the ride itself were part of the test? What if Jessica's comment about throwing her out wasn't as much a threat as their actual plan? Dizziness or not, she had to keep track of where they were. Fortunately, she didn't need her eyesight to do that. She just had to stay calm.

She drew in a deep breath through her nose and closed her eyes. Actually, shutting them alleviated the burning sensation, and it wasn't like she could see anyway. She took another breath and focused on the vibration of the tires against the pavement. She released that breath and let the murmur of Jessica and Brooklyn's voices fade into the background. She didn't need to listen to them. They weren't going to say anything important while she was within earshot. Forget them. Forget…As Chloe's mind drifted into

Pat Esden

a peaceful place, she sent out a plea. *Hecate, show me the path, show me where we are. Be my eyes, be my guiding light in the darkness. Show me.*

Threads of orange and gray broke the darkness behind her eyelids: A distant sunset over Lake Champlain with the more distant mountains of New York State. Below her, a black ribbon of interstate stretched, headlights and taillights, bright gems flickering in the twilight. Stars appeared. Straight ahead the Little Dipper twinkled. The North Star. Her favorite star.

They traveled eastward, then turned in the opposite direction. An interstate off-ramp. City lights glimmered off to the south, nothing more than specks of brightness becoming a blur as they crossed a causeway or a river, water on both sides. More turns. A narrow road with trees close on either side. No headlights or taillights. No stars anymore.

Thump!

A bump in the road snapped Chloe's head back against the seat, jolting her out of her trance. She blinked and a foggy-gray outline of Jessica's head came into focus. That was good. She couldn't see well, but hazy vision was better than nothing.

She rolled her head, testing to see how dizzy she felt. Like her eyesight, that was a little better. This was great, except she could barely remember what she'd seen in the trance. In truth, it was so disjointed she might have imagined it. She more than likely had even passed out for a while, like for quite a while. Wherever they were, the drive had lasted long enough for the mushroom spores and magic to begin to wear off. Unfortunately, it also meant she was totally lost.

Cold sweat slithered down her back, leaving her shivering. *Shush*, she told herself. *Stay calm. This is just an initiation. Devlin knows about it. Athena helped plan it. Nothing bad is going to happen.*

The car slowed and stopped. A door up front opened, then closed. Footsteps crunched on loose gravel, stopping to her left.

A second later, cold air whooshed in and Jessica snarled, "Get out."

Chloe swallowed hard. This was it.

She held onto the doorframe, feeling her way as if she couldn't see at all. No sense in letting them know she was regaining some of her senses.

Jessica grabbed her wrists and yanked the duct tape from around them. A sharp sting of pain ripped across Chloe's wrists. She rubbed the burn from her skin. "Fuck, that hurt."

"It wasn't that bad." Jessica snickered.

Chloe bit her tongue to keep from calling her a bitch. But fear whispered in the back of her mind. What if this wasn't the initiation? Neither Jessica nor Brooklyn had said it was. No. It had to be. They were just doing a damn good job of scaring her.

"Let's get going." Brooklyn's voice came from a few yards away.

Jessica shoved Chloe ahead of her, away from the car and onto uneven ground. A band of foggy brightness fanned the air ahead of her, breaking up the landscape of gray shadows and indistinct shapes. Chloe wasn't sure, but she suspected Brooklyn was walking behind Jessica and her and the brightness came from a flashlight she was carrying. She caught a strong whiff of rotting apples. An orchard, that had to be what they were walking through.

As they went down a short incline, the smell of apples faded under a cedar-scented breeze. The air cooled. The gray foggy outlines vanished, replaced by blackness and the fan of the flashlight's brilliance. A forest trail.

"Tell me there aren't bats out here," Brooklyn said.

"Shut up," Jessica huffed. She nudged Chloe in the shoulder. "Hurry up."

Chloe quickened her step, blindly fast-walking forward. Her toe hit something. She stumbled and went down onto all fours. Something hard sliced into her palms. But instead of focusing on the pain, she let her fingertips interpret the ground her eyes could barely see. Hard-packed sand, crisscrossed with roots and long, sharp stones. A lakeshore trail. Now that she thought about it, the chill in the air held the same scent from earlier, when she was at the waterside park with Keshari. Lake Champlain.

Jessica wrenched Chloe to her feet. "Keep going. We don't have all night."

They marched forward for a couple more paces. Abruptly, a breeze whisked the hair back from Chloe's face. Foggy grayness instead of sheer black now stretched ahead of them, as if they'd left the shelter of the cedar trees and stepped out into the open—a large opening that smelled like water.

"Stop," Jessica commanded, her voice echoing.

Chloe did as she asked. She was certain they were close to the lake, very close. But she couldn't hear waves and the ground under her feet wasn't beach sand or pebbles. It was solid, smooth, and grass free. A flat rock ledge—

The breath seized in Chloe's throat as all at once she understood what was about to happen: the tarot card. The Fool. The man with the rod and bag about to head off into a new phase of his life, about to step off a cliff.

A freaking cliff! They expected her to jump off a cliff, skyclad and blind, into Lake Champlain. Were they nuts? There could be rocks below.

Chloe's pulse slammed in her ears, telling her to run. Get out. Go. Hide. This must have been what the orb's warning was about. Betrayal. Betrayal.

She clenched her teeth and willed her body to stop shaking. Jessica and Brooklyn were trying to make her chicken out. There was no way they would really risk her death—and she really wanted to be a part of the Northern Circle. *Magic and medicine.* Devlin liked her. He wouldn't risk her life either.

Jessica's fingernails dug into Chloe's arm. She leaned close. "Listen carefully. This is a test of your magical abilities, and your trust and connection to the coven."

She nodded. *Hecate protect me*, she prayed.

Jessica's voice hardened. "You came to our home. You ate at our table. You enjoyed our magic. You say you want to join us. Then trust us."

Chloe clasped her hands in front of her, waiting for the command to remove her sweater and jeans. It would be colder, but it would make swimming easier.

"This is called the Devil's Leap. No one has died here."

"That we know of," Brooklyn said, her voice trembling.

Jessica kept going. "Step forward into the darkness, into the void, without fear. Then reach out with your magic. Find our circle on the shore, connect with us, come to us—leave your past behind and become one with us."

Leave your past behind, the words repeated in Chloe's head. This wasn't some random initiation choice. Athena knew her past. They all did, including Devlin. They'd chosen water and this dangerous leap to remind her of the horror of that night. But they didn't know what she knew. Jumping into the water wasn't the hard part. Drowning wasn't something to fear. It was worse to be on the shore and see the shape of a body floating on the water. Worse to bring someone back to life, only to discover death might have been kinder.

"Go on. Step forward." Jessica paused. She cleared her throat. "Um— actually, I suggest you get a running start, then leap as far as you can."

Chloe swiped her arm across her face, wiping her eyes in an attempt to further clear her vision. To hell with them, it wasn't like they were going to penalize her for trying to improve her chances at this point. She blinked and her vision cleared a bit more, the shape of the ledge, its edge, and the expanse of fathomless darkness beyond them coming into focus.

Blowing out a long breath, she took a dozen steps back, then shot forward like a runner taking off from a starting block.

"Jump!" Jessica shouted. "Like the Fool. Jump into your future."

And Chloe did.

The world shifted into slow motion. *Feet first,* her inner high diving instructor whispered. *Arch your back. Prepare for shallow water.* But maybe she was wrong about this whole thing. Maybe it wasn't water below. Maybe they'd created a net of magic. Maybe death waited. It would be the perfect justice.

She never saw the boy slip into the pool, only his body floating in the water. She raced down the stairs, the red sequined dress twisting around her legs as she dove off the edge of the pool...

She hit. Water. Cold. Her body plummeted deep. It kept going. And going. She kicked her legs and pulled with her arms, propelling herself upwards. The weight of her clothes twisted around her body, fighting against her. She kicked harder and finally broke the surface.

Air hit her lungs. She gasped for breath and wriggled out of her sweater, kicked her way free of her jeans and sneakers.

Less restricted, she began treading water. Her eyes didn't sting any more. Her vision was almost normal. Fantastic, except she was surrounded by absolute darkness and needed to find the shore. It couldn't be far. She'd just jumped in.

She stopped moving, bobbing upright in the water for a moment. If she held still, the waves would pull her toward the shore. But the water was as smooth as graveyard marble, no current whatsoever. She spun in a circle, determined to find an answer. The water was deep and colder than she'd expected. The high cliff she'd jumped off was steep enough that the coven was certain she wouldn't hit anything on her way down. The top of the cliff had been as flat as—

A sick feeling came over her. *Oh, fuck.* This wasn't Lake Champlain.

"Hello!" Chloe shouted to test the theory forming in her head.

"Hello. Hello..." Her voice echoed back from all directions, the way Jessica's voice had echoed from up on the clifftop. It was as if she were inside a box—or a flooded quarry.

Chloe had seen a TV show about Vermont's quarries, abandoned and filled with water from natural springs, hidden swimming holes with sheer rock walls. When Chloe had first moved into her apartment, Juliet had mentioned going to one.

Chloe started treading water again, the cold water numbing her skin. She needed to find a way out before hypothermia set in. But how? '*Reach out with your magic. Find our circle on the shore, connect with us, come to us,*' Jessica had said.

Rolling onto her back, she stared up into the darkness and took a deep breath. She shivered, the quake running from her ears to her chest. She shouldn't have taken off her clothes. But she couldn't change that now. She just had to get going.

Chloe drew up her magic, releasing it with her breath, and reached out for the sensation of the coven's magic, that intoxicating vibe...

She felt nothing. Total numb-cold, nothing.

Panic stole her breath. She gritted her chattering teeth and tried again, this time concentrating on the memory of Jessica's nastiness. Again, nothing.

She searched for Brooklyn's stormy energy, like she'd sensed at the gathering. Nothing, other than a sense of creeping dread working its way into her bones. *Shit.* She was a good swimmer, but not immortal.

To hell with magic.

"Hello!" Chloe shouted again, listening more carefully to the echoes this time. She had to be close to the cliff. Once she found it, she'd swim in one direction until she discovered a way out.

"Hello, hello. Hello," the echoes came back to her. One much quicker than the others.

In practiced strokes, she swam toward it, until the sheer wall she'd jumped from loomed a yard in front of her. She switched to the side stroke, keeping her eyes on the rock as she paralleled it.

But what if she was swimming in the wrong direction?

Chloe flipped onto her back, floating as she reached out again with her magic, searching this time for the thrum of Devlin's energy. She couldn't be sure he was here, but Jessica had mentioned the circle, which meant most likely there were more than just her and Brooklyn on the shore. As Chloe sucked in another breath through her nose, she didn't sense him. But she smelled something very distinctive. The aroma of weed and something sharper, coming from the opposite side of the quarry.

Pushing fear aside, she turned away from the cliff, and switched to the breaststroke, swimming in the opposite direction, sniffing the air each time she rose, then going under again in hard, fast strokes.

The moon broke free from the horizon behind her, glazing the quarry in faint light. In the distance more sheer cliffs rose, topped with the outline of evergreen trees. What if the burning weed smell had come from up there? She could swim toward it, but that didn't mean there was a place for her to climb out.

Blocking that thought from her mind, she pushed on, sniffing the air every few strokes. A prickle of intuition now urged her on. A sensation that reminded her of the night when Devlin had slid the invitation under her door. He was here, and he was thinking about her.

Her pulse picked up, her body warming. Her connection with him was faint, but it was growing stronger even as the smell of the weed faded. The vibration of other magic reached her too, Brooklyn's and maybe Jessica's.

Ahead, a deep V-shape cleft in the cliff's outline appeared. Maybe it was an outlet formed by water or a rockslide, a place where the sheer cliffs had given way. Whatever it was, there were no specks of brightness on the shore, like from flashlights. No welcoming bonfire to dry off beside.

Chloe dove under the water and came up. Cramps pinched her jaw muscles and made her hands claw-like. Still, she was giddy-happy. This wasn't so hard.

Somewhere in her brain it registered. The giddiness. The claw-like hands. They weren't good signs. The cold was getting to her. She had to hurry.

A shiver rattled her teeth, then another—

Something hard and bony jabbed her foot.

Chloe yelped and instinctively lowered her legs, whirling in a circle to see what she'd hit. Her feet kicked something else. Hard. Angular. A rock. A wonderful, glorious rock!

She dog-paddled forward, into shallower and shallower water, over blocks of abandoned marble, closer and closer to the V-shaped cleft. When the water became too shallow to swim, she belly-crawled, using her hands to pull herself over the slick rocks, forward toward what she now could see was a dense wall of pine trees—and in front of them, an exit from the quarry.

Slippery rocks were under her hands now. She rose from the knee-deep water, trembling in the cool night air, colder in truth than the water.

A whisper came from the evergreens. A spark of light flashed, followed by the glow of an ember and the smell of burning weed. A giggle.

"Shush," someone grumbled.

Chloe stopped, ankle-deep in the water. She took a deep breath, then let her intuition and the smell lead her in a straight line. She reached the shore and stumbled into the trees.

Shivering, she folded her arms across her chest and stared into the darkness. They were here. Very close.

"Booyah!" Devlin shouted.

A circle of candles flamed to life, illuminating a tiny clearing in the pines. In the center of the ring, four people waited. Devlin, Jessica, then Brooklyn and Matt.

As Chloe staggered toward them across the prickly forest floor, Devlin passed a joint to Brooklyn. Jessica scowled at him. "You lit one when she was in the water, didn't you? You used the smell to help her cheat."

Devlin glared at her. "I wouldn't talk, after last night."

"That was Athena's—"

"Go ahead, say it." Devlin's voice rumbled, a threatening tone infused with magic. "Are you forgetting this coven has a high priestess—*and* a high priest?"

Even at a distance, the power of his tone reverberated into Chloe's bones, bringing her to a halt mid-stride. Devlin was the Northern Circle's high priest. It made perfect sense. In fact, she should have considered the possibility before. Most often, covens had both a high priest and priestess. But it wasn't uncommon for their level of involvement in the coven to vary greatly, especially if one took on the coven management role as their full-time employment and the other had an outside profession—like with Athena and Devlin.

Jessica sliced a glance at Chloe. "I get it now."

"Leave it be," Devlin said.

Chloe stared at him as he pivoted away from Jessica and strode toward her. She wanted to say something, but the warm blanket Brooklyn was draping around her shoulders stole her attention. It was amazing, its magic-enhanced comfort soaking into her like sunshine.

"Wonderful," she murmured, snuggling into it. Her voice rattled like castanets. She could barely feel her feet.

Brooklyn tsked. "Jessica's right—you're a total wimp."

Matt thrust a steaming travel mug into her hands. "Nothing fancy, just mint tea. But it should help."

Devlin was next to her now. He rubbed his hand down her back, his fingers sliding about her waist as he urged her forward. "We need to get you to a warm car."

Happiness radiated through Chloe. She leaned into him and rested her head on his shoulder. "I'm fine, really."

His breath nuzzled her ear. "Congratulations, by the way."

"Thanks," she mumbled.

Chapter 11

*We would have thought the box nothing more than a stone,
entangled in the oak's roots, if it weren't for the runes
that brought us to that circle of earth
and for the solstice moon that illuminated it.*
—Journal of Chandler Parrish
June 21st, Isle of Anglesey

When they arrived back at the complex, Brooklyn took Chloe up to Athena's personal suite, a series of rooms on the second floor of the main house, and directed her into the most amazing bathroom in the universe. Candlelight reflected off mirrors and moonlight-blue tiles. A stemmed glass and an open bottle of May wine waited next to a steaming whirlpool bath. Chloe's chills had subsided thanks to the roaring heat vents in Devlin's BMW. Still, as soon as Brooklyn left her alone, Chloe stripped off her wet underwear and slipped into the water.

She rested back, closing her eyes and listening to the drift of Celtic harp music coming from the nearby bedroom, and sipped the wine. She could have floated off to sleep in about a half a second, except Brooklyn had told her that once she was dressed, a circle would be cast and a ritual performed to welcome her into the coven. Soon she'd be a part of a group who could help her make everything right.

She wove her hands through the water, letting it flow between her fingers as she replayed everything that had happened at the quarry. The surrender of jumping off the cliff, going under the water—the terror of realizing it was a quarry, not the lake. Despite the warmth, she shivered as she remembered the moments when she was certain she was going to die.

Loneliness. Determination. But mostly fear. Then the joy of succeeding. She was certain Devlin had helped her do that, thrown her a lifeline. Still, she'd really done it on her own. She'd noticed the smell. She hadn't given up. He'd just been like a guardian spirit.

A mix of happiness and desire washed over her. She scooched deeper into the water, remembering the protective strength of his hand against her waist, his warm voice close to her ear. The harder, stronger voice he'd used on Jessica. There was something going on there behind the scenes. But more importantly Devlin was the Circle's high priest. Standing behind Athena, letting her take the reins. Still, he was there and vigilant. And beyond gorgeous and sexy.

Chloe finished the wine and was about to give in and take a quick nap, when the bathroom door slid open partway. "It's just me," Athena said quietly. She opened the door the rest of the way and stepped inside. "I've brought a heated towel and your robe for the ceremony."

"Thank you." Under normal circumstances, having someone she barely knew walk in while she was bathing would have felt uncomfortable to Chloe. But with all that had happened and the serene gentleness of Athena's voice, it felt natural. In fact, shyness would have felt odd.

Athena pulled the vanity chair up next to the tub and sat down with the towels and Chloe's ceremonial robe in her lap. She was dressed in a similar robe with her black choker around her neck and rings on every finger, all carved with symbols of the Craft and accented with different types of stones. Her hair was piled on top of her head, held in place with gold pins and a band of embroidered white cloth. With the steam of the bath and the harps playing in the background, Chloe had no trouble visualizing Athena as an ancient high priestess, perhaps even a queen.

"I'm so happy you're going to join us." Athena rested her hand on the foot of the tub. "I was afraid you might change your mind."

Chloe laughed. "I was afraid about that too—especially right before I jumped."

"But you did." She looked down at her hand, fiddling with one of her rings for a moment. Her voice hushed even further. "My parents never would have allowed me to join a coven like the Circle, something new, something they don't understand. I'm not saying they didn't love me and Devlin, quite the opposite. But holding your children back isn't right either. Children need to be given wings. Chloe, you astound me—how you reach for what you deserve."

Chloe pulled her washcloth up close to her chest, more self-conscious now. "I wouldn't be here if you hadn't invited me."

"Perhaps that's true." Athena hesitated. "Parents like ours aren't evil or hard. It's just...They think we are too inexperienced to handle our powers. They're afraid we will end up shunned by the witch community."

"Yeah." Chloe totally got what she meant. It was a large part of why her parents had insisted that she live at home and get her undergraduate degree at a community college. It was a nice surprise to learn that she and Athena had something in common besides the Craft. Not to mention how wonderful it felt to talk to someone who came from the same place, but was brave enough to bring innovative ideas to the Circle. However, a part of Athena's story didn't quite add up. "But your mother surrendered the coven to you."

"She did. But she'd never have done it if it weren't for her own fear of failure—and selfish interests outside her duties." Athena refilled Chloe's wine glass. "I'm so happy for you and for us. Together we're going to do great things." She got up and set the robe on the chair but kept the towel. "Now we should get you dressed, everyone is waiting. They're all so excited about you joining."

"All of them?" *I'm not so sure about that*, was what she wanted to say. But passing judgement on other coven members didn't seem the best way to start a new relationship, no matter how close she felt to Athena.

"What's wrong?"

Chloe shrugged. "Nothing, really."

Athena raised an eyebrow. "Is Jessica giving you problems?"

"I'm not sure. She seems..." Man, this was impossible to say out loud.

"If you're thinking she's jealous, you'd be right. If you think her feelings are only toward you, you'd be wrong. She doesn't warm up to new people quickly. She's equally uncomfortable about Em joining. Perhaps more so since Em is pansexual."

Chloe's face heated, surprised by the level of Athena's laidback straightforwardness. At the same time, it was a huge relief to know why Jessica was giving her attitude, and that Athena was aware it was a problem.

"Jessica and I have occasionally been lovers." Athena shook out the heated towel, letting it fall open in an invitation for Chloe to get out of the bath and wrap up. "Don't worry about her. She'll come around."

"I hope so." Chloe set her wine down and got out of the tub. She liked Athena a lot, but Jessica didn't have anything to worry about in the romantic area.

Athena moved behind Chloe, enveloping the towel around her body. As she snugged the towel tight, her hands stopped on Chloe's upper arms. "We have no issue with coven members becoming involved, casually or seriously, like Brooklyn and Matt. I'd like nothing more than to see my brother involved with someone like you."

Chloe stiffened. Athena didn't sound angry, but there was a note of warning in her tone. "Nothing's happened between us. You know that, right? Like the other night after the gathering?"

"I don't care about that. I love my brother. I want to see him happy." She picked up Chloe's wine glass and handed it to her. "It's you, not him, I'm concerned about. He's—when he was in prep school—"

Not even daring to breathe, Chloe waited for her to go on. What the heck had Devlin done?

Athena motioned to the vanity chair. "Sit. Let me do your hair while we talk."

Chloe hurried to do as she asked.

In silence, Athena stroked the brush down her hair. She sighed. "He's a lot like our father."

Chloe shuddered, a chill going straight to her heart. He couldn't be. Devlin couldn't have fooled her to that much of a degree. He was sweet and kind, not at all like his father.

"Have you ever been with a witch?" Athena asked.

Chloe frowned, unsure what that had to do with anything. "I've been with guys, if that's what you mean," she said, though she suspected it wasn't what Athena was getting at. Her parents had been dry and straightforward when it came to talking about sex. But one afternoon, when she was far too young for it, she'd stumbled across a dog-eared book in her older sister's room. *The Witch's Way of Love.* That had been an eye opener. Another whole realm that explained the late-night moans and throbbing energy reverberating from her parents' bedroom. A realm beyond anything she'd come across since then in her dating experience with normal guys.

"The thing is"—Athena gave her hair an absentminded stroke with the brush—"hooking up with an empowered witch is as wonderful and as different as you've heard—and as addictive, more quickly than most are willing to admit. That, I believe is the root of Jessica's jealousy. And something she and I need to work on."

Chloe's nervousness subsided and she took a long sip of wine to relieve the dryness in her mouth. So this wasn't about Devlin being an asshole then. Relief spread through her body. This was about his witchy bedroom skills, and that wasn't exactly a turn off. "Oh, I never thought of that."

"It's not just that." Athena rested a hand on Chloe's shoulder. "Guard your heart. When it comes to relationships with women, Devlin isn't good at commitment. I don't want to see you hurt."

Chloe nodded. No doubt, Athena was trying to be nice. But her advice hardly put Devlin in an unusual category. That sounded like ninety-five percent of the guys she'd dated.

Athena's voice lightened. "Enough serious talk. This is your night. What do you say we get you into that robe? I'm sure everyone is wondering where we are."

Since Chloe's clothes were at the bottom of the quarry and her underwear was still wet, she pulled on her robe with nothing underneath. It felt rebellious and new. As a rule, her family wore clothes under their robes. Athena, however, confided that she preferred going skyclad as a way to feel closer to nature. Chloe smiled at Athena's preference. It didn't surprise her in the least.

Once she was ready, the two of them went downstairs and out into the garden, where Midas and Devlin waited on the bridge. Chloe barely had time to catch Devlin's eyes and share a smile before Em and Chandler arrived. Seeing all of them in robes, knowing that Em and Midas had also chosen to join, eliminated the last speck of wariness Chloe had about her decision. Joining the Circle was the right path for her, she was sure of it.

She walked next to Athena on their way to the teahouse. Her robe whispered against the glowing path. Overhead, the stars sparkled, more brilliant than ever. Chloe's fingers rubbed at her wrist, unconsciously reaching for her charm bracelet that was back at the apartment on the coffee table. A bittersweet feeling flittered through her chest. Ever since she could remember, she'd worn the bracelet for Sabbats and rituals, whenever she worked the Craft. It had been lengthened as she'd grown. Charms had been added on special occasions. It felt odd not to have it with her now.

Inside the teahouse, Jessica, Brooklyn, and Matt stood around an altar draped in white cloth. Candles representing the four directions—north, east, south, west— and a smoking incense burner awaited on the altar, along with as a bowl of water, a chalice, and what appeared to be Merlin's crystal.

As the ceremony began, Athena and Devlin worked together to cleanse the room and cast the circle. Chloe dipped her head, listening and enjoying the heady sage scent that permeated the air. The words they used were slightly different than what she was used to, but not so much that she couldn't adjust and join in. A warm sense of safety and timelessness enveloped her as the coven's magic filled the room.

"Chloe, come forward," Athena called out. "Come forward, Emily and Midas."

Keeping pace with the others, Chloe approached the altar. As was traditional for a blessing, she held her hands out with the palms up.

Athena dipped her fingers into a bowl of water, touched Chloe's palms, then forehead. "Blessings and welcome to the Northern Circle, Chloe," she intoned.

"Blessings and welcome, Chloe," all the other members repeated the words in unison.

Athena moved on, repeating the blessing for Em and Midas. Then she raised her hands and voice. "Tonight, we are not only blessed with new members. We are also on the cusp of a new beginning." The pitch of her voice dropped, each word becoming concise and rhythmic, as steady as the hypnotic pulse of a metronome. "We step out. As the Fool off his cliff. As the Wizard from the dark of the winter solstice. A new beginning. A new path for the Northern Circle." With a flick of her wrist, a slender silver knife appeared in her hand. With another flick, she sliced her palm with its blade.

Chloe cringed. This wasn't any ritual she was familiar with.

"Athena?" Devlin said in a hard whisper. "What are you doing?"

Ignoring him, she held up her hand and turned in a slow circle, revealing the stripe of welling blood on her palm to everyone. "I welcome you all to pledge as I am doing. Rededicate yourselves. To a new age. A new way. A new path." She turned to the altar and rested her bloodied hand on Merlin's crystal. White and purple light exploded outward, followed by a wave of surging energy. The walls of the teahouse rattled. Bright light flashed again and Athena's voice roared, loud and powerful as a thunderstorm. "I offer myself. I rededicate myself. To a new path. To Merlin's return."

"Athena." Devlin's voice cut sharply through the room, the surge of energy freezing in midair—Chloe had never seen him turn on his magic full force like that before, but now she understood to a greater degree why he was the high priest.

Her gaze darted to him, then back to Athena. What had she said? *To Merlin's return.* That made no sense.

Athena wheeled toward Devlin, her jaw set, her gaze unflinching. "If we wish to search for things lost to history and do it safely, we need the wisest guide we can find. Unlike all the other great witches and wizards, Merlin is not dead. He is merely sleeping. Why do you think we went to such lengths to acquire the stone?"

"Certainly not this." His voice rumbled, so thick with magic and anger that Chloe felt it right down to her toes.

Her body went cold, colder than when she'd emerged from the quarry. She couldn't have moved even if the teahouse were on fire. She now fully grasped what Athena had meant the first night, when they'd seen the crystal. Athena hadn't lied. She hadn't even avoided the truth. But she sure as heck had hidden it.

"...with this item, guidance, and the right coven members...the Northern Circle can be used to accomplish the unheard of."

By guidance, Athena had meant they could explore the past and discover lost magics literally with the help of Merlin—after they used his crystal to awaken him and return him to this world. Athena had never meant—or even actually outright said—the crystal alone could be used for incorporeal time travel. And, clearly, Devlin hadn't known about awakening Merlin either.

Athena softened her voice, once again taking on a slow measured beat. "What are you afraid of, Brother? Afraid of losing your position to a more powerful man? Are you so self-centered to put yourself before the coven—and before the welfare of mankind?" She stepped closer to him. "Have I ever not supported you?"

"Of course not. I—" His voice broke, and the surge of Athena's energy that had hung frozen in the air broke with him, cascading like a wave through the teahouse and swirling in a giant eddy. The power of its return made Chloe's head swim and she had to fight to regain her equilibrium.

Athena thrust the knife handle-first at Devlin. "Brother, join me. We need the strength of the entire coven to succeed. This alone will not bring Merlin back. This is merely the first step of that journey."

His fingers clenched into a fist. Indecision and fear flickered across his face, followed by desire and a desperation Chloe couldn't understand. Slowly, he unclenched his fingers and reached for the knife. In one swift motion, he drew the edge across his palm. Blood gushed to the surface, flowing down his skin.

"Blessed be our new path," Athena intoned as he pressed his palm against the crystal. "May it lead humanity into a new age."

Jessica strode forward next, followed by Em. Chloe watched as one after another the members dedicated themselves to the new path. Inside, her intuition whispered for her to not do it. *Run*, it screamed. But she'd jumped off a cliff only a few hours earlier to prove her commitment and loyalty to the Circle. Only moments ago, her soul had soared when Athena blessed her and welcomed her as a new member.

An image of the Vice-Chancellor's son lying in his hospital bed wavered into her head. That same hospital bed that she'd put him in five years ago. She could still feel that red dress twisting around her legs. See him lying motionless in the water. Feel his icy, clammy skin against her own. Taste the cold of his lips as she blew the life back into him. If she did this, then she'd be able to help him, to make up for her wrongs and absolve the shame she'd brought upon her family.

Merlin. He was one of the most revered wizards in history. Powerful. Loved. What harm could come from his return?

She stepped forward, half-dazed, took the knife from Athena and sliced her skin, a fast cut that left her lifeline bloodied.

Chapter 12

He clasped my face between his palms. I believed he wished nothing more than to guide my lips, to show them how to form the spell. But he was nothing more than the basest of thieves.
A thief of innocence in wizard's robes.
—Nimue, Lady of the Lake

Once the ritual was over, Chloe relaxed on one of the floor mats with everyone else, sipping a hot mulled cider and reveling in how amazing her life had become. She was part of a coven that was going to rediscover lost cures under Merlin's guidance. In retrospect, the panic that had come over her before she cut her palm had been ludicrous. Athena was right. Under Merlin's guidance, they were going to change the world. Of course, that came with a large sticking point. How were they going to make the cures available to mankind while retaining the witching communities' sacred anonymity? Not to mention hide Merlin's existence. She might have asked Athena those things, but she was bone-tired, drained to the glorious point where everything felt trancelike. Even the thought of getting up didn't appeal to her.

Devlin sat down next to her. His knee brushed hers and warmth radiated up her thighs, spreading through her body and settling into a delicious ache below her belly. She smiled and laughed with the conversations whirling around her, but in truth she was too lost in the sensation of his closeness and the joy of the moment to hear a word.

His fingers touched hers, slowly, softly, sending tingles up her arm and throat. She nestled in closer to him. He rested his hand on the floor behind her and she leaned her head against his shoulder. Across from them, Matt lay down with his head on Brooklyn's lap. Chandler told a funny story involving her son's third birthday and the flying monkeys on the complex's gate. Everyone laughed. Athena took over, something else about the metal monkeys and an issue Chandler had when she'd used her magic to weld them.

Chloe didn't dare breathe as Devlin stroked a finger along the neckline of her robe. He whispered, "Want to get out of here?"

Desire throbbed inside her, so strong she trembled. His eyes shone in a way that told her he felt it too. Without a word, he took her hand and drew her to her feet and out of the teahouse. The cool air refreshed her super-heated face. The blue glow of the path filtered through a low mist. Stars. Moonlight. Everything was perfect. Impossibly so.

She pulled him to a stop on the bridge. He was so gorgeous. So smart and powerful. What if her exhaustion and the afterglow from the magic had made her read his signals wrong? It seemed impossible, but what if he was just offering to drive her home? She didn't want to say or do something stupid.

Devlin caressed the side of her face, a light touch. "You okay?"

"Yeah." She glanced back at the teahouse. "Aren't Em and Midas going to need rides?"

"It's not my night to watch them," he said coolly. He grasped her by the shoulders, bringing her in close to his chest. His voice became husky. "Do you know what I'm thinking about?"

She tilted her head up, her lips parting of their own accord. "That you want to kiss me?"

He smiled, beautiful, slow, luxuriant, full of promises. "And?"

Heat flared south of her stomach, branching from one nerve ending to the next. She licked her lips and slid her hands down his chest. "That you want to go someplace more private?"

His cheeks dimpled. "Definitely."

His lips met hers, moist and hungry. She matched his kiss, the strength going out of her legs from the energy tumbling through every part of her being. His strong hands swept down her arms, moving up onto her ribcage. She slid her fingers down his back, feeling his corded muscles, broad shoulders, and tight butt. Oh Goddess, his amazing tight butt as naked under his robe as she was under hers.

"Come on," he whispered in her ear, and she remembered they were still on the bridge, in full view of the teahouse.

Chloe let him draw her down the path, flying past the waterfalls and gardens. They were almost to his door when his retriever—Henry— came bounding out of the dark. For a moment the spell was broken and self-consciousness came over her, as they stepped out of the moonlight and into the brightness of his apartment, the dog insisting on pets and treats before settling down on the couch.

"I've been dreaming of this since that first night at your apartment," he murmured, moving up close to her.

She shivered and bit her bottom lip. "So have I."

He leaned in, his lips meeting hers, a slow, lingering kiss, a promise of something more. His fingers caressed her face, her throat, the sides of her breasts. She tilted her head back, opening her mouth and surrendering to the movement of his lips and body. He pressed harder against her, urging her backwards to the bed.

Together they fell onto the quilts. His hand slid under her robe, the kiss growing hotter as his fingers explored her thighs. Shudders of pleasure rippled through her.

He pulled back. His hands cupped her face, his smoldering gaze searching hers. "Have you ever been with a witch?"

She wriggled free of his hands and laughed. She couldn't help it. "Your sister asked me the same thing earlier."

"And?"

"No." Her voice came out more breathless than she expected. *No* she hadn't, but she had wanted to. Oh, how she wanted to. "You're the first."

He kissed her forehead, drawing a finger down to the corner of her lips. "Then we'll take this slow."

She stopped his finger with her own. "I don't mind fast. And I like wild, too. And condoms—I insist on them."

He chuckled and glanced at his bedside stand. "No problem."

Tension pulled at her stomach. It was great he was prepared. She wasn't looking for a commitment. But he answered that question almost too fast, like he did this a lot.

As if he could read her mind, he gently stroked her hair back. "I bought them this morning."

She laughed. "You're bullshitting me now."

"Seriously, Chloe. I was hoping."

Dear Goddess. The nervous tension in her stomach melted away. She nodded, wondering how she'd landed here with this beyond amazing man, in this too-good-to-be-true dream.

His lips were on hers again, hands moving up under her robes, pushing them off. She wiggled free from the loose cloth, the cool air sending shivers across her bare skin. She found the hem of his robe, pulled it off over his head.

The warmth of his powerful body enveloped her. His hands once again caressed her inner thighs, stroking inward, magic fluttering in their wake. She gasped as he trailed a finger down her spine. His tongue awakened her breasts, her nipples. She moaned and squirmed away, taking a deep breath, pushing energy into her hands, experimenting with her own touch against the strong planes of his chest.

"Chloe," he moaned. He leaned forward, crushing his lips against hers, a hungry kiss, alive with magic. The world faded, into a dance of sensations. The moist heat of his breath. The hum of his body, his fingers teasing the sweet spot between her legs, bringing her to the brink and holding her there. She wriggled down his body, kissing his chest, his abs, exploring the planes of his stomach with her fingertips, the soft down of his belly hair. Pushing magic into her breath, she teased his cock with a gentle exhale.

His cock twitched with pleasure. But he pulled her back up. "Chloe..." His voice was ragged, strained as though the effort it took to stop her was physically excruciating to him. "Not this time. Tonight's about you. Just you."

He moved slowly down her body, as she'd done to him. His magic-infused breath purred against her skin, awakening every inch of her. She could smell it too. The scent of power. The smell of witchcraft. Ancient. Overwhelming. He parted her legs, his mouth on her, kissing, licking. She shuddered and arched, closing her eyes as delicious tension took her to the edge of oblivion. The pulse of his magic grew stronger. An escalating rhythm. A rhythm that wouldn't be denied. She let go, shockwaves of pleasure taking her, over and over again.

She fell back into the cloud of quilts, lost in a mix of serenity and exhilaration, and throbbing desire for more. What they said about witches was true. This was nothing like it had been with any other guy. Not even close.

Devlin slid up next to her and reach toward the bedside table. "You still okay with this?"

She could barely nod. And when he entered her, it wasn't just with his body. His magic thrust into her with equal force, a swell of energy that vibrated and hummed into every cell in her body. Electrifying. A thousand times stronger than any drink or drug she'd ever had, stronger than any spell she'd ever worked. Her magic roared and flared inside her, a wildfire with no wish other than to rush into his being, to pleasure him. He might have wanted tonight to be about her, but she couldn't hold back. She released her energy, and he shuddered and groaned. Their magics collided in a tsunami of waves and they both came in a blur. Then time stood still for a moment, sparks of energy hissing along her damp skin, joy shuddering though her, until the sensations slowly calmed into blissful oblivion.

She nuzzled up next to him, her head on his chest. He brushed her hair back from her damp face. "Chloe, you're so beautiful," he said. "Not just your body. Your soul. Your magic."

"You too," she murmured. She closed her eyes, tears burning at the edges. *Yes, it was true what they said about witches,* she thought once more. Her body already craved more of him and his magic. A magic that made her feel both powerful and weightless at the same time. Maybe not now. But soon the ache would become unbearable.

She opened her eyes and gazed in awe at his gorgeous face. Then she closed them again and silently built a wall around her heart, a border to protect her from falling any harder for him and his magic. A magic that she was afraid may have just ruined her for any other man.

Chapter 13

Blood from the living. Blood from the dead.
One takes you forward. The other brings you back.
—From *'The Grimoire of Conjurations and Spirit Wisdom'*
Translated from Old French by B. Remillard

A phone was ringing.

Barely awake, Chloe felt her way across to the edge of the bed and located the phone on the bedside table. "Hello?"

"Who am I speaking with?" an older man said.

She rubbed her eyes, working to clear away her sleepiness. "This is Chloe. Don't you know who you called?"

"Chloe who?"

"Winslow," she said, a tad sharply. Her voice was groggy from sleep, but how could they not know who she was? They'd called her.

"One of *the* Winslows from Connecticut? Your father's in the botanical supply business?"

"Yeah. Who are you?"

The man chuckled. "Zeus Marsh. Devlin's grandfather."

Jolting fully awake, Chloe held the phone out and stared at it in abject horror. It wasn't her phone. It was Devlin's. Her gaze darted from the phone to the other side of the bed. No Devlin. She desperately threw back the twisted blankets, hoping to find him. No such luck.

She brought the phone to her ear. "Ah—nice to meet you? Give me a second, I'll get Devlin for you."

"That's all right. It might be better if I talk to you." He chuckled again. "I do have to say, bravo to Devlin. The boy seems to be finally getting away from his drafting table and on the stick. I was starting to worry about him."

Chloe glanced toward the open bathroom doorway. No one was there. She scrunched to the end of the bed where she could see the rest of the apartment. No Devlin there either. "He must have taken the dog for a walk. Can I have him call you when he gets back?"

"Don't you let the boy escape. He's a smart one. He'll be rich one of these days. Quite a catch."

"It's not like that. He and I just—" Chloe snapped her mouth shut before she got herself in deeper. "Sorry—ah."

"Don't worry about it. I was young once. I don't think any less of you for having some fun. Bravo, I'm quite pleased. But there's something I want you to tell him for me." There was silence on the other end for a second. "Devlin and I have had a wee misunderstanding. You don't mind giving him a message, do you?"

"Sure, I guess." It wasn't like she could just hang up without coming across as rude.

He cleared his throat. "Tell Devlin he shouldn't listen to rumors. I didn't do anything and neither did Uther. Tell Devlin he can't run away from the truth. We didn't kill anyone or have her killed."

Killed? A chill went through Chloe. She couldn't have heard that right.

"You still there, Chloe?" he said.

"Yeah." The front door scraped opened and Henry came zinging around the corner, knocking over a pool cue case that was leaning against a wall and leaping onto the bed. Chloe muted the phone and held it up so the dog couldn't grab it. She called out to Devlin, "Your grandfather is on the phone."

"My grandfather?" Devlin frowned as he came around the corner, his face flushed from being outdoors or perhaps from taking a run.

"His name's Zeus, right?" His grandfather's name was hardly easy to forget.

Devlin took the phone and walked away from her, the dog trailing an inch behind. "What do you want?"

As Devlin listened for a moment, Chloe slid out of bed, took one of his button-down shirts from the back of a chair, and shrugged it on.

"She's not my"—Devlin glanced back at her and cringed as if totally embarrassed— "Yes, she's smart. Pretty, too. Yes." His closed his eyes and glanced skyward as if trying to keep his patience. "My personal life isn't any of your business."

Chloe righted the pool cue case that the dog had knocked over, faking interest in it as Devlin paced toward the kitchen. It was hand-tooled leather with his initials stamped into it. Apparently he was serious about the game.

Devlin's voice lowered. "This isn't why you called. You told her what? You shouldn't be getting her involved. I've got to go now."

She padded across the sun-warmed floor to where he'd slumped down at the kitchen island, and settled onto the stool across from him. Henry immediately shoved a wet tennis ball onto her lap. She gingerly clutched it and listened as Devlin's voice became increasingly tense.

"You should talk to Athena about that. I'm going to hang up now. Goodbye, grandpa." He thumped the phone down on the island and shook his head. "Sorry about that. My grandfather can be a real ass."

"It's fine, really." Henry nosed her hand and she carefully lobbed the tennis ball across the kitchen. As he bounded after it, she considered not mentioning what Devlin's grandfather had said. On second thought, however, holding back made no sense, so she plunged ahead. "He said something about wanting you to know that he and Uther weren't responsible for someone getting killed?"

Devlin huffed out a frustrated breath. "He's talking about Saille Webster, the Circle's high priestess who died back in the nineteen-eighties. At the time, my grandfather and Uther Davies were both in the running to take over administrating the coven." He scrubbed his hands over his face. "There are people who still think one of them murdered the priestess, most likely my grandfather. Truthfully, I wouldn't be surprised if he did."

Chloe looked at him in surprise. "You really think that?"

He nodded. "My father was messing around with Uther's daughter, Rhianna. They were both young teenagers. She got pregnant."

"I'm guessing your grandfather wasn't happy about it?"

"Neither he nor Uther. From what I gather, the high priestess announced a pending engagement without anyone's consent. It turned into a nasty and very public mess. My father got sent away to boarding school. Then, around the same time, the priestess died and Rhianna lost the baby."

"A regular soap opera."

His jaw stiffened, his words coming out strained. "It didn't end there. My father hooked up with Rhianna years later—a high school reunion or something. She's the reason my parents split—along with about a dozen of his other girlfriends." Henry shoved his muzzle under Devlin's arm. Devlin gave him a few strokes before continuing. "Everyone knowing about my dad's infidelity was bad enough. Then, while I was away at prep school, the rumors about my grandfather and the high priestess' death started up again. I'd always admired Zeus, before that."

Chloe reached across the island, resting her hand on top of his. "That must have sucked." She lowered her voice. "My dad told me about the priestess dying, but I didn't know the part about your grandfather being connected."

"If Grandpa Zeus had walked away from the Northern Circle instead of taking over as high priest, he wouldn't have looked so guilty." Devlin hesitated. His lips quirked into a smile and his voice shifted abruptly. "However, right now, a large part of me is grateful my grandfather took over. If he hadn't, I might not have ended up here and met you."

Chloe glanced down, away from his steady gaze. "Personally, I'm shocked your grandfather didn't bitch at you for getting involved with someone like me."

"Why would you think that?" he said, clearly baffled.

"Your grandfather might be tangled up in a bunch of old rumors, but the gossip about me is totally founded."

Devlin frowned. "You can't be talking about the Vice-Chancellor's son. Everyone knows that was an accident." Sudden understanding crossed his face. "That boy, his near drowning—that's why you want to go to med school. It's why you were so eager to join the Circle."

Chloe nodded, relieved that it was out in the open. "If I could find a way to heal the damage that was done to his brain, then I could make up for everything. Maybe, if I'm really lucky, Merlin already knows a way." A sinking feeling balled in her stomach and she fell silent for a moment. It was the same gut level not quite right sensation she'd felt last night when she watched the coven members press their bloodied palms against Merlin's crystal. But it didn't make sense, Merlin was the answer to her prayers. His awakening was a way for the coven to resurrect their reputation. It would help humanity. Still, she couldn't help feeling something was off. "How do you really feel about bringing Merlin back?"

"There's a lot of good that could come out of it." He shrugged. "Right now, I'm mostly worried about Athena. It isn't like her to be manipulative and evasive."

"You think waking Merlin is the right thing to do, though?"

"If we succeed, it could lead to some incredible re-discoveries." He rested back on his stool, studying her intently. "Do you mind if I ask you something?"

"Yeah, sure."

He shifted forward again and folded his arms on the island. He licked his lips. "Why did you come all the way up to northern Vermont? Why UVM? With test scores like yours, you could have taken the classes you need almost anywhere. You might have known that the Circle existed. But we've kept our interest in ancient medicine to ourselves."

She stroked her wrist, toying with her absent charm bracelet. "Honestly, I had no idea that the Circle existed. All I knew was that I didn't want to live close to home, but I wasn't sure what to do or where to go. So I got out an atlas, dangled my crystal pendulum over a map of the world, then asked Hecate to guide me. She brought me here."

He smiled, his eyes brightening. "That's wonderful, perfect. Something your parents couldn't argue with either."

"Exactly." She closed her eyes for a moment. "When I first moved to Burlington, I was so lonely. I thought I'd made a mistake. But now—" She gathered her nerve, and then let the rest out. "Last night with you was amazing. But I'm fine with just having fun. Seriously, I'm not looking for a commitment. More than anything, I don't want to mess up my relationship with the coven."

Henry returned, this time shoving his tennis ball at Devlin. He pushed the dog away and leaned further forward, his gaze solely focused on Chloe. "We need to get a few things straight. First, I don't jump into bed with every woman that turns me on. Chloe, you're special to me and that will always be the truth. Secondly, it may take a while but—with or without Merlin—we will find a way to help that boy."

Emotion—one she couldn't quite name—welled up inside her. Sure she might do something stupid like cry if she tried to speak, she bit the inside of her cheek and nodded. She longed to believe he cared about her that much, but she couldn't afford to forget Athena's warnings about him. And then there was the witch sex. More than likely her magic had messed with him as much as his had enthralled her. No matter what, sitting here alone with him wasn't the place to attempt to untangle how she felt, especially with his bed only a few yards away.

He rested both hands on the island and pushed himself up onto his feet. "Now maybe you'd like some of my hangover cure. I could sure use some." He glanced at her again, a bit sheepish. "After that, I've got to take Henry for a walk to the lake. It's a Sunday tradition. He won't let us have any peace until I do. You're welcome to come with us."

"A walk sounds great." She smiled, feeling calmer already. Fresh air always made her feel better.

Ten minutes later, they'd chugged the hangover goop and she'd changed into clean jeans and a light sweater that Devlin had borrowed from Athena, along with her own underwear. Apparently, that's where he'd been coming back from when Zeus had called.

With Henry tugging at his leash, they headed outdoors and down a path that ran alongside Devlin's apartment and toward the rear of the complex property.

Morning sunshine glistened off the dense brush and scrubby trees that grew close on both sides. Chloe breathed in the crisp air, feeling more enlivened with every step. She wasn't surprised when they reached a gate and a chain-link fence that blocked the path. It wasn't like the coven could leave the complex accessible to everyone. However, it was unlikely that most people would ever notice or even sense the sheer wall of rippling green magic coating the fence and gate for added security.

Devlin pointed at the gate. "Open," he said, sending a quick burst of energy toward it, similar to the way she snuffed out candles.

The gate swung open, closing again after they passed through.

Chloe glanced back. "That's cool."

"The Circle was lucky to get this property," Devlin said. "It's right on top of a major lay line. Between that and the lake's magic, we can do some pretty unique things."

After they walked a few more yards, the path intersected with a wide paved trail that ran in both directions. Chloe took a guess. "The city bike path?"

He nodded. "Go right and you'll eventually come out downtown. We're going left, Oakledge Park and Henry's favorite swimming spot. There's also a clock there that I think you'll like."

"A clock?" She glanced at him, inquisitively. "Like a clock shaped garden? A miniature Big Ben?"

"No clues. You'll have to wait and see."

What remained of Chloe's hangover and exhaustion evaporated, replaced with sheer happiness. Her footsteps felt light as if moss and petals carpeted the path under her feet. For the most part, they walked alone. A few bikers passed by and a pair of joggers, smiling and saying good morning. Chloe suspected they mistook her and Devlin for a real couple out walking their dog on a Sunday morning. And, it felt good. Even if it was a temporary fantasy.

"I owe you another apology." Devlin slid his free hand around her waist as they walked. "I feel awful about the quarry. We drew names to see who would be in charge of each initiation test and Jessica got you. I couldn't do anything about her choice." Her body warmed as his hand glided up onto her shoulder. "All I could do was insist on being on her team."

"It's okay," Chloe said, though she had wondered about this. "Leaping into the water felt right."

"I was hoping the water hadn't cooled down too much." He let go of her, bent down and unhooked Henry from his leash. The dog rocketed off down the bike path.

"It's okay to let him run loose here?" she asked.

"Not really, that's why I bring him down before the park opens. The lake's just ahead."

She brushed her hand down the sleeve of his quilted jacket until her fingers meshed with his. "Jessica was right, though. You lit that joint on purpose?"

He gave her fingers a squeeze. "But I didn't inhale. I was the designated driver after all."

Chloe laughed. "I'll never forget seeing you in those woods. I was so relieved."

They went around a curve and the path opened onto a mowed lawn with a view of a rustic beach and a wide stretch of slate-gray lake. But her gaze only stayed on the water and Henry for a few seconds, before straying to a circle of standing stones that was about forty feet across. A miniature Stonehenge. Even at a distance, her skin tingled from the energy wheeling off it.

"That's incredible," she said. "Does the coven use it for rituals? I mean, it is a public park."

"That's the clock I wanted you to see. It's the Burlington Earth Clock. Local Wiccans and Pagans come here to celebrate the solstices and other events." He led her across the lawn toward the stones. "We use it late at night sometimes. That's one reason we're lucky to have Matt in our coven. Since he works for the city park department, he can make sure those ceremonies remain unnoticed."

Chloe counted the stones, fourteen in all. With their rough surfaces shadowed by the early morning light, she had no trouble imagining wizened faces staring out from them, craggy and gnarled by time. She strolled to the closest stone and pressed her hand against it, letting its energy soak into her palm, echoes from past rituals and the circle's vibrations mixing and rising from the lay line below. For a second, she wondered if Juliet came here with her Wiccan friends. *Juliet.* She was probably super pissed at her right now for pulling a no-show on pizza night.

She made her way over to an information board, scanning to get the most important details. Apparently, there was a flat stone sundial at the center of the circle. If someone stood on it, their shadow would tell the time of day. If they looked west across the lake, the five standing stones on that side of the circle marked where the sun set on solstices and equinoxes. The days when dark and light gave way to each other. Darkness and light.

She stepped closer and reread the solstice part. Darkness and light. Yin and yang. Could the orb's warning have been referring to this place?

A creepy-crawly sensation slithered up her spine. She shuddered, and then froze motionless as she realized the feeling had nothing to do with recalling the orb's warning. The sensation hung thick and heavy in the air around them, as if someone had opened a grave on this sacred ground. Disturbed magic. Not at all like the positive wheeling energy given off by the stones.

Her heartbeat slowed, dread pounding inside her. Slowly she turned around, searching for Devlin. She saw him striding toward the nearby woodline, holding something in his hand. He tossed it into the bushes. The creepy-crawly sensation vanished immediately.

"What are you doing?" she called out.

"I found a dead bird. I thought I'd do everyone a favor and put it someplace more respectful. It didn't smell very good, either." He glanced at his fingers. "Come on, let's go down to the lake. I want to rinse my hands off." He strode through the circle of stones, aiming for the beach where Henry was tugging on a chunk of driftwood.

She started after him. But as she passed the circle's most westerly stone, the hair on the back of her neck prickled. She followed the tug of her instincts, her gaze swinging to where tufts of small black feathers speckled the grass at the stone's base. A sick feeling built in her stomach as her gaze traveled upward. Blood smeared the rock's rough surface, as red and gray as the ash berries and owl bones Jessica used to divine the future.

"Devlin!" she shouted. The bird hadn't died of natural causes or even been killed by a predator. That kind of death wouldn't leave behind such a heavy sensation of dread and magic, not to mention blood all over a stone.

Devlin jogged back to her. "What's wrong?"

"The bird you found—someone sacrificed—" Her voice stuttered as she gestured at the feathers and blood. "You must have felt the magic." A fresh chill went through her. He touched the bird. With his level of power, he couldn't have missed the energy.

"Damn," he mumbled. "I didn't see that."

"But you did sense it? The bird you found—was it—*mutilated*?"

"I didn't sense dark magic if that's what you're worried about." He slipped his arm around her shoulder, turning her away from the stone. "It could have been an offering with good intentions. Some practices call for live sacrifice, like us putting our blood on Merlin's crystal."

"I guess, I wasn't expecting to see something like that...especially not here." She snuggled into his warmth as they walked away from the circle of stones and toward the beach. It could have been a practitioner of any of a number of crafts, or even someone with latent powers messing around and giving life to a spell without even realizing it. Still, it was unsettling. "I thought the coven knew all the empowered witches in the area."

"We try to. But the Earth Clock is a tourist destination." He nudged her teasingly with his elbow. "You know witches do take vacations." His voice quieted. "The bird looked pretty nasty. Its head was gone, but the magic was fading quickly. I didn't want to show it to you and spoil the mood. I really enjoy being with you, Chloe Winslow."

She gave him a peck on the cheek. "Same here, Devlin Marsh. And you're right. I wouldn't have wanted to see something like that."

The corners of his mouth twitched into a slight smile. Warmth flushed her skin and a sense of contentment blanketed her. She glanced out over the lake, past the bright line of autumn leaves and seaweed staining the high-water line, beyond Henry, to the gray rhythmic waves, their white crests as fine as a woman's hair, as misty as faces materializing out of stone.

Chapter 14

Hi Mom, These were made by Double Infinity Glassworks.
I thought they were really elegant. I hope they're what you wanted.
Classes are going great. Loving my cozy apartment.
XOX, Chloe
—Note in package to Joy Winslow

Late in the afternoon, Chloe got a ride back to her apartment from Devlin. "Thanks for everything. Last night, this morning—all of it was beyond amazing." She hesitated, uncertain whether she should lean in for a kiss. Their relationship had flown right past the handshake stage, but there were people on the sidewalk and a dozen young guys barreling out of a van right ahead of them.

"I'll text later," he said.

Her breath stumbled as his gaze met hers. What was she waiting for?

She bent toward him, a thrill rushing through her as his fingers stroked her cheek. His lips met hers, firm and moist. She wriggled in closer, enjoying the warmth of his body, the purr of his magic bathing her skin. His lips parted and grew more demanding. She tilted her head back, murmuring with pleasure.

Someone outside the car hooted. One of the guys banged on the car's hood and gave a thumbs-up. Devlin returned the thumbs-up without taking his lips from hers. She trailed her fingers up his thigh, teasing. He stroked the side of her breast. She closed her eyes, losing herself in the pleasure for another moment before pulling back, breathless as a teenager on prom night.

"Mmmmm. We should say goodbye more often," he said. He glanced down, his smile fading before his gaze met hers again. "I'm going to be busy for the next few days. A big project for a new client. But maybe we could get together later in the week?"

A lump formed in Chloe's throat. Everything he'd said and done indicated he wanted a relationship with her, but her past experiences shouted that *busy* and *maybe later* translated into the exact opposite. "Ah—yeah, that would be great. I've got a lot to do for school. Reading, papers..." Her voice trailed off.

"Okay, then"—he gave the steering wheel a meaningful pat—"I better get going."

Sadness tightened her chest. She opened the door and got out, then turned back. "Athena will let me know when the next gathering is, right?"

"Of course." He shooed her off with a wave. "Go. Get your work done. If I know Athena, you're not going to have a lot of free time in the near future."

"I can't wait," she said, delaying the inevitable for another heartbeat before she shut the car door. He waved again. She waved back as he pulled away, the BMW vanishing down the street. She caught one last flash of orange as it turned toward downtown. Then she sighed and scuffed toward the apartment house. But when she reached the front door, she realized she had a big problem. She hadn't been home since Jessica and Brooklyn kidnapped her. She didn't have her keys.

She tried the doorknob. It didn't budge, locked as tight as usual.

"Damn it." She took a deep breath. She could buzz the Rescue Twins and they'd let her in. But that still wouldn't help her if her apartment door was locked. The only tenant the landlord entrusted with a master key was Juliet.

She pushed Juliet's buzzer and waited. As a rule, Juliet stayed home on weekends. But no doubt she was pissed about the pizza night no-show.

Stepping back from the front door, Chloe looked up at Juliet's apartment windows. One of her Persian cats glared down like a pudgy-faced gargoyle. Behind the cat, the lights were on. How long was Juliet going to make her wait before she answered the buzzer?

The front door flung open. Juliet stood there with her hands on her hips, her face as furrowed with irritation as the cat's. "I was starting to think you'd been kidnapped or murdered and tossed in a dumpster."

Chloe held her hands out in surrender. "I'm sorry. I was planning on coming to your place for dinner, honestly." She sidestepped past Juliet and into the foyer. "Forgive me?"

"The Twins were more worried than I was. They had rescue squad duty last night and expected you to turn up in some alley raped or in the emergency room. Even Greta was worried. We checked your room to make sure you hadn't had an accident."

"I really am sorry." Chloe edged closer to the stairs.

Juliet narrowed her eyes. "I assume this involves *him*—the guy from the coven. He asked you out? You tracked him down?"

"It was kind of a surprise thing." She started up the stairs walking backwards, trying to escape without appearing unfriendly. "Seriously, I would have told you if I'd had time.

Juliet prowled up the stairs, not letting Chloe gain any distance. "I didn't hear the door buzzer."

It had been less than twenty-four hours since Chloe left her apartment, but in a way it felt like decades. More than anything, she wanted a hot shower and time alone to think.

"All right." She surrendered, as they reached the door to her apartment. She wouldn't get any peace if she didn't. "It was the guy from the coven."

Juliet stabbed the master key into the door's lock. "Inside, now. You're going to tell me absolutely everything."

"I'm exhausted. Can we talk about this later over some Chinese? My treat. You can order whatever you want."

"You're not going to buy your way out of this that easily." Juliet opened the door and propelled them both inside. Once the door was shut, she plopped onto the couch and patted the spot next to her. "Sit. I want details. All of them. Then maybe Chinese."

Chloe sunk down on the edge of the coffee table. "His name is Devlin. He's really nice."

"Older?"

"Not that much. Twenty-four. Maybe twenty-five"

"You didn't ask him?"

"There wasn't exactly time."

Juliet's eyes bulged. "So he's as cute without his clothes on as with?"

"Well, yeah." Chloe hugged herself. She was dying to tell someone. Juliet would figure it out eventually. "He's amazing, but it wasn't just about him. I disappeared because there was this initiation. I joined the Northern Circle."

Juliet rose partway to her feet, like a cat ready to jump and claw. "You were supposed to go to the Wiccan meeting with me on Wednesday. You said you were going to give it a chance before you went all fancy-snobby coven on me."

"The Circle's not like that. They're into discovering ancient cures, medicine and magic. That's something I'm interested in. They've been around for a long time. They know what they're doing." She closed her eyes for a second, then added one last defense. "I didn't join because of him if that's what you're thinking."

A red bloom of anger slashed across Juliet's cheeks. "Medicine. Ancient cures. Didn't you ever think I might be interested in that?"

Chloe swallowed hard. *Shit.* She shouldn't have mentioned the coven's mission. Juliet was aiming to be a veterinarian, as long as the cat toy business didn't intervene. Chloe thought fast. "The coven's not into animal medicine."

The lameness of her reasoning wasn't lost on Juliet. "In case you're wondering, I'm not an idiot. I could have gone to an Ivy League university if I wanted—Cornell or Harvard. I was valedictorian of my high school class—and it wasn't some hick school either." Her eyes burned into Chloe. "Or am I too ugly or weird for your rich-witch friends?"

"Of course, not. I—It sounds self-centered, but I never thought about you. You've got the Wiccan group. You seemed happy."

Juliet huffed. "I am. But that doesn't mean I'm not curious about the Northern Circle." She leaned forward, her voice going quiet. "One technique cults use is isolation, building walls between people and their friends."

Chloe closed her eyes, a dull headache beginning to pinch behind them. The last thing she needed was for Juliet to become convinced that she'd been brainwashed by a cult and tell the university administrators or health services—or, worse yet, call her parents and tell them about the Circle. She forced a level tone into her voice. "How about if I ask the high priestess if you can come as a guest?"

"You'd do that?" Juliet gaped at her.

"It might not always feel like it to you, but you are my friend. One of my only ones." Chloe contemplated how she could pull this off. She'd have to explain the situation to Athena, then bring Juliet by the complex for some May wine or tea—maybe not Athena's special ginger tea. They could tour Chandler's art studio. Athena could lie, tell Juliet that they weren't taking any more members for this year. Let Juliet down easy.

A loud knock sounded on Chloe's front door. "Which one of you morons left the downstairs door open?" Greta shouted from the hallway. "Do you want every creep in the world to get in?" She stomped off.

"She really needs to mellow out," Chloe whispered.

Juliet pressed a hand over her mouth, stifling a laugh.

Relief washed over Chloe. One of the good things about Juliet was that she never stayed angry for long. Unfortunately, she wouldn't be as quick to forget about the Northern Circle.

* * * *

The next morning, instead of sitting in the front of Folklore class, Chloe sat in the back with Keshari. When the class finally ended, they hurried out of the room ahead of everyone else.

"You won't believe everything that's happened," Chloe said, as they went outside into the sunshine. "I planned on calling you last night. Actually I planned on doing a lot of things, but I was so exhausted I fell asleep super early."

"Don't worry about it." Keshari smiled broadly. "I was busy myself. My neighbor's appendix ruptured. They rushed her to the emergency room. She isn't good with English, so I went to the hospital to help translate. *Friends look out for friends, even when they don't ask for it.*" She said the last part like a motto, then dismissed the story with a wave of her hand. "Enough about that. Everything is fine with her. Tell me what happened to you. You are talking about the initiation, yes?"

"That and more." Chloe patted her messenger bag, indicating the package she had safely tucked inside. "I need to drop something off at the Mail Center. It's for my mother and I'd like her to get it right away. Want to go to the café after that and talk? I could use a coffee in the worst way."

As they headed across the campus green toward the Waterman building, Chloe gave Keshari an overview about what had happened at the quarry and about spending the night with Devlin.

When they reached the building's front steps, she glanced around to make sure no one was close enough to hear, then told Keshari the news about Merlin.

Keshari stepped back, almost stumbling off the steps. "You are not serious. Merlin? The Merlin."

Chloe nodded. "The one and only."

"Are you sure they are capable of something of that scale? You would think, if it were possible, some larger and more powerful coven would have done it by now."

"It's not just about power. No one else knew his staff crystal still existed. Athena's planning on using it somehow."

Keshari lowered her voice even further. "Are you sure the act of bringing Merlin into this world won't disturb the balance of the universe? Yin and yang. This could be connected to the orb's warning."

"I don't think so. But, maybe." She blew out a loud breath. "You're making my head spin."

"Good. You have much to think about. This is huge."

Chloe went into the building first, leading the way through the busy hallways to the Print and Mail Center. The idea of taking time to send her mom a package right now felt totally out of step with the rest of her life. But her mother was going to love the straws. Hopefully they'd also make up for the fact that she didn't want to call home right now. She didn't want to lie to her mom about what was going on in her life, but it wasn't like she wanted to tell her the truth either.

Once the package was sent, they went back out into the hallway. Keshari pulled out her phone, reading the café lunch specials as they walked. "Pumpkin soup. Braised kale and feta pizza..."

A sharp crackle of nearby magic prickled Chloe's skin. She snagged Keshari by the arm, pulling her to a stop. "Did you feel that?"

Keshari went stock-still. "What?"

Chloe cocked her head; beneath the hubbub of voices and footsteps she heard a slight snap-crackle. Magic for sure. She focused on the sound, scanning through the crowd of students and office workers until she pinpointed it. A burly guy with long dreadlocks lounged against the frame of a closed door with his back to them. A backpack hung over one of his broad shoulders. At first glance it looked like he was focused on his phone, his thumb moving against the screen. But then—despite the fact he'd angled himself in an attempt to shield it from view—Chloe noticed that his other hand rested on the door's keycard lock. She was also certain who he was now.

She pulled Keshari into a doorway where they could still see him but weren't quite so obvious. "That's Midas."

"He was an initiate too, yes?"

"Yeah and he's really skilled."

Keshari craned her neck, taking another look. "You think he can pick that lock with magic?"

"Definitely. He used it combined with physics and magnetism to get through the maze." She took another look. "It doesn't make sense though. I don't know him very well, but he doesn't seem like the kind of person who'd risk getting thrown out of the university for something stupid like breaking and entering."

"People do strange things for strange reasons," Keshari said.

"That's true, but what do think he's after?" She licked her lips, thinking for a moment. "That door's right next to the Administration offices. There might be computers. Files. Student records."

As they watched, Midas opened the door a crack, tilted his head as if listening for a second. Then he opened the door wider and crept inside, leaving his backpack in the doorway so the door couldn't swing shut all the way and lock again.

"Let's go see what he's doing." Chloe glanced back at Keshari. She did a double take. Keshari was clutching something that looked like a short celery stalk with tiny bells glued onto it. "What's that?"

"Protection," Keshari whispered.

Chloe shook her head. She couldn't imagine what the celery stalk thing was, but this wasn't the place or time to ask for details.

With Keshari beside her, she pushed the stalk from her mind and strolled down the crowded hallway to the door. No surprise, the sign on it read: *EMPLOYEES ONLY.*

She nudged the door open a little wider and peeked inside. The windowless room was small and cramped, every inch jammed floor to ceiling with bins, file cabinets, and stacks of boxes. Faint light, voices, and general office hubbub trickled in from an open doorway in the furthest wall. But there were no signs of life in this room, only the steady tick of a clock.

Sweat dampened Chloe's armpits, but she hoisted her messenger bag up higher on her shoulder and crept inside. Midas had to be here somewhere.

A rustle came from near the distant doorway.

Chloe's breath caught in her throat. She inched a few more steps forward, then craned her neck, looking around the closest stack of boxes. Near the doorway, a coat rack and a couple of work carrels sat against the wall. Midas was hunched in front of the carrels, rummaging through a large, tangerine-orange handbag. It had a gold clasp and the initial *J* decorated one side. What the heck was he looking for?

Tension pinched between Chloe's shoulders as she watched him unzip a side pocket and dig through it. She needed to get out before he spotted her or before some office worker came in to get something. But she had to know what he was after. Money. Credit or ID cards. If he was ballsy enough to steal like this, he'd swipe stuff from the coven for sure.

She snuck forward, around the stacked boxes. She had to get close enough to see better. This was really horrible. She liked Midas. Devlin did too. It seemed unlikely, but maybe Midas was doing something innocent.

The pad of light footfalls sounded behind her. Keshari. Damn it. One person spying on Midas was bad enough, two doubled their chances of getting caught.

As if in rebuttal, Keshari's words came back to her. *'Friends look out for friends, even when they don't ask for it.'* Chloe gritted her teeth. Maybe it was time for Keshari to scrap that motto for something safer or at least not take it so seriously.

Midas turned the bag upside down, his face fraught with desperation as he shook everything onto the floor. Lipsticks, pens, tampons…spewed across the floor. He snagged a phone from the rubble and shoved it up his sleeve. He straightened up, as if readying to leave.

Chloe's pulse flew through the roof. She wheeled, shoving Keshari ahead of her as she rushed out the doorway and back into the hall. She grabbed Keshari's arm, towing her into the flow of people. They had to blend in, play it cool.

Keshari brushed her arm. "Do you think he saw us?"

"I don't know. But I bet he heard us leave." Chloe glanced back. There were a lot of people, but she couldn't see Midas anywhere.

As she turned back around, shock crushed the air from her lungs. No more than a dozen yards ahead, walking down the hallway in the opposite direction with a group of older women was Jessica, dressed in conservative slacks and a dressy blouse.

Chloe did a double take. Jessica's formal clothes. The women she was with. No jackets. No backpacks. Unhurried strides. Plus, she couldn't help but think of the orange handbag with the initial *J* on it, as in Jessica. Everything screamed that she and the women worked in the building.

Chloe started to duck her head and look the other way. But it was too late for that; Jessica's icy gaze was already slithering over her.

A sour taste crept up Chloe's throat, she swallowed it back and met her cold stare. When they got close to each other she flipped a friendly wave. "Hey, nice to see you."

The group of women kept going as if in a hurry to get back to their offices, but Jessica paused.

"I didn't realize you worked here." Chloe plastered on a smile.

Jessica jutted her chin in the direction of the Administrative Offices—the ones attached to the room they'd just escaped from. "I've been here since last winter. Boring but the pay's good."

"A good paycheck never hurts." Chloe was stunned by how calm she sounded, despite the sweat flooding down her sides.

Jessica's gaze flicked to Keshari, then back to Chloe. "I'd love to stay and chat, but some of us have work to do."

Chloe forged another smile. "See you later."

Neither Chloe nor Keshari said a word as they walked down the hallway and around the corner. The further they went, the more certain Chloe was that the phone Midas had swiped couldn't have belonged to anyone other than Jessica. He must have been keeping track of her and waiting for the perfect moment to strike. But why would he do that and risk being caught or worse, thrown out of college and the coven?

A lump lodged in Chloe's throat. Why was she even worrying about Midas? Holy crap. Jessica hadn't seen Midas, but she had seen her. She was sure to discover her spilled handbag and missing phone. What if Jessica thought she stole it?

Chapter 15

There is light and darkness within all of us, controlled by will or breath—
or tongues, let us not forget them,
a weapon with more power than all the rest,
except perhaps the heart.
—Soliloquies of Merlin

"If Jessica thinks I took her phone, she's not going to be satisfied with getting me thrown out of the coven," Chloe said, as she and Keshari sat down at a table in the café, "At a minimum, she'll screw with my college records. She'll go after yours, too, if she figures out who you are."

Keshari cradled her tea, her voice low. "Can you talk to Devlin about it?"

"I could, but I'm wondering if I should confront Midas first." She rubbed her wrist, thinking. "The only thing I know for sure is that we weren't Midas's intended targets."

"What do you know about Midas?"

"Not much, really. He's a graduate student. Kind of domineering. But Devlin seems to like him. Why?"

"Are you certain the phone he took belonged to Jessica? It could be his girlfriend's. The *J* could stand for Jasmine or Jade. Stealing it could be part of an elaborate prank."

"Do you honestly believe that?" Chloe's phone chirped. She glanced at her messenger bag where the phone was stashed, then at Keshari. "You don't think that's someone texting about the phone, already?"

Keshari's eyes mirrored her fear. "It could be. But it cannot be Jessica, unless she borrowed a phone from someone."

"Guess we'll never know if I don't look." Chloe took a steadying breath, retrieved her phone, and glanced at it. "It's from Athena."

Gathering this afternoon about Merlin. Can you come?

Keshari scuffed her chair up close to Chloe, peering at the phone. "What are you going to do?"

Unsure if she should go or not, because of Jessica, Chloe texted back: *I have a class until 4.*

It's fine if you're late. But we could use your help.

Chloe raked her hair back, thinking out loud. "I could call Devlin and tell him what we saw, or I could go and tell him then."

Athena sent another text: *Don't worry about dinner. I've ordered pizzas.*

Chloe gritted her teeth. Why was she even considering not going? To hell with Jessica. It wasn't like she'd done anything wrong. She texted back: *Sure. If late afternoon is okay.*

I'm so grateful we can count on you. See you soon.

Keshari frowned. "I don't like this."

"If Jessica accuses me, Devlin will be there. He's on my side."

"Don't forget," Keshari said, "you can always call me—for any reason."

As Keshari settled back in her chair, Chloe caught a flash of the mysterious celery-like stalk peeking out from her pants pocket. She nodded at it. "Okay, I'm dying to know. What *is* that?"

A proud gleam sparkled in Keshari's eyes. She slid her hand into her pocket and pulled out a keyring. A small atomizer was attached to it as well as a thick, braided length of celery-green plant stems decorated with pinhead-size copper bells. She lowered her voice to a whisper. "The atomizer is filled with special water-soluble incense. One spritz will temporarily scramble a demon's brain. The stems are a lotus-stalk wand. It won't make a sound until I channel my magic into it, then watch out."

Chloe shook her head. "That's unbelievable. Your own miniature arsenal."

"Much like yours?" Keshari slanted a look at Chloe's charm bracelet.

She laughed. "We do make a good team"—she gave the tiny wand and atomizer another study—"but don't you think taking it out to follow Midas was overkill? I mean, you didn't really think we were going to run into demons?"

"Better safe than sorry, yes?"

"I suppose." Chloe wrapped her hands around her coffee cup, focusing on the sensation of its moist heat against her skin. As worried as she was about the situation with the stolen phone, it was wonderful and a huge relief to have someone like Keshari she could talk to openly.

Chloe didn't text Devlin right away to ask him when he'd pick her up for the gathering. She didn't want to come across as clingy. Besides, he *had* said he was going to be busy. But when it got to be three o'clock and she still hadn't heard from him, she gave in and sent a text. An hour later, her phone was still silent. Feeling more and more like a clingy girlfriend—and not liking it one bit—she texted again, then started walking toward home.

The day had turned sharply cooler, the temperature dropping a good ten degrees, and a strong breeze pushed leaves across the sidewalk. As she joined a crowd of people waiting on a curb for the crossing signal to change, she glanced at her phone again. Still nothing. Yesterday, she'd felt uneasy when Devlin had been all into her, then flip-flopped by saying they wouldn't be able to get together for a few days. Now here she was again with crazy thoughts flying around in her head, all because he hadn't made the time to text back. But the truth was, he could have. No one was that busy.

The hiss of a bus pulling up to a nearby stop drew her attention. To hell with waiting. She had on worn jeans and a casual sweater. A little informal, but covens were like family, right?

Her messenger bag slapped against her side as she made a dash for the bus. The seats in the front were taken, but she found an empty one halfway back and claimed it. The bus lurched into traffic, barely slowing at the next stop. It wouldn't take her any time at all to get downtown at this rate. She'd change buses and be at the complex in maybe twenty minutes at the most.

She scrunched down in her seat, resting her head back and staring out the window at the passing traffic. This had been a good idea. A damn good one.

The bus hissed to a stop, doors opening to let a group of people file in. As they crammed their way up the aisle, Chloe moved her messenger bag off the empty seat next to her and onto her lap. Her gaze settled on the pocket where she kept her phone. While she had the chance, she should text her mom and tell her to expect a box in the mail.

Someone stopped in the aisle next to her seat. She looked up. A woman in a stylish trench coat gawked down at her.

Chloe's mouth fell open. "Jessica?"

Jessica harrumphed. "Twice in one day, who'd believe it." She nodded at the empty seat next to Chloe. "Do you mind?"

"Sure." Chloe scooched over, a queasy feeling tumbling in her stomach. Of all the people in the universe, why her?

Jessica claimed the spot, stretched her legs out, and rested her handbag on her lap—a big tangerine-orange handbag with a gold clasp and the initial *J*—for Jessica— decorating one side.

The queasy feeling in Chloe's stomach crept up her throat, but she somehow managed to keep her voice steady. "Are you going to the complex?"

"Of course." Jessica gave her a tight-lipped smile, one that conveyed that she knew things Chloe didn't, like perhaps about tonight's gathering.

Chloe's jaw clenched, her anxiety flashing to sudden anger. She didn't like being toyed with. She didn't deserve it either. If Jessica was determined to mess with her head, then she'd mess right back. She leveled her eyes on Jessica's and sweetened her voice. "I owe you thanks."

Jessica stiffened. "I can't imagine what for."

"I know you've read my records." She kept her voice calm. "I'm grateful you did. If it weren't for you, I might never have been asked to join the Circle."

"Oh"—Jessica's lips remained pursed, but her chest puffed out proudly— "I never looked at it that way."

"Seriously, I know we got off on the wrong foot. But if you're worried about me being mad, that's far from what I feel." Chloe's middle finger itched to make a gagging gesture, but this was going better than she could have planned.

Jessica blinked at her for a second, then dropped her gaze as if she couldn't bear to meet Chloe's any longer. "Oh, okay. Whatever."

Chloe smiled. "Friends, then?"

"I didn't think we weren't." Jessica opened her handbag. "I need to tell Athena I'm running late." She took out her phone casual as anything.

Chloe stared at it. Had Midas somehow managed to return Jessica's phone or was this a different one? Or was Jessica suspicious and toying with her again? Either way, she needed to be sure. "Can you tell Athena I'm coming too? I—misplaced my phone. I remember setting it on my coffee table, like I always do. But when I went to grab it before I took off for class, I couldn't find it."

Jessica gave her a sidelong look. She surrendered a tiny smile. "Have one of your housemates phone you. I thought I'd lost mine earlier today and that's how I located it."

"Good idea." Chloe clenched her teeth, resisting the urge to smile.

"Some idiot knocked my bag over while I was at lunch, spilled everything. For a while, I thought they'd swiped my phone. I was certain they were going to figure out how to drain my bank account. It was a good half hour before I thought to have someone call me. Turned out, the whole time it was on my desk under some papers."

"That was a good thing," Chloe said, unable to contain her smile any longer.

A sense of joy lifted her spirits. Thank Hecate, one disaster diverted. She stole another look at Jessica's orange bag. Still, Midas's perfectly timed theft-and-return didn't explain why he'd wanted the phone in the first place.

A disturbing possibility seeped into her head. After that night at the Vice-Chancellor's house, her father had caught one of his employees rummaging through his office. The employee claimed the High Council's Bureau of Special Investigation had hired him as a spy, to make sure her father's botanical business wasn't dealing in anything illegal. It seemed like a remote possibility, but what if Midas was a council spy? He knew about Merlin and the crystal. He knew she was a new member. Worse, he knew what they were planning to do and not making the Council aware of such monumental plans was definitely against their spy rules. She had to tell Devlin about the possibility, as soon as she could get him alone. Maybe Midas was innocent. Still, stealing and going through someone's personal belongings was not okay.

* * * *

After a few blocks, they switched buses for the rest of the ride. Chloe was thankful Jessica knew exactly what to do and which stop to get off at. However, their walk up the complex's driveway and under the monkey-covered gateway consisted mostly of uncomfortable silence.

When they reached the main house, they found Athena and Chandler in the lounge. They both had on plum-colored robes and were sipping glasses of burgundy.

Chloe scanned the room. No Matt or Brooklyn. No Devlin. She frowned. "Where is everyone?"

"Just us dedicated few tonight." Athena breezed over to them, her ring-covered fingers and black beaded choker glimmering in the candlelight. She hugged Jessica. "You look tired. Long day at work?"

Jessica rolled her eyes. "And then some."

"I'm sure once you have a cool drink, you'll feel refreshed." Her gaze went to Chloe. "Devlin had to run over to the Adirondacks for a couple of days. He's working on a waterscape for a new client. He didn't tell you?"

Chloe faked a weak smile. "I knew he was busy, but I didn't realize he was going out of town." She took the hug Athena offered, its warmth and the hum of her magic lending a measure of solace. She stepped back as another almost more interesting absence piqued her curiosity. "Midas isn't coming either?"

"He's with Devlin. Something to do with his thesis—waterfalls and power generation. I don't know about you, but I'm looking forward to tonight being just us girls." She steered Chloe toward where Chandler was opening a fresh bottle of wine. "I truly appreciate you making time to come."

"No problem. I'm sorry I couldn't come earlier. Is Em going to be here?"

"She's out in the teahouse gathering some supplies for later." Athena shot a meaningful glance toward the glass doors. "If you wouldn't mind, she probably could use a hand carrying things in."

Chloe hurried out into the garden. A girls' only night might not be a bad thing. Part of her not feeling comfortable around Jessica was Jessica's fault. But she was also partly to blame. She'd been so focused on Devlin that she hadn't put much effort into getting to know anyone else. A gathering without the guys would force her to make up for that lapse. Besides, Midas not being around might be a good thing, though him being with Devlin meant she couldn't just text Devlin about her concerns. There was no telling who might end up seeing her message.

When she reached the bridge, her mind drifted to the kiss she and Devlin had shared right there on that very spot. She pressed her fingers against her lips, letting her mind relive the sensations. Warmth spread through her body and thrummed in all the right spots. Maybe a girls' night would be fun, but she really wished he was here—

The faint odor of something burning broke through her thoughts. She frowned and sniffed the air. Smoke, and nearby. Not the complex's main building or teahouse, the wind's direction was wrong for that.

She sniffed again. It wasn't sharp or overpowering, like the first hint of an electrical fire. It was natural like the smell of pipe tobacco. Letting her eyes and nose guide her, she followed the smell, looking upstream from the bridge to where a waterfall trickled down a man-size standing stone, partly screened by juniper trees. A tiny flash of red sparked in the branches. It vanished, then returned brighter than before.

Chloe dashed off the bridge and crept up the edge of the stream, heading for the junipers. The glow could have come from an indicator light or something else mechanical having to do with the manmade water features. But that didn't explain the burning odor.

The wind lifted, blowing back her hair. She shivered and tucked her hands into the sleeves of her sweater. As cold as it was now, it was hard to believe she'd dove into the quarry the other night.

She stepped around a statue of a nymph, then again glanced toward the junipers and the red glow.

The glow was gone, and the smell had faded.

"Waning," someone whispered behind her.

Pulse racing, Chloe swung around.

No one was there.

"Waning," the voice whispered all around her now. *"Waning. Waning."* Her brain engaged. She knew that voice. The orb.

She turned back toward the junipers. The orb was fleeing into the trees, shimmering in the depth of their branches, then stopping for a moment before moving on, as if begging her to follow. She sprinted across the distance, pushed the branches aside, and stepped into a natural grotto with an altar at its center. The place hummed with the energy of recently cast magic.

A sense of guilt made Chloe retreat a step. This was someone's sanctuary, their private place of worship. She shouldn't intrude. But the orb had brought her here for a reason.

One slow step at a time, she stole forward to where the orb hovered above the altar. On it sat a basin filled with black stones and marigold blossoms. Next to them, a cone of incense smoldered. That explained the burning smell.

There was something else on the altar as well. Something the same color as the dark stones and about the size of a wild plum.

Her whole body went cold. A blackbird's head. Just the head. Its beak crusted with blood. Its beady eyes staring back at her through a gray skim of death. A head, like the one missing from the bird at the Earth Clock. Also, now that she was closer, she recognized the incense's fragrance: myrrh, rosemary…a pinch of vinegar intended to ward off spirits.

"Yin and yang. The Circle. Protect the Circle. Banished. Banished…" The orb's hoarse whisper faded as the last wisp of incense smoke disappeared.

The orb's light throbbed one last time, then died.

Chapter 16

LAKE PLACID—*Teenage girl found chained inside a van after police respond to reports of a dog left in a vehicle with blacked out windows. According to police when they arrived at the New Sun Conference Center they heard whimpering coming from a van owned by the Violet Grace Psychic Medium Show…*
—From The Upstate Tribune, August 9

Chloe backed out of the grotto. She'd only been in there for a few minutes, but twilight was now descending, the trees and shrubbery darkening, the pathways glowing blue. She glanced across the gardens and at the windows in the main house to make sure no one had watched her come out from the grotto, then she dashed for the bridge.

Athena had banished the orb from the house, so it made sense that she'd done this ritual. But why would she—or anyone for that matter—do such a thing to a spirit whose only wish was to protect the coven?

An image of the bird's dead eyes staring at her flashed into her mind. Chloe hugged herself and made for the teahouse. She couldn't help but wonder if Athena was responsible for the head here and the body at the Clock. No matter if that was true or what the reason, the idea of sacrificing and dismembering living creatures made her utterly uncomfortable. Intellectually she got that these things were normal in some magic practices. Like Devlin had said, intent was what was most important. She hadn't sensed evil or darkness around the ritual, only intense power. It was also possible she was interpreting the whole thing wrong. Maybe the orb had been a trickster or something. Still, the whole thing bothered her.

Brightness stung her eyes as she opened the teahouse door. Em was in the back of the room rummaging through a glass-fronted apothecary cabinet. She glanced over her shoulder at Chloe, her eyes looking even more distressed than usual. "Do you know what apple twigs look like?"

"Yup!" Chloe scanned the boxes and jars, some labeled in Latin, others unmarked. She noticed a bin of red-black twigs, about six inches long and neatly tied into bundles. She took out a bunch, scraped off a fleck of bark with her fingernail and tasted the raw wood to be certain. Apple for sure.

"Here you go," she said, handing it to Em.

"Thanks. I couldn't have found the right ones in a month of Sundays. Could you grab me a couple more? I need three in total."

"Don't feel bad. I grew up working in my parents' botanical supply business. We harvested things like this with my aunts." She handed her the additional bunches, then tucked her hands into her jeans pockets. "Do you mind if I ask you something?"

"Is something wrong?"

"I saw that orb you called the other night, just now out in the garden. It's a spirit, right?"

"Yeah, but are you sure that's what you saw?" She clutched the bundles of twigs against her chest. "I haven't seen or sensed any spirits since Athena banished that one."

Chloe gave a half-hearted shrugged. "I guess it's possible I could have imagined it. There's lots of reflections from the house and stuff." She glanced back at the apothecary, pretending her question was a passing fancy. "Why don't you tell me what else you need? It'll go faster that way."

"That would be great." She set the twigs in a gathering basket that was on the floor and took out a list. "I need a variety of crystals. One of each. Medium size."

As Em read the list, Chloe dug through the cupboard and handed her the stones. She paused as she passed Em a piece of smoky quartz. "Who was the orb spirit, anyway? Someone you know or someone related to the coven?"

"I was so nervous that night. I kind of latched a hold of the first soul I sensed. It wasn't a smart thing to do. I could've drawn someone malevolent." She set the crystal into the basket. "Maybe Chandler knows. If I'm not mistaken she has at least some psychic ability, and she wasn't as nervous as I was."

"Good idea. But I hate to bother her with everything that's going on, especially since I might not have seen anything."

Em's gaze touched hers. "I've slept like a baby ever since I moved in. I wouldn't be able to do that if there was a threatening presence nearby."

"You're living in the complex?" It surprised Chloe, though it made perfect sense. Em had been in a halfway house in New York State. It wasn't like she could have gotten a job and afforded an apartment so quickly.

Em nodded. "It's a great deal. No rent. Free meals." She gestured at a round floor mat, maybe six feet across and made of what looked like braided straw. "Athena wanted me to bring this too. While I roll it up, do you mind finding a piece of twine for me to bind it with?" Her voice went serious. "You should ask Athena if you can live here. There's lots of space. You'd never know there were five of us here."

Chloe did a double take. "Five of you? I thought there were only four—you, Athena, Chandler, Devlin."

"Jessica lives here too. She's got her own suite."

"I didn't realize that." It was interesting that Jessica had neglected to mention that.

"Athena's the one who arranged for me to stay here," Em continued. "She didn't have it easy when she was young. She totally related to my situation." Her voice quieted. "We were both runaways at one point."

The sad tone in Em's voice went right to Chloe's heart, but a suspicion nipped at the back of her mind. The other day, Athena had compared their childhoods as well. That seemed a little odd, especially since she couldn't see how this comparison jived with what she knew about Athena and Devlin's childhoods. Still, she guessed it made sense. What reason would Athena have to lie about something like that? She gave a sympathetic nod. "I'm sorry you had it so rough."

Tears glistened in Em's eyes. "My aunt and mother...they started dragging me from town to town when I was eight, maybe nine years old. *Violet Grace, the World's Youngest Psychic Medium*—that's who I was."

"You're kidding me? You worked at fairs when you were that young?" She'd seen TV shows about young girls being taken on beauty pageant circuits, movies stars, athletes, but not child psychics.

"It wasn't a carny kind of thing. My aunt liked to think she was highbrow. They put on shows in conference centers, Las Vegas, Atlanta—" She pressed her knuckles over her eyes as if forcing back the memory.

Chloe rested her hand on Em's forearm. "If you ever want to talk about anything, I'm a good listener."

Em lowered her knuckles, her lips curving into a trembling smile. "Thank you. Same goes if you need a friend."

Once they got back to the house, Em stayed in the living room with Jessica and Chandler to get the mat and supplies situated, while Chloe headed for the kitchen to tell Athena they were back.

Athena beamed when she saw Chloe. "Perfect timing." She set a squatty loaf of dark bread on a wooden tray, the sleeve of her robe fluttering lightly. "I'll get the juice and we'll be ready to go."

As she opened the refrigerator door, the question Chloe had planned on keeping to herself came flooding out. "Em told me you ran away when you were a kid?"

Athena swung around, a carafe of dark purple juice held white-knuckled in her hand. "We each have our own stories, Chloe. None of us with magic have had normal childhoods."

"I'm sorry. I shouldn't have pried. I was just surprised."

"What I said to Em was that my parents used me, like her family used her. Most of it is Devlin's, not my, story to tell. Our parents were so wrapped up in the Circle, and their parties and cheating, that I ended up having to be a parent to him."

"But you're not much older than him."

"That's right. What's important now is that you and I and everyone else support Em. The more she feels welcome and accepted by all of us, the better the chance of her becoming strong and whole. The damage done to her runs deep."

A thick sense of shame weighed in Chloe's chest. She should have kept her mouth shut, instead of making assumptions about other people's pasts. She rubbed her fingers overs her bracelet, every charm a gift from someone who had raised her with love. "I never realized how lucky I was to have my parents." She swallowed hard. "I was the one who screwed things up for them."

Athena nodded. "Now you have a chance to make everything right, and I'm proud to be able to give that to you." She set the carafe of juice on the counter, took Chloe by the upper arms, and looked her square in the eyes. "That is what you want?"

"Yes," she said meekly. "More than anything."

Athena released her arms. Her voice hushed. "Chloe, I'm going to ask if I can use your magic tonight, not like Em's parents did to her. But as your witch-sister and high priestess. As Merlin may ask of us all once he returns."

"What do you need?" she asked, breathless.

"After we complete a ritual connected to the awakening, I want to do a healing spell for Em. It will require a great deal of energy from all of us." She glanced at the bread and juice as if considering her plans and whether to go into more detail or not. "When I was in Wales, we managed to communicate with Merlin. He led us not only to the crystal, but to an ancient grimoire that contained one of his spells. Old magic. A forgotten technique to heal a wounded psyche. I'd like to try it on Em. Will you help?"

Healing psyches. It wasn't the same as reversing damage done to a brain, but it was part of the answer. "Of course." Chloe humbled her tone. "I really am sorry about bringing up what you told Em. That was between the two of you. I should have trusted you without asking."

"I understand. You were curious. But what I don't understand is why you started to make excuses earlier when I texted to ask you to come help."

Chloe's face heated. "Um—I."

"We need to get one thing straight." Athena's voice toughened. "Your college studies are important. But nothing can take priority over the Northern Circle. After tonight, everyone will be needed, every night until the new moon when the main ritual will happen. Even personal relationships must be put on hold, understand?"

"This new moon? That's Saturday. I—" She started to say she couldn't believe they'd be awakening Merlin so soon, but Athena silenced her with a raised finger.

"I'm counting on you—the entire coven is. If you have an issue, this is the time to bring it up. Not later."

"Ah—there isn't anything. I'm ahead at school." Slightly panicked, Chloe breezed through her mental checklist again to make sure. There was only one problem that she could think of. Though it seemed like something she could avoid until Saturday, she didn't want to hold anything back. "There's a woman in my apartment house who's Wiccan. She knows about the Circle and wants to meet you. Not that I think she should join, quite the opposite. I know this is the wrong time, but she's driving me nuts."

Athena laughed. "Why didn't you say something sooner? Her interest is natural, something that should be encouraged to a degree. Perhaps you can"—she waved her hand over the carafe as if putting a spell on the contents—"invite her to visit us, then make sure she isn't feeling well enough to come. As you said, this isn't the time to deal with her."

Chloe blinked at Athena. "That's a great idea. You're not kidding, right?" It sure wasn't a suggestion she expected to hear from a high priestess.

"Do what you need to." Athena wrapped an arm around her shoulder, cradling her in warmth. "Think about it, Chloe. In less than a week, you and I will be students of Merlin—one of the greatest wizards of all time. Did you ever dream such a thing would be possible?"

She took a deep breath and closed her eyes, savoring the possibilities that lay ahead. "No. Not in a million years—certainly not this soon."

* * * *

Chloe carried the bread out to the living room, while Athena took charge of the carafe. The room was darker now, lit only by the flicker of candlelight. The smell of applewood smoke permeated the air.

Near the staircase, Jessica and Em had stripped down to their bras and panties and were putting on plum-colored robes that matched the ones Athena and Chandler wore. The whole atmosphere felt warm and relaxed. Chloe supposed it was like a slumber party, something she'd missed out on as a kid.

She followed Athena to where the round mat had been laid out on the floor. They set the bread and carafe in the middle of it where the crystals had already been arranged.

"Here you go," Chandler said, handing Chloe a robe.

Chloe got undressed and slipped on her robe, then she set her clothes on a side table with everyone else's. She was about to head to the mat where Em and Jessica were settling down to form the beginning of a ritual circle when she caught a few words of hushed conversation coming from the lounge.

"I'm not comfortable with this," Chandler whispered. "Unleavened bread. Unfermented juice."

"Have I ever misled you?" Athena asked.

"No. I owe you everything. But necromancy?"

Chloe's eyes widened. Necromancy? She pressed her fingers against her lips, smothering a gasp. But now that she thought about it, she should have realized it herself. Dark unleavened bread, unfermented wine—also known as grape juice—were traditionally referred to as *lifeless foods*.

Pretending to be busy rolling up her sleeves, she edged closer to the lounge.

"The old ways are darker than what we're accustomed to. But because we walk the razor's edge to free Merlin, it does not mean the path is wrong."

Though she was only listening, Chloe caught herself nodding in agreement. It didn't take a college-level Folklore class to know the early tales about the Craft were darker, harsher, and more powerful than what was practiced nowadays. Plus, symbolic use of death—whether it was unleavened bread, blood smeared on a stone, or parts of a dead bird—were a long way from true evil.

"You're right," Chandler said. "It's just—"

"Frightening? An unfamiliar path most often is."

As they stopped talking, Chloe quit fiddling with her sleeve, made a beeline for the mat, and sat down next to Em. A second later, Athena and Chandler appeared.

Athena placed the cloth-covered tray she was carrying down next to the bread and carafe. As she did, Chloe's stomach growled loudly. Everyone glanced her way.

She grimaced. "I should have had a snack before I came. I was expecting dinner."

"And we shall feast," Athena said. "But this ritual isn't about consumption for bodily needs. It's about preparing ourselves for the next leg of the journey we have embarked on, the journey to awaken Merlin who now treads in darkness, but will culminate on the new moon, as waning turns to waxing, the time for awakening and opening doorways."

She removed the cloth from the tray, revealing a low earthenware bowl. The bowl was a size that might normally have been used for cereal, but this one contained Merlin's crystal and a mix of crushed fresh herbs. She took the crystal from the bowl, set it at the very center of the mat, then poured juice from the carafe into the bowl of herbs.

Raising the bowl skyward, Athena chanted in a low monotone. The sound reverberated in the room, energy soaring and swirling in the air. The power of it tingled against Chloe's skin, exciting her senses and sending adrenaline rushing into her veins.

Athena lowered the bowl and brought it with her as she scooted backwards to sit between Chloe and Chandler at the edge of the circle. After another short incantation, she raised the bowl up, then lowered to her lips and took a sip. As she passed the bowl to Chandler, puffs of rosemary-scented mist wafted from it. The strangeness and power of the ritual tightened a knot of fear in Chloe's chest, especially since Athena had passed the bowl counterclockwise, against the natural flow. But it thrilled her as well. Merlin. Magic and medicine. They'd soon be learning so many new things. She smiled to herself. That was silly. They were already doing things she'd never experienced. Performing the ritual counterclockwise also made sense. This was a first step toward undoing the spell that had imprisoned Merlin.

The bowl made its way around the circle, from Chandler to Jessica. Chloe started to worry that the bowl might be empty by the time it got to her. It wasn't very deep. But a small puddle remained when Em passed it to her.

Chloe raised the bowl as everyone else had done, then used her lips to strain the juice from the herbs and took a sip. The bitter tang of the herbs and unsweetened juice bristled on her tongue. Her mouth puckered. She started to hand the bowl to Athena, but her fingertips scraped across a rough ridge that spanned the bowl's bottom. An odd blemish for an otherwise smooth piece of earthenware. Curious, she took a closer look at the bowl.

"Skull!" The word leapt from her mouth, breaking the solemnness of the ritual. Not pottery or just any skull, a human skull, or the dome of one.

Athena snatched the bowl from her fingers. "It's a summoner's bowl," she said reverently.

Heat flushed Chloe's cheeks. "I'm sorry I reacted that way. I just—I've seen stoneware versions of them, but never the real thing. How old is it?"

"It's belonged to the Circle since the time of our origin, back when we worshiped in oak groves under the guidance of the Fair Folk. It's one of the few objects the High Council didn't confiscate."

Awe overcame her embarrassment and her gaze scanned the bowl, studying it intently. "I'm glad the Council didn't take it. It's amazing, really."

"We are blessed to have it." Athena set the bowl back in the center of the circle and took out the loaf of black bread. She broke off a piece, ate it, then passed the loaf to Chandler.

As the bread made its way around the circle, the solemnness returned. Chloe snuck a look at Athena. Her hands peacefully rested on her knees, palms up while she waited for everyone to take their turn. Back straight. Neck taut, perfectly enhanced by the dark line of the choker. Chloe's parents and aunts were highly knowledgeable and skilled at the Craft, as were all the High Council members she'd known. But they were wrong in assuming someone as young as Athena couldn't comport themselves with the maturity and dignity of an elder high priest or priestess. She deserved her title and to oversee a coven, as much as any of the older generation did.

Not long after that, Athena brought the ritual to an end with a clap of her hands. "Now"—she removed the carafe from the center of the circle and set it on the floor behind her— "we are going to attempt a spell that belonged to Merlin himself, the first spark of the greater goods we will accomplish once we are under his tutelage." She took Merlin's crystal from the center of the circle and cupped it in both hands. "Our witch-sister Emily's spirit and energy are hampered by hardships her psyche has endured. Together we can heal that wound." She gestured at the remaining crystals. "If each of you will take the first one that calls to you."

Excitement jittered inside Chloe, so strong that her hands trembled. Merlin's magic. A spell he'd done himself. A healing spell. Psyche spell. Not that far from the sort of spell she'd dreamed of finding.

She scrunched forward, fingers outspread, and closed her eyes. She slowly circled her hand overtop the stones until a gentle tingle feathered up her fingers. Without looking she snatched the stone and sat back, only then opening her clenched fingers to look. Clear quartz crystal, smooth except for one rough side.

Once everyone had selected their stone, Em took off her robe and laid down in the center of the circle with her blue crystal clasped against her stomach. Then Athena held out the crystal in front of her and began to chant. Chloe couldn't understand the words, but they hummed in her ears like a choir of voices. Chandler and Jessica held out their stones and joined in. Suddenly Chloe felt the words rise from the well of her magic. She held out her crystal, her entire body shaking as the words soared from her mouth.

The energies flowed from one person's crystal to the next, around the circle clockwise, spinning faster and faster, mixing everyone's magic and the power of the different crystals into one explosive circle of color. Dizziness whirled in Chloe's head. Power crackled through her hands. She took a deep breath and pushed as much magic as she could into the stone.

Slowly, without breaking the energy's flow, Athena rose to her feet. Her movement tugged Chloe and everyone up, as if they were all mirror images of Athena. The power spun in front of them, a multicolored ring of magic, shooting from crystal to crystal, through the staff crystal and around again.

Athena moved forward until she was close to Em. As she knelt and laid her crystal on the mat, Chloe and everyone else did the same, the colored ring now an egg-shaped halo of magic racing around Em's body.

"Air. Fire. Water. Earth," Athena called, looking skyward. "I call on you. Gods. Goddesses. Gatekeepers. Take the wound from our sister. Release her from the past. Free her. Restore her. Bless her."

In an explosion of colors, the racing halo shifted direction, flooding inward toward the blue crystal Em was holding. It streamed downward into her body. Em's torso humped upwards, thrashing and twisting. Gray fog steamed out from her pores, clouding the room.

Chloe clamped her hands over her ears as the air pressure in the room rose, singing higher and higher. Just when she thought she couldn't it take anymore, the pressure subsided.

Jessica and Chandler leapt to their feet, grabbing bundles of apple twigs and sage, lighting them and fanning the air.

Athena ran to the garden door and flung it open. "Out! Out! I command you."

Before Chloe could even gather her wits, the gray fog cycloned out the door and the energy drained from the air. She turned to check on Em.

Em sat cross-legged on the mat, her head in her hands, swaying like a child on a swing. She looked up, eyes bright. A smile spread across her face. "I feel lighter...free."

Chloe scooted to Em and pulled her into a hug. Everyone joined in, a giant group hug. Joyous. Uniting. Amazing.

Chapter 17

Pink bow in her hair. Little white shoes on her feet.
The child warned me about my husband.
The spirits see his soul. Dangerous. Violent.
"The girl needs to get a better shtick," he said. But her words were true.
—Anonymous, one month after a reading by Violet Grace, age 8-1/2

After Em's healing, Athena ordered the pizzas. Chloe settled onto the couch, her knees pulled to her chest, her toes burrowing into the cushions as she sipped a glass of burgundy and listened to Jessica tell another story about their trip to Wales, about hiking paths once taken by Merlin. When she got to a part about spending a weekend at Gladstone's Library, Chandler took over.

"That's when I got this," she said, pulling down the neck of her robe to reveal a watercolor tattoo of a Welsh dragon rising out of an open book. "Obviously not at the library. But the artist's shop was close by."

Em got up from her seat to take a closer look. "That's gorgeous."

Deep happiness unfolded in Chloe's chest, a surreal feeling of being in a moment that she knew she would remember forever. It was the kind of moment she'd expected to find at the university with her classmates and professors, even with her neighbors in the apartment house. But here it was, even better than she'd dreamed, because these women got her, really got all of her, both the witch and the woman. It was a powerful moment, like the night when she'd lain on the bench outside Devlin's door, looking up at the stars.

She sighed, wishing Devlin was with them.

Jessica turned on the TV and Athena streamed an old movie. The Hallmark version of *Merlin*. Chloe curled up under a throw blanket, too happy to move.

"*Magic has no power over the human heart*," Merlin or someone in the movie said.

"Guess the producer wasn't familiar with love potions." Em snickered.

Chloe laughed along with everyone. But her thoughts once again went to Devlin. His apartment was so close by. If only he was there, then she could crawl naked into bed with him. Run her fingers over his beautiful jawline. Touch his lips. Feel his lips against her body. Get lost in the purr of his magic and make love until they were both exhausted. Wake up next to him and do it all over again.

"Want a refill?" Jessica said, bringing her attention back to the room.

"Sure." She held out her glass. "I think I like this better than the May wine."

"No accounting for taste," Jessica teased.

Em shifted forward in her chair, staring at the TV as if hypnotized. "What do you think Merlin will look like? Old or young? Handsome or not so much?"

"Merlin can shapeshift," Athena said, popping open another bottle of wine. "If I were to guess, early thirties, old enough to look wise, young enough to attract the ladies."

Chandler scoffed. "We'd be safer with a wise old crone version of him, then."

"Speak for yourself," Em interrupted. "I like the sounds of young, hot, and magical." She cut a look Chloe's way and giggled. "You like them that way too, right?"

Chloe looked down, her face burning. There was no question everyone knew she and Devlin had gotten together, but she wasn't used to her hookups being made so public. In a way it felt good. She laughed. "I'm with you about the hot and magical. But not so much when the guy's my teacher. I mean, that is technically what Merlin's going to be."

Athena turned the sound down on the TV. "It's fun to joke about these things. But we need to remember that Merlin will know nothing of our world. We'll be as much teachers to him as he is to us, at least at first."

She turned the volume back up and Chloe closed her eyes, listening to the movie and everyone's hushed voices as they commented on it. And Chloe drifted into sleep and dreams.

A line from the movie echoes in her head: "He will bring people back to the old ways."

"Magic was more common then," Athena whispers in her ear.

Chloe is at the quarry, standing on the diving ledge. Below her, the half-moon's reflection shimmers on the gray water. But the reflection isn't normal. It forms the shape of a luminescent yin and yang, absolutely perfect, unmistakable. On the distant shore, the pine trees stand motionless. No wind. No sound. Everything is waiting for her to make a choice. To jump. Or turn and leave.

Excitement sends a chill across her skin. She leaps, plunging downward, her motion cutting the stillness of the air, her feet and legs an arrow piercing the heart of the yin and yang. She plummets into the watery world, an otherworldly blurred place with waterfalls and bridges. The entire Northern Circle is there, their magic trailing out behind them like a school of phosphorescent fish. Midas's eyes glisten gold. Jessica clutches a basket of blackbirds. Athena holds a staff that looks like Merlin's in the movie. Devlin stands in the middle of them all with his back to her. But when he turns around, she can see it's not him. It's Merlin. Young. Hot. Magical. Just like Em wanted. His eyes flash from green to blue like embers deep within a fire, secrets waiting for her to discover them, ancient grimoires begging to be opened.

Something vibrates in her pocket. Her phone.

She reminds herself that it's important to answer such things even in dreams. The voice on the other end might tell her what this is all about. It could be Devlin. She'd get to hear his voice. She could tell him about Midas and Jessica's phone.

She presses the phone to her ear. "Hello?"

"Chloe Winslow?" Devlin's grandfather's voice says.

Whereas a moment ago she could breathe despite being underwater, now the lack of air sears her lungs.

"Don't forget the boy," he says.

She knows he means the Vice-Chancellor's son.

And all she can think about is how the boy must have felt, his lungs filling with water, unable to breathe, blood vessels bursting in his brain. Someone should have been able to stop that. Someone like her, with magic at her fingertips.

She races for the water's surface, breaking through. She gulps air. But there's no yin and yang of moonlight now, only velvety darkness as silent and eternal as the inside of a casket or the sheets on a hospital bed.

Chloe woke with a start. She lay on the couch in her underwear, shivering from the cold. She found the throw blanket on the floor, wrapped up in it, and snuggled back into the couch cushions.

Traces of early dawn brightened the room. Used wine glasses and bottles lay on the floor. The end tables were covered with pizza boxes and candles burnt down to their stubs. But despite the room's disarray, she felt good. No hint of a hangover. Well-rested. Utterly peaceful. Undoubtedly that was an off-shoot of the healing ritual's magic combined with having some downtime. The only thing that could have made her feel better was if she had woken up next to Devlin.

Taking the blanket with her, she got up, hunted around, and found her clothes and messenger bag waiting on the side table. She took out her phone, her heart sinking when there weren't any messages from him. But there were a ton of texts from her mom.

You okay? the last one said.

Not bothering to read the rest, Chloe checked the time: 7:15. Her mom would be up.

She slumped back on the couch and made the call.

Her mom answered on the first ring.

"Hey, Mom."

"Chloe, you're all right."

"Of course, why?"

"You didn't answer my texts."

She rubbed her free hand across her eyes, wiping away sleepy seeds. "Did you get mine—about the box? You're going to love the straws."

"Yes. I'm sure. When you didn't answer, I was afraid something happened to you. I tried calling."

Chloe thought fast. "Ah—I was studying. My phone was turned off."

"I was afraid it might have had something to do with that awful coven. Your dad told me they invited you to—"

"They aren't evil, Mom. They're nice people. Serious witches."

"You didn't go to that event, did you?" she said, aghast.

A headache began to pulse in Chloe's temples. She pinched the bridge of her nose to stave it off. The truth was, Devlin's grandfather knew she'd been at the complex. If he mentioned it in passing to his witch friends, it would get back to the High Council. In turn, her father would inevitably hear about it. "It was my choice to make. You'd like them. They're smart." She swallowed hard, then took a chance. "They are exploring ways to integrate ancient magic into modern medicine."

"Please tell me you didn't do something foolish like join them?"

"Don't worry." She closed her eyes and regrouped. "You should get the box I sent you tomorrow or the next day."

"That's wonderful, dear. But promise me you won't jump into anything you'll regret. Act responsibly."

"I'll be fine. Love you, Mom. I have to go."

"Love you, baby." She hesitated. "Please, no more disasters."

Chloe stashed the phone in her bag and stared out across the room. The crystals they'd used to heal Em glistened in a bowl on the coffee table. She thought back to the rainbow-colored magic racing around Em and streaming into her body. It seemed almost unbelievable in retrospect. Merlin's magic. They were going to awaken him, then change the world. Old magic. Cures for modern diseases and conditions that had been lost to time. The wisdom and magic of Imhotep, Hippocrates…Her breath caught in her throat, her pulse thrilling at the thought. Then a prickle of fear crept in.

What if that powerful of a magic was too much for mankind? There were reasons the old ways were gone. Darkness. Light. Yin and yang. Walking the razor's edge. What if the Circle's plan did turn into a huge disaster?

The coven would be disbanded.

The High Council would blame her parents for her failure. They'd be shamed in the witches' community. No one would buy botanicals from her dad.

Devlin would be shamed, too. He and Athena would be stripped of their ability to work magic.

And, the boy…

Chloe covered her face with her hands, a heavy feeling collapsing over her like dirt crumbling into a grave as a memory came back to her.

A week or maybe two weeks after that night at the Vice-Chancellor's house, she'd slumped on a chair outside the boy's hospital room. She scuffed her sneakers back and forth, back and forth against the yellow tiled floor until her legs ached. Everyone had gone in to see him, but she wasn't allowed. He wouldn't know she was there anyway, they said. She was too restless, too noisy, too…She knew the truth. His parents, her parents, no one wanted to look at her. Brain damaged. He was there because of her.

But when they left the room to discuss things, she pushed open the heavy door. He lay there, tubes running in and out of him. So much plastic. White sheets. White walls. His pale face.

"I'm sorry," she whispered. "I wish it had been me."

She touched his hand. His tiny, cold fingers—

That day she'd thought she had the answer. She'd thought she could cure him, thanks to an ancient Book of Shadows she'd found in her dad's office.

But she'd been wrong.

Shamefully so.

Chloe flung on her clothes and grabbed her messenger bag. She bolted for the stairs. Maybe she loved it here. Maybe she loved being with Devlin. But her intuition kept insisting that something was wrong. The orb's warning. Athena's evasiveness. Midas's spying. The dead birds. Jessica's sly smiles and the blood swearing. As much as she didn't want to face it, she'd jumped into this too fast. Just like her parents always warned her. Just like she always did.

Her head throbbed as she flew out the front door and down the driveway, eyes on the ground, fast-walking under the flying monkey gateway, her tight jeans tugging at her thighs the way the red dress had done that night at the Vice-Chancellor's house.

Chapter 18

You can leap off a cliff like the Fool,
but it's what you do once you reach shore that determines who you are.
—Athena Marsh, high priestess, Northern Circle

The warmth of the morning sun soaked Chloe's skin. All around her blackbirds chattered in the weeds. *Don't go. Don't go,* they seemed to cackle. *You belong here...*

She blocked out their voices. This had been a wonderful dream, the coven, Devlin, magic and medicine. But she'd been foolish. Irresponsible. Shortsighted. She'd heard those words about herself enough over the years to know it was the truth.

Not slowing her pace, she texted Keshari.

We need to talk. Meet after class, okay?

Putting her phone back in her bag, she jogged the last few yards to the end of the driveway, then up the street to the bus stop. Commuter traffic flooded by. Sweat soaked the back of her shirt. Hopefully, a bus would show up soon. She needed to get out of here. Bury herself in her studies. Prepare for her MCAT exams. Move on. Not look back. Do the sane, smart thing. She'd find a cure for the boy on her own, someday, somehow. What they'd done for Em with the crystals gave her a place to start.

The smothered chirp of her phone vibrated through her bag. She let out a relieved breath. Thank goodness for Keshari.

She retrieved her phone. As she checked the message, a sick feeling twisted in her stomach. Not Keshari. A text from Devlin. Damn it.

Without reading the message, she buried the phone in her bag, deeper this time. She had to do this. She had lost sight of the path she'd been on.

She'd tone down the witchcraft side of her life. Stick to meditation. Basic rituals. She'd use the Tears of Tara salt to keep the Circle or anyone from spying on her. She'd lie to Juliet. Tell her she was taking a break from the Craft.

A crushing tightness squeezed her chest. She glanced over her shoulder, toward the complex. Only a couple of windows in the main building's top floor were visible in the distance. Joining the Circle had been a dream come true. But it had to become a brief memory, before guilt and regret ruined it. It had to be replaced by sanity.

Two women joined her at the stop.

A second later, the hiss of the city bus's brakes sounded down the street. Chloe spotted it, moving with the traffic, stopping to drop off and pick up riders, then working its way closer. She lowered her gaze and focused on her feet, scuffing at the street-side gravel and crumpled leaves, waiting for the seconds to pass.

She raised her head as a car pulled up to the curb a few yards away.

Her mouth went dry. Dear Goddess. Not just any car. An orange BMW coupe. Devlin's car.

He lowered the passenger window and smiled. "Need a ride?"

The bus hissed up behind his car. Chloe patted her ear, gesturing like she couldn't hear him over the noise.

"Got to go," she shouted.

His smiled widened, dimples forming. He motioned for her to get into the car. She looked away from him and toward the bus, time slowing down, each second taking on a surreal importance.

The bus's doors whooshed open. A tall, goth guy with long, straight black hair strolled down the steps. His gaze met hers, his eyes as vivid blue and deep as a frozen lake on Candlemas Eve, a clairvoyant's gaze. As he started past her, he paused and whispered, "He that dares not grasp the thorn should never crave the rose."

Dumbfounded, she could only blink at him. The quote was from one of her aunt's favorite Anne Bronte poems.

With a nod, he moved on and the surreal moment ended, the world crashed back to life.

"What's wrong?" Devlin's distant voice reached her ear.

She turned toward him, drawn by a force as irresistible as gravity or moonlight. A force that had everything to do with her heart and nothing to do with logic.

"Get in." Devlin leaned across the passenger seat and opened the door. "If you don't hurry, Henry will get out," he said as firmly as if *no* wasn't an option.

He was right too. She hadn't noticed the dog in the back, but now he was whining and climbing over the passenger seat, begging her to come with them, his eyes as big and brown and as sweet as Devlin's.

She looked at the bus again. The two women who'd been waiting with her vanished inside. The door started to close…A memory from her first night at the coven, the maze test flashed through Chloe's mind: Em sitting on the stairs with her earbuds in, setting herself up for failure.

Chloe dashed for Devlin's car.

Screw it. Maybe the Circle would fail or be disbanded. Maybe she and Devlin wouldn't work out. Maybe her intuition was right and something was dangerously wrong.

But if she didn't try, if she didn't dare the bite of those thorns, that, even more than the shame of failure, is what she'd really regret.

Chapter 19

Burlington's flying monkeys.
The originals were crafted out of steel decades ago.
I created mine out of car parts and garden tools
as a gift to my son on his third birthday.
Truly, if I could have made them fly, I would have.
—WPZI interview with artist Chandler Parrish

When Chloe and Devlin reached his apartment, they went inside and left Henry outside to burn off some energy.

"Tell me, what's going on?" Devlin said, leading her to the couch.

Chloe sank down and curled forward, elbows on her knees. "Lots of things. Nothing." She closed her eyes, squeezing them tight. "I thought I could remake my life once I moved up here. When I found the Circle and you, I thought…Everything felt perfect. But my gut's telling me something is about to go horribly wrong."

His voice gentled. "When they sent me away to prep school, I thought I was going to remake myself. I ended up expelled and…If it weren't for Athena, I'd have ended up rotting in juvy."

She glanced at him. "That's not exactly reassuring. You mean, juvenile detention, like jail?"

He grimaced. "Where do you think the Circle's bad reputation came from? It wasn't just because of my father or grandfather—or because my mother emptied the coven's bank account on vacations in Belize."

"You didn't do anything that wrong, did you?"

"Selling pot mostly. I had an impressive operation going. I thought I was king of the campus. Then I got even stupider. Some friends and I broke into an old equipment shed. We set up a hydroponic system in it, grow lights, automatic fertilizing, the whole works."

She shook her head. "You were pretty industrious." But in a way, she could see him doing it. Literally, a gardener with a magic touch. She softened her voice. "Juvenile detention must have sucked."

"I wasn't there long. Grandpa let me suffer for a few days, then he stepped in and got me out. But Athena knew I was in trouble long before the shit went down. She yelled at me. Told me not to ruin my life because of the anger I had toward my parents. She encouraged me to follow my real dreams—and to not be afraid of what people might say or of failing."

"I can see her doing that. She really has a gift for knowing the right thing to say." Chloe thought back to last night and when she'd picked up on Athena telling her and Em different versions of her childhood. Athena hadn't twisted the truth to prove or gain anything; there was a kind heart and truth at the bottom of her actions.

"Athena's always been that way." Devlin scooched nearer to her. The warmth of his closeness soothed away her tension. He ran his hand down her back. "My point is, life didn't come together for me until I blocked out other people's bullshit, took a chance, and aimed for my dreams. You should have seen my grandfather's face when I told him I wanted to design waterfalls for a living."

She laughed. "I can just imagine."

"The thing is, Chloe, I've never told anyone my whole dream. When I listen to a stream or the beat of waves, when I design a waterfall or stream to play a certain song, I feel relaxed, renewed. I think—"

Her own worries faded a little as she waited for him to go on. "Yeah?"

"I think once we have Merlin to help guide us, we might be able to rediscover ways to heal with the sound of water. Your friend, Keshari, her family heals with singing bowls and chimes. Can you imagine healing diseases by creating specific rhythms with water? We could install fountains in hospitals that cured people. Ever since I was a boy, I've believed it was possible."

She stared at him. She hadn't considered until now why he was as into medicine and magic as she was. But this...Devlin was the most amazing person she'd ever met. Still—"But what if we succeed and bringing Merlin back causes some huge disaster? If his power is too much for modern witches to handle? What if —"

His hand cupped her chin, raising her gaze to his. "What you've chosen to do by joining the Circle and being a part of this path has nothing to do with conceit, like what I did when I went to prep school. You have a dream backed by sincerity and good intentions." His lips touched her forehead, more of a blessing than a kiss. He released her, his tone deepening. "If you knew you couldn't fail, what would you do with your life?"

Magic. Medicine. Not just for the one boy, for other children, for old people, for everyone.

Whereas a second ago Chloe's intuition had still screamed for her to run before something horrible happened and she shamed her family even more, now she felt a seismic shift in the universe, a larger sense of purpose that was more important than her fears. The sunlight flooding through Devlin's apartment windows was sharper, brighter. Under her fingertips, the couch's upholstery was softer. The trophies on his shelf glistened, as silver and gold as stars.

She swept her fingers down his cheek, trailing magic over the silk of his freshly shaven skin. "If I knew I couldn't fail—I'd stay here."

His lips were on hers with a fierce intensity that made her gasp. Heat raged into her blood. She kissed him back, mouth opening. Teasingly he nipped her bottom lip, then trailed kisses down her neck. Her neck tingled and throbbed with heat. She slid her fingers under his T-shirt, relishing the sensation of his kisses and the warmth of his skin.

Abruptly, they both pulled back, faces flushed.

She laughed; she had to do something to break the spell or they'd be in bed in a second and there were still things to talk about, serious things.

Devlin anxiously rubbed his hands down his pants legs, then gave her a guilty look. "About yesterday, I planned on getting in touch with you once I got to the Adirondacks," he said. "I didn't realize I was going to be in a dead zone. It was hard to believe, a gorgeous multimillion dollar log cabin but no cell service or Wi-Fi. Once I got back to the real world, dozens of texts downloaded. Most of them from Midas."

"From Midas? Athena said he went with you."

"He was supposed to. He backed out at the last minute." Devlin frowned. "Speaking of which, you don't have classes today?"

"Yeah, but I already missed most of them." She took a deep breath.

He folded his arms across his chest. "Now tell me what else is bothering you, all of it."

She told him about her and Keshari catching Midas stealing the phone and her fear that he might be working for the High Council.

"Ahem"—Devlin cleared his throat, interrupting her story— "I already know most of this. Midas told me. He knows you saw him and that you ran into Jessica."

"I can't believe he confessed. Did he tell you why he took the phone?"

"He was mad about Jessica getting into his files. He planned on looking for a photo or something he could use for blackmail to keep her from prying or messing with his records."

An unexpected flare of anger sizzled in her veins. "I can't say that I blame him."

"I understand how you feel. It's one of the ways the Circle's always investigated initiates, but that doesn't make it a good policy. However, it's also the reason I can reassure you he doesn't work for the Council."

She breathed a sigh of relief, but then pushed her shoulders back and sat up taller on the couch. "That's only part of the problem. Coven members are supposed to trust each other implicitly, honest and open. But someone's performing rituals on the sly. And I'm not talking about average ceremonies." Even if it wasn't evil, she suspected he didn't know. "There's an altar in a grotto near the bridge."

"Yes. What about it?"

"Last night, I saw the orb again. It led me there. There was incense burning, some other objects and a blackbird's head—just the head. It was a banishing ritual to get rid of the orb."

"Damn it." He raked his fingers through his hair. "Athena is…since she's come back from Wales she's been micromanaging everything. Doing things without discussing them first. She's always liked to be in charge, but she never was this much of a control freak."

"Like doing sacrifices at the Earth Clock and in the grotto? Could her impulsiveness be what the orb wanted to warn you about?"

"No. What Athena's doing may be old magic, but it's not dark. It's more like she doesn't trust anyone else to get it right."

"How about Merlin? We're planning on awakening a wizard who's been gone from this world for eons. What if bringing him back affects the balance of energy? What if that's what the orb's warning was about?"

"We're righting a wrong that was done to Merlin centuries ago. We are freeing him from a prison made of dark magic."

Righting a wrong. Prison of dark magic. Chloe stroked her thumb across her charm bracelet and let the words play in her head. She hadn't thought of it like that. "You could be right. Maybe I've been looking at the orb's message the wrong way. It could have been trying to encourage us to restore the balance between light and dark."

"Protect the Circle could refer to making sure our ritual circle is warded well," Devlin said.

Even as he said it, her heart felt lighter. That was what the orb had been trying to tell them. It made sense. It was how she'd felt about the Circle and their path when she'd first heard about it, before she'd started to overthink and panic.

Chapter 20

Beauty is not the seat of Nature's power. I learned that in the Everglades.
Nothing survives unless it's armed with brute force or cold indifference.
Death of the weak is as inevitable as the survival of the fittest.
—Matt Dominic

A tough job, but someone has to do it, Chloe thought dreamily as she kissed her way down Devlin's abs and belly to the belt line of his chinos. Last time they'd made love, he'd insisted on it being all about her. This time she turned the tables on him.

She undid the button on his fly, then teasingly strummed a trail of magic over his clothed groin.

He squirmed against the couch cushions, his magic purring. "Dear Goddess, you're horrible."

She looked up at him, a wicked glint in her eyes. "You don't know the half of it."

Scrunching down, he caught her face between his hands and moved in to kiss her. She nipped his lip playfully, and pushed him away.

"Bed," he said, staggering to his feet. But before they were halfway there, she had his chinos around his ankles. She slapped his butt. He grappled with her, pulling her with him as he stumbled and fell onto the bed, rolling and laughing. He kicked his pants and briefs the rest of the way off. She shimmied out of her jeans. He tugged off her shirt, kissing between her bra-cupped breasts, before undoing the clasp and releasing them.

She trembled under the chill of the air and the thrill of his magic. Her mouth moistened. She longed to pull him closer, but she shoved him back against the mattress and straddled him.

An impish smile twitched on his lips, dimples forming. She leaned forward, her chest caressing his as her lips eagerly found his. The tip of his hardening cock nudged between her legs. Her breath hitched, and a coil of tension pulsed inside her, almost unbearable. All she had to do was move backwards a few inches and—

No. She slid off him, determined to make him suffer a little longer.

"On your stomach," she commanded, tough as a drill sergeant.

He grabbed her by the wrists, pretending to fight against her, both of their bodies growing hot and slick with sweat. He surrendered, rolling over and letting her mount the small of his back.

"You're going to pay for this later," he growled.

The rumble in his voice went straight to the sweet spot between her legs. Excruciating need throbbed and spread through her body, still she pressed him hard against the mattress, bent close to his ear and whispered, "I'm counting on that."

She took a deep breath, mixing her magic in with the air. Then she let it out as she nipped and nibbled her way from his ear lobe down along the side of his jaw. He moaned and writhed from the torturous pleasure, his muscles snaking beneath her. She shuddered with pleasure and moved on to kiss the base of his skull, her fingers slowly skating down his spine, igniting each synapsis one at a time. She kissed and licked her way south, fingers splaying over his ribs, then waistline. When she reached his tailbone she lingered, teasing it with a fierce vibration of magic while her lips massaged the dimples in his butt.

He groaned in ecstatic agony. Then in one powerful twist, he threw her off him and onto her back. He fumbled for a condom and put it on with lightning speed, thrusting into her with a groan. Their lovemaking was urgent with hunger, a bonfire demanding release. An explosive moment later, they fell apart, exhausted and laughing at how fast it all had ended.

"Shower?" he suggested.

She grinned. "Definitely."

* * * *

Chloe decided not to worry about classes for the rest of the day. Instead she and Devlin spent what remained of the morning enjoying each other, and taking a walk to the Earth Clock with Henry. This time there were no encounters with dead birds.

In the afternoon, she went to the main house to watch Chandler's son while she and Athena finished preparing food for the gathering. By dinnertime everyone had arrived, including a rather withdrawn Midas, and Brooklyn and Matt. The only people missing were the elderly couple and the off-the-grid witches who Chloe had met the first night. Athena explained they weren't being included in the Merlin plan for the sake of expediency.

When they sat down at the table, Chloe took the chair between Devlin and Chandler. The rich smell of the homemade bread and simmering lentil soup had made her hungry for hours. She was more than ready to get the blessing over with and dig in.

Athena tapped her wine glass with her knife, the ringing sound silencing everyone. "I'd like to have a word before we begin." She set the knife down. "With the new moon only four days away, I think it's time to relate the details of what the awakening ritual will entail. To start, everyone will need to be here for various rituals from sunset until one a.m. every night from now until then."

Devlin half-rose out of his chair, glancing at Midas and Brooklyn. "I'll be glad to give either of you rides if need be, or you're welcome to spend the nights here. We have plenty of extra beds."

Warmth radiated in Chloe's chest, her pulse beating an ecstatic rhythm. He hadn't included her in his offer, which could only mean one thing. That he thought of them as a couple and rightly assumed she'd want to stay with him.

Athena took over. "There will be a ritual dinner and a ceremonial cleansing, but we won't attempt to awaken and draw Merlin to us until midnight. That's the moment when the stars and moon are best positioned to help us open doorways to enchanted places." She folded her hands in front of her. "We'll be performing the ritual at the heart of the Earth Clock."

"Isn't that a little public?" Chloe said, though she wasn't shocked by the location. In fact, perhaps preparing for that was what the first bird sacrifice had been about.

"We happen to have a city park employee on our side." She nodded at Matt. "He's been assigned the less esoteric but no less important role of making sure our ritual isn't disturbed by outsiders. The Earth Clock itself is perfect. Powerful, and it has all the attributes of the stone circles Merlin is familiar with. We've also already anointed it."

Matt raised his glass. "I personally guarantee there won't be any journalists to worry about this time."

"Journalists?" Devlin's sat forward in his chair, frowning. "Did I miss something last night?"

Athena waved off his comment. "Matt's talking about that other initiate."

Tilting her head, Chloe listened closely. She vaguely remembered a fourth.

"I thought he left before the first gathering?" Devlin said.

"I can't believe I forgot to tell you what happened." Athena paused, her brow wrinkling as if thinking deeply. "Oh, I remember now. I intended on telling you later that evening. But first you ran off to take Midas home, then you had a house guest." She shrugged. "It must have slipped my mind. I've had a lot going on."

Jessica snickered. "The man was an idiot. I overheard him in the bathroom talking to his editor on the phone. He swiped an invitation from a real witch and was planning on joining, then writing an article from the inside." Her voice turned nasty. "The bastard is going to get his wish, just not the way he planned."

A chill raised the hairs on Chloe's arms. "What do you mean?"

Athena's voice went saccharine sweet. "Let's just say the journalist was more than willing to make a small donation for violating our sanctity. In exchange, we agreed to not curse his family for his trespass." She picked up her wine glass, twirling the stem between her fingers as she relaxed back in her chair. "We didn't ask for much, some hair and blood, a few fingernail clippings, things we needed for the ceremony."

Even without looking at him, Chloe sensed the tension go out of Devlin. "I see where you're coming from," he said. "I just wish you'd told me."

Midas huffed. "Would someone mind filling me in?"

"To prevent the Lady of the Lake from discovering Merlin's escape, something must be left in his stead," Athena explained. "Part of the spell must be made of human."

Midas nodded. "Oh, you mean an offering."

"Essentially." Athena raised her wine glass in a toast. "To the journalist and all those who have in small and larger ways been a part of this journey."

Jessica was quick to raise her glass.

"To them all," Matt and Brooklyn said, raising their glasses.

Chloe raised her glass as well, but she didn't take a sip. She understood that spells worked that way with one thing representing another, parts from a human used to create the illusion of a human. Still...she couldn't help feeling that threatening people into offering was a step back into that gray zone between dark and light.

* * * *

Chloe's uneasiness about the journalist lessened after a hearty bowl of soup and bread, washed down with a robust lager. No one else acted concerned. Devlin certainly wasn't. She relaxed, getting into the chanting session that followed as well as an intricate ritual designed to get them used to focusing and entwining their magic as a group. She didn't go back to her apartment that night. But in the morning, Devlin woke her up early and made sure she arrived at campus in time for her first class.

It was noon before she finally straggled back to her apartment house. As she went inside, the antiseptic odor of the cleanser the Rescue Twins used to sanitize the foyer hit her nose, making her sinuses prickle. She sprinted upstairs and into her apartment, letting out her breath once she closed and locked her door.

But the air inside wasn't pleasant either, musty with a hint of men's athletic shoes. It was as if in her absence, the apartment had reverted to smelling like the previous tenant.

She lit a cinnamon candle and set it on the kitchen bar. As much as she needed to study, the first thing she had to do was take Athena's advice and create a spell or potion to keep the Juliet situation from becoming a problem, at least until after Saturday night. And she had just enough time to do that before Juliet would return home for the day.

Guilt about putting a spell on Juliet feathered the back of her mind as she used the Tears of Tara to cast a circle, then lit a beeswax candle and went to work. She'd decided on a spell that Brooklyn had recommended, involving using the candle's melted wax and her athame to write Juliet's name and a couple trigger words on a piece of parchment. In this case, *Northern Circle* seemed like the perfect words.

With that done, Chloe folded the paper and held it over the candle's flame as she intoned, "Honey and ash. Words are my weapon. From my lips to her mind, a force irresistible. Sleepy, tired, in need of a nap. Eyes must close. Sleep must come. Honey and ash..."

The spell's theory was simple. Once she made tea that included the paper's ash, sweetened it with honey, and convinced Juliet to drink it, then anytime Juliet thought or heard the words *Northern Circle*, she'd be overwhelmed by the need to sleep. Essentially, the spell worked like a hypnotic suggestion and would make Juliet want to stay home in bed instead of socializing.

She brewed a pot of jasmine tea and fixed two mugs, one with special ingredients and one without. Juliet loved tea almost as much as she loved talking. If she added a few chocolate chip cookies from her mom's last care package, she'd for sure be able to convince Juliet into having tea instead of lunch.

Chloe padded to her front door and opened it an inch, just far enough that she'd be able to hear if anyone came up the stairs from the foyer. She got out the tin of cookies and was contemplating popping the mugs into the microwave to reheat the tea when the clomp of footsteps echoed in the hall. A second later, a knock reverberated on her door. She took a deep breath and opened it.

Keshari stood there with a woven bag tucked under her arm. "I decided to check and make sure you were okay. Didn't you get my messages?"

"How did you get through the front door?" Chloe said sharply. She grimaced. "Sorry, I didn't mean to be rude. I am glad to see you, just surprised. I thought you were Juliet."

As if summoned by her name, Juliet bounded out from the stairwell and down the hallway. "It seems I'm not the only one wondering what happened to you." She gave Chloe a Cheshire cat grin. "Were you with that guy?"

Chloe shot a look at Keshari.

Keshari dipped her chin, wide eyes begging forgiveness as if she were guilty of talking to Juliet about Devlin. She gestured at the mugs. "That smells wonderful."

"Jasmine tea and honey from my aunt's hives." Chloe grabbed the tainted mug and thrust it at Juliet. "Come on in. I'll tell you everything."

As Juliet headed for the afghan-draped end of the couch, Chloe handed the other mug to Keshari. "I'm so glad you stopped by. Go, sit. I'll get us some cookies."

Juliet raised her voice. "So, will I get to meet Devlin when we visit the complex?" She lifted her mug, hiding a conniving smile before she took a sip, then another.

Anticipation fluttered inside Chloe and her hands trembled as she placed the tin of chocolate chips on the coffee table. "I talked to the high priestess. She said I can bring you by the *Northern Circle* complex anytime."

Juliet blinked. "Really?"

Keshari frowned. "Are you sure?"

"It surprised me too." Chloe made herself comfortable on a floor cushion, stretching out her legs as if she didn't have a care in the world. "The priestess said even tonight would work."

"Wow, that's fantastic." Juliet dipped her fingertip in the tea, then sucked off the liquid. "I'd love to do that. But this weekend would be better. I'm not doing anything on Saturday. Do they have any cats? I bet they do."

"I don't know about cats. But Devlin has a dog." Chloe clawed her fingernails down her pants legs. Why was the spell taking so long? Brooklyn claimed one sip and the trigger words would work instantly.

Keshari put her mug aside and opened her bag. "I meditated about your new path while I created a mandala, blessing and prayers for you." She took out what looked like a quart-size mason jar filled with muddy-colored sand, and held it out for Chloe to see. "I finished this morning. Now I need to release the sand. Would you like to do it with me?"

"Sure. What do you mean by 'release'?"

Juliet sat up straighter. "You release the sand by pouring it into a lake or river. I saw a demonstration once. The water carries the prayers to the ocean and—" She stopped talking and rubbed her eyes. "Phew, all of a sudden I feel really tired."

Chloe faked a yawn, patting her mouth to add to the effect. "I'm exhausted too. This is the first chance I've had to sit down since I got back from the *Northern Circle*."

Juliet's mouth opened in an impossibly wide yawn. "Wow. I can't believe this." Holding on to the arm of the couch for support, she staggered to her feet.

"Are you all right?" Keshari asked.

"I'm fine. I just need to take a catnap, a couple of winks, a siesta..." Still babbling, she wobbled out the door.

Once Chloe heard Juliet's apartment door shut, she jumped up and closed hers quietly. She turned back to Keshari, everything bubbled out. "I confess, the tea was bespelled. I had to get her off my back about going to the complex."

Keshari shook her head. "I'm not certain if I should laugh or yell at you."

"Don't worry, I feel horrible enough for both of us." She joined Keshari on the couch. "But, honestly, I feel worse about not answering your messages. Everything's been such a blur. When I texted you, I was going to back out of the coven. Except everything the Circle is into feels right to me, even more so than the future I'd planned out for myself. It's kind of terrifying."

"I'm so happy for you." Keshari smiled. "I also totally understand why you didn't have time to text."

Chloe pulled her into a bear hug. Then she sat back and told Keshari everything she knew about the awakening ritual: the who, where, what, and when. She even went into the part about the journalist. "I'm scared shitless and excited. If that makes sense."

"I'd give anything to see it." Keshari laughed. "Who am I kidding? I want to meet Merlin. He may not be part of my heritage, but I love the stories about him and Camelot."

"I wish you could be there too. But we could fail. This isn't exactly something that's been done before." She hesitated, then used the unsettling phrase that had repeated in the back of her mind for days, like the tolling of a bell. "It's on the razor's edge between dark and white magic."

"You have only good intentions. You want to help others by finding cures."

"Yeah, but bespelling Juliet wasn't exactly white magic. I didn't hesitate about doing it either. It was easy, too easy."

"With your abilities, you could have chosen to do a permanent and much more harmful spell." She took a breath. "The Dalai Lama said, 'Compassion is a wish to see others free from suffering.' You are a compassionate woman, Chloe. As long as that is your aim, you don't have to worry about turning toward evil."

"You really don't think I'm jumping into this too fast?"

"No. I think you are brave."

Chloe smiled. Brave was one word no one had ever applied to her. Crazy seemed more accurate.

Chapter 21

I thought of her, that night alone in the cell,
the gentle stroke of her magic on my forehead, soothing away my fear.
And I vowed to always be there for her.
—Devlin Marsh

Not long after Keshari headed home, Chloe noticed the jar of mandala sand left forgotten on the floor. She slumped down, cradling it between her hands. It would have been nice to have those extra blessings and prayers, but releasing the sand would have to wait. She'd already received a message from Athena asking if she could come early tomorrow to help before the evening session:

Morning would be better. If it works for you. Before sunrise would be best.

Chloe knew "if it works" was an attempt to be polite. Athena meant she was *expected* to be there before dawn, and to bring extra clothes because she wouldn't be home until Sunday morning at the earliest.

As she expected, the next few days and nights were a haze of gatherings and rituals, of robes and strange foods, and chanting in the teahouse until they fell asleep on the mats, their magic and bodies exhausted and entwined. Together they summoned fog from the lake. Called wind from the calm sky. Sprouted leaves on bare branches, and created energy-balls with their minds and magic. Things that she'd been told were way beyond the grasp of witches her age.

To a large extent, the passing days felt as much like daydreams as reality. It was the most incredible, glorious, and energizing time she'd ever known. No question, she'd found the home of her heart. Even if right now it didn't afford her and Devlin much alone time.

Saturday evening arrived and the dizzy haze of her excitement subsided into stillness under the weight of what lay only a few hours ahead. Along with everyone else, she put on her black robe and went to the teahouse for a meal of dark bread and juice freshly pressed from pomegranates and white grapes.

The shadows and brightness cast out from a dozen candle lanterns flickered against the walls. In the background, slow chanting music played. Almost everyone was talking softly as they ate. But Chloe found herself falling into profound silence. Her gaze drifted to Devlin's profile. A spark of desire burned inside her as she took in the beautiful slope of his jawline and classic nose. He stopped talking with Midas, glanced her way and smiled, as if he'd sensed her watching. Then he turned back and continued to chat.

She closed her eyes, concentrating on the music and letting everything else fall away. Her thoughts wandered to a different night:

Music drifting. The shimmer of light on smooth blue water.

She'd swiped her finger across the screen of the e-reader. Page 44. The red dress. She was rising from the poolside lounge chair and floating into the house. Her toes brushed the carpet. Twenty-two treads to the top of the stairs. The closet door swung open. The coat hangers jangled. The dress snugged her hips.

Glass breaking. Her pulse leaping. Terror. Running. Shards glittering under the pool lights, like the gleam of sequins, like water. Like the floor in a hospital. Like spittle at the corner of a boy's mouth—

Chloe bit down hard on her lip, holding the image of the boy in her mind and praying more deeply than she ever had. *Dear Hecate. Dear every God and Goddess, please be with me. Guide me. Not for me. For the boy. For my parents. For the Circle. Bless my gifts and help me use them wisely.*

As she released her lip and opened her eyes, the room returned in sharper focus: everyone talking, the rustle of robes and the clink of glasses. But she remained in her own world for a second longer, studying everyone's faces, memorizing them. Chandler and Em. Jessica and Midas. Devlin and Athena. A sad sense of melancholy seeped into her bones. No matter what happened, tonight was bound to change them all.

Athena rose to her feet, her robe swirling out around her. The candlelight glittered on her cheekbones and the rigid line of her neck, encircled by the darkness of her choker. Around her, the air rippled with energy, then stilled.

Goose bumps tingled on Chloe's arms. Seeing auras or a witch's energy wasn't one of her gifts. She'd have thought it a trick of light, except she'd noticed the same thing the first time she'd met Athena. What was it?

She glanced again and realized—with surprise—that she'd once more lost track of time. Only a few minutes ago, Athena had been in deep conversation with Brooklyn and Matt. But now they were both gone.

Adrenaline jumped into her veins. This could only mean one thing. They'd left to take up their positions, closing off the park and bike path to outsiders. It was time. This was it.

"All right, everyone." Athena's voice rose, taking command of the room. "If you'll all grab a lantern, we'll begin."

Devlin handed one to Chloe, its handle hot against her fingers. "Are you doing okay?"

She nodded. Her whole body buzzed with excitement. "I just hope I don't screw anything up."

"Listen to Athena. Follow her lead and you'll do fine."

With Devlin walking next to her, Chloe followed everyone else down the path to the complex's back gate. A chill hung in the air. Darkness crowded in around them. But their lanterns formed a tunnel of brightness, opening before them and closing behind.

By the time they arrived at the Earth Clock, Chloe's eyes had adjusted to the light. Instead of sheer darkness, the world beyond her had transformed into a web of leafless trees and shades of gray. The standing stones themselves brightened and dimmed in the lantern's flickering light, creating the illusion of ghostly faces and skulls glaring from their rough surfaces.

Chloe shivered, fear and excitement quivering under her skin.

Em bent close to her. "I can't believe we're doing this." Her voice hushed even further. "When I was a kid, I used to dream about running away to join the Knights of the Round Table."

"I wanted to be Merlin," Chloe whispered. Then they both fell into respectful silence, watching as Athena and Devlin cast the ritual circle.

Once that was done, Athena laid out a crescent of votive candles at the circle's center and placed what looked like a damp bird's nest inside the curve.

A whiff of rancid blood reached Chloe's nose. Her stomach cinched, the taste of bile creeping up her throat. Not a real bird's nest. Most likely it was a nest created out of the journalist's hair and fingernail clippings, soaked in his blood.

She swallowed back the nausea. There was no reason to be repulsed. She'd known these things would be used. What they were doing called for powerful magic. It took sacrifice.

Athena placed Merlin's crystal inside the nest. "Bless our circle tonight. Grant us the strength of the old ways. As waning gives way to waxing, doorways open—"

Jessica leapt forward into the circle, raising her hand to silence Athena. "Wait. I heard something, someone—" She bolted across the circle and into the darkness beyond the stones, like a wolf on the attack. Devlin and Midas took off after her, one step behind.

"Over there," Midas shouted.

There was a crack-snap of dry branches breaking.

Chloe's mouth dried. Fear pounded in her chest. It wasn't Brooklyn or Matt. They weren't stationed this close. Maybe an animal. A dog. Henry. Or the journalist that Athena had sent packing.

Em stepped closer to her. "What's going on?"

"I don't know," Chloe whispered.

More breaking branches. The crunch of leaves.

Jessica shouted, "Son of a bitch."

Sleigh bells jangled.

Chloe gasped. Bells. It couldn't be—

A thud. A grunt. A whimper. A second later, three outlines appeared out of the darkness and into the circle of stones, Jessica and Midas hauling a woman between them. As they reached the center of the circle, the air went out of Chloe's lungs, her suspicion confirmed. It was Keshari.

Oh Goddess, no.

"Look what we caught," Midas said, gripping Keshari's arm tighter.

Athena clasped Keshari's chin, forcing her face up until their eyes met. "I know you. You chose not to join the Circle. Now you're spying."

"Let me go," Keshari pleaded. "I won't tell anyone." Her terrified gaze lit on Chloe, then darted away as if to pretend they didn't know each other.

"Friends look out for friends, even when they don't ask for it." Keshari's motto rushed through Chloe's head. That's why she was here, she was certain of it.

Chloe raced over to them. "She's not a threat to us! Let her go."

"Please"—Keshari's voice trembled—"I promise, I won't cause any trouble."

Chloe's heart squeezed. This was beyond horrible. She straightened her spine. "Seriously, she won't tell anyone. It's almost midnight. We don't have time for this."

Devlin strode back into the circle, his voice firm. "Chloe's right. We need to get back to the ceremony."

"I agree," Chandler said.

Athena tilted her head as if thinking. "True, we don't have time to spare." She slowly stroked her finger down her throat, a deliberately languid movement that sent a chill zinging through Chloe. "I suppose this could be an innocent mistake. Then, again, perhaps not."

"She didn't just stumble across us," Jessica snarled. Her glare narrowed on Chloe. "You and her were together the other day. You can't deny it."

Chloe ground her teeth. "So what—that doesn't mean I told her anything."

"Bullshit." With her free hand, Jessica reached into her robe and pulled out a hunting knife. Its thick blade glinted in the lantern-light. "Same crime as the journalist. Same punishment."

"No!" Keshari shrieked. She thrashed against Jessica and Midas's hold. They grasped her harder, magic crackling from their fingertips until her knees buckled.

Terror choked Chloe's voice. "Athena, please. If Matt and Brooklyn had been doing their jobs, she'd never have made it this far."

"Shush." Athena turned her back on Keshari, swiveling toward where the crescent of candles sat with the nest and crystal inside its curve. She bent over, placed her palm on the crystal and murmured, "Master, I beseech thee, grant me your power."

"Athena," Devlin said sharply. "Don't—"

Red light shot out from the crystal, its spears knifing between Athena's fingers. With a sweep of her hand, she scooped the light into a crackling energy-ball. Tossing the energy from hand to hand, she turned back to Keshari. She smiled, then hurled the energy ball straight at her.

Jessica released Keshari and leapt out of the way. Midas ducked. Keshari did the same, but she was too late. The energy-ball caught her upside the head. Red light exploded, every vein in her face illuminated stark white. Her eyes slammed shut. She folded to the ground, unmoving.

Chloe dropped to her knees beside Keshari. Keshari's skin was ashen, her lips purple. But she was breathing. There were no visible wounds. "What did you do?" she screeched at Athena.

Athena shrugged. "Don't you think it's kinder that she doesn't feel it when we slice her veins?"

Chloe's voice trembled with rage. "I don't think we should do anything to her."

"Fresh blood will ensure our success. You want that, right?"

"Of course I do. But not like this."

Chandler cleared her throat. "This girl and her family are local. They're not powerless. This isn't like the journalist."

"Exactly," Devlin said. "I vote to have Matt escort her out of here. He was supposed to be taking care of security."

Athena rubbed her choker. "I agree with you two, willingness and anonymity must always be a high priority. But I also agree with Chloe's earlier point. We don't have time to waste." She held out her hand to Jessica. "Knife, please."

Jessica grinned. "I sharpened it this morning. It has been getting quite the workout lately."

Devlin snagged the knife before she could pass it. "I'll do it. First we need to get her over to the nest." The icy look on his face froze the breath in Chloe's throat. She didn't recognize this Devlin, but she also wasn't sure if the look was real or a put-on. Either way, she couldn't take a chance.

In one motion, she leapt to her feet and thrust her arm at him. "Cut me. I accept the punishment for Keshari's crime. Use my blood to bring Merlin back."

Anger flashed across Devlin's face as if he were mad at her for offering, then every hint of emotion dropped away. "Are you sure about this?"

"A willing sacrifice is stronger than one that's forcibly taken, right?"

Athena licked her lips. "Very true—"

She stopped talking as footsteps sounded from the darkness. A second later, Matt appeared. "Fuck," he said. "I don't know how she got past me."

Athena waved him off. "Don't worry about it. Just get her out of here." Her gaze rounded on Chloe. "If you're willing, then as high priestess, I accept your offer."

Chloe nodded, barely paying attention to Athena's words as Matt scooped Keshari up in his arms and started out of the circle. As they were about to vanish into the darkness, Keshari stirred and hooked her arms around Matt's neck. Chloe let out a relieved breath. Thank goodness, Keshari was going to be okay. Matt would give her a ride home or call a taxi once the magic fully wore off. Everything would be all right. It had to be.

"Now let's get back to work." Athena glanced skyward as if checking the position of the stars. "We only have a few minutes."

While Devlin had Chloe kneel and place her wrist on top of the crystal, Athena began the ritual in earnest, chanting until the air vibrated with her magic. Everyone joined in. Their voices echoed out between the standing stones, into the leafless trees and across the lake.

"Close your eyes," Devlin said. His voice lowered to a whisper. "Hold still. I need to make this a clean cut."

Chloe did as he asked, squeezing her eyes even tighter as he placed the cold edge of the blade against the inside of her wrist. She focused on the chanting, letting her voice and magic join the others, losing herself in the intoxicating sensation of the entwining energy. They were so close to what she wanted. *Magic and medicine.* They'd all be students of Merlin soon. No regrets. Not now.

Devlin pulled her arm out straight, a fast tug that brought her out of her trance. "Accept this offering, a sacrifice for disturbing the sanctity of the Circle."

Athena's voice spoke over top of his, dominating his cadence. "Take this blood, this token, take it. Open the doorway. Bring him to us, leave this sacrifice behind to balance his light. An offering to leave in his stead."

The blade moved. Pain streaked across her wrist. She clenched her teeth, white-hot agony shooting up her arm. Devlin had cut her. Not hesitantly. Not superficially. He'd cut her swift and deep.

Chapter 22

Protect my heart from love not returned and trust misplaced.
Guide me into the warmth of true friendship and kindness,
and away from loneliness and sadness.
—Chloe Winslow, entreaty to the Goddess

Blood bubbled from her wrist, cascading down her palm and off her limp fingers. Devlin chanted, his voice thundering across the circle of stones. Athena took up a higher note. Everyone joined in, their voices melding into one.

Vertigo made Chloe's head spin. She curled up on the ground, the hazy crescent of candles orbiting in front of her face like a miniature solar system. Devlin had cut her. She could bleed to death. She'd end up dead and in the ground. Maybe that's where the journalist was.

Heat clamped her wrist.

Her pulse jolted and began to jackhammer. She twitched. She thrashed. Sweat soaked her skin. But the darkness retreated and the candles settled down and came into focus.

"Look," Em gasped.

It took all the energy she had, but Chloe lifted her head.

The ground all around her shimmered with orbs, eerie and luminescent, colors as rich as stained glass. The orbs glided and shuffled, forming a runway in front of her. At the end of their path, a single standing stone wavered into focus, shadowy in the orbs' strange light.

As though in slow motion, Chloe floated to her feet and drifted toward it. But Athena, Chandler, Em…none of them glanced her way to see where she was going. Instead, their gazes remained fixed on the ground in front of them.

Chloe glanced to see what they were looking at.

Her body lay curled on the grass. Devlin knelt beside it, his hands clamping her wrist, his eyes closed. She would have thought she was dead, except if she were a ghost, then Em would have seen her. Still, she wasn't in her body.

Her intuition tugged at her, turning her around, drawing her down the orbs' path toward the stone. More orbs floated up from the ground, glistening red ones, bumping against each other, merging into one larger sphere.

A hazy sense of relief spread through her. She knew this orb. This spirit might have been banished from the complex's house and garden, but it wasn't gone.

It glided to her and lit on her cupped hands, as cold as death and as red as sunrise.

Holding the orb, Chloe let herself be pulled to the standing stone. She passed through it, as if it were no more solid than cascading water.

On the other side, she came out into a cavern. Long stalagmites hung down from the low ceiling. Thick, cool mist filled the air, glistening red from the orb's glow. All around her magic wailed an ancient ballad, words that hissed against her skin and whistled in her ears.

She crept forward. A salty-bitter taste of minerals coated her tongue. The ground under her feet grew slick with algae. The slow drip of water echoed in her ears.

Odd that a bodiless person could sense so much, she thought. But more than anything, it warned her to be cautious. Most likely other sensations such as pain were possible in this place, despite her out-of-body state.

Ahead, an opening to a second chamber arched. She tiptoed toward it, excitement and fear fluttering in her chest. Merlin had to be here somewhere.

The orb crackled in her hands, shooting out rays of light as she went under the archway and into the chamber. A few dozen yards ahead of her, a stone platform rose from the floor, carved with symbols and unfamiliar runes. On it the outline of a tall person lay, shrouded in a thin white veil. A robed man. Long white hair. White beard. He clutched a staff against his chest. Merlin. She was as certain of this as she was that he needed to be awoken.

A stench wafted in from the chamber she'd just left. Burning hair. Blood. Her ear caught the drone of the coven's voices, a chanting chorus underneath the wail of the cavern's magic.

Athena's voice climbed above all the rest. "Take these tokens. Open the doorway. Bring him to us, leave this sacrifice behind. An offering to leave in his stead."

The coven's voices grew louder, battling the wail of the cavern's magic. The burning stench stung her lungs and stole her breath. But she kept moving forward, slowly, closer to Merlin. He was why she was here. No matter how terrifying everything was, she wanted this. *Medicine and magic.*

The orb lifted from her fingertips. "Yin and yang. Yin and yang. Beware!"

She frowned at it. What was it warning her about in here? Outside there were people, some she trusted less than others. But in here there was only her and Merlin.

The coven's chant intensified. Its magic vibrating in every molecule of air, subjugating the wail. But beneath those noises her ears picked up on a much closer sound. A slight hiss. An exhale of air beneath the louder maelstrom.

Her gaze went to Merlin. Had the sound come from him?

Like a ghost arising, Merlin's shroud drifted upwards, floating away into the mist and leaving his robed body exposed. Another hiss. Then something black, glossy, and the size of a paring knife poked its way out from inside Merlin's chest. Four more protrusions joined the first, groping and clawing. A hand with long, black-tipped fingernails. The crown of a misshaped head appeared, veiled in a pus-green caul. Shoulders followed. The creature slithered and seeped the rest of the way out from Merlin's chest, like a giant jaundiced eel creeping from a carcass.

Paralyzed by fear, Chloe watched the grotesque creature free itself from Merlin and wriggled off the platform. It hunched, writhed, and pulled itself upright into the shape of a lanky man, draped in a cloak of glistening black feathers. With a lazy rake of its hand, the creature tore the caul away from its face, strings of mucus trailing from its fingernails. Hollowed cheekbones. Bone-thin nose. Long white hair.

Chloe slapped her hands over her mouth, silencing a gasp. For all the world this creature looked just like the still-sleeping Merlin, unchanged despite the beast's emergence.

The creature grinned down at Merlin and whispered coldly, "Enjoy your slumber. I shall not be returning any time soon."

The orb brushed Chloe's ear. *Yin and yang. Tell Devlin. Protect the Circle.*

Dear Goddess. Save them all. Yin and yang. Black and white. A creature and Merlin. She now knew what the orb meant. How could she have missed it? She'd known the legend since she was a child. This wasn't totally about her or the coven taking a dark or light path. It wasn't even about the human psyche. Merlin's mother was human. His father was a demon. He literally had a dark and light half. The ritual hadn't awoken Merlin. They'd summoned his shade!

She scuffled backwards, away from the Shade and closer to the stone. "Hecate, guardian of the gateways, get me out of here. Now!"

The Shade yanked the staff from Merlin's hands and swirled to face her. "While the weak sleep, the powerful shall claim mankind."

She pivoted and raced toward the archway and the other chamber, the orb fleeing ahead of her, the Shade only a step behind. She had to get back. Warn everyone. A shade. Merlin's Shade. Loose in the world. Even if he helped the coven discover lost cures, there'd be costs to pay. Horrible costs to the coven and all of humanity.

He seized her arm, knife-like fingernails shredding her ethereal form in an attempt to hold her back. "Why do you flee?" Merlin's Shade cooed. "I heard your voice with the others. Your blood roused me. You are a blessed one who shall stand beside my throne."

"No!" she shrieked, running for the stone she'd come through. Shoulder to shoulder, they passed through it and into fresh air.

Chloe dropped to the ground, her ethereal form reentering her body. She blinked her eyes open. Next to the crescent of candles, the Shade crouched, the lantern light flickering off his very solid and Merlinesque form. He shuddered, then languidly pulled himself up to his full height, lifted the staff skyward and bellowed, "Tonight is the most glorious of dawns!"

Dear Goddess, what had they done?

Chapter 23

Take me, sweet slumber.
Give my flesh to the Shade. Give my breath to the sky.
I have no use for either. I crave neither thorns nor rose.
—Note found on a self-mutilated body
Lakeview Cemetery, Burlington, Vermont

Chloe woke up. She was laying on her back in a bed with her head propped up on a pillow. She felt woozy and her left arm was cold and numb from the fingertips to her shoulder. Her gaze darted to her wrist. A wide, white bandage wrapped it. There was a line of stain where blood had oozed out from the cut, yellow-brown and fresh-red.

She glanced around. She was in Devlin's apartment. Alone in his bed. She wasn't sure how she felt about that or him right now—he'd cut her wrist, fast and hard with no hesitation. Still, at least she was somewhere familiar rather than in an unknown spot.

Her gaze went to the windows. Judging by the slant of the light, it was early morning. Seven, maybe eight o'clock. She was shaky and weak, but that didn't matter. She had to get out of here. Quick.

The murmur of voices came from Devlin's kitchen: Athena and the Shade.

She clenched her teeth, anger seething. She might not have remembered much of what had happened after she returned to her body, but she'd never forget the ritual and watching the creature crawl out of Merlin. Goddess help them, they'd summoned a shade.

Their voices moved closer. Chloe clamped her eyes shut and held perfectly still, pretending she hadn't woken up. However, when they stopped in the living room, she glanced out through the veil of her lashes. The two of them stood next to the couch. The Shade looked the same as when she'd last seen him. Tall. White haired. Like anyone might picture an ancient wizard or sorcerer, except he was now dressed in all black from his shirt down to his pants and boots. Only his brocade vest glistened with a hint of blood-red. If she hadn't known better, she'd have assumed he was a vampire-goth version of the Merlin they'd planned to awaken—at least the Merlin she'd intended to awaken. She wasn't so sure about Athena's intentions anymore. For that matter, she wasn't sure who she could trust—or if anyone would believe her if she claimed he wasn't Merlin.

"I suspect this will please you." Athena bowed her head submissively, then handed the Shade what appeared to be a jewelry box.

He touched her chin, lifting her face. "My dear, I'm quite certain it shall—as long as you followed my instructions. I trust he was in his twenties. Physically fit? Attractive? Healthy? A pleasing sacrifice."

"Yes. Very much." Athena giggled, a childish sound that seemed totally wrong coming from her mouth.

"Then let me examine your artistry." The Shade slowly opened the box. He looked at the contents for long moment, then poked it. He scowled, the air filling with a hiss of his magic, a skin-crawling sound like a nest of angry vipers.

Athena paled. "Did I do something wrong?"

Chloe swallowed dryly. What the heck was in the box?

The Shade plucked out a leather bracelet. "I would have preferred if it were more supple," he said. "But how it works is more important. Would you do me the favor of securing it?"

He held out his wrist. As Athena fastened the bracelet on, the air around him rippled with energy, vibrating so violently that it obscured him for a second. When it settled, the white-haired Merlin was gone, replaced by a tall, twenty-something guy with long, straight black hair. A guy Chloe instantly recognized.

Terrified, she bolted upright and scrunched back against the headboard, trembling. A leather bracelet. A transformation. "*I trust he was young, like you. Physically fit? Attractive? Healthy?*" No. It couldn't be. Human skin.

The Shade swiveled to face her, his intensely blue eyes pinpointing her, eyes she'd only seen once. Eyes of the clairvoyant goth at the bus stop.

"That's—You killed him," she stuttered.

He smiled. "You've been spying on us, haven't you?"

Ice cold sweat drenched her back. Maybe the real Merlin could shape shift, but what the Shade had done had nothing to do with an inborn ability to shift. Necromancy. Dark magic, that's what this was. The Shade even sounded different, a voice that reminded her of the lines of poetry the goth had spoken.

The Shade flicked his fingers dismissively. "Technically, I didn't kill the boy, though I will admit to being party to the death and skinning—as a conductor is to a fine orchestra." His smiled broadened. "Quite an effective spell, wouldn't you say?"

Chloe clutched her numb-cold arm against her chest and stuttered the first thing that came to mind, "I—I—Where's Devlin?"

"Doing something useful, I would assume." The Shade's attention returned to his bracelet. He gave it a stroke. "Yes. This will do nicely."

As if to answer her question, the front door swished open and Devin loped into sight with Henry at his side. Chloe started to let out a relieved breath, but sucked it back in. As much as she was glad to see him and her heart screamed for her to trust him, she couldn't afford to. Not anymore. Not anyone. At least not until she was sure.

Devlin glanced at the Shade. His brow wrinkled. "You're—Merlin, right?"

"Perceptive, boy. I believe you will prove to be quite trainable." He waved at Henry. "However, that slobbering beast must go. This is a surgery, not a kennel."

Devlin's jaw tightened. "Actually, this place is neither of those things. This is my home and the dog lives here."

"Devlin," Athena said warningly. "These rooms are whatever Merlin wishes them to be. For all practical purposes, he's the coven's high priest now."

The Shade smiled, a slow, dangerous smile. "On second thought—" He crouched down and held his hand out to Henry. "Come here, boy."

Devlin's face paled, as Henry bounded over to the Shade and obediently sat in front of him, tail happily pounding the floor.

The Shade scratched him behind the ear. "He is rather sweet, innocent... malleable, especially his brain." He glanced meaningfully toward Chloe. "Brains interest you, don't they?"

A chill swept Chloe's arms, but she held perfectly still, her mouth tight shut, afraid if she said or did the wrong thing that something horrible might happen to Henry.

"Cat got your tongue?" The Shade snickered.

"Ah"—she wet her lips—"Brains are fine. But I prefer them right where they belong, inside his head."

"Why, of course. But you miss my point." The Shade clamped his hand hard on the top of Henry's skull, his black-tipped fingernails digging in.

Henry's eyes went wide, pleading for help, but he seemed unable to move.

"My point is," the Shade continued, "simple creatures have simple brains, easy to manipulate." The vibration of his magic sang in the room, fast and hot, a high-pitched squeal gaining momentum. Henry's ears went back. His ruff stood up, a low growl vibrating in his throat as his glare homed in on Devlin.

"Stop it!" Devlin shouted, striding toward them, his magic rumbling. "Henry, good boy."

The Shade let go of Henry's head—and the dog hunkered down, tail between his legs as he apologetically wormed toward Devlin. The Shade straightened to his full height. "As I was saying, simple brains are easily manipulated. Witches' brains take more finesse"—he glanced at Athena—"right, my dear?"

Athena nodded her agreement. But the Shade slanted a look toward Chloe, the glisten in his eyes hinting his words weren't perhaps just about what Athena and he had done to fellow witches; they were also about what he'd done to Athena. Chloe glanced toward Devlin to see if he'd caught the innuendo as well. But he wasn't paying attention. He had Henry by the collar, dragging him toward the front door.

"Well," the Shade said, sanding his hands as if readying to move on from the current topic of conversation. He stopped mid-rub, his gaze once again going to Chloe. "What you might want to take away from this small demonstration is that I am capable of teaching you how to cure your worst nightmare. However, the same skills and spells could also be used to create new ones, say for your simple-minded and non-witch friends, if I so desire."

His eyes remained on hers, as if to burn his point into her soul. She didn't look away and—beneath the raw terror that his words had inspired—a pulse of anger grew, fierce and determined. No one, not even one of the most powerful wizards to ever walk this earth—or his shade—was going to threaten her friends like that and get away with it. No way in hell.

Abruptly Merlin's Shade turned away from her, the air seeming to lighten as his attention went to where Devlin was returning from letting the dog out.

"Now that he's gone," Devlin said, "maybe we can get on with the healing?"

The honesty and concern in Devlin's voice stole a measure of Chloe's anger and fear. But she reminded herself that she couldn't afford to be stupid, especially when it was a certain sexy feeling just south of her belly that kept insisting she should trust him.

She wriggled forward. "Are you talking about healing my wrist?" she asked. "How bad is it?"

Athena shrugged. "Don't worry. We have a cauterizing spell that should make it as good as new."

"You're not cauterizing any part of my body," Chloe said, clasping her arm against her body.

"We'll see about that." The Shade strode to the bed, snatched her arm, and pulled it away from her body. His grip was so powerful, there was no way for her to resist. He unwrapped the bandage. "Your boyfriend may be a skillful enough witch, but he lacks ability in the healing arts. This whole thing is an untidy mess."

Devlin stabbed him in the back with a dirty look, his jaw tensing as if he were struggling to keep his thoughts to himself.

"Does this hurt?" The Shade poked the wound with one of his black-tipped fingernails.

Despite being frozen, pain ricocheted up Chloe's arm. She winced in agony. "Yes! A lot."

"Hold still," Athena snapped.

Chloe gritted her teeth and focused her attention on her wrist. An oozing wound gaped across its entire width, swollen and scabless. Maybe it wasn't a perfect healing job, but Devlin had successfully stopped most of the bleeding, though the Shade's poking had partly reopened it.

"In the end" —the Shade yanked her arm out straighter—"the outcome of this healing depends on your threshold for pain."

"That's not exactly comfort—" she started to say.

But before she could finish, the Shade flicked his fingers, sending a spray of cold magic at her wrist, freezing her arm until she couldn't even sense the numbness. He glanced at Athena. "Fetch my staff and we'll get this over with."

Chloe closed her eyes and sunk down against the pillows, lightheaded and nauseous. A shade was about to heal her. A wielder of dark magic.

"Don't worry," Devlin's voice said, gently. "I promise, nothing bad will happen to you."

Opening her eyes, Chloe glared at him. He grimaced and slunk up close to the bed, next to the Shade and Athena.

Athena handed the Shade his staff. The amethyst crystal now crowned its head, held firmly in place by a set of claw-like prongs. He rested the head against Chloe's wrist.

"Naturally, I could do this more quickly by myself. But at least, by allowing everyone to participate, we can turn a botched mess into a teaching opportunity. Now, if you all will focus your magic on the crystal, we'll begin. Pay attention to the rhythm of my magic, memorize the pattern."

A flutter of something other than fear took flight in Chloe's chest. There was one good side to this. With a messed up wrist, she wasn't much good to anyone, including herself.

She took a deep breath, mixed it with her magic, then focused on the crystal and waited for the next command. She strongly suspected this *teachable moment* had as much to do with the Shade reserving his own energy and using theirs as it did about teaching healing techniques.

The Shade looked away from the crystal, turning to Athena. "After we're done with this, I would like to take closer look at those winged monkeys. That witch, Chandler, said she created them out of scrap metal." He smiled wistfully. "One particularly dull Christmas Eve, we animated a suit of armor. It was most amusing."

Athena's eyes widened. "You can do that?"

"Of course, though it would be considerably more work than this mundane task." He cast a hard smile at Chloe. "But the welfare of the *faithful* members of our Circle comes first."

Chloe lowered her gaze submissively, expecting him to look away. But his stare intensified until it reverberated inside her skull. She furrowed her brow, building up a wall of magic around her brain, sealing it away from him. Maybe he could feel her resistance. Maybe not. But as much as she wanted her wrist healed, she wasn't about to sacrifice her brain or will to do it.

His voice deepened. "Those who loan their magic and obedience to our causes shall reap rewards—cures, miracles, powerful gifts." He broke off his gaze and the vibrations left her skull. He chuckled, but she wasn't sure if his amusement was at her attempt to resist him or because his plans for using medicine and magic to manipulate humanity filled him with glee. "Needless to say, we won't give away these gifts for free. There shall be costs—reverence being the first of many."

He gripped his staff in one hand and laid the other lengthwise. He began to chant, "Flesh and flesh. Knit and mend. Blood to blood. Muscle to muscle. Return as thou were. As thou were meant to be..."

Chloe repeated the words in unison, then she let her magic flow into the crystal and entwine with everyone else's. As the conjoined magic flooded her wrist, the sensation of cold left her arm, replaced by intense burning. "Knit and mend. Blood to blood. Muscle to muscle."

She closed her eyes and clenched her teeth, willing herself to not feel the pain, to not show the Shade a speck of vulnerability. The squelch and hiss of the magic knitting her wrist closed sounded loudly in her ears, above the sounds of their voices.

Something else occurred to her, something so profound it stole her breath away. If she focused even harder, she could separate out the threads of each person's magic, sense each of their energies, almost taste them. Hers was not weaker than the rest as she'd assumed. Hers was raw but just as strong as Athena's or Devlin's. She sensed a new level of power unfolding inside her, filling her body. Like a slumbering beast uncurling, shaking itself out, getting ready to awaken. She wasn't sure what sort of gift it would grow into, but she knew this much: the Shade wasn't the only thing awakened last night. The ritual had roused something inside her as well.

* * * *

The healing took less than an hour and left Chloe's wrist perfect, except for a little temporary stiffness and a pale scar.

The Shade draped an arm over Athena's shoulder. "How about we go see those monkeys now. After that, I wish to meet Chandler's boy. I like children. They are quite biddable."

As Devlin tailed them around the corner and toward the front door, Chloe slipped out of bed, retreated into the bathroom, and locked the door. Her suitcase and messenger bag were still on the bench where she'd left them. She yanked on her jeans and a long-sleeved shirt, then got out her phone.

A soft knock sounded on the bathroom door, followed by Devlin's voice. "They're gone. I'll make us coffee." A second passed before his voice came again. "Chloe, I'm sorry about everything. I'm sorry…about cutting you. I—"

Anger leapt into her veins, making her blood roar. She flung the door open. "You're sorry? You didn't even try to hold back."

"Chloe, calm down." He scrubbed his hands over his face. "No, don't calm down. I deserve it. But I had to cut you. I couldn't fake it. Did you want Athena to ask Jessica to do it?"

Her anger subsided, but only a bit. She wasn't sure why she'd lost control so quickly, other than that she loved being with him and now she hated him for confusing and deceiving her. Then again, he'd jumped down the Shade's throat about Henry, like he was totally oblivious to the nature of what he was dealing with.

She narrowed her eyes at him. "You do know what we awakened, right?"

He looked at her blankly. "Merlin. Why?"

"No, not him—at least not all of him." She closed her eyes for a second, regaining her composure. Devlin's voice was too full of truth to be lying. "You figured out that I went through the stone, right?"

"Merlin told us. He knew you willingly sacrificed, but he didn't seem to trust you. That's why I was losing my patience with him. That, along with Henry, and…He's not like I'd thought he'd be. Wise. Compassionate. He's an asshole."

"He's a shade, Merlin's dark half. Yin and yang. Incredibly dangerous."

"Shit." Devlin dropped down onto the edge of the bed, shaking his head as she told him about waking up and leaving her body, about meeting the orb again, how the orb had led her inside the standing stone to where Merlin's body lay. And when she got to the part about the Shade emerging from Merlin's body, she shuddered, goose bumps rising on her skin.

"There's something else." Chloe rubbed her bracelet hesitantly. It was possible she was wrong. But if she was right…she couldn't keep this to herself. "Did you notice how Merlin's speech was really modern, even before his transformation—which is another rather terrifying topic on its own?" *And condemning*, she thought.

Devlin lifted his head, a confused expression crossing his face. "You're right. Technically, he should be speaking ancient Welsh or some Celtic language. He's been asleep for eons." His mouth fell open. "Oh, I see where you're going with this. You think he's been communicating with someone who speaks modern English."

"Athena's the only one who would make sense. This plan was her idea from the start. She and the Shade act like they are old friends, like they've been involved with each other for a long time already, before tonight."

He jumped to his feet and paced away from her, toward the living room, shaking his head. "No. It couldn't be. She wouldn't. She's a good person." He stopped as if frozen, staring blankly out the window.

She went to him and rested her hands on his shoulders. "I don't want to believe it either. I like your sister. I agree, she's a good person. But I have been worried about the path she's led us all down."

He shook his head. "She's always been the stable one. The smart one."

"Smart. Caring. Those attributes don't mean a person can't be tricked. You saw how he controlled Henry. Sure he was asleep, but he could have entered Athena's dreams. Bespelled her somehow. Insinuated himself into her life. He's a powerful sorcerer's shade."

Devlin thumped a fist against his leg. "I can't believe it. Not Athena."

"The orb told me to warn you, about danger, not her. It said to protect the Circle. It knows something."

He spun to face her, jaw clenched. "We don't even know who the orb is. Maybe it's in league with Merlin's Shade, trying to turn us against her."

Chloe held up her hand, palm flat as if to fend off his anger. "Athena found the crystal, something historians and archeologists didn't even know existed. Who told her about it? Who helped her find it—and don't say Jessica and Chandler. They're smart, but Athena was in charge on that trip to Wales."

He closed his eyes. A vein pulsed in his tightly corded neck. "I've been worried about Athena since before that trip. She hasn't been herself since early last winter. I—I thought she'd gotten too obsessed with awakening Merlin. I hoped—honestly, I thought we'd fail. Then we could look for different ways to discover cures and she'd relax, go back to her old self."

Chloe stroked her hand down Devlin's arm, moving in closer until her chest rested against his. She looked up. "We'll figure out what's going on with her. We'll break the spell or whatever hold he has over her. But first, we need to find a way to put the Shade back where he belongs."

Devlin smiled down at her, his fingers cupping her chin. "You're amazing, Chloe Winslow."

"More like I'm terrified." She wanted to get lost in his eyes, to let the warmth of his touch turn into a kiss, but she needed to keep her head. She stepped back. "I have to tell you something else, about how the Shade transformed himself. Then we'll have to gather all the help we can, but I'm not sure who we can trust. There's Keshari—" She slapped her hands over her mouth as her mind flashed back to the scene at the ritual, to the energy ball Athena flung at Keshari. Keshari crumpling to the ground. The last thing she remembered before the pain from the cut on her wrist stole her senses was Keshari hooking her arms around Matt's neck as he carried her off—"Dear Goddess, I need to make sure she's okay. I feel so horrible about her getting hurt."

Devlin rested a reassuring hand on her shoulder. "Matt said she's going to be fine." He blew out a breath. "I wish she'd never shown up there. I feel bad that she got caught in the middle."

A sick feeling crept up Chloe's throat. She had to confess. "I'm the one who told her what we were doing. Jessica was right about that."

Surprise flickered in his eyes, but his tone was quiet. "Don't be too hard on yourself. She's the one who decided to come. Right?"

"I suppose. I'm still going to check and see how she's doing." Chloe headed back into the bathroom to get her phone out of her messenger bag. Keshari had probably already left a message for her.

Fear tangled with her confidence when she discovered she was wrong. No texts. No missed calls. No messages of any kind. She glanced at the time: seven forty-five. Almost eight hours since she'd last seen Keshari.

She typed a quick message.

Hey. I feel bad about last night. How are you doing?

"She's probably sleeping off the effects of the magic," Devlin said. "She was pretty dazed."

"I don't know. I have a bad feeling about this." Chloe double-checked her messages, though she knew full well that she wouldn't see anything new. "Did Matt specifically say she got home all right?"

A worried look passed over his face. "No, but I trust Matt." He scrubbed his hands over his head. "Matt was supposed to watch the perimeter while we did the spell, though. He could have left her in his truck to rest—"

Chloe waved him into silence. "Can we just stop speculating for a minute? There are enough bad vibes floating around as is." She set her phone on the edge of the sink, then held her arm out to him. "Can you undo my bracelet? I've got an idea."

"What are you thinking?" he asked, undoing the clasp.

"I'm going to use my pendulum to locate Keshari. If she's home, then we'll wait for her to get back to us. If she's not, then at least we'll know where she is." She took the bracelet from him and pointed out the crystal charm. "It's tiny, but it's never let me down. All I need is it and an aerial map of the city. I can get that on my phone. It'll work. I'm sure of it."

Devlin started toward the living room. "I've got a better idea. Let's use my laptop. Bigger map, better resolution."

While she settled down on the couch, he put the laptop on the coffee table, brought up an aerial map. "How's that?"

"Great." She pushed the laptop's screen as flat as it could go, then she held the bracelet so a length of chain and the crystal dangled freely. "Once I locate the general area where she is, I'll need you to enlarge the map. Don't worry about my concentration, just keep enlarging it every time the crystal stops swinging and starts to circle."

Breathing deep, Chloe cleared her mind and brought up an image of Keshari. Two more breaths and she reached into her core where the new level of power had awakened. She drew it upward, letting it surge hot and fast, then flow down her arms, through her fingers, and into the bracelet and crystal. "Show me where Keshari is," she murmured. "Guide me to her."

As the crystal began to swing, she moved it over the laptop screen, fanning from the city's old North End—where Keshari lived with her parents—toward the complex, Oakledge Park, and the Earth Clock.

When she reached the park, the crystal began circling. Devlin enlarged the image, tree tops and the stones of the Earth Clock now visible. Chloe swore under her breath. Keshari hadn't made it home.

She closed her eyes, focusing all her energy. "Show me."

Beneath her fingers, the tug of the crystal swung in a tightening circle. Then it pulled downward, until the point of the crystal touched the screen.

"Got it," Devlin said, bringing her back to her senses. "Come on. Hurry. We'll take the path. She's closer to the Earth Clock than the parking lot."

Chloe threw on her sweater and he grabbed his jacket.

Outside the front door, they found Henry waiting, looking a bit cowed. Devlin snapped a leash on his collar. "I'm not leaving him here with Merlin—that fucking shade around."

"I don't blame you," Chloe said. "I'm worried about Chandler's son, too."

"So am I." He took a firmer grip on the leash. "I'd also like to know why you're worried about the Shade's new appearance."

As they jogged through the gate and down the deserted bike path, Chloe gathered her nerve and told him about the leather bracelet: how Athena had presented it to him in a box, how when he put it on the air around him had rippled violently with energy, obscuring him as he transformed. Her voice trembled as she explained that the Shade now looked exactly like a goth she'd met at a nearby bus stop, the same vivid blue eyes, the same voice. She skirted around the worst of the story, but finally couldn't hold off any longer.

"I'm sorry, Devlin. The Shade said he orchestrated the goth's death—" Her voice caught in her throat. "But Athena did it." She couldn't bring herself to mention the skinning.

Devlin kept walking, his gaze straight ahead, his fingers fisted around Henry's leash. His face had gone as white as a candle at dusk on the winter solstice, at the start of the darkest night of the year.

"I can't believe that," he said. But his bleak tone told her he did believe.

* * * *

When they reached the Earth Clock, Chloe was glad Devlin had a few minutes to recover from the shock, not that anyone could ever get over hearing his sister most likely had committed a murder and used black magic to create an object like the bracelet. But he at least seemed to be trying to hold it together—which was doubly good because they weren't alone. A couple was wandering around the circle of stones, tourists judging by how they were photographing everything.

"We need to focus on finding Keshari," Devlin whispered. It sounded like he was saying it as much for his benefit as hers. "We don't need someone else spotting her first and calling the police."

They walked fast past the tourists and into the Earth Clock, the shortest way to the line of trees and an overgrown area where the pendulum had indicated Keshari would be. As they passed through the middle of the clock, a chill raised the hairs on the back of Chloe's neck. Even if the goth was still on her mind and she hadn't spotted the dribbles of candlewax and the stain of her blood on the leaves, the shadow of magic in the air once again drove home how real the danger was. Thanks to her, a powerful, murderous shade now walked the world and her friend lay here somewhere, dazed and alone.

"Keshari! Keshari!" she shouted as if she were searching for a lost dog. Henry turned to look at her, concerned.

Devlin jutted his chin to where weeds and piles of windswept leaves gathered against a tall fence that separated the park property from an old industrial site. "Cross your fingers she's on this side," he whispered.

A sick feeling churned in Chloe's stomach. She took off her bracelet, allowing the pendulum to dangle. "Show me where Keshari is."

Straight and true, the pendulum pointed ahead of her, in the direction they were going. But when they got there, there was only a thicket of bright purple asters, goldenrod, and fallen leaves, nothing even vaguely human shaped.

Chloe's gaze went to the fence, tears of frustration welling. "He must have thrown her over." Worry clogged her throat. "Dear Goddess, she can't be dead."

Henry whined, tugging on his leash.

"What is it, boy?" Devlin glanced back as if checking to see if the tourists had left, then he let go of his leash. "Find her."

Tail flagging, Henry plunged into the weeds and started barking. Chloe ran to him and dropped to the ground, shoving leaves aside, not caring about the dirt and bits of leaves sticking under her fingernails. Devlin joined her, digging furiously.

Something glinted with in the bed of leaves. Keshari's keyring and bell-studded wand.

Chloe sat back on her heels, scanning the ground ahead of them. Keshari had to be right here.

A yard away, patchwork squares of pink and orange all but blended in with the bright autumn leaves and weeds. Keshari's jacket, camouflaging her body, curled up in a fetal position.

Chloe scrambled over to her. "Keshari! Keshari, are you okay?"

"Is she alive?" Devlin asked hesitantly.

"I don't know." She pressed her fingers against Keshari's throat. She was warm. There was a pulse. "Keshari, can you hear me?"

Keshari moaned. Her eyes flickered open, dark and unfocused.

Chapter 24

The magic burst from the small stone,
shooting upward like a butterfly taking flight,
casting off smaller magics as it took wing.
It was entrancing, a new shade of power,
a prismatic hint of the possibilities he offered.
—Reflections by Rhianna Davies

The gray-bearded tourist dogged Chloe and Devlin as they half-carried Keshari down the bike path. "I'm calling 911," he announced.

"You don't need to," Chloe said. "She just had too much to drink. That's all." Sweat drizzled down her temple, plastering her hair to her cheek. The man was probably right. Keshari didn't look good at all.

The tourist turned to his wife. "Don't you think she needs an ambulance?"

"No." Devlin shot a glare at them. "I'm going to get my car and take her home. She just needs to sleep it off."

Chloe readjusted her grip on Keshari, her feet now scuffing the ground as she attempted to walk instead of simply being dragged along.

Keshari raised her head. "I be all right. Just sick," she slurred.

"Hmpf. I doubt that." The man took his wife by the arm and stormed away. But when Chloe glanced back, they were huddled together and the man had his phone out.

"Keshari," she said, "We need your help. Can you try a little harder to walk on your own?"

"Hell with this." Devlin picked Keshari up in his arms and strode down the bike path toward the park's entrance.

Chloe grabbed Henry's leash and jogged ahead to make sure the coast was clear. It was early Sunday morning, so chances were the park employees hadn't arrived yet. But if anyone were around it might be Matt, and that wouldn't be good at all.

She glanced skyward and said a grateful prayer when they found the entrance area deserted, except for a couple boys on bikes, and a single car in the parking lot that most likely belonged to the tourists.

Devlin lowered Keshari onto a curbside bench. "Can you sit up?"

She nodded as if she could, but Chloe quickly sat down and put an arm around Keshari to give her a shoulder to lean against. "Hurry back," she said to Devlin.

"Don't worry. It'll take me maybe ten minutes at the most."

As he and Henry sprinted down the road, Chloe's mouth dried. Not worrying wasn't going to happen. She glanced back toward the Earth Clock. She couldn't see the tourists, but she was certain they'd called 911. Even if they hadn't, most likely they'd walk back this way to get to their car. Keshari was more alert than a few minutes ago, but not enough to convince them that she was fine. If an ambulance showed up, no rescue worker in their right mind would blow Keshari's state off as normal.

Her mouth went dry. Rescue workers. *Shit.* What if the Rescue Twins were on duty? Dear Goddess, no. Anyone but them.

Keshari snuggled closer and mumbled, "Can't go home. Dad kill me."

"Don't worry. Devlin will take us to my apartment." Chloe located Keshari's phone in her jacket pocket and fished it out. "I'll text your mom and tell her you fell asleep at my place last night studying."

Keshari nodded, then slumped down until her head was on Chloe's lap.

Despite her shaking hands, she typed the text in record time. She'd just sent it when the crunch of car tires came from nearby. It was too soon to be Devlin.

She glanced up and almost died.

A police cruiser.

She ducked her head and nudged Keshari. "Wake up. Cop."

Keshari shifted upright, swaying as if her head were too heavy for her neck. Chloe cringed. There was no way to make her appear simply tired or a tiny bit drunk. There was no getting out of this.

The cruiser pulled up to the curb, right in front of the bench. A lone male officer got out and swaggered around the car to them, one beefy hand resting on his holstered gun. Why did he have to be patrolling here? Why couldn't he have been doing something else, like been off somewhere discovering the goth's body? Except, that would be worse for the coven. Much worse than this.

"Nice morning," Chloe said. Her smile strained her cheeks and she was certain it looked as forced as it felt.

"You ladies have IDs?" His gaze scanned Keshari, then swung her way.

"Ah, sure." Chloe fumbled in her pocket. "We're waiting for a ride." She gave him her Connecticut driver's license and college ID. Hopefully, he wouldn't ask them to get up. Keshari could barely stand, let alone walk a straight line or count backwards.

The officer studied Chloe's IDs and handed them back. He nodded at Keshari. "Does she have an ID?"

"Oh." Chloe dug into Keshari's pocket, produced her ID, and handed it over.

"What are you doing here this time of morning?" He handed the IDs back to Chloe, then pulled a Maglite out and shone its light at Keshari's eyes. "What's she on? You can tell me the truth."

"Ah—" Yeah, that wasn't going to happen. "She was at a party last night. I don't know what she took. She's okay, really. My boyfriend's going to be here any minute." She wanted to do something with her hands, to wipe them down her jeans or rake them through her hair. She picked at the corner of her license, then forced them to go still.

"Do you mind turning your pockets out for me?"

"No problem." Chloe did as he asked, nothing other than her phone and keys. Relief stole some of her tension as Keshari began rooting in her own. Thank goodness she was coming out of it, and just in time. But what if she pulled out something weird by mistake?

Keshari stopped and gaped at the officer. "My keyring," she slurred. "It's missing. I dropped it—" She stopped, rubbing her lips as if thinking. "Someone—stole it."

Chloe thought back. She'd seen it in the leaves, the bell-wand and homemade atomizer. Not something they needed the officer looking for, especially with the bloodstain in the circle. "Devlin has it," she blurted, though she wasn't positive.

A flash of an orange car appeared down the road. Chloe jumped up from the bench. One eye on Keshari to make sure she stayed put, she waved at the car. "That's him, my boyfriend," she said to the officer.

Devlin swung the car up to the curb and leapt out, opening the passenger door before he even strode over. "Good morning, officer. Thank you. I was worried about leaving them alone." He frowned at Keshari. "Like it or not, we're going to Urgent Care."

"That's a good idea," the officer said.

Devlin swooped his arm around Keshari, hoisting her to her feet. "I was so pissed when they called me about this. Thank you again, officer. Don't worry, you won't be seeing her like this again." Half-carrying her, he headed for the car.

Chloe lowered her gaze, trying to fade into the background as she followed.

"Not so fast," the officer's voice rumbled. But as Devlin loaded Keshari into the passenger seat, his tone changed, and he switched to making alternate suggestions about where to take her, as if he'd realized someone else was saving him work and potentially from having vomit in his squad car.

Still, Chloe didn't let out a relieved breath until she, Keshari, and Devlin were out of there, across town, and inside the apartment house. She was equally grateful when the Rescue Twins didn't come out while they were crossing the foyer or dragging Keshari up the stairs.

She unlocked her door and was about to let Devlin and Keshari go in first, when Greta's apartment door flung open. She stomped out into the hallway, hands on her hips. "Do I need to ask about the front door?"

Chloe swiveled toward her. "Don't worry, we shut it." The whole conversation sounded ludicrous, considering Keshari was currently sinking toward the floor, despite Devlin's efforts to keep her upright.

"And locked it?" Greta's asked. Her gaze winged to Keshari, like she'd just noticed her. "I don't even want to know about that."

"She's fine. Just drunk." Chloe nudged her door open wider with her foot and Devlin propelled Keshari inside.

"For all I care, you can drain her blood and drink it. But no candles or chanting." Greta folded her arms across her chest and glared darkly. "It's enough that I've got to put up with Juliet's yowling cats."

"Promise, as quiet as mice." Chloe pasted on a smile, backed into her apartment, and slammed her door without waiting for Greta to retreat.

While Devlin helped Keshari lay down on the couch, Chloe beelined for the kitchen and poured a glass of water. "First, we need to get her comfortable and hydrated."

He slid a pillow under Keshari's head, then took the glass and held it while she took a sip. His gentleness struck Chloe and her heart tightened thinking about the emotional turmoil he had to be in, but the phantom sensation of the knife against her wrist sent a chill down her spine. *Trust him*, her heart murmured. *Don't let the sorrow and glitter blind you to the darkness behind your back*, a ping of uneasiness whispered.

Devlin set the glass on the coffee table, then took Keshari's keyring from his pocket and tucked it into her jacket. "I wish I had a gift for healing. Unfortunately, the Shade's right, mine's minimal at best."

Chloe frowned. That was bullshit. "When I left my body, I saw and felt you holding my wrist. It was your magic that stopped the bleeding. So what if you didn't do a perfect job? If it weren't for you, my spirit wouldn't have had a living body to return to."

He shrugged halfheartedly. "Water is my element. It's liquid. Blood's liquid. That didn't have much to do with real healing."

"So you did what—pretended my blood was a river and you were plugging a hole in a dam?" Despite how serious the situation was right now with Keshari and everything, she couldn't help but roll her eyes. It was ridiculous.

"Something like that." He grinned. But the brief break in the tension faded as all the water she'd given Keshari dribbled back out her mouth and down her chin.

Chloe wiped the water off. "You all right?"

Keshari nodded. "Tired. Head spinning."

"Hang in there. We'll figure this out." Chloe glanced at Devlin, telegraphing her worry. "If we had Merlin's crystal, maybe the two of us could do something. It worked on my wrist. When you were away, we used it to heal Em's spirit too."

His eyes brightened. "We could make a staff crystal. Midas and I checked it out the other night. It's essentially nothing more than an amplified generator crystal. All we'd need to do is recreate it."

Chloe laughed. "Is that all?"

"Chloe?" Keshari's weak voice stole her attention.

She crouched, brushing the hair back from Keshari's heated face. "What is it?"

"Mandala. Blessings. Prayers."

Adrenaline shot into Chloe's veins. "You're talking about the mandala sand, right?"

"Shaman use it. Many ways."

Chloe flew to her feet and retrieved the jar of mud-colored mandala sand from next to the other end of the couch. She showed it to Devlin. "This is what she's talking about."

"Sand is crystals. Infused with prayers and magic, it should work," he said.

"Plus," Chloe began as she went to her windowsill altar where she kept her favorite crystals, "I've got an idea of how we can ramp the sand's power up even more."

As she took off the jar's lid and added the smallest crystals in with the sand, the light sparked against them, casting rainbows across the room. She replaced the lid and gave the jar a good shake, mixing everything together. After that, she gathered the rest of the supplies they'd need. Apple twigs and sage for a smudge stick. A bowl of larger crystals for Devlin and Keshari to choose from.

Devlin opened a window. "We don't want your neighbor smelling anything."

"Good idea. It's kind of stuffy in here, too." She peeled off her sweater. Maybe the morning had been crisp, but the day was rapidly turning stifling. Another thought came to her.

"Can you wedge a chair against the door, too? Juliet has the master key. We don't need her walking in."

He did as she asked, then together they helped Keshari to the middle of the floor. Once she was lying comfortably, they cast a circle around her using the Tears of Tara to ensure that the Shade and Athena wouldn't sense they were working magic.

"Hold your crystal in two hands." Chloe placed the stone Keshari had picked out at the base of her rib cage.

"On the third chakra," Keshari murmured, closing her eyes.

Chloe and Devlin knelt on opposite sides of Keshari. Chloe took a deep breath and another, bringing up her magic. The other night when they'd healed Em, she hadn't understood the words Athena had chanted. But she knew their sound, a vibration in her ear like a choir of voices. She brought up that memory, letting the incantation flow off her tongue, old magic, the kind the Shade and Merlin knew. Devlin joined in, their voices echoing off the walls.

Blocking out every thought of failure, Chloe held the jar out in front of her. Devlin did the same with the crystal he'd chosen. Even as the power of the magic engulfed her, Chloe could sense Devlin following her lead. She thrust the jar out even farther and the energy from his crystal was there to connect with the jar's contents. The magic roared between them, a humming current spinning faster and faster. Her head swam from the crackle of its power. She breathed deep, pushing even more magic into the jar.

The power screamed in the room, then shattered into swirling colors. Without warning, the colors rejoined and transformed into something Chloe hadn't seen the other night: a whirling mandala, a shimmering temple, and layers upon layers of prayers to Gods and Goddesses etched into every grain of sand. The mandala blurred, colors blending and shifting until the circling rainbow returned.

Chloe pulled the jar away from Devlin's crystal, the rainbow still circling over Keshari even as she lowered the jar to the floor. She looked skyward. "Air. Fire. Water. Earth," she intoned. "I call on you. Gods. Goddesses. Gatekeepers. Take the wound from our sister. Release her from the spell's magic. Free her. Restore her. Bless her."

In an explosion of colors, the racing energy shifted direction, streaming down toward the crystal Keshari was holding and into her. An instant later, the energy reversed direction, gray colors rising out of her and fogging the room.

Chloe jumped up, seized the smudge stick, and lit it. Even with the open window, there was no way Greta wasn't going to smell something, but tough luck for her.

"Turn on the vent over the stove," she shouted to Devlin.

Waving the smudge stick, Chloe chased the fog out the open window. When all of it was finally gone, she let out her breath and turned back.

Devlin was helping Keshari to sit up.

"How do you feel?" Chloe asked.

Keshari pressed her hand against her chest and blinked. "I am not sure. Exhausted. Drained." Her eyes widened and brightened. "Clean. Clear-headed. I can hardly believe it. I feel well. Oh, so many blessings to both of you. So many blessings."

"Frankly, I'm surprised too," Devlin said. He glanced at Chloe. "Your magic felt different. Stronger, even without the jar."

"Ah—Well, something happened to me at the awakening, not just to Merlin." Since she hadn't really tested out her theory, she drew up a burst of energy and flung it from her fingertips at the tray of votive candles on top of her dresser. The candles flared to life, all ten of them lighting without effort. She curled her fingers toward her body, gesturing sharply. Without a word, they flickered out.

"Nice," Devlin said. His voice deepened. "I'd rather stay here, but I have to get going. It's too warm to leave Henry in the car much longer. Also, someone needs to watch over Athena and the coven until we find a way to put the Shade back where he belongs."

Keshari's eyes bulged. "Shade? I feared something dark might happen. That is why I went to the ritual: '*Friends look out for friends.*'" Her hand went to her mouth smothering a gasp. "Oh, no. Merlin's father was a—"

"A demon." Chloe finished, then she told Keshari the rest of the story, stopping when she caught herself launching into her thoughts on the length and extent of Athena and the Shade's relationship, not to mention the goth and the leather bracelet. It would be easier to keep everything emotionally on an even keel if those subjects were left untouched for now.

"Ahem." Devlin cleared his throat. "There is something else you both should do." He grimaced apologetically at Chloe. "Remember the hangover cure I gave you?"

"The honey and liverwurst stuff. What about it?"

"Um, you should make some. Have it on hand in case—" He licked his lips. "I'll tell you how to make it."

Her emotions tumbled into a confused free fall: fear, anger, trust, love, sympathy, all spinning together into a messy whirlpool. Whatever this was about, it didn't sound good. "First tell me why."

His chest rose as he took a deep breath. "You need it to counteract the Circle's magic. Its buzz is over-the-top, not natural. I've been taking the cure as a preventative, for a while now."

Keshari glared. "And you did not tell Chloe about it?"

"Chloe, you have to believe me." His eyes met hers, their dark depths full of remorse. "I confronted Athena about the buzz. She convinced me the magic's enhanced strength would help you and the other initiates relax. But I gave you the cure anyway, to help with the hangover and to protect you." His hands fell to his sides as if surrendering to his guilt. "I also suspected that someone had messed with the sake and tea. I thought that was solely Jessica's doing, until that night at the quarry when Jess claimed Athena had put her up to it. But I swear Athena wouldn't intentionally harm anyone—not even if someone seduced her into doing it."

"Devlin, I do not wish to say anything against your family," Keshari said. "You have been a blessing to me. But these are not things a high priestess does to build up a coven. These are things that are used to destroy one."

The cords in Devlin's neck tightened, taut as if he were holding back a scream. A bead of sweat glistened on his temple.

Chloe jumped in, her voice straining. "Keshari, please. We need to focus on what we can change, not things we can only guess at." Keshari was right to be angry, especially after what happened to her last night. But she didn't know anything about Devlin's relationship with and devotion to his sister. Chloe suspected she didn't even know the half of it herself. But in truth, the extent of his loyalty cast a shadow of doubt deep inside her. Still, her intuition said she could trust him on this. She rested her hand on Devlin's arm. "Once we make this preventative-cure, should we take it right away?"

"No, wait until the last minute. It'll dull the rush from the power. It's a sure bet the buzz from the Shade's energy is even stronger, capable of lulling even a powerful witch into submission before she can even sense it."

She knew who he meant by *a powerful witch*. Athena. And maybe he was right, but there was also the possibility that she'd become involved with the Shade of her own volition. Both Athena and Devlin had told her their childhoods hadn't been the easiest.

While Devlin told her and Keshari how to make the cure, Chloe jotted down notes in her Book of Shadows. It was a simple recipe and spell. But simple roots often gave rise to the most powerful potions.

When he was done, he touched her cheek. "I really have to go. Don't text me or call—or use any sort of magic link. I don't want to give them an excuse to not trust me."

Chloe pressed her fingers over his heart. She wanted to tell him not to leave. But she knew if she held him back, he'd never be able to live with himself. "Be careful. Midas is probably on our side, and maybe Em. But I don't know about anyone else. Maybe just trust yourself."

He smiled. "Are you forgetting about Henry? Even biscuits can't buy him, especially after what the Shade did."

She laughed. Keshari joined in weakly. But the energy in the room rang with their joined fear and the shadow of doubt about Devlin's loyalty burned inside Chloe as if it were made of smoldering embers. But it was not just where his loyalty lay that made her afraid.

"Ah—What about me? I mean, the Shade's going to notice I'm not around. Do you think"—she swallowed around a lump in her throat—"do you think he'll come looking for me?"

Keshari let out a sharp exhale. "I did not think of that. Your blood woke him. He healed your wrist. In his mind, you two are bound—"

Devlin raised a hand to stop her. "I'll make excuses for you. Keep his mind elsewhere. Later, I'll find a way to come back. Meanwhile you need to make that cure as fast as possible." He squeezed both of Chloe's shoulders. "If I can't get away, I'll send you a direct message on Facebook. If someone takes my phone, they're less likely to look there."

Chloe stepped closer and placed her hands on his chest, raising her face to him. He lowered his head and pressed a tender kiss on her lips. She gripped his head gently, pulling him closer, tilting her head and deepening the kiss. A sense of urgency surged inside her. Devlin responded, matching his desperation to hers. A desperate kiss, one that could quite possibly be their last.

Chapter 25

Lightly pack a pint jar with fresh rosemary tips.
Fill to the top with unrefined coconut oil.
Seal and set in the sun for two weeks.
Strain and add four drops of rose or lavender essential oil.
—Rosemary Hair Oil, Chloe Winslow's Book of Shadows

"I'm with Devlin on that point." Chloe paused for a second to light the burner under her chafing dish, also known as the best substitute for a cauldron ever. "Why would Athena want to destroy the Northern Circle? She's worked for years to rejuvenate it." She stared at the burner's flames, thinking back to what she'd learned this morning. "The Shade's fully capable of controlling people and animals, some more easily than others. But I don't think that's what is going on in Athena's case. There's nothing zombie-like about her."

Keshari shrugged. "Why else would she want to wake up the dark half of Merlin and not his entire being?" Her nose twitched. She bent over the chafing dish. Fanning the air with her hand, she sniffed the chunky slurry. "That is the most disgusting cure I've ever smelled."

"Wait until you taste it. That's even worse. Still, it's better than the alternative." Chloe dropped a handful of marjoram leaves into the dish and stirred it with her athame. She sighed heavily. "I'm not saying you're wrong about Athena's goal. It's just counterintuitive to everything I believed about her."

"You can't even guess why she might do such a thing?"

"No, not in the least." Now that Devlin was gone, she couldn't lie. "But I'm not convinced Devlin isn't still a little blind when it comes to her. They've always been super close." A hollow sensation spread in her chest, a mixture of guilt and downheartedness. If only her relationship with her sisters and brothers had remained as close as Devlin's and Athena's, close like she'd been with them before she messed up. "Do you think I'm making a mistake? I don't mean us creating this cure. I'm talking about not telling my family and the High Council about the Shade. He's beyond dangerous to everyone, not just us and the Circle."

Keshari remained silent for a long moment, pulling her hair over her shoulder and stroking it distractedly. "I don't know. I once watched my grandfather vanquish a demon that was possessing a woman. It was not easy, even for a skilled shaman like him. This Shade, he is a more complex being. He is not contained within a body or restrained in any way."

"But if I tell, they might think I'm making it up to get attention—at least at first. Either way, the High Council would send a special investigator."

In her head Chloe could see the chain of events that an investigation would lead to, one thing leading to another like a runway of orbs pointing at a standing stone. Devlin and the coven members would be shamed for bringing the Shade into this world. Her family would be too, just because of their connection to her. Just like with the Vice-Chancellor's son. Without a doubt, the Circle would end up disbanded. The Council would seize members' assets: mystical objects, books, even businesses and homes… Worst of all, since Devlin was the Circle's high priest, they might vote to have his ability to work magic permanently removed, and curse his genes so the restriction would last for generations.

Keshari nudged her with the jar of mandala sand and crystals. "Why don't you add some of this to the cure? It will make it more personal to us."

"That's a good idea," Chloe added a pinch, her fingers shaking from the worry in her mind. She set the jar down and folded her arms across her chest, rubbing the cold from her skin and thinking once again about her family. "The thing is," she said, "even if the Council or my parents and yours combined could get rid of Merlin's Shade, the Northern Circle is screwed. And the one thing I believe wholeheartedly is the orb's message. The Circle needs protecting. It needs to survive. I feel that in my soul."

Keshari pulled her into a hug. Resting her head against Chloe's, she whispered, "You are a good person, Chloe. The gods and goddesses speak to you, I think. I also believe you should follow what feels right"—she released Chloe and looked her in the eyes—"and you do not walk this path alone. I am with you. This is the right thing to do."

Keshari's words only deepened Chloe's fear. Keshari was a true friend. But she wasn't sure she was someone anyone should follow. Her parents were right; she jumped into things too fast and didn't use good judgement. She'd brought heartache and disgrace to people she cared about. Now she'd been involved with bringing a shade into this world. Still...

The new level of power inside her pulsed, a strong, confident beat. She drew a long breath, exploring the feeling. Maybe her parents were right about her. Maybe she hadn't been the sort of person friends like Keshari should follow—and the way she'd failed to protect Keshari last night certainly proved that. But perhaps it was time she became the person Keshari believed she was, even if she had to fake it for a while.

She pushed her shoulders back. "Well, then, witch-sister, once we're done with this, what do you think our next step should be?"

"I am glad you asked, sister." Keshari grinned, a secret twinkling in her eyes. "We aren't the only ones who the Shade's escape would have angered. There is the Lady who imprisoned Merlin to start with."

"Oh my Goddess. You mean, Nimue, the Lady of the Lake, right?" Of course, that was it. Except—"I've never heard of Nimue being seen outside Great Britain or France. Then again, the Shade came through one of the Earth Clock stones."

"Nimue has many sister lake spirits, like Gemu in Tibet. A beautiful lake like Champlain must have its own native spirits. Even if our entreaty doesn't draw Nimue, another Lady might help."

A burbling sound came from the chafing dish, signaling the cure was done. As Chloe stirred it one last time, the grains of sand speckling the thick liquid gave her an idea. "We're planning on pouring the mandala sand into the lake, so it can carry the blessings back to the ocean. Do you think the sand has enough power to draw a Lady's attention, especially if we offer it near the Earth Clock?"

"Very much so." Keshari shuddered. "I don't like the thought of going back to that place."

"I'm not really wild about it myself. There's another issue, too. After we left, the tourists probably told the cop we were messing around near the Clock. If he spots us there again, he's not going to overlook it, especially if the tourists showed him the blood and candlewax. But"—she lifted her eyebrows, pleased with her next idea—"I could lend you some different clothes. I have the perfect hooded sweater. It might be a little too warm and you'd have to roll up the sleeves. But it's camouflage green and should fit. You'd look totally different."

"That's a good idea." Keshari's chin dipped. "But clothes won't help that much. He saw my ID. He might have even asked around the community about me and my family."

Chloe slung an arm around Keshari, leading her to the dresser. "We'll have to be extra careful, then. I hate to wait. But, honestly, I'm bone tired. How about if we rest up, maybe do some research, then go to the lake just before dark?"

"I didn't want to say anything, but I am exhausted. We could take turns napping. I do not think Devlin would be able to dissuade the Shade if he took it in his head to find you."

"Unfortunately, I agree," Chloe added, fear settling deep in her chest.

* * * *

While Keshari got changed and took a nap, Chloe used the Tears of Tara to create fresh protection wards. If the Shade showed up, the salt wouldn't hold him off for long. But it would help.

Once that was done, she funneled the preventative-cure into ampules that she normally put her homemade hair oil treatments in. She ended up with six for her and an equal number for Keshari. She'd just finished setting out some folklore books they could use for research when Keshari got up from the bed.

She stretched and yawned. "That helped a lot."

"You couldn't have slept for very long."

"Mostly I meditated. Truly, I feel much better."

Chloe shook her head. "I'm not sure I could sleep. I'm so overtired, I feel wired."

"You should at least try." Keshari nudged her toward the bed. "Even if all you do is close your eyes."

Chloe curled up on top of the blankets, her cheek against the warm pillow. She closed her eyes as instructed and listened to the pad of Keshari's feet as she sat down on the couch, then the rustle of Keshari opening one of the research books and turning pages. Chloe stretched out, careful not to lay on her newly healed wrist. It was amazing how good it felt, even the stiffness was almost gone. She took a deep breath, and another. The rustle of turning pages faded as she fell asleep and slipped into a dream.

The Shade's voice whispers in her ear: "I heard your voice with the others. Your blood roused me."

She lies in a hospital room, curled up in a bed. She's naked. Devlin is spooning her, his chest against her spine, one arm holding her close. The rhythm of his breath warms the nape of her neck. He's deep asleep. But she's wide awake, the fast pounding of her heart bordering on panic.

White curtains circle the bed. She's certain the boy lays beyond them. But the fear pulsing inside her drives her to lift Devlin's arm, to slip out from under its warmth and from the bed to see if she is right. The floor is smooth and cold against her bare feet. She steps toward the curtain. She doesn't want to open it, but her fingers close on the rough fabric. She slides it aside. The walls of the room beyond are white. The floor is as black as unleavened bread, as shiny as unfermented juice. Lifeless foods.

In the center of the room, the boy lies in a bed identical to the one she just left. Silent tubes run into him and out. Oxygen. Blood. Drugs. Beside the bed, silent machines stand sentinel. But the boy is not dead. He's waiting. For her. To help him.

She realizes her fingers are closed around something small and cold. An ampule.

The cure.

The right cure.

She steps toward the boy. But something draws her to glance back toward the bed she left. Devlin lies there, tubes now run into him and out. Silent machines stand sentinel on either side.

Tick. Tick. Tick. The machines are all ticking now like clocks. Like time running out. Beep. Beeping a warning now. She has one ampule. She has one. Only one.

She looks back at the boy. The Shade stands between her and his bed, long black hair, pale face, blood-red vest. She pivots to glance at Devlin. The Shade stands there too, between her and him.

The room goes dark, except for the flicker of a circle of candles around her and the Shade. He's only an arm's length in front of her now. In a flash, his blue eyes go dark, as black as the water in the quarry. He steps forward, tilts his head, and leans in as if to kiss her. He stops, his moist breath touching hers.

She wants to flee. She wants to run. But her legs can't move. She has the red dress on. It cinches her thighs. Imprisons her.

The Shade seizes her wrist. A knife appears in his grip, Jessica's knife. Pain rips up her arm as he slices her forearm, peeling back a strip of skin. There is no blood. Just pain and the sight of her naked flesh. He slices again, but this time it's not a strip. Her arm has become a book, each slice creating a new page. A Book of Shadows. Her Book.

He wets his finger in an open wound and turns a page, devouring her with his eyes. Spittle glistens at the corners of his mouth. He smiles up at her and whispers, "Let me heal the boy. You know I can do it. Let me finish this chapter for you."

Something pokes her leg, as sharp as a thorn. Her gaze darts from the Shade to the floor. Dozens of metal monkeys surround her, dancing in the candlelight, their sheet metal wings gleaming, their knife-blade fingers coming closer and closer, darting out to slice her legs.

A scream comes from her mouth—

In the back of Chloe's head, it registered. The scream hadn't come from her. Keshari.

She snapped awake.

Keshari shoved something into her hand, an ampule. "Drink it. Quick!"

"What's going on?" Chloe vaulted from the bed, popped the ampule open, and downed it in one gulp.

"It was awful. A monke—" Her eyes bulged. She gestured wildly at something behind Chloe. "It's back!"

Chloe pivoted. One of Chandler's flying monkeys crouched on the ledge outside her windows, its nut and bolt eyes and sheet metal wings now animated as if alive. She flung her hands over her mouth, holding back a scream of terror. It couldn't be. She had to still be dreaming.

The monkey latched ahold of the window screen, ripped it off, and flung it aside. With a shriek of delight, it raked its knife-blade fingers down the windowpane. A squeal rang out, like a bow scraping across a hideously out of tune violin.

No, this wasn't a dream. This was real. Horribly real.

Chloe's gaze streaked to something else. The window next to the one the monkey was perched on was open.

"Shit!" She leapt to her feet and dashed for the open window. The monkey met her there, only a thin mesh of screen separating them before she slammed the window shut.

The monkey hissed at her, canines showing. She glared back, magic simmering inside her, begging to be let out. She squeezed her hands tight, resisting the urge to blast him with an energy-ball. No way was he going to tease her into doing that. One shot and not only would the window break, but the wards would be damaged as well. For a brainless creature, the monkey was far too clever.

The monkey stopped moving and cocked his head as if listening. A second later, a low bee-like buzz came from somewhere beyond the window. Chloe might have thought there was a drone flying over the house, if it weren't for a sense of foreboding in the air. This was exactly how she'd felt the night Devlin delivered the invitation, like someone powerful was thinking about her, only this time it definitely wasn't him. The Shade.

Bang! The noise reverberated up from downstairs, and the monkey took off, vanishing around the side of the building.

"I do not like this," Keshari said.

"Me neither." Chloe grabbed the remaining ampules off the bedside stand, handed half to Keshari, and stashed the rest in her jeans pocket. "I doubt one is going to do the trick, but we need to try to make them last."

"Yes. Good idea."

The bee-like buzz grew sharp, keening almost, vibrating inside the building. Its intensity increased, getting louder and louder as if a swarm of bees were flooding up the stairs and into the hallway outside her door.

Then everything went silent. Dead silent.

A long second passed. Then someone knocked on her door. Once. Twice. A moment later, the Shade's voice said, "We know you're in there."

Chloe swallowed hard. They had to do something. The wards wouldn't keep the Shade out of the apartment for long, not if he took it in his head to get through them.

A door slammed down the hallway, followed by Greta's piercing voice. "I don't know how the hell the two of you got in here or what's going on with the freaky noises. But if you're not out of here in ten seconds, I'm calling the cops—"

The Shade murmured something, too quiet to hear.

"Oh, I'd like to see that." A familiar voice said. Jessica.

Chloe charged toward the door. She had to put a stop to this.

Keshari dove in front of her, blocking her way. "You're not going out there alone. Where's my wand and atomizer?"

"It's me he's after. You have to stay here. It's safer." Chloe moved to push Keshari out of the way, but stopped. *No.* What she needed to do for once was stop and think. To be the kind of witch and friend Keshari thought she was. Besides, she could use Keshari's help. "Devlin put your wand and atomizer back in your jacket."

"Great. There has to be a way out of this." Keshari stepped to one side, grabbed her jacket off the arm of the couch, and tossed it on.

Chloe scanned the room. The jar of sand. It could amplify her power, though the Shade's skills and strength would still far outweigh hers…She clenched her hands. No negative thoughts. She could do this. She had to.

She snagged the jar and tucked it into her hoodie's extra-large pocket. "We've taken Devlin's cure, so that will help. But we still don't stand a chance against him in a test of sheer magic. We're going to have to bluff our way out of this."

"Make him think we have more power than we do, yes?"

"Exactly. I'll strike hard and fast. When I say, *now*, I'll need you to channel as much energy as you can into the jar to give me a boost. If that doesn't drive him off, use your spray and run. But first, I'm going to try to talk our way out of this."

"Sounds good." Keshari gaze darted to the door. "Should we leave it open, in case we need to retreat?"

"Good idea. If we get separated, I'll meet you at the lake."

Eiowell! A cat's yowl pierced the air.

A shudder ran up Chloe's spine. She glanced at Keshari. "Time to get going."

Taking a deep breath, she flung the door open and stepped out with Keshari an inch behind.

The Shade stood in the middle of the hallway with Jessica. One of Juliet's cats was pinned under the tip of his staff, struggling to get free. Greta glared at him from a few yards away.

"We wouldn't want the wee puss to escape and get hit by a car, now would we?" the Shade said. His gaze lingered on Greta, then he slowly turned to face Chloe, a languid set of movements that made everything around him fall still for a moment. "Ah, there you are, lovely as ever."

Juliet flew out from her apartment. "What's going on?"

The Shade's eyes remained on Chloe, but he tucked the staff into the crook of his arm, bent down, and picked up the cat. "Such a pretty creature."

Sweat beaded along Chloe's upper lip, her pulse pounding hard. "Put the cat down."

"As you wish." An amused smile played on the Shade's lips as he gently handed the cat to Juliet. His voice deepened and took on a rhythmic cadence that reminded Chloe uncomfortably of Athena leading one of their nightly chants. "I have always wondered what it would be like to be a cat. Haven't you?"

Juliet beamed at him. "I can't imagine anything more wonderful."

Greta wrinkled her nose. "Litterboxes. Canned tuna. Sounds disgusting to me."

"I'm with you." Jessica grimaced.

The Shade gripped his staff in two hands and smiled at Juliet. "It's possible. More easily done than you might think."

"Really?" Her wide blue eyes took on a distant look. She smiled dazedly.

The bee-like vibration once again reverberated in the hallway, pitching higher and higher as the Shade stroked his hand down his staff.

"This is not good," Keshari whispered in Chloe's ear.

Chloe slipped her hand into her pocket. Fingers tightening around the jar, waiting for the right moment to pull her bluff.

Greta growled. "Enough with this creepy mumbo-jumbo. I want everyone out of here. Now!"

Without taking his eyes off Juliet, the Shade held up a hand to shush Greta. "Be quiet, wench."

Greta glared at him. "Don't give me orders. This is my home."

"Greta," Chloe said softly. "Go back into your apartment. Please. I'll take care of this."

"Fuck you," Greta snarled.

The Shade stepped closer to Juliet. "You would like her to be silent, wouldn't you?"

Juliet nodded. "Yes, please."

"No, Juliet." Chloe's voice rasped. "Don't encourage him."

The Shade spun on his heels and in a few swift strides he was nose-to-nose with Greta. He leaned against this staff, glanced leisurely over his shoulder at Chloe and smirked. "Some are simpler than others."

"Stop it!" Chloe shouted.

His free hand clamped Greta's face. Her eyes bulged, but she seemed unable to move. The Shade's magic screeched in the air, a whining hornet's nest of power. "Leave us," he crooned. "Fill your bathtub. Kneel in the water, then…"

The air went out of Chloe's lungs. Water. Silence. Drowning.

"*Now!*" she shouted to Keshari. She yanked the jar from her pocket. Taking a deep breath, she pulled up the full force of her magic and channeled it into the jar. Focusing again, she entwined that magic with Keshari's, and released it all at once.

A blinding flash of energy exploded outward from the jar, streaking toward the Shade. He let go of Greta, wheeled, and deflected the blast with his staff.

The energy splintered into razor-sharp pieces, then knifed around the hallway like a saw-toothed tornado. The floor shook. The air squealed. Lightbulbs shattered. Windows exploded. A side table flew around the hall and smashed against a wall. Debris sliced Jessica's face and arms, tossing her screaming to the floor. The cat streaked toward the staircase. Juliet and Keshari dropped down, hands over their heads as if an earthquake had hit. Chloe stumbled back against a wall, the jar tumbling from her shaking fingers.

"Stop!" the Shade bellowed.

The tornado of debris froze in place. Motionless pieces of lightbulb, splintered table, droplets of blood, shards of window glass, all hanging suspended in midair. Even the air itself was unmoving.

The Shade strode toward Chloe, cutting a path through the immobilized debris with furious sweeps of his staff. His gaze trapped hers.

She squared her shoulders and refused to look away. Then his power hit her, jackhammering against her forehead, screaming to be let in, an unrelenting force... She slammed her eyes shut, gritted her teeth and struggled to drive him back. Blood trickled from her nose and down onto her lips. Its coppery tang filled her mouth. Her heart, lungs, throat...every inch of her screamed from the very real the possibility of his magic breaking through her resistance and the cure's protection, of it reaching her brain.

She collapsed to her knees, her face and body slick with blood and sweat. Still his magic pummeled her skull. Flashes of darkness and light pulsed before her eyes. She gripped her head with her hands, the agony overwhelming. She couldn't hold out much longer—

The Shade's magic released her, quick as turning off a light switch.

All around her the room came back to life, bits of lightbulb, wood, glass...everything that had hung suspended in the air now rained down. Even droplets of blood splattered them all.

Jessica scuttled toward the staircase.

"We have to do something," Keshari said, her voice quaking.

Chloe's head throbbed. Her mind spun. She could barely think, let alone be rational.

The Shade strolled to where the jar of mandala sand had rolled. He nudged it with the end of his staff. "Blessed sand and crystals. Interesting." He smiled at Chloe. "I give you credit for an innovative bluff. With my guidance you could go far." He swept his hand, indicating the destruction left behind from the tornado of energy. "But presently you're untrained. A danger to yourself—and even more so, a danger to your friends and family. Shall I demonstrate further?"

Without letting go of his staff, the Shade swooped to where Juliet huddled, grabbed her by the throat, and yanked her up until her feet dangled in the air.

Juliet thrashed against his grip, gasping like a fish out of water.

"No," Chloe shrieked. She stumbled to her feet. "I'll go with you. I'll do whatever you want. Just let her go."

"You've made a choice to shun me. Now others will suffer because of your action. Friends. Family. Strangers. People you've met. People you've never known. Animals." His smile widened into a grin. "And mark my word, they will suffer, long and painfully without the luxury of death—all in your name. Until I decide to let you join us again."

The Shade lowered Juliet until the balls of her feet touched the floor. Then he craned to one side, looking at Keshari.

Chloe scrambled in front of Keshari, blocking his view. "Don't even think about it."

He laughed. "You are brave." His eyebrows raised. "And a dark one at heart. Two things I very much admire."

Her hands clenched into fists. "I'm not into dark magic. You can't tempt me, either."

"I don't need to. You already took that path long before you joined the Circle."

Keshari was on her feet, hand on Chloe's arm. "What's he talking about?"

"He's talking bullshit."

The Shade's gaze went back to Keshari. "Don't let this one fool you. She has walked in the valley of shadows."

"I have not!" But a dark memory that few except her family and the High Council should have known pushed its way into her throbbing head:

A week or maybe two after that night at the Vice-Chancellors house, the night she'd gone to the hospital with her parents, she'd snuck into the boy's hospital room. Tubes ran into him and out. So much plastic. White sheets. White walls. His pale face.

"I'm sorry," she whispered to the boy. "I wish it had been me."

She touched his hand. His tiny, cold fingers.

Taking a deep breath, she reached into her pocket and pulled out a slender bottle of oil. She'd found the recipe for it inside a locked drawer in her dad's office, in a Book of Shadows, so ancient the ink was faded and the pages crumbling. The potion wasn't exactly right for the boy's condition, but it was powerful and the closest she could find. It was worth a try.

The oil warmed in her hand, heating further when she pressed her palm against the boy's cool forehead. As she said the incantation, the spell crawled over her skin, its power primordial and shadowy. The room filled with the stench of rotting flesh and pus-green haze—

The door to the boy's room fanned open and the Vice-Chancellor's wife walked in. She screamed, a shrill piercing sound that brought Chloe's parents and a half-dozen High Council members racing to see what had happened.

Chloe jolted out of the memory. It had been sheer luck that the Council members had been able to reverse what she'd set in motion.

The Shade grinned at her. "Yes, I'm aware of that occasion and a great deal more." He winked. "Don't worry. I am a kind judge of character."

He cleared his throat and tilted his head toward Greta's apartment door. "You might want to check on that other friend of yours, though I suspect you're too late."

Greta. The bathtub. Drowning.

Chloe gasped. Not that!

She took off at a run. She'd never been inside Greta's apartment before. It was larger than she'd expected. Living room. Kitchen. Study. Where was the bathroom?

On the far side of the bedroom, she found it. Greta knelt in the overflowing tub. Her head was under the water. Bubbles streamed from her mouth, rising to the surface. Chloe grabbed her by the hair, yanking her head up and out of the water. Keshari had Greta by the armpits, helping Chloe haul her from the tub.

Greta fell on all fours, coughing and spewing water. Suddenly, she stopped. Her gaze darted to the bathtub, then up at Chloe. "You tried to drown me!"

"No. That's not what happened."

Greta scuttled away from her, backing into a narrow space beside the toilet. "Get out of here. I'll kill you, I will."

Keshari edged toward her, holding out her hand. "It is okay. You are all right now."

"No." Greta grabbed a plunger and swung, connecting with Keshari's shoulder. Keshari yelped and fell back. Greta snarled and got to her feet, advancing on both of them. But the anger in her eyes looked normal, and no hint of the Shade's magic buzzed in the air.

The Shade.

Chloe's pulse skyrocketed. She turned to Keshari. "Juliet! The Shade still has her."

They flew out of the bathroom, back through the apartment. She could use the spell she'd put on Juliet. Say "Northern Circle" and Juliet would fall asleep. That would keep her from talking to the Shade. That would work.

They sped into the hallway.

It was empty.

Nothing, except debris—a pair of bejeweled kitty slippers and trail of blood droplets, leading toward the staircase.

A chill settled over Chloe as she slowly glanced through the open door to Juliet's apartment, hoping to see her standing there, though she knew with all her heart that Juliet was gone.

They will suffer until I decide to let you join us again, the Shade's words replayed in Chloe's head. She pressed her hands over her eyes, rock-hard fear and guilt weighing down on her. Some things are worse than death, like near drowning or being held hostage by a merciless and powerful shade.

"You need to tell Devlin what happened," Keshari said.

"I don't know about you, but the Shade almost broke through my resistance. Can we be sure his magic hasn't gotten to Devlin? The cure's better than nothing, but it doesn't work as well as we hoped." Her voice sounded shaken even to her own ears. "We have to stick to our plan."

Keshari took Chloe by the arm and led her back into the apartment. She washed the blood from Chloe's face. Most of it had come from the nosebleed. But both she and Keshari were covered with cuts and slices from the flying debris, not to mention the damage Greta had inflicted on Keshari's shoulder. Still, by the time they'd washed and changed into clean clothes, a renewed sense of determination was building inside Chloe.

Damn the Shade. She wasn't going to let him torture Juliet or Greta, or any of her other friends or even strangers, like what had happened with the goth. She wasn't going to let him destroy the Circle. Or her chance to help the boy. Or be with Devlin. *No*. She was going to find a way to send him back. Even if it killed her—or worse.

Chapter 26

Come to me, sweetheart, lay in my arms.
Whisper your secrets and I'll give you my charms.
—The Seduction of Merlin

Sunset rapidly settled into twilight as Chloe and Keshari hurried toward Oakledge Park. They were too late to catch a bus and didn't want to risk taking a taxi in case the driver might be in Athena's pocket, so they took off on foot, zigzagging their way through side streets and avoiding going near the complex, entering the park on the south end.

From there, they made their way through the fading light to a tree sheltered rock outcrop, overlooking the broad lake and the cove where the Clock stood near the shoreline. The roundabout route they took seemed wise, better to avoid running into any Circle members until they knew who was on their side.

Devlin slipped into Chloe's mind and her heart fumbled. His relationship with Athena was so much closer than the one she had with her siblings. In fact, it was strange how quickly and easily her brothers and sisters had distanced themselves from her after everything went down with the Vice-Chancellor's son. If it came down to it, could Devlin do the same to Athena? If his sister remained loyal to the Shade, would he take sides against her? Judging by the Shade's power, it would probably be wiser for him if he didn't.

Focus, Chloe told herself. She couldn't afford to worry about Devlin right now. As much as her heart hated the idea, this was bigger than their relationship. Plus, it felt wrong to even think about him having to choose sides.

Chloe found a flat rock at the water's edge and set down her flashlight and messenger bag. The crisp air drifting off the still lake cooled her face and helped her move toward a more meditative zone. She inhaled deeply, taking in the scent of water and cedar, similar in many ways but subtly different than the smells from that night at the quarry. How long ago that felt now.

"Ready?" she said to Keshari.

Keshari nodded. "I hope we will not call a lake demon or trickster by mistake."

"We won't," Chloe said confidently. But a fresh trickle of sweat slid down her spine. That was something she hadn't considered.

With that new possibility weighing heavy in her mind, she opened her messenger bag and took out their supplies, everything specifically chosen to appeal to Nimue: blue candles, a chalice of white wine, jasmine oil, a perfect apple.

Chloe lit the candles, then pricked her finger with her athame and let the droplets fall into the water. Once that was done, Keshari poured the mandala sand and crystals onto the same spot.

The last traces of sunset stretched amber along the western horizon, quickly seeping into gray. Closer to them, the reflection of stars broke the water's darkness. No moon. Just fading twilight and stillness.

Together they intoned, "We call upon the Lady of the Lake. We seek your wisdom. Come to us…" While Keshari kept up the entreaty and jangled her bell-wand to add to the magic, Chloe sliced the apple in two and set it in the water. Pale and perfect, the slices shimmered in the low light. They bobbed for a moment, drifting inward until they tagged the rocks. Then they floated outward more rapidly than seemingly possible in such still water. Chloe's heart leapt, wondering if the movement meant a Lady was nearby.

With her eyes trained on the water, she waited. The last colors vanished from the horizon, city lights now glimmering along the lakeshore. She straightened, pushed past the growing nervousness in her stomach, and raised her voice. "We call upon you, Lady Nimue. Hear our plea."

A flutter of wings broke the silence as a restless bird sped away from the Earth Clock and into the trees behind them. Somewhere beyond the park a dog barked.

Keshari's fingers entwined with hers, giving them a squeeze. "I don't think this is working. She wants more."

The sinking feeling of impending failure settled over Chloe. Keshari was right. The apple represented Nimue's island home of Avalon. It would please her. The sand was full of power, and so much of Keshari's heart. But neither was really a sacrifice on Chloe's part. The blood she'd offered had been tiny compared to what had awoken the Shade. She had to give more. Something that would hurt.

A painful ache gripped Chloe's chest and tears misted her eyes as she undid the clasp on her charm bracelet. Her father had special ordered and had the tiny pentagram engraved for her tenth birthday. Her aunt had given her the crystal pendulum on her eleventh, her mother had...

"What are you doing?" Keshari whispered.

"It's connected to my heart and witchcraft, to the Craft the Lady and I share." She cupped her hands around the bracelet and lifted it skyward, toward the dark velvet night and starlight. "Nimue, I entreat you. High priestess of the water. Will you speak to me? Counsel me?" She crouched, dipping her fingertips into the lake and letting water pour into the chalice of her hands. "Please, Lady, take this offering, as a poor man's copper penny into a well, as a warrior surrendering his sword into the depths. Come to me. Bless me with your presence."

She opened her hands and watched with sadness as the bracelet sunk downward and out of sight.

A long moment passed, then another. No breeze. No vibration of magic. No glimmer of anything rising from the lake's depths. Nothing.

Disappointment weighed in Chloe's heart. She sunk to her knees. *Please, Lady. Please.*

Another moment passed. And another. Just when she was about to give up, a faint tingle of magic swept Chloe's neck.

"Did you feel that?" Keshari whispered.

Chloe nodded and scrambled to her feet.

In the distance, the water rolled, rising and falling in undulating waves. The surge moved toward them, pushing whitecaps against the rocks, falling backwards in a crash and roar.

Chloe held her breath as a tall Lady rose up from the water in front of them. Symbols of the Craft gleamed on her skin. Her seaweed-entwined hair swirled out around her like solar flares. Her eyes shone with fury. Chloe's bracelet shimmered on her wrist.

"You"—she pointed a long finger at Chloe—"you came to my cavern. Your blood released him."

"Are—are you Nimue?" Chloe's voice quivered. She hated to ask, the spirit didn't sound happy. But she wasn't going to make a mistake now, especially after Keshari mentioned the possibility of them attracting a trickster.

The Lady glowered. "You have the audacity to question who I am? Of course, I am Nimue of the Lake."

"I—I'm sorry. I had to be certain." Chloe blinked at the Lady, totally awestruck. It was really her. Nimue. She raked a hand through her hair, struggling for the right thing to say. "I didn't mean to release the Shade. I mean, my blood was used, but now I want only to return him to you."

"You expect me to believe that?" With a flick of her fingertips, Nimue swiveled away, nose up in the air as if disgusted.

"She's telling the truth," Keshari pleaded. "We need your help."

Chloe stepped to the very edge of the rock, the whitecaps snaking over her shoes. "Tell us how to send him back. Please. I'll do—I'll give you anything you want. I just—" Chloe clenched her teeth, searching for the deepest truth she could give. "I want to make up for my wrongs."

Nimue spun back, a shrewd smile rippling across her lips. Her eyes glistened. "If there are truly no limits to your willingness, then there is a way." She held both arms out. As she raised them, mist streamed upward from beneath her feet, a ghostly blue luminesce that reminded Chloe of the garden paths at the complex. The blue grew more intense, vibrating with hot-white energy. Then a spear of light burst upward, its brightness blazing out in all directions. Nimue grasped the glowing rod by its end, slashing it through the air until it took on the shape of a small sword and dimmed to a steady glow.

"This," Nimue said, "is the only weapon that can rejoin two halves that have been split."

As Chloe's eyes took in the rapier-like weapon, the mythic proportion of what she had to accomplish sunk in. She humbly lowered her gaze. "What do I need to do with it?"

Nimue pointed the sword downward and thrust its narrow blade back into the water. It blazed to life again, light flashing outward, illuminating all that lay below: fish, seaweed, rocks.

She withdrew the blade and smiled. "It's simple. You must impale the Shade with it."

Chloe stepped back, closer to Keshari. Stabbing the Shade wouldn't be easy, but it sounded straightforward enough. Still, in folklore, tasks were never as simple as they seemed at first. And the Shade certainly wouldn't give up without a fight.

"What else?" Keshari asked, as if she'd read Chloe's mind.

Nimue laughed and tossed her head back, her hair dancing like candle flames. "After what was done, do you think the solution would be simple? The sword can slow the Shade, but only for a few heartbeats." Her cool eyes landed on Chloe. "You must then stab the sword into the stone through which the Shade emerged into this realm." She fell silent; a finger lifted to indicate there was more.

"And...?" Chloe asked, her mouth drying.

"Both these things must be accomplished before the hour the Shade emerged. If more than one full day passes between that time and when the sword pierces the stone, then he shall remain forever free to roam this realm."

Chloe gaped. "That's less than four hours from now." She slanted a look toward Keshari to get a confirmation.

Keshari shrugged. "Don't ask me. I do not recall anything after the energy-ball."

An eerie stillness came over the lake and Nimue's voice lowered to a hush. "Be warned before you take this sword. The act of purposely using such a weapon against another being—even a shade—is an act of dark magic. Whoever stabs him will never be the same. There is no way to reverse that. By nature, killing or intentionally harming another imbalances the soul." Her gaze bore into Chloe's as if to etch the words into her being. "Understand?"

Chloe bowed her head. "I do."

Chapter 27

It wasn't until I became the person I thought I wanted to be
that I realized who I was.
—Chandler Parrish

As Nimue placed the lightweight sword into Chloe's outstretched hands, the warnings played all too clearly in her head. Strangely, she had no desire to flee or turn away from the task before her. In a way, the price seemed just.

"Promise I won't fail," she said to Nimue. It sounded like what a fool from a fairy tale might say. Coming from her mouth it sounded like a lie.

"We shall see about that." Nimue twirled around, arms outstretched, hair a wheel of flames and mist. She brought her arms together over her head and sank into the water, illuminating what lay below for a moment, before vanishing.

Chloe's adrenaline kicked in. She pulled off her sweater and wrapped it around the sword. It wasn't as if they could wander around with it glowing like a beacon. Even if it didn't freak out anyone they happened across, the Shade would catch onto what they were up to the second he spotted it.

"What do you think our first move should be?" Keshari asked, flinging the strap of the messenger bag onto her shoulder. She snagged the flashlight. "It's almost eight forty-five already."

"Like it or not, we've got to go to the complex first." Chloe tucked the wrapped sword under one arm, its brightness leaking out as they started up the rocks to the path.

"I do not think the Shade will be there. I suspect he is still touring the town."

"But Devlin could be. With his help and a car, this whole thing would be a lot easier. We'll just have to make sure no one else sees us." She led the way, fast-walking past the Earth Clock, down the bike path toward the complex's hidden gate.

Keshari lengthened her strides, a faint jangle of bells sounding as she came up next to Chloe. "Um—I am worried about Devlin."

"I am too." Chloe glanced at Keshari. "We should take some more of that cure before we head into the complex. I'm not sure if there's a maximum dose, but I'd rather risk it. I'm hoping Devlin downed gallons of the stuff." She took an ampule from her pocket and swallowed the contents.

Keshari did the same. "If we survive tonight, I am going to talk to your boyfriend about doing something to improve the flavor of this stuff."

Chloe laughed, glad for the relief. "It gives disgusting a whole new meaning." Her face heated when she realized what Keshari had said. "He's not actually my *boyfriend*."

This time Keshari laughed. "I have seen how he watches you. And, you, your magic radiates when he is near."

"Time will tell." Chloe kept her voice light. She didn't dare think about Devlin in that way right now. She couldn't afford to let anything sway her from her plan, even him. As if echoing her need to stay the course, the sword warmed against her side.

Ahead, the magic ward enhancing the complex's back gate and fence rippled in the darkness. Keshari looked up at it and shook her head. "We should have gone through the front. It will be impossible to force our way through something this strong without our presence being detected."

"Maybe. Maybe not." Chloe rubbed her neck, thinking. "Devlin opened it with a simple flick of his fingers and a command. I'm willing to bet all coven members can do that—and I just happen to be a coven member."

Focusing on the gate, she drew up her magic. It surged hot and ready to sail from her fingertips. It was strange how already working with her amplified power felt more natural than dialing it back. Still—

She hesitated, her magic receding a little as she reached up and touched a fresh cut on her throat, one she'd gotten after the Shade deflected her super-charged power and created the tornado of debris. She suspected this was another instance where letting her magic rip wasn't the wisest choice. Like Keshari said, everyone in the complex would sense that kind of energy burst. She needed to play it cool.

"Hold this for a second." She gave Keshari the wrapped sword, then turned her back on the gate and shook out her arms to eliminate even more of the magic she'd built up. Calming her thoughts and energy, she swiveled around. "Open," she murmured, lightly flicking her fingers to send the slightest burst of energy at the gate.

Please, Hecate, please, she prayed.

The gate swung slowly open and she let out her breath.

"I would never have guessed that would work," Keshari said, as they hurried through.

"I'm just grateful it did."

Chloe took the sword back from Keshari and started toward the complex. After a couple of yards, motion lights blazed to life, brightening the path ahead of them. In the distance, a dog began to bark.

"Shit. It's Henry," Chloe whispered. "He'll alert everyone."

Keshari moved in closer to Chloe. "I was bit when I was little. This one, he is friendly, yes?"

"Don't worry, Henry's a sweetheart."

With Keshari next to her, Chloe sprinted toward the complex, ready to unsheathe the sword if the Shade or anyone else emerged from the shadows. As they reached the end of the path and started past Devlin's coupe, Henry appeared on the other side of the parking lot. A ferocious snarl reverberated from his mouth. Hackles raised. Teeth bared. He charged at them, like a hungry wolf.

"Run!" Chloe shouted. "The car."

It was the closest option. Thank the Goddess it was unlocked.

Keshari dove in first, Chloe close behind. She tossed the sword to Keshari and yanked the door shut, just in time. A loud *bang* reverberated as Henry slammed into the outside of the door. He leapt, hitting the side window, snarling and snapping. Saliva slid down the glass.

"I swear, he was fine the last time I saw him," Chloe said, panting for breath.

Keshari hunched in the driver's seat hugging the sweater-wrapped sword, lips trembling. "What are we going to do now?"

"Don't worry. I'll think of something." Chloe glanced at the ignition. No keys. Of course, it couldn't have been that easy. Her eyes went to Devlin's apartment, a dozen yards away. There were no signs of life coming from inside, no lights shining from a window, no glow of a TV. She scanned the main house. It was also dark, except for one faint light that looked to be more decorative than functional. At least they didn't have to worry about Henry's barking alerting anyone. But that wasn't really a good thing. Even if they managed to escape from him, there was no one here who could tell them where the Shade was, and it was impossible to stab something she couldn't find.

Henry circled the car, once, twice…Finally, he slunk away and hunched down in the shadows as if daring them to try to escape.

Chloe took out her phone. "I'm going to check Facebook and see if Devlin left us a message. He could be coming back anytime."

She flicked her fingers over the screen. No message. In fact, there wasn't anything new on his Facebook page. Not for weeks. Her gaze went to the time. Nine fifteen. For the love of Hecate, they had less than three and a half hours.

Holding her breath, she checked for a text, even though Devlin claimed he wouldn't do it. Nothing. No missed calls either. No voicemail. No emails. She checked for a direct message on Twitter. Nothing again. She gritted her teeth in frustration. They couldn't just sit here and watch their time run out.

She scoured the car's interior, looking for a weapon. She didn't want to hurt Henry, but there might not be another choice. Nothing. The place was as empty as a steel cage.

Like a cage—or a box trap.

Chloe smiled. "Unless your demon spray works on bespelled dogs," she said to Keshari, "I think we only have one choice—get us out and him trapped inside the car."

Keshari shuddered. "I am pretty sure this is a bad idea."

Chloe held her hand out. "Give me the sword. On the count of three, I'll open my door. When Henry starts to charge, I'll shout *go*. You get out your side as fast as you can, leave your door open, and run around and close my door. Hopefully, I'll be a second behind you with all my body parts intact."

"I do not like this, not one bit."

"One," Chloe said, before she could lose her nerve. "Two. Three."

Chloe opened her door. And Henry charged, Keshari flew out her side. Chloe was a second behind, Henry snapping at her shoulder as she escaped and slammed the door in his face.

A second door slam echoed in the air, followed by Henry's frantic barking as he bounded from seat to seat.

Keshari laughed. "We did it. I can't believe it."

"Hurry. We should check to see if Devlin left a note for us." She beelined toward his apartment, but as they reached the door a new fear hit her. She put out a hand, stopping Keshari from opening it.

"What's wrong?" Keshari asked.

"He could be in there. But…" She couldn't bring herself to say the rest out loud. The Shade could have gotten to him. He could be lying in wait for them like Henry—or dead on the kitchen floor...*No, don't think like that*, she admonished herself. They didn't have time for negative thinking. Just time for doing. "Try the door. If it's not locked, open it. But let me go inside first."

Keshari slowly wrapped her fingers around the doorknob and turned it. She glanced at Chloe, nodding to confirm the door was indeed unlocked. As she began to ease it open, Chloe took a fresh hold on the covered sword, wishing for a moment that she'd taken fencing; even a vague idea of what she was doing would have been better than her drop the wrap, stab, and run plan. Still, she swallowed hard, slipped through the open doorway, and into the apartment.

Light filtered out from a salt lamp near the TV. No movement. No sound. No strange odors.

Chloe sprinted to the living room. She checked the bedroom alcove and the bathroom. No one.

"What now?" Keshari asked.

"I can feel Devlin and the Shade's magic faintly, and Athena's. But it's residual. It could even be from when they healed me." She set the sword down on the kitchen island next to a dirty shot glass and a half-full decanter of Devlin's cure. "At least it looks like he followed his own advice."

"Let's hope he took enough," Keshari said.

She pulled out her phone. "I'm going to check for messages again. Can you look around for car keys? Maybe he has a set for something other than the BMW."

"Even if we find keys and the right car, we don't know where the Shade is."

Chloe sunk down on the end of Devlin's bed. She rocked forward, head in her hands. "I don't know. Maybe I should just call Athena and pretend I'm begging forgiveness—simply ask where they are."

Her phone chirped, adrenaline pounding into her veins when she saw it was a Facebook message from Devlin. A link and one word: *Instagram*.

She followed the link. A photo Devlin posted five minutes earlier showed a scrap metal monkey perched close to a fountain in City Hall Park with its wings outspread and its fangs bared. Two minutes ago, he'd added an image of the Shade leaning on his staff, glaring down a living statue of *The Thinker*. There were other familiar faces in the background. "Found them."

"Where?"

"Church Street. All of them, including Juliet." She blew out a relieved breath, Juliet hadn't sprouted cat's ears or something—and if Devlin was leaving a breadcrumb trail of photos, that meant he hadn't succumbed to their magic, at least not yet.

Still, the damage the Shade could cause in the busiest part of the city was unimaginable, especially at night, with people heading to restaurants and bars. Even if he didn't physically or mentally screw with everyone he met, it was only a matter of time before the Shade and his monkeys were all over the Internet. Then, whether she'd told her family and the High Council about the Shade or not, it wouldn't make a difference. The Council would see the news. They'd send an investigator. He or she would shut down the Circle...But worse than all of that, in a few hours there would be no way to send the Shade back. Plus, she had the sneaking suspicion there were a few questions she should have asked Nimue, like were there ways to kill him if she failed, or was he immortal?

The feeling of dread returned, squeezing her chest until she could barely breathe.

Stay calm, Chloe. You've got this. You can do it, she repeated sternly to herself.

"I am not finding any keys," Keshari said.

"We should go see if there are any cars parked in front of the main house. With all the craziness, maybe someone left one with the keys in it. If not, we're going to have to take a chance and call a taxi."

As Chloe got up from the bed, Keshari stepped to one side, knocking over Devlin's pool cue case by mistake. Chloe's eyes zeroed in on the case, an idea sparking. She snatched it, dashed to the kitchen, and began using a butter knife to wedge out the plastic divider that was intended to hold the pool sticks in place.

Keshari stared at her, a mystified look on her face. "What are you doing?"

"We can't exactly wander around Church Street with a glowing sword, can we?" Chloe pushed with all her might. The plastic let out a loud snap and gave way. With it gone, she went back to the island and unwrapped the sword. The whole room brightened as if lit by a white-hot sun, then returned to darkness as she shoved the sword diagonally into the case. It was a tight fit, but she didn't sense any resistance from the sword's tip, like the sword didn't have an issue with close quarters.

She slung the case's strap over her shoulder. "Let's go look for cars."

"Sounds good."

They dashed outside and into the parking lot. As they passed Devlin's car, Henry bounded from seat to seat, foam flying from his mouth.

Chloe's chest ached. She hated seeing him like this, having to leave him locked up in a car, even if it was cool and one window was slightly cracked open. He was such a good dog. Devlin's baby. Damn the Shade and his cruelty.

She veered sharply away from the car, sprinting across the parking lot with Keshari keeping pace. They jogged through a puddle of floodlight, then back into the surrounding darkness. She could see now that there were two lights on in the main house, the faint one she'd noticed earlier and another down in the basement. But she didn't bother to give either of them a second glance. No one was home. She'd seen everyone in Devlin's photos.

As they skirted the house, an uneasy feeling fluttered in her stomach. In truth, she'd only studied the photos for a moment. She could have overlooked someone.

Clank! The metallic sound came from somewhere just ahead of them, followed by a creaking noise, like rusty hinges.

Keshari snagged Chloe's arm, pulling her to a stop. She bent close. "How many monkey sculptures were there to start with?"

The uneasy flutter in Chloe's stomach transformed into an acidic burn. There had been a lot more monkeys on the gateway than the two they'd seen at the apartment house. Dear Goddess, not more monkeys. The first ones had been terrifying enough, and they been held back by wards and a windowpane.

A whisper came from the darkness off to their right. Or was it the swish of a metal wing?

Chloe thought for a second, orienting herself. They were near Chandler's workshop. She'd created the monkeys.

Another creak and the interior light of a sedan illuminated the front of Chandler's building. The dark outline of a wide-shouldered woman heaving a suitcase into the sedan's backseat appeared, then she helped what looked like a half-asleep boy into the seat next to it. Peregrine and Chandler. What was she doing? And why wasn't she with the rest of the coven?

Chloe re-evaluated the scene and a possibility dawned on her. Chandler was escaping. But it couldn't be. She and Athena were longtime friends, coven-sisters attached at the hip.

Keshari elbowed Chloe and tilted her head toward the main gate, signaling they should keep going. She was right, it was smarter to escape while Chandler was too busy to notice them, safer to assume she was still on Athena and the Shade's side. Except it didn't look that way—and Chandler had a car.

A piece of gravel crunched under Keshari's foot. Chandler wheeled, a bright red energy-ball forming in her hands. Logic said the darkness they stood in should have hidden them from her sight, but Chloe could sense that Chandler's magic had homed in on their location. The ball's crackling power grew, throwing off sparks. Lit by its glow, Chandler's face revealed a single emotion: sheer terror.

Chloe threw up her hands in surrender. "Stop. Please. It's me and my friend, Keshari." She stepped forward. "We aren't going to try to stop you. But we need a ride—desperately."

Chandler scuffed backwards, closing the car's rear door and opening the driver's. "Stay away." Her voice rasped. "You can't have my son. Never."

What had the Shade done to her—or the boy? Chloe dared another step. "We don't want your son. We want to send the Shade back. But we need your help."

"No. You're trying to trick me. Athena, Merlin—that creature...They're trying to enthrall everyone. They've been doing it for months. You can't lie to me about it. I asked Athena, and that Merlin monster had my son chained in the basement—" A pained expression swept over her face. She dropped the energy-ball and clamped her hands against her temples as if to push back a blistering migraine.

"We have a cure that will help you resist their magic." Keshari crept past Chloe, her voice soothing. She took an ampule from her pocket and held it out. "It will ease the confusion. Here. Have it. Take it for your son's safety. You should not drive without drinking it first."

Chloe hung back, crouching down to look less threatening as Keshari inched forward. The warmth of the sword against her back reminded her of the seconds that were passing. But another feeling tightened in her chest. They had to help Chandler. She was a coven-sister. She was in pain and danger. She needed them.

Chandler rested her hand on the driver's door, as if preparing to launch herself into the seat. Her voice lowered to a snarl. "Don't come any closer."

"Please." Keshari leaned down and rolled the ampule toward her. It tumbled across the pavement, stopping short.

Chandler eyed it, but she didn't move.

Thinking quick, Chloe drew up a spritz of magic and let it out with her breath. The magic wisped across the distance, touching the ampule and rolling it forward until the vial hit the toe of Chandler's work boot. "Please, Chandler, for Peregrine," she said. "Trust us. Trust your instincts."

The air went still, surreally quiet. Even the sound of Henry's barking silenced.

Then Peregrine began to cry.

In one motion, Chandler swooped down, took the ampule, and chugged it. She stared down at the pavement for a second, then a fleeting smile crossed her lips. "Thank you." She hesitated, then continued, "The Athena I knew—the high priestess I dreamed about the future with, about the amazing things we could do once we awoke Merlin—this Athena isn't her, any more than this Merlin is who I expected."

"That's because he's not Merlin," Chloe said. "Athena tricked everyone. She used our powers and blood to help her awaken and summon Merlin's Shade."

Chandler gasped. "Goddess forgive us."

"Please." Keshari clasped her hands together, begging. "We want to stop this, but we need a ride."

Chandler nodded to the old Cherokee parked beyond the sedan, yanked a ring of keys from her pocket, and tossed it to Keshari. It landed halfway between the two of them, the clink of metal chiming against the pavement. "Take it. It has plenty of gas."

"Keep in touch," Chloe shouted to Chandler. "Email Devlin. He'll tell you if we succeed. The coven needs you."

Chandler raised her hand in an abbreviated wave, but whether it meant she would stay in touch or not, Chloe had no time to worry about it. She snatched the keys and hurtled for the Cherokee's driver's seat. Keshari scrambled in through the other side.

Chloe gunned the gas, gravel spraying up behind them as they squealed under the gateway, now only decorated with a few unanimated monkeys.

Chapter 28

Curiosity. Intention. Focus.
These are the most powerful tools and weapons of our Craft.
—A Witch's Study by Zeus Marsh

According to the car's clock, it was almost ten when Chloe careened into a parking spot near the fountain—the one in Devlin's photograph with the monkey perched nearby.

She shuddered. Maybe not all the Circle members were loyal to the Shade, but the monkeys weren't going to let her send him back without putting up a fight. She yanked the keys from the ignition and shoved them into her pocket. "Has Devlin posted any new photos?"

"Not in the last half-hour. You do not think he gave in—" Keshari cringed. "Sorry."

"Go ahead, say it—that the magic finally got to him—I wouldn't be surprised." She snagged the pool cue case and slung it over her shoulder. "But we can't worry about that. We've got one goal: stab the Shade and then get the sword back to the stone before it's too late." She said it more for her benefit than Keshari's, to reinforce the plan in her mind.

You can do this, you have to, she told herself.

They sprinted away from the Cherokee through streaks of watery streetlight. The trees that had been bright with autumn colors when she'd come here to the farmers' market now stretched skyward with bone-bare branches. But despite the night's eeriness and the fact that it was a Sunday, the streets hummed with traffic and people hurried everywhere, as if racing to wring as much life as they could out of the night before winter's cold closed in.

"Excuse me," Chloe said, jogging through a group of dressed up couples. The cue case slapped against her side as she veered around a guy walking his golden retriever. Her mind flashed to Devlin and Henry. She pushed the thought aside. No distractions, though she hoped distracted was exactly what the tour of downtown Burlington was doing to the Shade.

She slowed when they reached Church Street, a shopping district that was closed off to car traffic. The sidewalk cafés and bars teemed with people. A heartbeat echoed from a drum circle up the street. Coffee, grilled sausages, beer—the place not only looked and sounded normal, it smelled that way too, unnervingly so.

Keshari panted up next to her. "We should find that living statue, *The Thinker*. He had to have seen which way they went."

"In Devlin's photo, he was in front of City Hall." She went up on her tiptoes to get a less obstructed view. It was hard to tell at a distance, but down the street a ways someone was sitting statue-still on a rock. "I think I see him."

They wound their way through the crowd. But as they neared, Chloe's instincts sent up a warning flare. *The Thinker* sat utterly motionless with his chin on his fist. His resemblance to the original statue was absurdly uncanny, every inch of his seemingly naked and muscular body tinted metallic shades of teal and black.

She snatched Keshari's sleeve, slowing her. "There's something off about him. Do you feel it?"

"I am not sure. He does give me the creeps." She studied him again, her forehead wrinkling as if she were sensing for magic. "Yes. Very creepy."

The cue case chilled against Chloe side as they crept closer to him. She pulled the case forward, ready to unsheathe the sword if needed. It wouldn't be smart to stab anyone other than the Shade with it, but that didn't mean she couldn't use it for threatening.

Her eye caught a shift in the energy around him. Not magic. This was a vibration she'd heard about but never seen before. Her breath stalled in her throat as a likely possibility came to her. She bent close to Keshari. "I think he's a shapeshifter."

"Like the Shade?" she whispered.

"No. I think this is inborn, not a spell."

With her heart in her throat, Chloe once again scanned the street, looking for other shifters or members of the Circle. No familiar faces. No indications of magic either.

She pushed back her worry and lengthened her steps, striding toward him. If this was a trap, so be it. It was the last place the Shade had been and it was the end of Devlin's short breadcrumb trail.

A group of teenage girls stopped in front of *The Thinker*, whispering to each other and snickering. A couple threw a five into his donation box, then continued on arm in arm.

"Watch my back," Chloe said to Keshari. Then she pasted on a cheerful smile and strolled up to him. "Hi, there. I hope you can help. This is a bit of a strange question, but we're looking for a long-haired guy carrying a staff. He would have been with a group of people—and a steampunk monkey. Did you happen to see them by any chance?"

The Thinker's expression remained stoically frozen. Not even an eyelash moved. Not even when she repeated the question.

She gritted her teeth, holding back the urge to give him a good shake. Desperation filled her voice. "There would have been a guy with dreadlocks and a taller woman wearing a choker with him. Please. It's important. All I need to know is which way they went."

A thought came to her and icy fear drained her anger. What if the Shade had done something to him, like turned him into a real statue?

She crouched down, leaning in close enough to see the slight rise of his chest as he breathed.

Keshari stepped up next to her and dropped a bill into the donation box. "Would a ten help you remember?"

His metallic lips twitched and his eyes shifted, indicating farther down the street.

"Thank you, thank you so much!" Chloe shouted, though she felt slightly embarrassed that she hadn't thought of giving him cash before she wasted so much time.

They fast-walked in the direction *The Thinker* indicated, but with each step the normalness made Chloe increasingly uneasy. No traces of magic hung in the air. No news vans rushed to investigate reports of flying monkeys. A thought prickled the back of her mind. The horrible things the Shade had done so far to people and animals, plus him bringing the monkeys to life and creating the tornado in her hallway, these things had convinced her that he intended to shock the world with a dramatic entrance, a manipulative show of cruelty and power, backed up with more bullying and threats.

But everything around them said differently. The Shade was covering his tracks, showing care and control that made the possibility of him having seduced Athena into releasing him much more plausible. She was an intelligent woman and a high priestess, sincere about acquiring magic and medicine to help mankind. Her devotion to Devlin proved she cared deeply for family as well as coven. Someone like her wouldn't have been easy prey, even for someone as powerful as the Shade.

Sweat trickled down Chloe's spine and a sick feeling settled in the pit of her stomach. She moved closer to Keshari. "You don't think the Shade manipulated Devlin into posting fake photos to mislead—or maybe lure us somewhere?"

"I would believe almost anything at this point," Keshari said.

Two younger guys hurtled up behind them. As they shot passed, Chloe caught a few words "…Not kidding, man. A dude with a mechanical monkey is buying drinks. All night."

Thank you, thank you, Chloe sent a shot of gratitude out to the universe. Such a coincidence had to have come from some god or goddess, or maybe even Nimue.

She grabbed Keshari's hand. "Come on! Let's follow them."

They took off full-tilt after the guys, chasing them to the end of the block, around a corner and up the street. Straight to the front door of Club Elysium, where the guys vanished inside. Chloe paused, her breath coming in short pants, stitches pulling at her sides. Beside her, Keshari had her hands on her knees as she gulped air.

Club Elysium.

I should have seen this one coming, Chloe thought, waiting for the pounding of her heart to subside. Elysium was the most popular club in town. It had a small barroom in the front and a back area with three or maybe four bars, raised dance floors, loads of tables. She'd gone there once with Juliet.

"We're looking for the guy with the monkey," Chloe said to the man at the door, flashing her ID.

"Isn't everyone? He's in the way back. The VIP section."

They slunk inside, heads down, moving along the dark edges of the room. Chloe prayed that no one from the coven would spot them. Not before she or Keshari found them first.

She stole a quick peek around. The bartender and a few patrons clustered at the far end of the bar. A couple of girls were playing pool. She focused on the club's energy and picked up on the buzz of the Circle's magic. Definitely coming from farther back in the club, amid the throb of the band and the roar of voices.

As they reached the short hall that connected the club's two rooms, she leaned into Keshari. "If we get separated, meet me back at the Cherokee."

Keshari slid her hand into the pocket of her sweater. The jangle of her bell-wand vibrated off the hallway's walls, sounding loudly. "Do not worry. I will stick close to you."

"No, I don't want you to do that." Chloe's pulse raced, sending thoughts of what had happened to Keshari at the circle of stones shooting through her mind. "Watch my back. But stay as far away from me and him as you can."

"If I daze him with my demon spray, you will have a better chance." Keshari's voice toughened. "This affects both of our magic communities. I want to help."

A knot tightened in Chloe's throat. She didn't like this, but there was something she hadn't thought about until now. If she failed to send the Shade back, Keshari's family would be among the first practitioners of magic to be affected by his presence, considering they lived in the city. "I'm just—I don't want anything to happen to you."

"I'm worried for you as well. But this is beyond us. Returning the Shade is more important than your welfare—or mine. If you fail, then all we love will be destroyed."

Chloe gave a slow, heavy nod. "I know. This just isn't getting any easier."

With heaviness weighing in her chest, Chloe took a fortifying breath, holding her magic back to hide her presence from the coven. Then she stepped into the backroom with Keshari an inch behind her.

For a moment, the loud music and flashing bolts of laser light disoriented her. She refocused on the coven's magic and shouldered her way between the people and tables, past the raised dance floors to the end of a bar. From there she had a clear view of the bathroom hallway that was just beyond the other end of the bar. After the hallway came a short ramp that led to the VIP section, for the most part hidden by sheer curtains.

She glanced back at Keshari. "Ready?"

Keshari nodded.

Keeping one hand clamped on top of the case to make sure the sword's light remained unseen, she undid its latch. Her pulse throbbed in her ears, louder even than the music as she moved along the bar. With each step, she could see more of the VIP section. Midas lounged on a loveseat with a girl on his lap. Jessica was talking with Juliet and someone she didn't recognize. The curtains obscured the rest of the coven members. Em's outline, maybe. The Shade and two winged monkeys, definitely. Even if his outline hadn't been familiar, she couldn't have missed the light glinting off the head of his staff, and the bee-like drone of his power. Actually, the intensity of his and the coven's conjoined magic tugged at her, urging her to join them. The buzz prickled her skin and pushed against her forehead. *Let go, let go,* it whispered in her skull. *Join us. Be one with us.*

She dug an ampule from her pocket, opened it, and chugged the vile liquid down, trying to not gag. Keshari did the same.

A guy sitting on a nearby barstool chuckled loudly. "Might want to take that in the bathroom," he said. His eyes went to the cue case and he frowned.

Chloe glanced at it. A fierce white glow leaked out from under her fingers. She grinned sheepishly and raised her voice. "It's a sword of light."

He waved her off. "Whatever, Princess Leia."

Keshari elbowed her, then tilted her head toward the VIP section. Someone had just come down the ramp and was striding into the bathroom hallway. Devlin.

Heat rushed through Chloe's body and for a moment she felt buoyant, as though floating above everyone—all the people who had no idea how much danger they were in. She glanced at Devlin again and the urge to run to him ached inside her. But she couldn't afford to do anything stupid. What if he was under the Shade's control? What if his breadcrumb trail had been a setup meant to specifically draw her in?

As Devlin reached the bathroom hallway, he paused and glanced back at the VIP section as if to check and see if anyone was watching. Then he hurriedly whipped out his phone and snapped a photo of the room.

Relief washed through Chloe. *No.* He was still trying to leave a trail and had gone out of his way to make sure no one saw him do it. He *was* on their side and they needed his help desperately. She bent closer to Keshari. "I'm going to talk to him while he's alone."

"Be careful," Keshari warned.

"Don't worry." But she was worried. If it came right down to it, she was certain she couldn't hurt him. Her heart wouldn't let her.

Keeping one eye on the VIP section, she strolled to the end of the bar and went into the empty bathroom hallway. It was dark except for the glimmer of the emergency exit sign, reflecting off the walls. Both bathrooms were single occupancy. She'd only have to wait for a moment for him to come out.

She studied the walls, stained with who knew what. The smell of stale beer wafted up from the floor. Each note from the band went on endlessly long. She shifted her weight, listening as the roar of a hand drier came on in the closest bathroom, only a couple of yards away. The door opened— Athena stepped out.

Chloe jumped back, her pulse jackhammering. But it was too late. There was nowhere for her to hide. Athena's eyes zeroed in on her face and a cruel smile appeared on her lips.

She strolled toward Chloe, closing the distance between them with the lazy gait of a panther who'd already won the chase. "Well, well, well, what do we have here?" She smirked. "Come groveling back to us, have you?"

The glacial tone of her voice made Chloe tremble. Athena didn't sound like herself. Her eyes looked odd as well, twin ovals of glistening onyx. Still, maybe Athena could break free of the Shade's magic. She *was* powerful.

Either way, there was one thing Chloe needed to know. "You knew we were going to summon the Shade, didn't you? Why did you do it?"

Athena scoffed. "Because I could—with the conjoined power of you and the coven." She caressed her throat, her fingers pale against the dark glimmer of her beaded choker. A black aura crackled around her, growing more intense. "Why do you suddenly care what side of light and darkness you're on? You can have what you want. My Merlin has the power to heal the Vice-Chancellor's son."

Chloe's voice splintered with anger. "Devlin told me how hard you worked to rebuild the coven. He told me how you were always there for him. This isn't like you. You're a good person."

She snorted. "Devlin will have his reward, the poor deluded boy."

Athena didn't appear to notice the other bathroom door opening slowly behind her, nor did she seem to sense Devlin as he slipped out.

"He was kind enough—not like the other men." Athena's voice rose, sharp and brittle. "They said they loved me. But they got what they wanted, then ran away. Then they promised the world and told me they'd come back, only to choose another woman—"

"Athena," Devlin interrupted her rant. "What's going on?"

She wheeled on him, the air hissing with her power. "Your mother is such a skank. I don't see why any man would want her." She stepped back, her spine now against the bathroom door. Chloe felt the weight of Athena's dark gaze on her, then Athena looked back at Devlin. "*My* Merlin taught me more as a child than your mother has ever known. He told me, 'Rhianna, sweetheart, you merely need to present the weapon. There is no need to kill.'"

"Shush." Devlin said, moving toward her slowly. "We need to go home. You don't know what you're saying."

The hair on the nape of Chloe's neck prickled, whispering that someone was behind her. She swiveled, glancing back toward the room. Keshari had moved closer, standing less than ten yards away at the end of the bar. She mouthed, "What's going on?"

Chloe shrugged and held up both hands to say that she didn't know. Athena was far too angry, too out of control to just be entranced. Drugged, maybe. Hallucinating. It was impossible to be sure.

"Come on." Devlin's voice gentled even further. "We can go out the emergency exit. Get some fresh air. Relax. I'll take you home."

Athena cackled. "The Queen poisons babies. Abort it! Kill it! It takes but seven Daucus seeds to clean a womb." She glared at Devlin, like a pit viper ready to strike. "You're so in love with your do-no-wrong sister you can't see the truth."

Devlin's eyes went flinty. The air rumbled with his magic. "What the fuck's wrong with you?"

"Poor boy." She flicked her hair back and slid a sideways look at Chloe. Her gaze dropped to the cue case and her voice went deadly quiet. "What's in there?"

In one swift movement, Chloe drew the sword. Blinding brightness engulfed the hallway.

Horror dawned on Athena's face. She scuffed deeper into the hallway, whimpering, so unlike the composed Athena that Chloe had come to know. "Merlin, help me!" she screeched, the sound rising above the music.

Chloe blinked against the sword's light, now mellowing to a fierce glow. "Devlin, back me up," she shouted. "I have to get to the Shade."

The air thrummed with Devlin's magic, stronger than Chloe had ever felt. Athena snarled at him, her power rising to an equal pitch. "Athena, please," he said.

She laughed, a rasping sound that grated on Chloe's ears.

But Chloe couldn't stay and help Devlin. Time was running out. She had to get to the Shade. She swiveled away, magic roaring into her blood as she readied to dash toward the VIP section—

Thunder rumbled. The floor shook. Lightning cracked and zigzagged through the club. Bottles of liquor exploded. They ignited, blue and green flames roaring up the walls and bathing the room in fire. Screams replaced the thump of music. Fire alarms squealed. Sprinklers went off, water raining down as the crowd stampeded toward the front room, unable to get to the emergency exit through the wall of flames. Midas fleeing. Jessica. Fire. Smoke. Explosions. It took Chloe a second to realize the bathroom hallway stood intact, as if quarantined by magic.

The Shade stepped out from the flames and smoke, strolling into the hallway toward Chloe. He rested both hands on his staff, his attention on the sword. "I see you made the acquaintance of my Lady Nimue."

Her brain told her to run for the emergency exit. To get out. But her witch-instinct held her still as he prowled toward her. His magic pressed against her forehead. It buzzed in her ears. She clenched her teeth, blocking it out as she braced herself, waiting for him to get close enough. She could hear Athena ranting as if she hadn't even noticed the Shade. Devlin's soothing voice.

The Shade's voice whispered, velvet-smooth. "I have no interest in killing you, Chloe. I wish to increase your talents, bring your dreams to life." He pointed his staff at her and smiled. "You have already walked in darkness. The braindead boy in his sickbed is proof of that."

Blood roared in her ears. "That's not true. I made a horrific mistake. But I'm not evil. I tried to save him. I tried to heal him."

Her attention flicked to a movement behind the Shade. Keshari was crawling across the floor, creeping toward him through a waft of black smoke. She held a rag over her mouth and nose while her other hand clutched her atomizer. Stealthily she inched forward, until she was less than a yard away from him. She dropped the rag, launched herself to her feet, and sprayed.

The mist hit the Shade's neck. Howling in pain, he wheeled away from Chloe, his staff aimed at Keshari. She hit the ground and rolled, screaming as cracks of his magic drove her back toward the wall of flames.

Chloe lunged forward and thrust the sword into the Shade's lower back. The sword hit bone. She shoved harder, driving it all the way through, and yanking it out.

Light burst from the wound. Red. Orange. White-hot flashes illuminating the hall like an exploding sun. The Shade crumpled to his knees, wailing like a banshee.

Athena flew to him, screeching so loudly that the sound of glass shattering could be heard somewhere beyond the flames. She glared back at Chloe. "What have you done!"

A hand clamped on Chloe's arm: Devlin, pulling her toward the emergency exit. "We have to get out of here."

She pulled against him. "Keshari. We have to find Keshari!"

The air was blazing-hot. Her eyes stung as black smoke billowed into the hallway.

Flames leapt toward them. The scream of emergency vehicles wailed outside.

"Hurry." Devlin yanked her out the exit, smoke streaming past on both sides.

Chapter 29

By the dark moon's light stitch beads of bone to skin dyed black.
Your skin against my skin, my shape becomes yours.
—Transformation Spell, traded to Rhianna Davies
Translated from Archaic Welsh by Magus Dux

"Keshari!" Chloe wailed as Devlin dragged her out of the building. The light from the bloody sword in her hand illuminated the smoke-filled alleyway, revealing a team of firemen thundering toward them.

Devlin flagged them on. "We're fine. But there's a girl trapped. Inside. Near the end of the hallway."

Chloe yanked free from Devlin and started to follow them. "I'll show you where."

He snagged her arm. His grip was firm as he pulled her away from the firemen and the emergency exit, through the smoke, up the alleyway toward the street. "Let them do their job. Keshari wouldn't want you to get hurt."

"No!" Chloe twisted, wrestling against him, trying to break free. "It's my fault she's in there! If it weren't for me, she wouldn't have come."

"Stop it, Chloe." Devlin took her by both arms and looked her square in the eyes. All around them emergency vehicles screamed, their blue and red lights strobing in the thick smoke. People ran past, shrieking, crying, zigzagging in every direction. Devlin nodded at the sword in her hand. "This isn't over, is it?"

She glanced back down the alleyway. Flames now crackled from the windows and eaves, illuminating the smoke. With all her heart and soul, she ached to run back and find Keshari. But there was something else in the air besides the smoke and heat, something even more powerful and horrifying than the fire. The Shade. She could sense his magic out there, somewhere, buzzing and snapping. She hated it, but Devlin was right. The firemen were already searching for Keshari. The rescue workers were everywhere. The words Keshari had said in the club's hallway reverberated in her head: *Returning the Shade is more important than your welfare—or mine. If you fail, then all we love will be destroyed.*

Devlin gave her a shake. "Chloe, snap out of it. What's going on?"

She clenched her teeth, drawing up her magic to bolster herself. Adrenaline pushed into her veins. She had to finish this. For the Circle. For her family. For Keshari and all she loved. "We—I have to get to the Earth Clock. The sword. Before midnight."

"Do you have a car?" Devlin asked, releasing her arms.

She pulled the keys from her pocket and thrust them at him. "The Cherokee. It's near the park."

Devlin nodded, the tips of his fingers grazing hers warmly as he took the key. "You might want to do something about that sword."

She shoved the sword under her sweater. Light leaked out from the loose weave, still it was less noticeable than before.

"Let's go," he said.

She took one last look down the alleyway. *Please, Gods and Goddesses. Please watch over Keshari*, she prayed. Then she turned and headed down the street.

They jogged between police cars and firetrucks, keeping their heads down, moving as fast as they could. Her throat burned from the smoke. Grime packed her nose. As they skirted an ambulance she spotted the Rescue Twins, helping a short woman onto a gurney. Chloe's heart stumbled. *Juliet.*

She took a second look. Not Juliet. The breath sucked from her lungs and the world once again seemed to collapse around her. Where was Juliet? Trapped in the building like Keshari? And Em. And Midas…How about the rest of the coven? Who was dead? Who was alive? Where were they?

"Keep going." Devlin seized her hand, linking them together, towing her along as she once again struggled to refocus. Firetrucks raced by. Car horns blared. A tide of people rushed toward the fire, impeding their progress. Chloe clutched the sword tight against her body, its heat and magic radiating into her, lending her more strength and conviction.

They turned onto Church Street. The smoke smell diminished. Only a few people passed by. *The Thinker* was gone. The park was empty. They dashed past the fountain…

"Devlin! Chloe. Wait," a woman shouted, just as they reached the Cherokee.

Chloe wheeled toward the voice. A tiny part of her prayed it was Keshari, though in her heart she knew that was impossible.

Em came flying up the sidewalk to them. No soot or filth on her face or clothes. She was out of breath from running, but otherwise appeared oddly unfazed.

Chloe gaped at her, shocked but delighted. "You weren't in the club?"

"I was at an A.A. meeting." Em raked her hands through her hair, talking fast. "It's been hard enough to not drink at the coven gatherings. I wasn't about to go to a club, no matter how much they badgered me." She took a breath. "I was there in the meeting, thinking...I got this feeling. At first I thought it was a ghost calling me, then I heard the sirens. I saw you and Devlin running. I have to tell you something, right away."

"Get in," Devlin interrupted. He flung open the driver's door and vaulted into the seat. "Hurry."

Chloe pulled the sword out from under her sweater, the air around them brightening like daytime as she jumped into the passenger seat and set it on her lap. Em dove into the back, not even as much as blinking at the sword. *No huge surprise*, Chloe thought. Em was the girl who spent her time talking to the dead. Why would a glowing sword alarm her?

As Devlin threw the Cherokee into reverse, Chloe briefly explained to them about the Earth Clock and what she needed to do. None of them mentioned the fire or who could be dead or trapped. Everyone seemed to understand they couldn't afford to think about those things.

Devlin floored the gas, zigzagging through traffic. Streetlights exploded on both sides of them. Ahead, the traffic lights flashed erratically. Fire licked along their wires, sparks sprayed down. The sword's glow intensified.

"Who's Rhianna?" Chloe asked bluntly, as Devlin took a shortcut through a parking lot. She wasn't sure she wanted to know. But Athena had called herself by that name when she was ranting. Now that she thought about it, Devlin had mentioned someone named Rhianna too. It had been right after she'd talked to his grandfather Zeus on the phone.

"Rhianna Davies?" Devlin's voice cracked. "She's the woman who was—" He frowned, a deep shadow darkening his eyes. "She was my father's first girlfriend, and later his mistress. My grandfather banished her from the Circle, way back when it was located in Saratoga Springs. She's powerful and crazy."

Chloe's head whirred, the pieces of a disturbing puzzle beginning to come together. This was beyond horrific, all the way to downright petrifying.

For a moment, Devlin didn't speak as they flew through another intersection and squealed around a corner. He let out a loud breath. "I'm not kidding about the crazy part. She's a registered sociopath."

Em leaned over the back of Chloe's seat. "You're thinking this Rhianna is behind everything?"

"Not exactly," Chloe said slowly, gathering her nerve to say what she really thought. Devlin wasn't going to be happy to hear it. "I think Rhianna is masquerading as Athena. The way the Shade changed his appearance."

Devlin stomped on the brakes, slowing before he veered around a stalled car. "I knew something was wrong. I thought she was obsessed. I thought...She manipulated all of us."

The anger in his voice sent a chill up Chloe's spine. She bit her tongue, holding in a question that would only deepen his rage. A question that sent nausea creeping up her throat. If Rhianna was masquerading as Athena, then where was the real Athena?

Em raised her voice. "You know that thing I wanted to tell you?"

Bang! Something heavy smashed against the windshield. The Cherokee swerved. Chloe's hands went to the sword, clutching it as Devlin swung the wheel, bringing the car back into the road.

Em screamed, "Monkey!"

Right in front of Chloe's face, giant nut and bolt eyes glared through the cracked windshield. Its knife-blade fingers yanked on the broken glass, ripping pieces free.

Devlin jerked the wheel hard to the right, steering into the curb again. The monkey slid across the hood, claws squealing against the metal. Its wings jackknifed open. Devlin stomped on the brakes and the monkey summersaulted over the windshield. Its body thumped against the car's roof.

Another thump sounded, this time at the back of the car.

"Shit, it's another one. Hold on!" Devlin hit the gas, tires squealing.

Em began to murmur a prayer. "Bless us. Protect us..."

Chloe swiveled and glanced out the back window. The silhouette of a monkey rolled across the pavement, illuminated by the headlights of a car behind them. A second monkey nosedived onto that car's hood, punching its fists against the window. The car swerved, skidding wildly from one lane to the other. As it careened under a streetlight, Chloe caught a glimpse of a sign on top of the car. A taxi. Not the Shade. Not Athena. And there were no other cars following.

"The Shade has to have recovered by now," she said, facing forward. "Where do you think he—and everyone else—is? They aren't behind us."

"Not far." Devlin stepped on the gas, streaking down the street. They'd be at the turn to the complex and park in a minute.

Em leaned forward, talking fast. "That thing I need to tell you. It's important, especially after what Chloe said about Rhianna masquerading as Athena." She gulped a breath. "Don't hate me, Devlin. I can't be sure. But there are murmurings."

"What are you talking about?" Devlin snapped. "Who's murmuring—about what?"

"The dead. They said…The orb loves you, Devlin. It loves the coven. That's the reason it didn't want to leave." Her voice quieted, almost to a whisper. "I think the orb is Athena's spirit."

Chloe clamped her hand over her mouth, smothering a gasp. *Where was the real Athena? Whose spirit was the orb?* Em's theory answered so many questions. Out the corner of her eye, she stole a look at Devlin.

His knuckles went white as he steered with one hand. He pulled his phone from his jacket and thrust it at her. "Tell my grandfather about Rhianna. That she—" His voice stuttered. "We might not make it out of this. Someone needs to know."

He slowed the Cherokee, steering around the corner. Chloe found his grandfather's number, but the call went to voicemail. "Zeus, this is Chloe. We think Rhianna might have done something to Athena."

"Tell the truth," Devlin snarled. "I'm going to kill her."

Thump! Something hit the roof as they passed the complex's driveway.

Em began to pray again.

Chloe clutched the phone, enunciating each word carefully. "Rhianna killed Athena. We're—"

Headlights blared against their shattered windshield. A pickup sped straight at them.

"Hold on!" Devlin shouted. He stepped on the gas, accelerating instead of swerving.

A scream tore from Chloe's mouth. She dropped the phone, hands flying to the sword.

Devlin jerked the wheel hard, throwing Chloe against the door. Metal screeched as they sideswiped past the truck. She caught a glimpse of the driver. Matt. Brooklyn beside him. The Cherokee jumped the curb, thumping into the roadside weeds.

"You okay?" Devlin asked.

Chloe had her door open, already climbing out. She nodded.

"I'm fine, too," Em said, joining her.

The pickup lay crumpled on the other side of the road. Half its hood was smashed flat against its windshield. A monkey wing protruded from the wreckage. Brooklyn leapt from the passenger side. She ran around to the driver's door, yanked it open, and hauled Matt out. She punched him square in the face. Matt staggered back against the truck, blood streaming down his face.

"What the fuck?" he stammered.

"Son of a bitch. You're not screwing with my coven." She punched him again, this time in the ribs. She kneed him in the groin and he sunk to the ground, swearing and groaning.

For an instant, Chloe couldn't believe her eyes. Brooklyn was going after Matt, like she was beyond pissed. Like she was on their side, not the Shade's. Either way, she didn't have time to figure it out. She had to get to the stone, before it was too late.

Leaving them behind, she raced down the road and into the park with Devlin and Em hot on her heels. Ahead, the circle of stones loomed, shadowy under the sword's eerie brilliance.

Tires squealed behind them and headlights fanned the path. An engine roared, closing in. The whine of a smaller engine joined the pursuit.

"They're going to run us over," Em shouted, veering off the path and into the trees.

Devlin snagged Chloe's arm, hauling her along with him. She pushed all she had into her aching legs, running faster than she ever had. She was almost to the circle, too late for even a car to catch up. The cars screeched to a stop. Doors opened and slammed shut. Midas's voice. Jessica. Shouting. Footsteps closing in. The snap of angry magic.

The outline of a monkey swooped from the darkness, its razor-sharp wings folded as it jetted toward Chloe. She skidded to a stop. Devlin let go of her, an energy-ball building in his hands.

"*Solvo fasciculos!*" Chandler's unexpected voice echoed nearby. A sizzling arc of light shot toward the monkey, slamming it in midair. Every weld on the monkey glowed white-hot. It broke into hundreds of pieces, arms, legs, eyes, wings…all rained down across the circle of stones, hissing against the damp grass, steam rising.

For a second Chloe was sure she'd gone crazy. It was crazy, everything that was happening. She took a fresh grip on the sword and a deep breath. *Focus*, she told herself. *No distractions. The sword. Have to get it to the stone on the far side of the circle—*

Lightning streaked from the sky, striking the ground directly in front of the stone. Smoke fanned outward and the Shade and Athena materialized.

An oozing burn covered his neck. His shirt was torn and charred, but the buzz of his energy made even the grass tremble.

He and Athena strode toward Chloe and Devlin. The Shade pointed his staff at her. "Well done. But I tire of this game..." His gaze slipped sideways to Athena and he wrinkled his nose as if he smelled something unpleasant. "My dear, strip off that foul artifice. Seeing you like that is most unsettling."

She smirked. "My pleasure. I'd like the boy to see the truth before he dies." She yanked the beaded choker off her neck. The rippling halo Chloe had caught flashes of before descended over Athena, like an iridescent burial pall. Then Athena vanished, replaced by an unnaturally blond and curvaceous middle-aged woman with stretched-tight skin that suggested she'd done far too many youth-spells.

"Rhianna," Devlin growled.

The Shade grinned proudly. "Wise child. Would you care to guess what—or should I say whom—the necklace was made from?"

"You bastard!" Devlin's voice bordered on hysteria.

Fear for Devlin thundered through Chloe, but she couldn't let anything take her mind off her goal. Twenty yards to the Shade and Athena. Twenty yards beyond them to the stone.

She drew up her energy until her body quivered with it. The sword heated in her hand. She set her jaw, eyes on the stone.

"Fuck you." The thwack of a hard slap came from behind her.

"Stupid bitch!" Jessica shouted.

Brooklyn's voice rose. "You deserved it, asshole!"

Chloe redoubled her focus, refusing to waver as all hell broke loose behind her. Jessica. Midas. Everyone yelling. Fists hit flesh. Magic hissed.

Devlin rocketed toward Rhianna, a wave of blue magic surging from both hands. She staggered back, her legs collapsing beneath her. But her hands were already gathering a blazing energy-ball. A foul burning smell filled the air, warring with an earthy scent of juniper.

Chloe extended the sword out straight in front of her, readying to race for the stone.

The Shade grinned. "You don't want to do that."

"Fuck you," she said, charging forward.

"Bow before me," he bellowed. His voice hit her, a seismic wave of energy pushing against her and demanding she drop to the ground. She locked her knees, no longer able to move forward but refusing to do his bidding. His magic pressed against her body. It drilled into her skull, screaming and cycling like a siren.

She clenched her teeth, straining to block out the sound. He wanted to break her and bring her into his fold. She clamped her eyes shut and focused on the heat of the sword in her hand. Damn him. He wasn't going to win.

A blast of cold air sliced across her face, as frigid as midwinter.

Her eyes shot open. What the hell was going on?

Fog blanketed everything now, so impenetrable it obliterated the trees and sky. It spiraled from the ground. It clung to her skin and clothes.

Chloe grasped the sword in two hands and turned in a slow circle. The sword's light reflected off the swirling gray and glimmering silver. The Shade's magic whispered and spun all around her like a million hornets, disorienting her.

Somewhere beyond the screen of fog, Devlin groaned. Em shrieked. But she couldn't see anyone, not even the Shade. No one. Nothing, including the stone she desperately needed to reach.

"Two more minutes," the Shades voice crooned. "Bow to me and live. Everyone else has."

She didn't believe that, but still she prayed, *Please Hecate. Please Nimue. Someone help me.*

"Too late for that," the Shade's magic whispered.

A shudder worked its way up her spine, morphing into a cold sweat as flecks of purple light sparked in the fog. Not the savior she'd wanted. It was the glimmer of the staff crystal. Merlin's weapon in the hands of his shade. Its light sparked and sluiced into the gray, mixing with it and whirling faster and faster on every side of her.

"Because of you, the boy will never recover," the Shade taunted, as the purple sparks spun like merry-go-round lights gone insane. "Listen, do you hear the squeak of a faucet and the splash of water? That's the sound of Greta filling her bathtub." He laughed. "Juliet would do anything I asked. Drink bleach. Drink hemlock. Hold Greta's head under the water—"

"Shut up!" Anger flooded Chloe's veins. She'd stabbed the Shade once. She could do it again. Drive that sword straight through him. "Bastard, I'll kill you."

"I'm right here. With that kind of fury you might just win the fight." He sniffed loudly. "Can you smell that—burning hair and flesh? Keshari's flesh roasting, her brain bubbling in the flames...Come. Do your best. Try to kill me."

The purple glimmers of the staff crystal drew together, forming into one bright blaze. A single spot. A purple beacon, telling her where the Shade stood.

Chloe couldn't see anything in the fog, except for that beacon and the glow of the sword. But she knew two things: The Shade wanted her to fight him and in doing so lose what little time she had left to get the sword to the stone. She also knew she hadn't sensed the Shade move from the spot where he'd last stood—twenty yards in front of the stone. Twenty yards ahead of her real goal.

"Em, the orb!" she shouted. She could only hope Em was alive and would know what she meant. Even the sword's light couldn't cut through the fog and the crystal's brightness. But maybe, maybe with the help of an angry spirit it could.

Em's voice murmured out from the gray. "Come to us. Come to our aid..."

An otherworldly hum reverberated and orbs shimmered up from the ground, forming a runway of lights in front of Chloe. At the end of that runway, a single red orb glowed, illuminating the outline of a stone.

Chloe shot toward it, running as hard as she could. The Shade lunged at her, his staff swinging toward her head. She ducked, pain flashing up her neck as the staff connected with her shoulders. He dove at her. He had her by the hip, his black-tipped fingernails clawing through her pants legs, dragging her to the ground like a hyena taking an antelope. "Surrender or die!"

Holding tight to the sword, she rolled onto her back, kicking wildly. Her foot connected with his arm. A *crack* resounded. He howled. She yanked her leg from his grip. She was on her hands and knees. Pain pulsed up her leg. The red orb—Athena—glowed ahead of her. Only a few yards to go.

"Be gone!" Rhianna's voice commanded.

The orb exploded into a shower of sparks, raining down all around Chloe. The air wailed and whirled like a tornado. Flashes of purple light ricocheted like lightning. She leaned against the gale of magic and, in a last burst of energy, stumbled to her feet, lunged forward, and thrust the sword into the stone. It sunk in deep, all the way up to its hilt.

The sword's light went out.

Everything around her went charcoal gray.

And, for a heartbeat, the only sound was the soft rush of waves against the shore and the rustle of dried leaves tumbling across the path.

In that frozen moment, Chloe became intensely aware of the razor's edge she'd stepped over—not when she'd failed to watch over the boy or when she'd carelessly tried to cure him in the hospital. This was different, intentional harm done to another being for her own gain, even if it was justified. How much easier would it be to take that sword in her hands again, or a different sword—or to wield her magic as a weapon? How much easier to kill now that she'd already crossed that line?

Cold chilled her to the bone. *Much easier*, she knew.

This was what Nimue had warned her about. The soul-deep change that had happened the moment she stabbed the Shade, though she'd only now truly felt the impact. Still she knew with all her heart that no what matter the cost had been, she'd done the right thing.

Chloe lifted her head and yanked the sword from the stone.

The Shade screeched as the stone cracked open and spears of light flared out. The air and fog around Chloe sucked inward toward the fissure. But she and everyone—and everything—stayed in place. Everyone, except for the Shade. He was dragged howling toward the light. His fingers plowed furrows in the earth. His eyes flashed with fury. His magic buzzed around him like a nest of hornets.

"No witch's spell can bind me forever!" he screamed. "You shall suffer and regret. Regret!"

His body heaved upwards, then twisted like a dishrag. The wet squelch of flesh and the snap of breaking bones rang out as his feet and legs and then his torso warped into a jelly-like mass. The spears of light encased him, drawing him inward.

"No!" Rhianna screamed, diving for the last traces of his fingers. Her hands went right through them. The light flared like the sun's corona, then it swallowed the last of the Shade, and retreated into the stone.

In the distance, the sound of sirens wailed, growing louder by the second. Police.

Chloe stumbled toward the lakeshore, sword in hand. She had to return it to the Lady.

Jessica fled past her, arm in arm with Rhianna, heading toward the park's entrance. Matt. Brooklyn. Chandler. Em. Everyone running…But she had to get to the water.

Beneath her feet, the grass turned to sand. She waded in, the icy waves lapping against her pants legs. "Nimue!" she shouted. "I return what is yours. The Shade and sword."

She threw the sword. Once again glowing, it arced through the air and landed flat on top of the water. A hand rose up and grasped the sword, hoisting it skyward. Then the sword sank downward, the water illuminating for a moment before its murky depths went dark and still.

Chapter 30

"Like stars scattered across the sky,
each witch has their own place in the universe.
Some gather in groups, others are solitary. Some bright. Some dark.
A few are as commanding as planets.
And, once in a great while, one shines as brilliant as the moon herself."
—Saille Webster, high priestess Northern Circle
Saratoga Springs, NY, 1979

By the time Chloe and Devlin got to the complex, Em, Midas, and Brooklyn were waiting in the lounge. They all looked beat-up, to varying degrees. Em was in the best shape, mostly just splattered with dirt. Brooklyn was acting cool, but her lip was split and crusted with blood, one eye was swollen shut. Midas was holding an iced beer mug against his jaw. No doubt, they all were still riding high off the magic, or else they'd have been dead on their feet instead of energized.

Chloe was the worst off of everyone. Her lungs ached from breathing in smoke. She had cuts, bruises, small burns, and scorched hair from sparks and magic, not to mention the painful marks where the Shade had clawed her thigh.

"The marks may not look like more than deep scratches," Brooklyn said, dragging Chloe to the downstairs bathroom. "But they were made by a shade's fingernails."

She instructed Chloe to take off her torn jeans and sit on the toilet, then she went to work washing the marks and rubbing in a special salve that supposedly would eliminate any demonic infections.

Chloe shifted her weight from one hip to the other. "Can you hurry it up a little bit? We need to get back to the lounge and discuss things with everyone. I'm worried about Devlin, too. He's putting up a good front, but I can't imagine how much he's hurting. He and Athena were so close."

"He's probably mostly angry. I certainly am." Her tone turned more biting, her fury undisguised. "Matt—that bastard—I had no idea he was going to try to run you guys off the road. If I'd known, I would have stopped him." She looked down for a second, focusing on the jar of salve. "I feel bad about being such a shithead the night of your initiation. Really, I'm sorry."

Chloe shrugged. "Don't worry about it. What's done is done. I'm just glad you're with us now." She meant it too. Everything was such a mess, their past, the future. She couldn't begin to unravel it all right now.

Brooklyn got out gauze and cotton bandages. "Rhianna, Jessica, Matt, and whoever else is tangled up with them—they're all going to regret it."

Regret. The word sent Chloe's mind reeling back to the Shade's last words. *"No witch's spell can bind me forever. You shall suffer and regret."* She already regretted a lot, especially one thing.

An image of Keshari surrounded by smoke and flames flashed in Chloe's head. The firemen had rushed right in to find her. But what if the smoke was too thick? What if the flames were too hot? Her heart murmured that Keshari had survived. But what if it was wrong?

Chloe reached down to the floor and grabbed her torn pants.

"Quit fidgeting," Brooklyn said sharply.

"I need to call Keshari." Chloe wasn't certain if she'd said it out loud or not. Either way, her voice strained and her hands shook as she took the phone from her jeans pocket. She wasn't sure she wanted to know the truth. It was easier to pretend everything was all right if she didn't. Still, waiting and pretending wouldn't make it any easier in the long run.

She braced herself for the worst, then decided to send a text instead of calling. What if Keshari's mother answered? How could she explain? What would she say?

Her fingers stumbled as she typed:

You okay?

It sounded stupid. But would anything have felt right?

"All done." Brooklyn finished by snugging the bandage tight. She nodded at a pile of folded laundry sitting on a small dresser. "If you find something that fits, take it. Athena always liked to have extra clothes like that on hand. Athena—the real Athena—always was giving things away. Food, clothes for the homeless." She closed her eyes as if holding back tears. Then she took a steadying breath. "If you're all set, I'm going to head back to the lounge. I could really use a cold beer."

Chloe nodded. "Me too."

After Brooklyn left the bathroom, Chloe tried to not think about her still silent phone as she tugged on a plain T-shirt and loose cargo pants from the pile. Finally, she surrendered and double-checked. Nothing.

An almost unbearable ache constricted her chest. *No*, she told herself. *This doesn't mean anything, Keshari could have lost her phone in the fire. She might have it turned off.*

Chloe clenched her teeth and shoved back her fear. She couldn't fall apart. She needed to stay strong. For Devlin. For everyone. For the Circle.

A minute later she was back in the lounge. She sunk down onto the couch next to Devlin. Brooklyn was with Midas at the bar, having her beer and watching TV.

She scanned the room. "Where did Em go?" Another absence struck her. "Has anyone heard from Chandler?"

"Chandler called," Devlin said. "She'll be back in the morning." He smiled, the sadness lifting from his eyes for a moment. "Em's fixing a special dinner for Henry. His favorite cheese biscuits laced with cure."

Chloe cringed at the thought of the flavor combination, but she found herself smiling with relief. "He's going to be all right, then?"

"I think so." Devlin brushed his hand down her arm, his fingers coming to rest gently on top of hers. She nestled against him, soaking in the comfort of his warmth and magic.

Suddenly Midas cranked up the volume on the TV. "Look at this!"

Screams of ambulances and firetrucks flooded the room. Film clips of flames leaping from the club's roof flashed on the screen. Mobs of people ran everywhere. Streetlights exploded.

"Shit," Chloe said, when she caught a glimpse of her and Devlin near the alleyway, unmistakable because of the glowing sword in her hand.

"Your back's to the camera, that's good," Midas said.

As Matt's wrecked truck with a monkey wing sticking out of its hood appeared on the screen, Devlin sprung up from the couch and hurried closer to the TV. "If this makes national news, there's no way the High Council will miss it."

Brooklyn shook her head. "Even if it does, this is only going to make us look like drunks and idiots. There's no connection to magic or the Shade."

Chloe frowned. The Council not discovering what happened was a nice fantasy, but she was with Devlin on this. It wouldn't just be the High Council, either. Her parents would hear about it too. Like it or not, she'd have to call them first thing in the morning, before her dad had a chance to watch the news.

The news switched to a live segment and closed in on a frazzled reporter. He walked over to where a power company worker waited and began to talk to him. "There are reports that the Russians are behind the city-wide electrical disruptions, that this was a test before they attempt something much larger. Is that true?"

The reporter held out a microphone to the man. He hooked his thumbs into his tool belt and bent close to the mic. "I don't know why this comes as a surprise. They hacked into Burlington's electric grid a few years ago by infiltrating a single laptop." His voice deepened. "The club fire was a cover-up. Our government wants us to think this was a bunch of nerds with light sabers. But mind me, it's the Russians."

Brooklyn raised her voice above the TV. "See, nothing to worry about. The conspiracy theorists are going to cover it up for us."

The reporter backed up as a young black man with librarian glasses and oddly hacked off hair shoved the power company worker aside. "Don't believe him," he slurred. "It was witchcraft!"

Devlin brandished his hand at the screen. "That's the journalist."

"It is?" Chloe jumped up from the couch, joining Devlin. "You mean, the one who was supposed to be an initiate?"

"I can't believe he's still around," Brooklyn said. "He was pretty fucked up after the bloodletting and the—" She clamped her mouth shut as if she had just realized that she'd incriminated herself as being fairly involved in at least some of Rhianna's schemes.

The man on the TV pushed his glasses lower on his nose, looking cross-eyed at the camera over the top of their lenses. "Witchcraft—and I don't mean Wicca or these modern Druids. I'm talking raising-the-dead, blood-drinking witches."

The reporter stammered. "That's—an interesting theory."

His voice faded as the reporter snatched the mic away from him, pulling it up close to his own mouth. "This is John Rogers, reporting live from Church Street. We'll be back in a moment."

The feed went dead.

Midas scoffed. "Russians. Can you believe that?"

Devlin glared at him. "You didn't."

"I did." He grinned proudly. "I might have been stoned on magic, but I wasn't about to ruin my career by letting photos of me and rumors of witchcraft leak out on the Internet." He shoved his dreadlocks back from his face. Then he sighed and shrugged. "I wasn't responsible for everything, just the cellphone blackout inside the club. The rest was Merlin. Um—I mean, the Shade."

Chloe scrubbed her hands over her face, her frustration growing. Russians. Power disruptions. The TV report hadn't mention the one thing she cared about.

"Did they say if anyone was hurt in the fire or—" She couldn't bring herself to say the rest.

Everyone went silent, the mood draining back to heavy somberness.

"At least two people are dead," Brooklyn said quietly. "Dozens were taken to the hospital." Her eyes widened as if something had just occurred to her. "Your friend, Juliet? She's okay, if that's what you're thinking. We escaped out the club's VIP exit at the same time."

Juliet. A wave of relief and guilt washed over Chloe. She sunk back down on the couch and took out her phone. She needed to check and see how Juliet was, and apologize. If it weren't for her the Shade would have never gone after Juliet. It was wrong too that she'd put Keshari's welfare so far ahead of Juliet's. They were both her friends, though putting her on the Shade's radar and the way she'd used the spell and trigger words to keep Juliet from coming to the complex didn't exactly prove that.

"Hello?" Juliet answered on the first ring, her voice groggy from sleep.

Chloe winced. She hadn't stopped to think about the time. "I'm sorry. I know it's late—or really early. But I was worried about you."

"It's three-thirty." There was a rustle and a creak that sounded like Juliet was getting out of bed. "I'm feeling better, I guess. It's all kind of a blur. The Twins think it was food poisoning, maybe spoiled chilies or the wrong kind of mushrooms. Greta's sick too. Hallucinations, even."

"Oh. I was worried about the fire."

"I kind of remember that. At the club, right?" Juliet was silent for a moment. "I'll talk to you later. I need to go back to bed. Okay?"

Chloe's pulse picked up. It was a long shot, but—"Wait a minute. You don't happen to remember seeing Keshari? She was at the club."

"Ah, yeah. The Twins were with her. They were taking her to the hospital."

Hope fluttered in Chloe's chest. "She was alive, then?"

"She was in rough shape, but she seemed okay."

* * * *

An hour later, Chloe and Devlin sat alone in the hallway outside Keshari's hospital room, waiting for the doctor to finish talking to Keshari and her parents. They'd found out a little about her condition at the nurses' station. She had burns on her neck and one shoulder, but they weren't severe. Smoke inhalation was the doctors' main concern.

"A penny for your thoughts," Devlin said, sliding an arm around Chloe's back.

She rested her head against his shoulder and gazed down the hallway at the line of patients' rooms, every one of them full. "I was thinking about all the dreams we had for the Circle, the things we could discover. The people we could help."

He sighed dejectedly. "I'd be lying if I said things weren't going to change, even if the Circle survives the investigation." His voice lowered even further. "There's something I haven't dared mentioned to anyone."

She stiffened, surprised he'd held anything back. "What is it?"

"Merlin's staff?" He got up and rubbed his hands nervously down his arms. "Rhianna has it."

Her mind rushed back to the moments before the Shade had been sucked into the stone. He hadn't had the staff with him. "You have to tell the High Council. It'll help prove Rhianna's guilt."

"Maybe. But I'm going to talk to my grandfather first, see what he thinks. I'm all for telling the Council everything. I intend to be totally aboveboard."

Warmth radiated inside Chloe. She slid to her feet and smoothed her hands down his arms. He was an amazing man. Strong. Sincere. He also was another person she owed an apology to.

"I—um—" She wasn't sure how to put it without offending him. "When you were downtown with Rhianna, for a while, I wasn't sure you hadn't given in to the magic. You left the photos for us to follow, but I thought they might be a trap."

He wiped his hands over his head. "I wasn't sure myself for a while. Athena…" His voice trailed off, profound sadness shadowing his eyes.

With all her heart Chloe wanted to switch subjects and make him smile, to tease him and see his gorgeous dimples form. But she couldn't disrespect the intensity of the truth he was having to face. The sister he loved deeply had been murdered, and by his father's ex-lover.

Tears wet the corners of Chloe's eyes. "I don't know what to say. But we'll figure out what happened to Athena."

He pulled her into an embrace, leaning down so his cheek was against hers. His voice quieted. "To tell you the truth, for months it's felt like I'd lost the sister I knew. Now I know why."

She hugged him harder, rubbing his back. "I'm so sorry, Devlin."

"Rhianna was right. I deluded myself." Tears dampened her cheek, moisture that she knew had come from his eyes. He lifted his hand, his voice hitching as he no doubt wiped his eyes. "Athena deserved better. She was wonderful. The best."

For a long moment, they held each other, even the hallway around them heavy with silence. Finally, he stepped from the embrace. The corners of his mouth lifted in a shaky smile. "I don't know about you, but I'm thirsty and starving. You want something to eat?"

"Sure. Snacks, breakfast…anything's fine by me." She suspected he wanted a few minutes alone to get himself together more than food.

"Good. I'll go see what I can find," he said.

She watched him lumber down the hallway, past all the patients' rooms and around the corner toward the nurses' station. So much of what he'd said was right, mostly that nothing was going to be the same.

Her phone chirped and Chloe answered quickly, not wanting to disturb anyone. No doubt it was Juliet or someone from the coven.

"Chloe?" her dad's voice said.

Dread rolled through her and for a minute she couldn't begin to think of anything to say. She dropped into a chair and rocked forward. "Hi. Ah. What a surprise."

"I bet it is." He sounded tense, even more than usual. He knew. No question about it. "Your mother and I are very disappointed. After all our warnings you had to go and get involved with that coven. What's wrong with your head?"

"They aren't like you think. They are—"

"I can just imagine. I'm not a fool, Chloe. I've heard about the Marsh boy." His voice went as hard and cold as it had been that night five years ago at the Vice-Chancellor's house. "This time your impulsive, irresponsible behavior has gone too far. You've risked exposure of our entire community."

"You don't know anything about what really happened. And don't talk to me like a child—"

"We'll discuss this further when I get there. Your mother's driving me to the airport at noontime. Once I get to Burlington, I'll grab a taxi and be at your place by three. I expect you to be there."

She clenched her teeth, anger boiling. When he got here, he'd demand she drop out of her classes and come home with him. But this was where she belonged. This was her life. "Don't worry about the taxi. I'll have someone pick you up at the airport. I'm not going to let you condemn my friends—my coven—without even meeting them."

"Chloe," he said warningly.

"See you at the airport, Dad. Goodbye." She hung up.

She stood there frozen for a moment. It seemed like she should feel shaken, terrified that she'd be facing him in a few hours. Shamed that she'd screwed up again. But instead a powerful sense of contentment had stolen over her. Relief that she'd spoken her mind. He might not like the coven or that she'd chosen to be with Devlin. But that didn't matter. She'd found her place and stood up for it, last night against the Shade and again just now.

Chloe took a deep breath and smiled. It felt genuinely good.

The door to Keshari's room opened and the doctor came out.

"Excuse me," Chloe said. She tried not to limp from the cuts and tight bandage as she walked over to him. "Is it all right if I go in and see Keshari?"

He scanned her, as if assessing her various wounds, perhaps wondering if she was another victim of the club fire. Seemingly satisfied, he nodded. "I'm sure she'll be glad to see you."

Chloe opened the door and went inside. Keshari lay in the closest bed. Her long braids were gone, her hair short, frizzled, and hooked behind her ears. A gauze bandage covered part of her neck and jaw. Another one peeked out from the neckline of her jonnie. Chloe wasn't sure if it was the low light in the room or her imagination, but Keshari's complexion appeared a little mottled. But mostly she looked tired.

Next to the bed Keshari's mother and an elderly Tibetan woman sat in stiff chairs. A man stood nearby; judging by his age and looks Chloe figured he was Keshari's father.

Keshari's eyes lit up and she smiled broadly. "Chloe, I am so happy to see you."

Chloe hobbled over to them, her heart soaring from the warmth of everyone's smiles. "I'm so glad you're okay. You are, right?"

Keshari nodded. "They want to keep me longer for observation. But, yes, I feel very blessed."

Her mother glided to her feet. "Thank you for coming, Chloe." She dipped her head. "Would you mind if Keshari's grandmother, father, and I left the two of you alone? It has been a long night. We could use something warm to eat."

"Take your time. I can stay as long as you'd like," Chloe said. She had no idea how much of the real story Keshari's family knew, but the welcoming tone of their words and magic was unmistakable and certainly not what she'd expected.

Keshari's mom helped her grandma across the room and her dad held the door for them to go through. Once the door closed, Chloe sat down and scooted the chair closer to Keshari's bed. She lowered her eyes. "I'm not sure your mom is right about me being a good friend. I left you in the club."

Keshari reached out for her hand. "You got to the stone in time, yes?"

Chloe nodded. She pressed Keshari's hand between both of hers. "He's gone."

"Then everything is good." Keshari's eyes brightened, a teasing twinkle. "Though maybe you owe me a coffee once I get out of here."

"Definitely." Chloe laughed and squeezed her hand. Then she took a deep breath, drew up her magic, and let it flow down her arms and out gently through her fingertips, lending Keshari as much strength as she could.

Chapter 31

Carve a pledge on the flesh of a fox.
Bury it in a graveyard on the thirteenth stroke after midnight.
It will not rot. It will not waste.
It will remain a gift, a promise between friends.
—Rhianna Davies's Book of Shadows

Chloe sat in Devlin's apartment with her feet up on the coffee table, staring blankly out the window at the garden. On the way back from the hospital, she stopped at her apartment long enough to give Juliet and Greta a vial of the cure and to change into nicer clothes, her skinny jeans, raspberry top, and canary-yellow gilet. She now felt moderately rejuvenated, not bad considering when they got back to the complex they found Chandler had returned and the police were questioning her about the reportedly stolen monkeys and the accident involving her Cherokee. To make matters worse, Devlin's grandfather was on his way over from New York State. Still, none of those things unsettled Chloe as much as counting down the minutes until her father's plane landed.

"Have I mentioned you look fantastic?" Devlin said. "That outfit reminds me of the first night you came here." He smiled, dimples forming. "I'm not going to lie, I enjoyed taking it off you."

She slapped his leg. "I was passed out."

"I didn't touch. But you can't have expected me not to look." He grabbed her hand, pulling her to her feet. "Come on, we have plenty of time before we have to go to the airport. Let's get some fresh air."

She let him drape a sweater over her shoulders. He might have been doing a good job of masking the heavier emotions inside him with a pretense of cheerfulness, but she knew the air and exercise were a relief he desperately craved.

With Henry pulling on his leash, they headed out by their usual route, the gate and path. Now that they didn't have to worry about avoiding cops, she was curious to see if any signs of last night's battle remained.

At first she didn't notice much, trampled grass, pieces of scrap metal monkeys being carted off by curiosity seekers…But, as they neared the middle of the circle and she got an unobstructed view of the stone, a chill swept the nape of her neck and across her scalp.

The stone's rough surface now bore a shadowy outline, the shape of a twisted man. It wasn't easy to see like the figure on the Shroud of Turin. This was a faint shape, a whisper of a man. If she hadn't studied the stone before, she might have passed it off as the glitter of darker minerals within the gray granite. But she couldn't justify this by calling it natural. There was no question about it: this was a scar left behind by the Shade's passing.

"Monkey!" a little boy shouted, grabbing a tin cup that probably had been a monkey's cap. His sister came running and tried to steal it from him. They raced around the stone.

Chloe threaded her fingers with Devlin's. Without a word, she let Henry led them away from the stones and to the water's edge. Waves washed the sand at their feet, and crashed over the rocks where she and Keshari had summoned Nimue only last night.

"Zeus is going to talk to the Council about Athena and Rhianna," Devlin said. He paused, half-turning away and looking out across the lake. The tension in his voice told her he wasn't pleased. "He's going to ask for their help to cover up Athena's disappearance—to keep the police out of it."

"You don't think that's a good idea?"

"I don't think we have a choice about that. But I also don't think the Council is going to take his request lightly. After all, this isn't our first high priestess to die under questionable circumstances. There was Saille Webster…"

As Devlin went into details that Chloe hadn't known about Saille Webster—the Circle's cherished high priestess who had died in the nineteen-eighties—Chloe's thoughts wandered to Rhianna. She'd been a young teenager back then and a member of the Northern Circle. While everyone else was arguing about whether Saille was murdered or not, Rhianna had become pregnant and lost the baby. She'd been engaged to, then deserted by, Devlin's father. There had to have been a lot of shame and isolation that went along with those things. In a way, it was the perfect setup for

Rhianna to become a victim of the Shade's temptations—or had he come first and then the coven's troubles began?

"Stop that," Devlin said, as Henry yanked against the leash, even harder than normal.

Henry glanced back, his eyes bright. He whined, then barked insistently.

"All right, you win." Devlin let go of the leash and Henry bounded along the edge of the water until he came to a rope of seaweed. He nosed it, looked at them, and barked again.

Chloe saw it first, sparkling against the stones and sand. Her charm bracelet.

"I can't believe it." She ran over and scooped it up. "I gave it to Nimue as an offering. She was wearing it."

"Looks like you've made a powerful ally," Devlin said.

"I guess. I'm stunned." Nimue certainly hadn't seemed like the sort to give back gifts. But here it was. Amazing. Overwhelmingly so.

She looped the bracelet over her wrist. Devlin stepped closer and reached for her hand. "Let me do that for you."

As his fingers warmed the inside of her wrist, she looked out over the lake. She expected to see a glint of light in the water or the gesture of a slender hand. But there were only blue shimmering waves and the distant view of sailboats and a slow-moving ferry.

She brought her gaze back to Devlin. Still holding her wrist, he lifted his eyes to hers and moved in even closer. The air filled with the purr of his magic. His hand brushed her cheek. She didn't need her intuition to tell her what was coming next. She just closed her eyes and waited for the kiss.

He stepped back, cool air coming between them.

"What's wrong?" she asked, opening her eyes.

A wind-blown strand of hair brushed across his worried face. "You realize, no matter what Zeus does, the Council won't overlook what's happened. The Circle violated too many laws this time."

She glanced down, not wanting him to see the fear in her eyes. "When the time comes, we'll deal with the Council and any investigators they send. Together. You and me, and the Circle."

"You do realize it'll happen soon."

"I know." She put her arms around him, resting her head against his chest as she stared out to where the lake's shimmering blue water was shading to stormy-gray.

Up Next in the Northern Circle Coven Series
Things She's Seen

Prologue

I walked in the mist between worlds,
a ghost among the dead,
a child more lost than those I freed.
—Journal of Emily Adams. New Dawn House. Albany, New York

Before

Slush splattered the police cruiser's windows. Em focused on the *schwup-shuwupp* of the windshield wipers and tried not to think about the stench of vomit coming from the seat beside her.

Her stomach cramped. She folded forward. The floor. She needed to hit the floor this time. But the target was a narrow space, and the wooziness in her head and the handcuffs biting into her wrists made it impossible for her to lean far enough forward.

Relax. Breathe deep, she told herself. *Sit still. Stay quiet.*

She swallowed back the taste of bile and turned slowly toward the side window, swiveling only her shoulders so the seat wouldn't squeak and the handcuffs wouldn't rattle. Beyond the slush-coated glass, motels flickered into view, darkness returning as they passed. An inn materialized. A life-size statue of a horse. Old-fashioned streetlights glimmered in the haze. Wet snow. Empty streets…

Her head bobbed, eyes closing. Her thoughts wavered toward oblivion. How much had she drank anyway? A bottle. Two. Wine. Vodka. Gin. She remembered them all. She remembered. A concert. They were going to one. Or everyone else had. No money. No ticket. Tired. Cold. A stretch limousine. Unlocked. She needed to lay down. Sleep for a minute. She'd be gone before the owners returned. The limousine's overhead light flashed on. Someone screamed. Security. Police. She didn't remember having drugs on her. No needles. Never needles. The cop had asked her about that.

Her forehead thumped the window, snapping her back to her senses for a moment. Slush and haze. Slush and haze. The rhythm of the windshield wipers. The world dipping and reeling—

A voice touched her ear. *You stand at a crossroads, my child.*

She jolted fully awake, her sixth sense screaming for her to look out the window.

In the haze, a ghost stood on the sidewalk at the entry to a city park. Congress Park, the sign said. An older woman. Modern. Not someone from the distant past. Statuesque. Stylish coat. Boots. A cashmere scarf flowed out from around her neck. Her gray hair piled on top of her head, defiantly exposed to the elements.

The ghost of a witch.

Em knew that's what the woman was with profound clarity, a lucidness that defied her drunken state. A lucidness that was as strong as Em's gift for seeing and speaking with the dead.

The witch's gaze locked onto Em's—and across the distance she offered Em a choice to either be accepted or refused in that frozen moment. No second chances. This was it. She could stay on the road she was traveling or take a new one. No promise the new road would be easy. It wouldn't be. But what Em chose to do would make all the difference.

Not just for her, but for the ghost on the sidewalk and others as well, the living and the dead.

Chapter 1

A ghost followed me home from the school bus stop.
We had a home back then, not an endless string of hotel rooms.
I can't recall the ghost's name. Mine was Kate,
back before I became Violet Grace.
Before the beginning. The middle. And the end.
—Journal of Emily Adams, age 22
Memory from second grade. Massachusetts.

190 days later

Em lengthened her strides, hurrying to get ahead of the crowd leaving the A.A. meeting. The last thing she wanted was for someone to offer her a ride home. Not that she didn't like the group. Since she'd left the halfway house in Upstate New York less than a month ago and moved to Vermont, they'd made her feel more than welcome.

She picked up her pace, jogging through the slush, across a narrow street and down the sidewalk. She totally got why they didn't like the idea of a woman walking home alone at night, especially someone as small and skinny as her. But she'd lived on the streets in much larger cities. She knew how to handle herself. She had a phone—and a knife, if worst came to worst. Besides, walking in the dark and slush was a good reminder of the night she'd bottomed out, of what life had been like before she chose to live sober, a choice that had led her to join the Northern Circle coven and live here in Burlington at their complex. On top of that, there was an even more vital reason for her to walk alone. During the A.A. meeting a spirit had reached out to her, asking for help. She needed to locate it and find out what was going on.

Em stopped on a curb, shifting her weight from one foot to the other while she waited for the crossing signal to change. Damp leaves shone in the gutter, their bright autumn colors darkened to brown and black. Some people might have thought this time of year gloomy, but she found comfort in everything about it: the lengthening nights and leafless trees, the pumpkins and cornstalks on the front stoops of homes and shops, all the witch decorations. She smiled. If only those people knew that all the powers they imagined around Halloween were real, that witches and psychic mediums with powerful inborn gifts were right here in their midst.

A lifted pickup truck with four-doors and oversized tires rumbled up to the intersection. Country music thudded out from the open driver's window. The driver glanced her way, camo cap pulled low over black curly hair. She couldn't see his eyes, but she could feel the intensity of his gaze, studying her as if she were someone he knew. But she only looked at him for a second before her attention flicked to the occupant of the passenger seat, an apparition so misty it was almost imperceptible, even to her.

A haunting, her sixth sense murmured.

Sadness gathered in Em's chest. In such a brief encounter it was impossible to know why the ghost was haunting that guy in particular. But without a doubt, the ghost was in turmoil over something it couldn't resolve. That was the heart of all haunts. In turn, its unrest would reflect in every aspect of the man's disposition—spikes of frustration, seething anger, restlessness…It was a horrible situation, and the fact that hauntings weren't common didn't make it any less so.

As the truck moved on, the ghostly outline swiveled to watch her out the pickup's back window. Em sighed heavily. If only she were in a position to help them. But the truck was already disappearing around a corner and she needed to focus on the spirit who'd reached out to her at the meeting. She was certain they weren't one and the same. The spirit at the meeting had felt small, young.

Traffic slowed to a stop and the crossing signal changed. Em dashed across to the other side, past a bookstore, and jewelry shop. She let her sixth sense pull her down Church Street with its restaurants and boutiques. The tug grew more insistent, the small spirit's pull becoming even more desperate and strengthening with each moment that passed.

She headed into blocks of apartment houses, bars, dim streetlight, vacant lots. Her focus narrowed, her vision of the world constricting into a tunnel. As late as it was, she was grateful the tug was leading in a direction that took her closer to the coven's complex, closer to home rather than farther away. But what if—

She shuddered as she remembered only a week ago when she'd been at an A.A. meeting and felt a similar tug only to discover the other coven members had been trapped in a fire at a nightclub. She should have left that meeting—and this one—sooner.

Something low to the ground slapped her ankle, claws digging in.

She wheeled around, backing up and glancing down.

A kitten. A ghost kitten. The small spirit that had reached out to her, she was certain of that.

It vanished into the roadside darkness, a vacant lot of rain-soaked weeds and tall grass. She followed, the tangle of plants taller than she'd expected, the darkness more encompassing. Muck sucked at her feet. Her teeth chattered from a sudden drop in temperature. Her breath became white vapor. Something was wrong here. Very wrong. One small spirit couldn't affect the temperature like that.

The kitten circled back, its ethereal glow urging her on. Another glow joined in. Then a third. A fourth. All ghostly kittens, their mews wailing in the darkness. Their tails swished like eerie torches, leading her farther from the street, past a shack, and up a coarse gravel bank to a line of railroad tracks.

Something black lay on the tracks. The size of—

A trash bag.

Kittens.

"Fuck!" Em shouted, running to the bag. No need to look for trains. The only light came from the kittens' glow. There had to be a live kitten in the bag. Why else would the ghosts have reached out to her?

She dropped to her knees, the railroad bed's sharp stones stabbed through her jeans. She clawed at the bag's drawstring, struggling to rip it open. It didn't give. She tore at the plastic with her fingernails, panic taking her until she remembered her knife.

Pulling the knife from her peacoat, she flipped it open. Carefully she cut the drawstring, then worked her way down, slicing the bag from top to bottom like a coroner opening a corpse. Garbage and stench spewed out. Milk cartons. Banana peels. Balled up paper towels. Rags. Meat wrappers—

A dead kitten. Its body cover with coffee grinds, stiff and gray.

Another kitten. Dead. Cold.

Her stomach lurched. Hot tears rolled down her cheeks as she rifled through the rubbish.

The ghost kittens' yowls circled her, panicked sirens, bringing on more tears. She winced as one of the ghosts batted her hand, claws slicing. Above their cries another sound caught her ear. The whistle of a distant train. Approaching. Quickly.

She grabbed hold of the bag to drag it to safety. But she'd sliced the bag in half and the contents tumbled out onto the rails. She dove her hands into the pile, feeling her way through the garbage. It was too dark to see well, just dim outlines—and stench.

Her fingers found damp, cold fur. Another stiff body. What if there wasn't a living kitten? What if the ghosts just wanted their murder discovered?

The clang of railroad crossing arms lowering echoed nearby. Another whistle sounded. Louder. This time.

Another sound. A soft mew. Not ghostly.

Her fingernails caught on wet things, hard things.

The train's rattling vibrated through the tracks on either side of her. The brightness of its headlights reached her, widening, surrounding her, moving closer.

Please, please, she prayed. *Please. Let me find it.*

Light brightened the wasteland all around her, the tracks, the garbage bag. Brightness growing stronger by the second. Rattling echoed in her ears.

She touched something tiny and warm. Her fingers found a second one. Lukewarm, gritty fur. Unmoving.

The train's whistle blared. The ghost kittens scattered into the weeds. She scooped up the warmer body, then the cooler one. Not wriggling, but maybe alive.

Another mew came from the rubbish.

With one hand, Em claimed the third kitten. Then she slid down the gravel bank and away from the tracks, just as the train's engine screamed past.

The ground shook, the train clattering and clanking behind her as she wiggled out of her coat and bundled the kittens up in it. She was sure they were alive, right now. But how close to death they were, she wasn't certain. They were far too still and quiet. And small.

She got out her phone and called the Northern Circle's complex.

"Hello." Chloe—a woman who was another recent initiate to the coven—answered.

"I need a ride," Em blurted. "It's an emergency."

"What's wrong?"

"I'm okay. Sort of. I found some kittens. They're in bad shape."

"Is that a train I hear?"

"Yeah. Hurry. I'll be on Pine Street. The north end." Now that she thought about it, she wasn't certain where she was. Sometimes when she was with ghosts it was like that, time and space evaporating as she reached into the ethereal. "If I'm not there, look down by the ferry docks."

"I'll be right there."

As Chloe hung up the last of the train cars rattled past behind Em, dragging their noise and vibrations with them as they moved on. The air stilled. Darkness settled back around her, except for the glow from her phone. She realized then that she could have used its light to help her find the kittens in the garbage. But she couldn't change that now. The important thing was that the ghost kittens had vanished, a sign that she'd found all the living ones. Living for now, at least. Truthfully, she might have been a skilled medium, but she was no kind of adept witch or healer. She'd never even had a pet. All she could do was keep them warm and hurry.

Em gathered up the coat, snugging it against her chest as she started back through the weeds. When she reached the street, half of her wanted to keep walking toward the complex. A wiser part pulled her under the safety of a streetlight to wait for her ride.

Minutes passed, then more minutes. Finally, a familiar orange BMW coupe appeared and pulled up to the curb. Em carefully climbed in with her bundle. The car belonged to the coven's young high priest, Devlin Marsh, but Chloe was driving. Em was glad about that. She really liked Chloe. She was not only pretty in a long-legged and fashionable-blonde sort of way, Chloe was also kind and headed for med school smart. Best of all, it wasn't just people Chloe cared about. She loved animals, especially cats and Devlin's excitable golden retriever. She'd know what to do for the kittens.

"How many are there?" Chloe asked, pulling the car away from the curb.

"Three. But one is barely moving." Em dared to open the bundle and take a closer look under the brightness of the car's interior light. Two sets of shiny eyes stared up at her. The third set were closed. The kittens didn't look quite as tiny as she'd thought. Still, they were really young.

"I messaged my friend, Juliet. She used to volunteer at a cat rescue. I'm sure she'll have all kinds of advice."

Em cradled the kittens closer. "I just hope they all make it."

"I do too." Chloe fell silent, then stepped heavily on the gas.

Em glanced Chloe's way. She'd expected her to ask how she'd found the kittens or to give her advice about what they should do until Juliet got back to them. But Chloe's attention was trained on the road ahead, her jaw working as if she were lost in thought.

"Is something wrong?" Em asked.

Chloe skimmed her hand along the steering wheel, leaving behind a slight glisten of sweat. "Yeah. Something happened at the complex while you were gone."

Em swallowed hard. There was only one thing the coven had been worried about that could have upset Chloe this much. Despite the upturn Em's life had experienced since she'd joined the Circle, the coven itself had gone through a terrifying upheaval that culminated on the night of the club fire. Actually *upheaval* was far too mild of word for what had happened, and for the depth of the threat it represented to the coven and complex.

Rhianna Davies—a middle-aged witch with a longstanding grudge against the Northern Circle—had murdered Athena Marsh, the coven's high priestess and Devlin's sister. She'd then used necromancy and strips of Athena's skin to create a necklace that allowed her to transform into a likeness of Athena. In that disguise, Rhianna had manipulated the coven members into awakening the wizard Merlin's demonic shade. The coven had managed to banish Merlin's Shade. But Rhianna had escaped, leaving the Circle holding the bag for bringing the Shade into this world, an incident the High Council of Witches and their legal system would never overlook.

Worry sent a chill up Em's arms, and she shivered. To make matters worse, awakening the Shade wasn't the only violation the High Council could accuse the coven of committing. Their battle to banish Merlin's Shade had caused citywide chaos and briefly exposed the existence of true witches and magic to the mundane world at large. No matter how good a cover story the coven created, it was still impossible for an entire city to overlook flying monkeys made out of scrap iron rampaging through the streets, not to mention glowing swords, energy balls and strange lightning that had caused the club fire.

Em steadied her voice. "I'm guessing you heard from the High Council?"

"Worse. They've sent a special investigator."

"What? You mean, the investigator is here already—without any warning?" Em rubbed a hand over the bundle in her lap, feeling the stir of the kittens' tiny bodies. An investigator. At the complex. That wasn't good. They could recommend the coven be disbanded for their violations. If they saw fit, they could even abolish individual coven members' ability to work magic and seize their assets—including things like sacred objects or the complex itself.

Though Em hated how selfish it made her feel, an investigation like this could also put an end to her personal plans. She'd joined the coven mainly so she could live in the sanctuary of their complex while she got her act together. Once she reached a year of sobriety, she intended on leaving and never being dependent on anyone or thing again. But right now, she wasn't ready to go. She didn't have any money, no job, no other place to live—other than returning to the hellish halfway house or the streets.

"The investigator is interrogating Devlin right now." Chloe's voice strained upwards, her anguish for her boyfriend undisguised.

"Shit." Em's chest tightened. Devlin was usually cool and collected, the epitome of the upwardly mobile guy that he was. But right now, he was suffering deeply, full of remorse and guilt, shaken by the loss of Athena, a sister he loved with all his heart.

The car's tires skidded as Chloe winged into the complex's driveway a little too fast. Anger tinged her voice. "I can't believe the High Council sent someone this soon. It hasn't even been a week. Devlin—all of us—are grieving. It's not fair."

"It'll be okay. Devlin can handle himself," Em said. A lump knotted in her throat. She looked down at the bundle of kittens. This certainly wasn't the best night for bringing home orphans.

Ahead, the outline of the complex's main building came into view, an old three-story brick factory that the Circle had transformed into an artsy group living quarters. Devlin and Athena technically owned it and the adjoining smaller buildings, all surrounded by a chain-link fence broken only by an elaborate and funky arched gateway—or more correctly, Devlin owned the entire complex now that Athena was gone.

Em's gaze went back to Chloe. "So what's the investigator like? A man or a woman? Suit and tie, by-the-book asshole?"

"You got the asshole part right." As Chloe drove under the gateway, she glanced through the windshield toward the peak of the gate where the remaining flying monkey sculptures stood sentinel, their non-animated wings glistening in the darkness. "I bet the inspector will have a field day quizzing Devlin about them."

Em cringed. "I feel so bad for Devlin. What's wrong with the investigator? Is he just old and crotchety?"

"No, not at all. He's only a little older than Devlin, maybe thirty. He's more of a backwoods enforcer, all alpha and bad attitude. Not at all like the elderly examiner that investigated my dad's business. His name is Gar Remillard..."

Chloe kept talking, but her voice faded into the background as Em's entire focus went to a vehicle parked by the front door of the complex's main building. Most likely the special investigator's ride. A vehicle that should have been unfamiliar to her. But she knew the big, lifted truck instantly. Its oversized tires made for mudding. The truck she'd seen right after she'd left the A.A. meeting. The guy with the camo cap, the black curly hair, and intense stare.

The haunted man.

DON'T MISS THE DARK HEART SERIES

A Hold On Me

Annie Freemont grew up on the road, immersed in the romance of rare things, cultivating an eye for artifacts and a spirit for bargaining. It's a freewheeling life she loves and plans to continue—until her dad's illness forces her return to Moonhill, their ancestral home on the coast of Maine. There she meets Chase, the dangerously seductive young groundskeeper. With his dark good looks and powerful presence, Chase has an air of mystery that Annie is irresistibly drawn to. But she also senses that behind his penetrating eyes are secrets she can't even begin to imagine. Secrets that hold the key to the past, to Annie's own longings—and to all of their futures...

Beyond Your Touch

Annie Freemont knows this isn't the right time to get involved with a man like Chase. After years of distrust, she's finally drawing close to her estranged family, and he's an employee on their estate in Maine. But there's something about the enigmatic Chase that she can't resist. And she's not the only woman. Annie fears a seductive stranger who is key to safely freeing her mother is also obsessed with him. As plans transform into action and time for a treacherous journey into a strange world draws near, every move Annie makes will test the one bond she's trusted with her secrets, her desires—and her heart.

Reach for You

A world of deception and danger separates Annie Freemont from her mother—and from Chase, the enigmatic half ifrit with whom Annie's fallen in love. But she vows to find her way back to them, before Chase succumbs to the madness that threatens his freedom. The only person who can help is the magical seductress, Lotli, a beautiful, manipulative woman...a woman who has disappeared...

Available where books are sold.

About the Author

PAT ESDEN would love to say she spent her childhood in intellectual pursuits. The truth is she was fonder of exploring abandoned houses and old cemeteries. When not out on her own adventures, she can be found in her northern Vermont home writing stories about brave, smart women and the men who capture their hearts. An antique-dealing florist by trade, she's also a member of Science Fiction & Fantasy Writers of America, Romance Writers of America, and the League of Vermont Writers. Her short stories have appeared in a number of publications, including *Orson Scott Card's Intergalactic Medicine Show*, the Mythopoeic Society's *Mythic Circle* literary magazine, and George H. Scithers's anthology *Cat Tales*. You can find Pat online at PatEsden.com, Facebook.com/PatEsdenAuthor, Twitter @PatEsden, and PatEsden.blogspot.com.

Printed in the United States
by Baker & Taylor Publisher Services